T0147073

TOUCHED BY A ROGUE

This time when Benedict reached for her, he knew precisely what he was going to do, where he was going to touch her. Softly, gentle as a whisper, he dragged the back of his gloved fingers down her cheek.

Georgiana sucked in a quick breath. "But...how will I know one when I see him? A rogue, I mean."

Benedict stared at her, heat flooding through him, all the desire he hadn't felt for Lady Wylde—for *anyone*—gathering in his lower belly and burning.

He wanted her mouth open under his, wanted it with such visceral hunger he could already taste her, sweet and warm on his tongue, quince preserves and something else, something unexpected, a hint of tartness, just enough to drive him mad.

But if he took her mouth now, he'd never let her go. So, instead he caught her fingers in his, lifted them to his lips, and met her gaze over their clasped hands.

Her black pupils had swallowed the warm hazel irises of her eyes. They stared at each other for a long moment, the space between them crackling with tension. "What...what will a rogue do?"

"A rogue won't be satisfied with kissing your glove." His voice was deep and husky, his fingers shaking as he turned her palm up, and with a gentle tug, peeled her glove back to bare her wrist. "He'll kiss you here . . ."

Books by Anna Bradley

LADY ELEANOR'S SEVENTH SUITOR
LADY CHARLOTTE'S FIRST LOVE
TWELFTH NIGHT WITH THE EARL
MORE OR LESS A MARCHIONESS
MORE OR LESS A COUNTESS
MORE OR LESS A TEMPTRESS
THE WAYWARD BRIDE
TO WED A WILD SCOT
FOR THE SAKE OF A SCOTTISH RAKE
THE VIRGIN WHO RUINED LORD GRAY
THE VIRGIN WHO VINDICATED LORD DARLINGTON
THE VIRGIN WHO HUMBLED LORD HASLEMERE

Published by Kensington Publishing Corp.

The Virgin Who Humbled Lord Haslemere

Anna Bradley

LYRICAL PRESS
Kensington Publishing Corp.
www.kensingtonbooks.com

LYRICAL PRESS BOOKS are published by
Kensington Publishing Corp.
119 West 40th Street
New York, NY 10018

All Kensington titles, imprints, and distributed lines are available at special quantity discounts for bulk purchases for sales promotion, premiums, fund-raising, educational, or institutional use.

Special book excerpts or customized printings can also be created to fit specific needs. For details, write or phone the office of the Kensington Sales Manager: Kensington Publishing Corp., 119 West 40th Street, New York, NY 10018. Attn. Sales Department. Phone: 1-800-221-2647.

Lyrical Press and Lyrical Press logo Reg. U.S. Pat. & TM Off.

First Electronic Edition: June 2021
ISBN-13: 978-1-5161-1039-1 (ebook)
ISBN-10: 1-5161-1039-0 (ebook)

First Print Edition: June 2021
ISBN-13: 978-1-5161-1043-8
ISBN-10: 1-5161-1043-9

Printed in the United States of America

Prologue

Oxendon Street, London
July 1780

Georgiana Harley was the third.

Lady Amanda Clifford heard the girl's name before she ever saw her face. Just rumors at first, a whisper here and there about a ragged orphan who spent her nights in Covent Garden, fleecing the pockets of every drunken rake in London.

Gossip had it the girl had the devil's own luck.

Luck. A destitute street urchin, lucky? Lucky in the way of chimney sweeps, hunchbacks, and hangman's nooses, perhaps.

Which is to say, not lucky at all.

Lady Amanda believed in a great many things—fate and chance, destiny and intuition—but luck wasn't one of them. If a street urchin was warming her palms with coins plucked from London's hardened gamesters, she possessed something more valuable than luck.

Guile, perhaps. Cunning. A talent for treachery.

Lady Amanda didn't make a habit of scouring London's streets for stray waifs, but when the rumors swelled to a fever pitch, she and her servant Daniel Brixton made their way to Oxendon Street to see the girl for themselves. It was, Lady Clifford would later recall, one of the few occasions on which she acted contrary to her habit.

It wouldn't be the last. Not where Georgiana Harley was concerned.

She was perched on the street outside The Crimson, a low gaming hell named for the crimson-colored door, the one bright object in a neighborhood of soot-blackened buildings and shadowy streets.

Lady Amanda didn't emerge from her carriage, but directed her coachman to wait. She lingered far longer than she'd intended, watching the girl through the carriage window in silent fascination.

She wasn't a cheat. Not in the strictest sense of the word.

But neither was she simply lucky.

She had a piece of rough board balanced on her lap, her eyes darting back and forth as she slapped the cards down with a deftness born of practice. One deck, two, half a dozen. The number of cards didn't seem to matter.

Back and forth, back and forth…

Counting, and calculating.

She didn't lack for culls. Men of all sorts, high born and low, penniless or flush, drunken or sober, paused for a game on their way past The Crimson. The meaner among them saw an easy mark, and were eager to strip the girl of her winnings. Others, those with the guineas to spare, were merely taken with the novelty of the thing.

Regardless, the pile of coins in the girl's lap continued to grow. When the weight became burdensome, or the dull glint of copper became too tempting to pickpockets, she'd scoop them up and secret them away in some hidden pouch, secure from thieving fingers.

She wasn't greedy. She might have fleeced her victims for every last miserable shilling, but she was restrained, judicious. This more than anything else intrigued Lady Amanda, as an existence scraped from the grimy London streets was more apt to drive one to avarice than subtlety.

Luck? No. Lady Amanda hadn't expected the girl's gift would turn out to be divine good fortune. But neither had she expected to find a ragged little waif spinning survival into an art with every twitch of her agile fingers.

An *artist*, in Covent Garden, crouched on the filthy street outside a gaming hell.

Then again, there was nothing remarkable in finding art at a museum, was there?

The real genius was in recognizing brilliance, even if one stumbled across it in the last place on earth they'd ever think to look for it.

Chapter One

Covent Garden, London
January 1795

"Five guineas, Haslemere. Put 'em into Perry's hat, and he'll see your rider mounted."

Benedict Harcourt, Lord Haslemere, tossed the handful of gold coins in his fist into Lord Peregrine's hat, then fell to one knee in the street and peered over his shoulder. "Right then, Perry. I'm ready. Get her up. There's a good fellow."

"Ready, love?" Perry plucked up the girl waiting on the pavement and settled her on Benedict's back. "Hold on tight, now. Don't want a cracked skull, eh?"

The girl took hold of Benedict's hair with a grip that made his eyes water, and kicked her heels into his flanks, squealing with delight when he pawed at the ground and snorted. "Look at mine, Susannah! He's like a real horse!"

"More like an ass." Lord Harrington steadied his own rider and smirked at Benedict. "He's got the face of one, if you ask me."

"No one *did* ask you, Harrington. Now, be quiet, if you please, while I confer with my jockey regarding our strategy." Benedict craned his neck to wink at the little red-headed chit on his back, then caught her legs to still her before she could unman him with her frenzied kicking.

Harrington snorted. "What bloody strategy? Run down to the bottom of the lane and back, and don't lose your rider. Whoever makes it back first wins the lot."

"Only the worst sort of blackguard curses in front of a young lady, Harrington." Benedict shot his friend a disgusted look. "Mind your manners."

Harrington rolled his eyes at Benedict, but he tipped his hat to the girls with a charming smile. "Beg pardon, ladies. I forgot myself."

Both girls giggled madly at this, and Benedict's rider, still overcome with excitement, gave his hair another vicious tug. He winced and reached up to disentangle her fingers. "Hands on my head, Sarah, but not in my hair, or you'll snatch me bald. Lock your legs around my waist, so you don't take a tumble. Yes, there we are. That's how a proper jockey does it."

The coins clinked together as Perry took up the hat for safekeeping. "Right, then. On your marks, gentlemen."

"Damn," Harrington said, already forgetting his pledge not to curse. "If only we had a pistol, to set the thing off properly."

"Clever idea, Harrington, shooting a pistol into the air at midnight in the middle of Covent Garden. What could go wrong?"

Harrington frowned. "I hadn't thought of that."

No, he wouldn't have, but Benedict hadn't invited Harrington along because he was a deep thinker. He was amusing enough, as far as London rogues went, but he had one of the thickest heads in England.

Perry waved Benedict over to the right side of the street and Harrington to the left, then took his place between them. "On my count, then, gentlemen, and, er...young ladies. On your marks, get set...*go!*"

A footrace had seemed like a harmless enough diversion at first, but like many of Benedict's antics, it proved to be trickier than he'd anticipated. The lane was narrow, the cobbles slick and uneven, and both he and Harrington were a trifle sotted. They careened forward, their boots slipping from underneath them, and just missed slamming into each other and toppling their jockeys to the ground.

"Go on, faster!" Sarah jabbed her heels into Benedict's stomach, squealing with glee as he raced down the lane. His heart shot into his throat when Harrington stumbled against him at the turn, visions of blood and twisted, childish limbs racing through his head, but they'd come too far to put a stop to it now, so he dug in and shot past Harrington to clear a safe pathway for himself and Sarah, his legs shaking and lungs burning.

"They're coming into the final stretch," Perry shouted as they drew closer. "And it's...Haslemere and Sarah, by a nose! That big beak of yours finally came in handy, eh Haslemere? Too bad, Harrington!"

Harrington came to a halt beside Benedict, still panting. "Blast! Susannah and I had it up until that last bit. Damn you and your long legs, Haslemere. Shall we go again? A ten guinea wager this time?"

"Yes, yes, let's go again!" Sarah clapped her hands. "That were such good fun!"

"Ten guineas?" Susannah breathed. "Cor, guv. That's a lot of blunt, that is."

"You're quite right, Susannah. It *is* a lot of blunt. Such high stakes demand a more adventurous race. What say you, Haslemere?"

Benedict recognized the gleam in Harrington's eyes, and his own eyes narrowed. "Determined to break a bone tonight, Harrington?"

Harrington, who'd had a great deal more port than Benedict, shrugged off his concerns. "Nonsense, it's safe enough. Ten guineas, but this time our jockeys ride on our shoulders, not our backs."

"Are you mad?" Benedict peeled a squirming, clinging Sarah off his back. "I nearly dropped her as it was."

"Oh, come now, Haslemere. It's fine. Look, I'll show you." Harrington crouched down, and Susannah slid off his back. "That's right, love. Now, lift her onto my shoulders, will you, Perry?"

Perry looked doubtful, but he grasped Susannah around her waist and lifted her onto Harrington's shoulders. "Hold on to her, now, Harrington. Get a good grip on her legs, and don't drop her."

"What do you take me for, Perry? A proper stallion never loses his rider." Harrington eased to a standing position with Susannah balanced on his shoulders, and turned to Benedict with a triumphant smile. "Now, stop grumbling, and get your rider mounted. Up you go, Sarah. Kneel down, Haslemere."

Benedict didn't move. "No. Not a chance, Harrington."

"For God's sake, Haslemere, what's the trouble?" Harrington's lips curled in the wicked grin that had wreaked untold havoc on London's belles. "She wants to ride again, don't you, Sarah?"

"Of course, she wants to ride. She's a child, and doesn't know any better, but *you* do, Harrington. These are little girls, not china dolls. If you drop her, you can't patch her back together with twine and paste."

Harrington huffed out a breath, but after a bit of sulking he gave in, and reached up to lift Susannah down from his shoulders. "You're a dreadful bore, Haslemere."

Benedict slapped him on the back. "I'll think of some other amusement to entertain you."

"You'd better," Harrington grumbled. "Not White's either, or any of the gaming hells, or I'll be quite cross with you. I want something new."

"I've never failed you before, have I? Now, Perry. The hat, if you please." Benedict held out his hand, and Perry handed over the hat. "My dear young ladies, we thank you for your delightful company this evening."

Benedict turned to the two girls and offered each of them an extravagant bow. "You're both admirable jockeys, and you've earned your guineas."

Susannah snatched up the coin Benedict offered her quicker than a frog with a juicy fly on its tongue, but Sarah made no move to take hers. She stared up at Benedict, her chin wobbling, and then...

Disaster struck. Sarah's eye twitched, her face screwed up, her mouth opened, and a deafening howl broke loose from her lips.

Harrington slapped his hands over his ears. "Good Lord. What's the matter with her? What's she doing?"

Perry peered down at the little girl. "Erm, she seems to be crying."

Harrington leaned down to get a closer look at her, then straightened with a wise nod. "I do believe you're right, Perry. My sisters cry on occasion, and it looks just like that."

Benedict stared down at Sarah, horrified. "For God's sakes, of course she's crying, you half-wits. But *why*?"

Susannah had been studying her guinea, as suspicious as any moneylender, but now she turned to Benedict with a shrug. "She wants to go for another horse ride."

"I want to go again!" Sarah stamped her foot, tears streaming down her cheeks. "That cove there said we might."

"But it isn't safe, sweetheart," Benedict protested. "Lord Harrington here is sure to drop you, and you'll end up with a cracked skull."

"*Me*? You're the one who'd have dropped her, Haslemere."

"She doesn't care about a cracked skull." Susannah balanced her guinea in her palm, as if weighing it, then shoved it into her skirt pocket. "Oh, quit yer fussing Sarah, and take yer guinea before these coves shove off."

But Sarah didn't stop fussing, not even when Benedict offered her the coin. He'd seen females weep before, but kisses and flattery—or jewels in the direst of cases—usually quieted them quickly enough. Little girls were not, it seemed, as easily soothed. "What do we do?"

"I've no idea, but I wish you luck with it, Haslemere." Harrington pounded him on the back, then turned away. "We'll see you at Gentleman Jackson's tomorrow, eh?"

Benedict grabbed his coat sleeve. "Tomorrow! You're *leaving* me here?"

Harrington shrugged him off. "You're the one who made her cry. I would have taken them for another ride."

"Damn it, Harrington."

Benedict made another grab for him, but Harrington stepped neatly out of his way, and shot him an infuriating grin over his shoulder. "Good luck, Haslemere."

"Bloody cowards!" Benedict shouted after them, but they disappeared around the corner without a backward glance. "Come now, Sarah, don't cry," he pleaded, crouching down in the street in front of the weeping little girl. "Here's another guinea, all right?"

"Just a minute, guv. I never got my second ride, neither," Susannah reminded him, holding out her hand.

"With pleasure, Susannah. As I said, you earned every shilling of it." Benedict was happy to give them the whole lot, if only Sarah would stop crying. He'd never been able to bear it when his younger sister, Jane, wept, and now this little chit had him wrapped around her finger, too.

He pressed the coin into Sarah's palm. "Now, Sarah, dry your eyes, won't you? Here's a nice guinea. Take it. You're a splendid jockey, and I beg your pardon for disappointing you."

It was the wrong thing to say. At the reminder of her bitter disappointment, Sarah let loose with a deafening wail that made Benedict's ears ring. Good Lord, it sounded as if someone were murdering the girl.

In desperation, he dropped to his knees on the wet street and took Sarah gently by her shoulders. "Right, then, how about this? I'll give you another ride on my back, shall I? Down to the bottom of the lane and back, and then you'll be off with your guineas."

Sarah's shrieks trailed off into wet sniffles. Bloody good thing, too, because another few minutes of that, and every night watchman in London would be upon them. "Ye'll take me for another ride?"

"One more ride only, yes. Help her up, will you, Susannah?" Best get the thing done quickly, before the Runners appeared and took him up for teasing little girls.

Benedict offered Sarah his back, then rose to his feet when he felt her thin arms wrap around his neck. "Right, then. Hold on tight, now. Here we go."

* * * *

Sweet, precious, blessed silence.

There was a reason some sage or other had described silence as golden. Georgiana couldn't recall precisely who'd said it, but one of the ancient Greeks, most likely. They were the cleverest ones.

She rested her head against the closed door at her back and surveyed her bedchamber with what she was certain must be a very unbecoming but satisfied smirk on her lips.

Everything was in its place. She'd sneaked upstairs after midmorning lessons to arrange her kingdom—that is, her queendom—just the way she liked it, without a single thought to anyone's comfort but her own. It wasn't often she had no one to please but herself, and she intended to wallow in her privacy like a sweet little baby bird snuggled in its nest.

A sweet baby bird that's pushed all of its baby bird siblings over the edge, that is.

She'd folded the coverlet on her bed into precise thirds, leaving a neat corner of the snowy white linens peeking out invitingly. She'd arranged her candle just so, and had a second one secreted away in her table in case she got swept up in her book and burned through the first one. Nothing was more tedious than having to drag oneself downstairs to fetch another candle.

In the table beside the bed, tucked into the drawer next to the candle, was Mrs. Meeke's *Count St. Blancard.* Georgiana had languished for months on the waiting list at Lane's Circulating Library for it. Now her turn had come at last, and just at the right time.

She crossed the room and sank into her bed, sighing with contentment as she pulled the coverlet up to her chin.

Heaven. She'd been dreaming of this moment all day long—

There was a brisk knock, then a voice floated through the door. "Georgiana?"

It was Winnie Browning, Lady Clifford's housekeeper.

Georgiana froze, eyes widening, then dove under the covers and pulled them over her head.

"Sorry to disturb, dear," Winnie called. "But you'd better come at once."

Come at once? But Count St. Blancard was waiting! A lady didn't keep a count wait—

"Georgiana?" Another knock, louder this time. "Are you in there?"

Georgiana buried her face in her pillow, defeated.

So close...

"Yes, I'm here." There was no sense in fighting it. "Come in, Winnie."

Winnie opened the door, her tea towel crumpled in her hands. "I've just been upstairs, and two of the girls are missing."

"What, *again*? Let me guess. It's Sarah and Susannah, isn't it?" Georgiana wasn't sure why she bothered to ask. It was *always* Sarah and Susannah.

"Yes, the wicked things. Lady Clifford is already at her wit's end with those two. I don't like to think what she'll do if she comes home and finds they've sneaked out again."

Georgiana was tempted to find out precisely what Lady Clifford would do, but if there was trouble afoot, Sarah and Susannah were sure to find it, and this was London. There was *always* trouble afoot. "Why does this always happen when Emma's not here?"

Emma could coax a terrified mouse from its hole and straight into the jaws of a waiting cat. She was much better at herding recalcitrant schoolgirls than Georgiana, who was more likely to shove a piece of heavy furniture in front of the mouse hole, dust her hands off and be done with it.

"I'm sorry, dear, but Emma and Lady Clifford are off on some mysterious errand, and Daniel with them. I'm afraid it'll have to be you."

Georgiana cast one last despairing glance at her book before giving it up for lost. "It would serve Sarah and Susannah right if I left them to their fate. It would teach them a lesson."

Winnie merely raised an eyebrow. Georgiana had made similar threats before without following through on them, and they both knew this wouldn't be any different.

"Oh, all right. I'm going." Georgiana threw the coverlet back, marched across her bedchamber into the hallway, and up the stairs to the third floor, where the Clifford School's youngest pupils had their bedchambers. There were six girls to a room up here instead of four, a circumstance that led to one-third more than the usual amount of mischief.

Georgiana had done the calculations herself.

A burst of smothered laughter met her ears from the other side of the door, and she charged into the bedchamber without knocking. "Well, good evening, girls. My, you're all quite cheerful tonight. Pray don't let me interrupt the joke."

Her brisk steps were loud in the hush that fell over the room. One, two, and…yes, there was little Caroline, on the other side of the door. That made three, and then Abby, over by the window, was four. Four heads, where there should be six. She was missing two heads—that is, two *girls*. "All right, then. Let's have it out, shall we? Where have Sarah and Susannah gone this time?"

Four pairs of guilty eyes opened wide before Abby, the oldest and by far the most cunning, spoke up. "Wot, are Sarah and Susannah gone, Miss Harley? Why, we didn't even notice, did we girls?"

"Is that so?" Georgiana crossed her arms over her chest. Like most street urchins, her girls were accomplished liars, but she'd been both a street urchin and a liar herself once upon a time, and she knew how to pry their secrets loose. "Let's ask Caroline, shall we? Come here." Georgiana beckoned to Caroline and pointed to the floor in front of her. "Did you see Sarah and Susannah tonight?"

Caroline was the youngest and tenderest of the girls, and the most easily worked upon. Occasionally Georgiana felt a pang of guilt for targeting the weakest animal in the herd, but when it came to wild schoolgirls, ruthlessness was a necessity. It was either devour or be devoured.

Caroline cast an uneasy look at Abby, but she came forward as she was bid, her lower lip trembling. Georgiana peered down at her, and let the silence stretch until the child began to squirm. "Well, Caroline?"

"Yes, Miss Harley. I saw 'em."

"Ah, I thought *someone* must have. When did you see them last? No, look at me, not at Abby." Georgiana turned Caroline's face toward her with a finger under her chin.

"At supper, Miss Harley."

Supper! That was hours ago. "What, not since then?"

"Nay, miss." Caroline darted an anxious look at Abby. "They ducked out the front door when Mrs. Browning went back to the kitchen. They said they fancied a walk, and—"

Abby let out a warning hiss, but Joanna pointed an accusing finger at her. "Abby went with them, Miss Harley! She sneaked back in just before Mrs. Browning came up. She just told us Sarah and Susannah went to Covent Garden."

"Covent Garden!" Dash it, those foolish girls! What did they think they were doing, sneaking off to Covent Garden after dark? London was rife with scoundrels and villains, but no place more so than Covent Garden. "*Where* in Covent Garden?"

Caroline heard the tight note in Georgiana's voice and began to cry, but before she could get her lungs into it, Abby, who could see the truth was going to come out despite her best efforts, pushed Caroline aside. "Stop your sniveling, Caroline, and let me tell it. Right, so it were like this, Miss Harley. We were on Henrietta Street, not doing any harm, mind ye, just watching the coves going in an' out of the hells and begging a penny or two. Not bothering no one, minding our own business, like, when—"

"Minding your own business, were you?" Georgiana snorted. "I suppose if I check your pockets, I won't find any silk handkerchiefs, then?"

Abby took a hasty step backward, out of Georgiana's reach. "Minding our own business, like I said, when out comes these three toffs, and oh, they were pretty ones, Miss Harley, I tell you! Fancy, with their waistcoats all shiny embroidered everywhere, and gold watch fobs and everything."

Oh, no. This was growing worse every minute. Of all the scoundrels one might encounter in Covent Garden, fashionable rakes were the worst.

They saw everything and everyone they came across as playthings for their exclusive amusement. "Aristocrats?"

"Aye, I'd say so, miss. Viscounts, p'haps, or earls. Lords, leastways. So, these toffs, they see Sarah and Susannah hanging about, and they ask them if they want to make a guinea each."

"A *guinea*?" Georgiana gaped at Abby in horror.

"Aye, a guinea. They were in their cups and laughing a good deal, so it was hard to tell what for, but Susannah and Sarah went off with them quick enough, as soon as they mentioned the guineas."

Well, of course they did. A guinea was a fortune to girls like Sarah and Susannah, who'd hardly ever had two pence to rub together, never mind a guinea *each*. A frisson of dread tripped up Georgiana's spine. If these rakes were offering that much, what did they expect from the girls in return? Sarah and Susannah were hardly more than children, but to a certain type of man, it didn't matter how old the girls were.

Or how young.

The thought turned Georgiana's stomach. "Where did the lords take them, Abby? Did you see which way they went?"

"Round the corner to Maiden Lane. But there's no need to take on so, Miss Harley. Sarah and Susannah know what they're about. Why, they're probably on their way back here now, with that toff's gold fob in one of their pockets."

The other girls nodded, and Georgiana wanted to tear her hair out in frustration. Because they'd managed to survive the streets this long, these girls thought they were invincible, but Georgiana knew the odds of Sarah and Susannah coming away unscathed from an encounter with three drunken rakes were poor, indeed. She'd spent too many years of her own childhood on the London streets to have any illusions about a girl's chances of survival.

She wasn't fool enough to think she could rescue every waif in London, but these girls were *hers*. She'd plucked them off the street herself, one after the next, much as Lady Clifford had plucked her off the street all those years ago. They were *her girls*, and God knew if she didn't take care of them, no one else would.

"No one sets a single toe outside this door. Do you hear me?" Georgiana looked from one girl to the next, and if she could judge by their expressions, she must have looked fierce, indeed. "Not one single toe."

The girls nodded, their eyes wide. "Yes, Miss Harley."

Georgiana whirled around, ran back to her bedchamber to tug on some clothes, then hurried down the stairs. She paused in the entryway to snatch her coat and hat off the hook, then rushed out the door and into the night in the direction of Covent Garden.

It wasn't far, just over a mile, but it was damp and cold, and the streets were slick. She skidded along, shivering in the icy January fog, curses and prayers dropping from her lips.

Those foolish, foolish girls! Please let them be safe...

When she reached Bedford Street without stepping in any puddles of blood or stumbling over any lifeless bodies, she forced herself to calm. It was all right. Of course it was. The girls were naughty, but they weren't naïve. They were simply on another adventure, that was all. She'd be with them in just another moment. She'd drag them back to the school by their ears, and all would be well.

By the time she turned the corner onto Maiden Lane, she'd just about convinced herself there wasn't a thing to worry about.

That was when she heard the scream.

Chapter Two

It was a young girl's voice raised in awful, piercing howls, as if a monster from her darkest nightmare had come to life and was threatening to drag her down into the deepest bowels of hell.

That shriek made every hair on Georgiana's neck spike with fear, but not a single sound passed her lips as she flew around the corner. She didn't shout, or gasp, or cry—she certainly didn't *cry*—nor did she pause to think, but charged forward, her heart bursting in her chest and ghastly images filling her head as she ran—a hulking scoundrel dressed all in black, his dagger pressed to Sarah's throat, or his massive hands wrapped around Susannah's neck, squeezing the life out of her, or a gang of banditti, their swords drawn, or—

This isn't a Gothic horror novel, for pity's sake.

Georgiana dragged in deep gulps of the frigid air to calm herself, but it was dark, as dark as a nightmare. Covent Garden was a blaze of light, but only a few glimmers reached as far as Maiden Lane, and she'd seen for herself how darkness could hide a multitude of horrors.

She flew down the street, her half boots skidding out from underneath her. She was nearly upon them before she noticed the shadowy figures at the end of the lane. Two were smaller, child-sized, but the other was tall, with the broad-shouldered bulk of a man.

No, not a *man*, but a criminal, a demon, the sort of wretch who preyed upon innocent children. Georgiana's first instinct was to leap upon his back and sink her claws into his scalp, but she came to a crashing halt, the fog swirling around her, and blinked into the darkness.

There was no bloody dagger, and no blackguard with his brutal hands wrapped around a child's slender neck. That is, there *was* a man, but he wasn't dressed in black. He wore a royal blue coat embroidered with an abundance of costly silver thread, and instead of the meaty, murderous paws she'd envisioned, his hands were long, elegant, and wrapped in a pair of flawless white gloves.

Susannah was standing beside him, eyes wide, and it looked as if…yes, it *was*. "Sarah! Get down off that scoundrel's back. *Now*."

"Scoundrel?" The man's dark brows rose. "I beg your pardon, madam."

"Oh, that's going to be trouble, that is," Susannah hissed. "Git down from there, Sarah, and right quick."

Sarah released her hold on the man's neck and slid down his back, grimacing at the look on Georgiana's face. "Good evening, Miss—"

Susannah scurried forward, cutting Sarah off. "Ye see, it's like this, Miss—"

"Not a single word from either of you." Georgiana pointed at them, her hand shaking. "Come here this *instant*."

Sarah shot Susannah a panicked glance. "Aw, Miss Harley, we weren't doing anything wrong. We were just helping this cove here with his—"

"*Enough!*" Georgiana grabbed an arm in each hand and pushed the girls behind her. She was furious with both of them, but that anger was tempered by relief at finding them unharmed.

That left the hottest of her rage for the miscreant in front of her. "I'm well aware you were led astray by this, this…*gentleman*." She fixed him with a glare. "I assume you do style yourself a gentleman, sir, despite your shameful antics this evening?"

Anyone with a pair of eyes in their head could see he *was* a gentleman, and an aristocrat. His elegant clothing, his manner, the scent of expensive port that clung to him gave him away. He was an earl, most likely, or even a marquess, for who else would dare to treat children so callously?

Any gentleman with a shred of decency would have been ashamed to look her in the eye, but this one seemed more amused than anything else. A wide grin curved his full lips, and there was an infuriating twinkle in his dark eyes as he swept his hat from his head and offered her a mocking bow. "Haslemere, madam. I'm delighted to make your acquaintance."

Haslemere?

He said his name as if Georgiana would recognize it, and indeed, she did. Everyone in London knew who *he* was. Benedict Harcourt, the Earl of Haslemere. What she knew of him wasn't to his credit, but he wasn't *quite* the despicable fiend she'd envisioned. He wasn't carrying a dagger or brandishing a sword. No banditti were lurking in the shadows, and Sarah and Susannah appeared unharmed.

Still, he was scoundrel enough. Haslemere was London's most infamous rake, notorious for his reckless wagering, shocking scandals, and an endless parade of beautiful, volatile mistresses.

Georgiana took him in, from the tips of his polished shoes to his smirking mouth, her lips turning down in disdain. Oh, he was pretty, wasn't he? No doubt he thought that thick auburn hair of his and those handsome dark eyes excused his appalling behavior, but *she* was immune to his appeal. "Tell me, Lord Haslemere. Do you make a habit of entertaining yourself at the expense of the safety of young children?"

"They were never in any danger, I assure you. They found it all great fun. Ask them yourself." The smirking lips curved into a crooked grin that no doubt charmed most ladies out of their bodices and into his bed.

But Georgiana wasn't most ladies. "They found it great fun, did they? Perhaps you'd care to explain why I heard Sarah screaming from four blocks away, then." It had only been a single block, but Lord Haslemere didn't know that.

"Certainly, miss…it's Miss Harley, isn't it?" He leaned toward her and lowered his voice to a conspiratorial whisper. "Sarah here was upset because I put an end to our footraces. Her shriek nearly melted the skin from my bones. I was just about to take her for a final spin when you appeared, screeching like a banshee, and accused me of being a scoundrel."

"Footraces." Georgiana had heard rumors about these notorious footraces. Young, wild aristocratic gentlemen, tired of playing at hazard and whist, had taken to wagering on footraces, and the more dangerous they were, the better. There were tales of drunken wastrels charging about Covent Garden with ladies of dubious virtue in their arms, tripping over passersby and generally making a great nuisance of themselves.

If she hadn't seen it with her own eyes, she wouldn't have believed it, but God knew there was no end to the stupidity of bored noblemen. Last month it had been wagering on the time it would take a drop of rain to reach the windowsill at White's. The month before that all the rage was wagering on whether or not Lord-whoever-he-may-be could carry Mr. So-and-So around the Serpentine on his back.

Nothing should surprise her anymore.

For her part, Georgiana was happy enough to let every foolish lord in London split their thick skulls open on the pavement. She couldn't care less if they broke their noses and sacrificed every tooth in their heads to their silly antics.

That is, until one of them dared to involve *her* girls in his absurd games. Then she cared very much, indeed. "You smell like you've been bathing in port, Lord Haslemere. Do you really think you have any business balancing a child on your shoulders in such a state?"

"Why, Miss Harley, I'm flattered you'd show an interest in my bathing habits." He winked at her, his lips quirking. "It was either another ride, or a burst eardrum. Besides, I'm not one to leave a young lady in tears."

Georgiana was exerting a great of effort to hold onto her temper, but Lord Haslemere was edging her closer to the brink with his careless winks and sly flirtation. "This is all just a bit of fun to you, isn't it, my lord? Just another game, an entertainment to while away an evening. What if one of these girls had fallen and broken a bone, or worse, cracked their head open? Would you have found it as amusing then?"

Her vehemence took him aback. "Now see here, Miss Harley—"

"We didn't ride on his shoulders, Miss Harley." Susannah and Sarah had been quiet until now, their curious gazes moving from Georgiana to Lord Haslemere and back again, but now Susannah spoke up. "Them other coves wanted us to, but this one here said as it wasn't a good idea."

"The *other* ones?" That's right. Georgiana had forgotten Abby had said there were three gentlemen.

"Well, of course." Lord Haslemere chuckled. "Did you suppose I was running races against myself? Really, Miss Harley, what fun would that be?"

Georgiana clenched her hands into fists to keep from boxing his ears.

"There was three of them." Sarah's tone was eager, as if she thought the addition of two more rakes could only help their cause. "One named Harry something—he was the other horse, ye see, and Susannah his jockey, and then the other lord, Perry something, who held the hat with the coins."

Ah yes, the infamous guineas. "Give Lord Haslemere back his money." No girls of *hers* were going to be beholden to a scandalous earl.

Susannah and Sarah both took a hasty step backward, and hid their hands—hands stuffed with guineas, no doubt—behind their backs.

"I don't want them back." A hint of impatience had crept into Lord Haslemere's voice. "The girls earned them, and should be allowed to keep them."

Georgiana ignored it, and him. "At once, girls."

Sarah and Susannah were reluctant to relinquish their riches, but they'd been at the Clifford School long enough to know better than to argue with Miss Harley. Susannah returned her guineas, but Georgiana was obliged to pry open Sarah's fingers and take the coins away from her. "Here you are, my lord. I believe that concludes our business."

She held out the coins to him, but instead of taking them, he crossed his arms over his chest. "This is absurd, Miss Harley. Give the girls back their coins."

Georgiana's eyes narrowed. "Are you *arguing* with me, Lord Haslemere?"

"Cor," Sarah breathed. "He's done it now."

"I don't see what harm there is in letting the girls keep their reward, that's all." Lord Haslemere gave a careless shrug.

"That doesn't surprise me. I imagine you're not much in the habit of considering consequences." Why should he be? There *were* no consequences for gentlemen like him. "Allow me to explain it to you. Sarah and Susannah are meant to be tucked into their beds. Instead they sneaked out to Covent Garden, at night, disobeying the rules and putting themselves at risk, and you're proposing I *reward* them for it?"

Lord Haslemere scratched his temple, grimacing. "Now you put it that way, it doesn't seem quite the thing. I didn't think—"

"No, you didn't. Not an unusual occurrence, I'd wager." With a flick of her fingers, Georgiana dropped the guineas into the pocket of his cloak. "I daresay you're not required to think much at all. Good night, my lord. I wish you a pleasant evening."

She didn't wait for an answer, but took the girls' hands in each of hers, and turned on her heel. She'd intended to stride off into the night without another word or a backward glance, but his low, amused voice stopped her.

"What a liar you are, Miss Harley. We both know you wish me straight to the devil."

* * * *

Good Lord, the woman had a viperish tongue. Benedict had thought Sarah's shrieking was intolerable, but it was nothing compared to the blistering scold that had just rolled off Miss Harley's lips. He couldn't recall ever having been so thoroughly chastised in his life.

It was strangely refreshing, even…dare he say titillating?

Given how few ladies bothered to scold him these days, there was a certain novelty to it, and this Miss Harley was magnificent at scolding. He'd always had a bit of a weakness for a lady with a tart tongue, and she had a mouthful of rhubarb, without the sugar syrup.

"Are you their governess?" She had a governess-ish air about her that put Benedict in mind of Miss Vexington, who'd been his sister Jane's governess for years. It was an unfortunate name for a governess, really, but he'd always liked Miss Vexington. She'd been a decent lady, if a trifle starchy.

Miss Harley turned to face him again, her lips pressed into a tight, forbidding line. "You *would* think that."

Benedict blinked, taken aback. He hadn't meant the question as an insult, but her quills were quivering like an outraged porcupine. "I would? What does that mean?"

"Never mind." She turned away with a little shake of her head. "It doesn't matter. Come along, girls."

"Wait, Miss Harley. What's wrong with governesses?" Benedict didn't give a bloody damn about governesses, but he didn't want her to leave yet.

She glanced at him over her shoulder. "Not a thing. The fault isn't with the governesses."

Benedict did his best to look affronted. "You mean to say the fault lies with me? You can't simply stroll off into the dark after so viciously maligning my character, madam. I demand to know your meaning."

"Very well, Lord Haslemere, since you insist upon it." Miss Harley turned back to him with a huff. "You seem to me to be the sort of gentlemen who sees every lady as either a potential mistress, or a governess—"

"That's absurd, Miss Harley. Sometimes they're housemaids, or nursemaids." Benedict waited for another lashing from that acid tongue, but the only sound that emerged from her lips was a peculiar click, rather like...

Teeth snapping together.

"Those ladies who don't excite your amorous inclinations must be—"

"My amorous inclinations?" Benedict choked back a laugh. "Is that the same thing as my—"

"Those ladies who don't excite your amorous inclinations," she repeated stubbornly, "must inevitably be governesses."

He cocked his head to the side, studying her. She wasn't fashionable, nor was she a conventional beauty, yet there was something tempting about her all the same. Perhaps it was only that she was so contained, so composed. The urge to rattle her—to pull out her pins and loosen her buttons—was maddening.

So, as he did with most temptations, Benedict gave into it. "Why should you think I wouldn't want to make you my mistress?"

Her mouth fell open. "I...that's not...I never..."

Benedict couldn't suppress his grin as she fumbled and stammered, bright red color rushing into her cheeks. Oh, she was a cross little thing, to be sure, but that blush was delicious.

I do believe my amorous inclinations have been aroused.

No one was more surprised at it than he. She wasn't at all in his style. With her hair scraped back from her face and that ridiculous cloak buttoned all the way to her chin she looked like a shorn sheep, but the few tendrils of her hair that had come loose from her hat were a pretty, chestnut color, and she had a distracting pair of darkly lashed...brown eyes? Were they brown or green? He squinted at her, trying to decide.

Yes, brown would do. They were closer to it than green, at any rate.

She noticed his perusal, and her lips pinched into a scowl. "Do you take anything seriously, Lord Haslemere?"

The grin on Benedict's lips widened. "Not if I can help it. Do you take everything *too* seriously, Miss Harley?"

Her chin rose into the air. "For pity's sake, why should it matter to you whether I'm their governess or not?"

"Well, of course it matters. What sort of gentleman would let these little girls wander off into the night with a stranger?"

"Oh, Miss Harley isn't a stranger, she's one of our teachers at the Cliff—"

"Never mind, Sarah." Miss Harley snatched up the girls' hands again, and without another glance at Benedict began marching back up the hill toward Henrietta Street.

"Wait!" Benedict stepped after them. "It's late. Won't you allow me to see you home in my carriage?"

"No, thank you. That won't be necessary."

"Come now, Miss Harley. There's no need to be so particular. It looks as if it's going to rain again." Benedict wasn't sure why he didn't just let her stride off into the fog with her charges and be done with her, but his dormant gentlemanly instincts seemed to be reasserting themselves. No doubt that blush of hers was responsible for all this tedious gallantry.

"Can't we please?" Sarah tugged at a fold of Miss Harley's skirts. "He must have a handsome carriage, being a lord and all."

"I do, very handsome, and a splendid matched pair as well. If you're truly concerned about the children's well-being, Miss Harley, you won't risk their safety on the dark, wicked streets of London."

But Miss Harley was having none of it. "I assure you, Lord Haslemere, these two girls aren't strangers to the risks of the London streets. I daresay they've spent more time on them in their short lives than *you* have."

True enough. He'd only ever spent one night on the London streets, and that was only because his coachman had lost track of him, and Benedict had been too sotted to find his carriage on his own. He was, alas, every bit the rake Miss Harley thought he was, but a man should do what he excelled at, and Benedict excelled at amusing others and entertaining himself. Otherwise, he was quite useless. "Very well, but at least let the girls shake hands, Miss Harley."

Miss Harley looked as if she was going to refuse, but Benedict beckoned to the girls, and they wrenched their hands free of Miss Harley's. He slipped his hand into his pocket and retrieved the coins as they darted toward him. He knelt on the cobbles, held out his gloved hand, and took each of theirs in turn. With a solemn nod he shook them, pressing the guineas back into their palms as he did. "Miss Sarah, you're a capital jockey, and Miss Susannah, a fierce competitor."

The girls' eyes widened when they felt the coins, but he gave them a subtle shake of his head, then released them with a wink.

"Come, Sarah and Susannah. Your friends will be wondering where you are."

Miss Harley took the girls' hands again. Benedict didn't try to stop them leaving this time, but stood on the damp street and watched as the darkness closed around Miss Harley and her two charges, swallowing them into its depths.

Chapter Three

Berkeley Square, London
Three months later

Georgiana scraped her spoon across the bottom of her dish, unwilling to sacrifice even a drop of her pineapple ice.

"I do believe you've gotten the last of it, Georgiana. You'll wear through the bottom of the glass if you keep digging like that. Shall I ask Tristan to go to Gunter's and fetch another ice for you?" Sophia was seated on the opposite side of the carriage, her feet resting on Cecilia's lap.

Georgiana peeked out the window where Sophia and Cecilia's husbands lounged against the iron railing, watching the elegant carriages passing on Berkeley Street and enjoying the spring sunshine. The gentlemen had chosen to ride to Gunter's so as not to crowd the ladies in the carriage, and they looked so elegant in their smart coats and trim breeches, they might have stepped off the pages of the *Gentleman's Magazine*.

"No, I'd better not." Georgiana leaned back against the plush velvet seat with a sigh. "I'll only want another after that, and then where will it end?"

Cecilia laughed. "Such a sweet tooth, Georgiana!"

"Not *so* sweet. I've just always been mad for ices, particularly pineapple." Georgiana shamelessly licked her spoon, searching for more of the tart, cool flavor that still lingered on her tongue.

"Ices, marzipans, sugared almonds, and peppermints." Emma began counting sweets off on her fingers. "Candied fruit, cakes, ice cream—"

Cecilia tapped her spoon against Emma's dish. "Hush, you teasing thing."

Fondness swelled inside Georgiana as she took in the bright faces surrounding her. Cecilia's recent marriage to the Marquess of Darlington hadn't changed her, any more than Sophia's marriage to the Earl of Gray had changed her.

They were both very grand now, to be sure, but to Georgiana, her friends would always be simply Cecilia Gilchrist, Sophia Monmouth and Emma Downing, her closest companions at the Clifford School, and as dear to her as sisters. One of them might be a marchioness and the other a countess, but titles and fortunes couldn't change their shared history, or erase so many years of friendship.

Distance, though, and too much time spent apart...

Georgiana glared down at the sticky remains of her treat congealing at the bottom of her glass and grit her teeth against the wave of melancholy washing over her. Goodness, how broody she'd become! Sulking was a dreadful habit, but despite her best efforts she'd been maudlin enough these past few months.

Selfish too, considering how happy her friends were.

"I've no idea where the sweets go after they've passed your lips, Georgiana." Sophia waved a lazy hand at her, then let it flop back onto her stomach as if the effort had exhausted her. "Do you know I can't squeeze into any of my gowns anymore? My belly has swollen to such scandalous proportions these last few weeks, I've taken to wearing Tristan's banyan everywhere."

Emma rolled her eyes. "Your belly is swollen with a child, not pineapple ices."

Sophia snorted. "It's swollen with both, I assure you. This is the third time I've been to Gunter's this week. It's a great pity I'm such a short, stubby creature. If only I had your height, Georgiana, I could eat whatever I liked."

"If you had my height, you'd also have my sharp elbows and shockingly large hands and feet." Georgiana had once hoped curves would replace her angles, but she was twenty-five years old now, and long since reconciled to her fate. "You're much better off as the sweet, petite little thing you are, rather than a bony spinster."

Georgiana winced as one by one, the smiles on her friends' faces faded.

Dash it, how did that dark note keep creeping into her voice? She *did* miss her friends, but she had more than enough work to keep her occupied. Lady Clifford had asked for her help with some ambitious plans she had for the school, and Georgiana had a pack of mischievous little girls to look after.

"How are you, dearest?" Cecilia reached across the carriage to squeeze Georgiana's hand. "You seem a bit glum today."

"Nonsense. I'm never glum." She wouldn't permit such a thing. "I'm as content as I've ever been."

Her friends exchanged skeptical looks, but she pretended not to notice. They'd only worry, and she really was perfectly well. If she missed them, and occasionally wished things might have remained as they were forever, well…she'd simply make up her mind not to indulge in such melodramatic nonsense.

She'd grow accustomed to the silence at home soon enough. Who'd ever heard of such a thing as too much quiet? Privacy was a luxury at a school packed to the rafters with unruly schoolgirls, so it was delightful, really, to have some peace for a change.

At least, it had been at first.

Lately the silence had taken on an oppressive quality, and it was about to become even quieter still. Sophia and Lord Gray were off tomorrow to spend a month in Oxfordshire, Cecilia and Lord Darlington were leaving for Kent at the end of this week, and Emma was going off to stay in Lady Crosby's townhouse in Mayfair on some mysterious business of Lady Clifford's.

The evenings, when the four of them used to read horrid novels aloud to each other, were especially quiet now that Georgiana was the only remaining member of the Swooning Virgins Society. Could it even properly be called a society, with only a single swooning virgin left?

"Very well, Georgiana. If you won't say it, *I* will." Sophia pulled her feet out of Cecilia's lap and heaved herself into a sitting position. "I miss our cozy evenings together. But Tristan and I will be back in London soon, and we'll get ices together every day then, Georgiana."

"Yes, of course we will." Georgiana knew her friends *did* miss her. It was just that they were so busy now, with new and exciting lives to live, whereas she, well…she'd never done well with being left behind.

Still, there was no sense pouting over it. Georgiana straightened her shoulders, impatient with herself. "There's no need to fret about me, though I do confess it's not as amusing to read horrid novels to oneself. It's far more entertaining when Cecilia does the voices."

"Well, you're in luck, then." A sly smile lit Emma's face as she drew out a book she'd tucked between the seat and the carriage door and held it up triumphantly. "Mrs. Parsons's *The Castle of Wolfenbach.* A wicked count and an impoverished orphan, and even pirates and a kidnapping!"

Georgiana seized the book from Emma's hand. "I've wanted to read this for ages!"

Emma winked. "I thought Cecilia might read it to us this afternoon."

"Indeed, she will, but not here. This carriage is too cramped, and I'm dying for a proper sprawl." Sophia stuck her head out the window. "Tristan, my love, we're ready to return to Great Marlborough Street now. Will you and Lord Darlington be perfect angels, and take our glasses back to Gunter's?"

* * * *

It was well past dusk by the time Georgiana returned to Maddox Street and settled down to work in Lady Clifford's tiny study.

She, Sophia, Cecilia, and Emma had spent the day at Sophia's townhouse in Great Marlborough Street, lounging in the library. They'd whiled away the hours, laughing and gasping over Mrs. Parsons's story and overindulging in warm biscuits slathered with Sophia's housekeeper's delicious quince preserves. Georgiana had sworn her fealty to Mrs. Beeson the first time those heavenly preserves had melted on her tongue. She was so stuffed she'd had to waddle home, but it had been a delightful afternoon.

If she *had* felt just a twinge of melancholy when they all parted, she'd scolded herself back to equilibrium quickly enough. The time would fly by, and if she did grow restless, she'd simply turn to Mrs. Parsons or Mrs. Radcliffe for adventures. She didn't need more excitement in her life than that. She preferred things calm, quiet, and in their proper order. In any case, she had enough to keep her occupied without wishing for distraction.

She turned up the lamp sitting on the desk beside her and bent over the school's account book, ignoring the cramp in her neck. She'd been poring over the book for too long already, but the blasted numbers refused to cooperate.

They'd never done such a thing before. Never, since Georgiana's love affair with numbers began, had they ever disappointed her. They'd been her constant companions for as long as she could remember. Now, all these years later, her lover had forsaken her.

That is, her *lovers*. Yes, that was more appropriate, given the rule of infinites.

It had all started innocently enough, but what began with simple figures in single digits soon grew into sums. From there it was a quick progression to multiplication and division, and then…well, once a lady succumbed to algebraic and geometrical delights, there was no turning back.

After twenty-five years, surely it wouldn't end like this?

She dragged the account book closer and arranged its bottom edge so it was perfectly in line with the edge of the desk, as if right angles could somehow change the figures swimming in front of her.

Savings per annum were listed in a neat row on the left side of the page, and savings to date in her precise script on the other…she squeezed her eyes closed as her finger landed on the number at the bottom right side of the page.

Was it too much to hope she'd misread it?

She popped her eyes open, and her shoulders sagged. It *was* too much to hope.

She passed a hand over her aching eyes, hunched once again over the accounts, and focused on the long columns of numbers. They were burned into her brain already, but she ran her finger down the rows once again, quickly adding up the pence, crowns, guineas, and pounds in her head as she went.

Again, and then again, until the figures blurred on the page and she shoved the book aside with a groan. It was no use. No matter how she calculated it, there wasn't enough money.

Since Lady Clifford had mentioned securing a second building, Georgiana had been floating along on visions of a spacious new school with girlish voices echoing throughout, but the numbers had betrayed her.

Her lover had proved as faithless and fickle as any other.

She eyed the open book in front of her. Perhaps one more look would reveal—

"My dear child, it's not good for your eyes to read in such poor light. Take heed, Georgiana, or you'll end up with a permanent squint."

Georgiana glanced up from the account book to find Lady Clifford standing in the study doorway, a familiar expression of exasperation tempered with affection on her face. "I'll fetch another lamp."

"Not now, dearest. I need you in my private parlor. We have a visitor."

"A visitor?" How long had she been poring over the account book? Georgiana glanced at the window and saw darkness pressing against the glass. "Now? It's the middle of the night!"

"Indeed. Rather curious. You'll think it even more so when you see who it is."

Georgiana rose from her chair, her curiosity piqued. Lady Clifford was as calm as ever, her face placid, but there was a rare air of anticipation about her. "Who is it?"

"Not the sort of visitor who's accustomed to being kept waiting." Lady Clifford turned, throwing a glance at Georgiana over her shoulder. "Come along, and see for yourself."

Georgiana followed Lady Clifford down the darkened hallway and into the cozy sitting parlor she used when she wished to be private. Their visitor was seated in the chair closest to the fire, her back to the door.

"I beg your pardon for the delay, Your Grace." Lady Clifford took the seat opposite their guest, and gestured Georgiana toward a small settee tucked into the corner.

Your Grace? Georgiana sucked in a quick breath. There weren't many people in London who could claim such an exalted title, but surely it couldn't be—

"This is Miss Georgiana Harley, Your Grace. I've asked her to come because I believe she's just the young lady to assist you with this business."

"Of course," the lady murmured, her gaze catching Georgiana's as Georgiana hovered beside the settee. "How do you do, Miss Harley? Please do sit down."

Georgiana wasn't one to be intimidated by a grand title, but then it wasn't every day one found a duchess in one's parlor in the middle of the night. She fumbled an awkward curtsy before dropping down onto the settee with a graceless thump. "It's a pleasure to meet you, Your Grace."

She'd seen the Duchess of Kenilworth a few times before, but always from a distance. She was younger than Georgiana had realized, her pale face smooth and her hair as yet unburdened by any strands of silver. It was an unusual dark auburn color, the same color as…

As her brother's.

Lord Haslemere, the rogue. How a scapegrace like Lord Haslemere could be the brother of the petite, ladylike creature sitting here with her hands folded daintily in her lap defied explanation. There was a similarity in their features and coloring, but no brother and sister could be less alike.

Despite her small stature, the duchess had a regal air that befitted a lady of her station, whereas her brother was a libertine of the first order, and looked every inch the part with his wicked dark eyes, disheveled hair, and that intolerable drawl.

After Georgiana's encounter with him in Covent Garden three months ago, he'd managed to creep into her thoughts more often than she would have liked. Just when she'd banished the memory of his smirking lips at last, he'd appeared on the doorstep of the Clifford School with Lord Darlington, who'd come to declare his love for Cecilia.

She hadn't seen the man since then, nor did she wish to. Nevertheless, he persisted in haunting her thoughts.

Why shouldn't I wish to make you my mistress?

Georgiana's teeth snapped together as she recalled his mocking drawl. He'd only said that to fluster her. It had worked, too, which made it even more intolerable. She didn't *get* flustered, ever. She didn't stammer, or fumble or blush for any man, but especially not for a man like *him*—

"Her Grace has come hoping we might help her find an old friend she's been searching for," Lady Clifford said, interrupting Georgiana's thoughts. "She hasn't met with any success on her own."

"Of course." The duchess hadn't seen fit to bring her brother with her tonight, so there was no reason at all Georgiana should be thinking of him *now*. "We'll be pleased to help however we can, Your Grace."

"The lady's name is Clara Beauchamp." A peculiar, wary expression crossed the duchess's face as the name left her lips, as if she were unaccustomed to speaking it aloud, and feared she'd be overheard.

Lady Clifford's expression remained carefully blank, but Georgiana recognized the slight arch of her eyebrow, and she knew she and Lady Clifford were wondering the same thing. If this were a simple matter of finding a missing friend, why had Her Grace come to them in the middle of the night, alone? A duchess didn't sneak about in the darkness unless she had something to hide.

A duchess with a secret, then. How intriguing.

"Miss Beauchamp and I met some years ago," the duchess went on. "We kept up a correspondence for a time, but then her letters stopped, and I haven't heard a word from her since. She, ah…she seems to have disappeared."

Lady Clifford nodded. "I see. When was the last time you heard from her?"

The duchess hesitated, then murmured, "Six years ago."

Six years? Georgiana's eyebrows flew up. "That's, er…quite a long time, Your Grace. Forgive me, but something must have happened to prompt your search. Did someone see her, or was she—"

"I did. I saw her, or…" The duchess's troubled dark eyes met Georgiana's. "Or I thought I did."

"Well, that should make this easier." Lady Clifford gave the duchess an encouraging nod. "Where was this?"

"On Albemarle Street. She was in a carriage outside Lady Tilbury's townhouse. It was dark, and I only got a glimpse of her. At first, I thought I'd imagined it, as Lady Tilbury never leaves her country estate in Herefordshire, but then I recalled she arrived in London this week with her grandson. The child is sickly, so she's come to consult with Doctor Cadogan regarding his health."

"Clara Beauchamp was—or is—acquainted with Lady Tilbury, then?"

"Lady Tilbury was a dear friend of Miss Beauchamp's mother. I thought if Miss Beauchamp *was* in London, Lady Tilbury's house would be the first place she'd go."

"You said you only caught a glimpse of her. Are you certain it was her?"

"I can't be entirely certain, Miss Harley, but I believe it was her. Miss Beauchamp's hair is a very fair shade of gold—nearly white. It's distinctive, and difficult to mistake."

Lady Clifford considered this, then asked the question that was hovering on Georgiana's lips. "Do you have any reason to suppose Miss Beauchamp is in danger?"

People didn't, after all, simply vanish for six years for no reason, regardless of whether they popped back up again.

"No, nothing like that." The duchess's reply was too quick, then she bit her lip, as if afraid she'd given herself away. "But she may be in some financial difficulties. I thought if I could find her, I might be able to help her."

Georgiana and Lady Clifford glanced at each other. This wasn't the sort of business the Clifford School typically involved themselves in. If the lady had been a victim of foul play, then perhaps—

"I understand you don't…that your services aren't generally…I realize this is a small matter." The duchess twisted her hands in her lap. "But I thought you might be persuaded to grant me this favor in the interest of a future friendship between us."

Georgiana took the duchess's meaning at once. Lady Clifford didn't take money for her services, but she did accept patronage. Her connections to the titled and powerful citizens of London had proved invaluable to the Clifford School. If they did agree to help the duchess locate Miss Beauchamp, they would continue to enjoy her support even after the matter was settled.

The Duchess of Kenilworth's patronage was nothing to scoff at.

"If that's not of use," the duchess went on, "perhaps my friendship with Lord and Lady Darlington might persuade you?"

Ah, now that made some sense, at least. Lord Haslemere and Lord Darlington were good friends, and the duchess had become friendly with Cecilia through her brother.

"I believe we can come to some arrangement, Your Grace." Lady Clifford gave the duchess a reassuring smile. "You mentioned Lady Darlington. Does she know about your search? Did she recommend you contact us regarding Miss Beauchamp?"

"No! That is, I didn't mention anything about Miss Beauchamp to Lady Darlington. She knows only that I have some business I wish to see resolved, nothing more."

"I take it, then, that this matter requires…discretion?"

"Indeed, Lady Clifford, it must be kept strictly between us. The duke is very busy, and I don't wish to worry him with something so insignificant."

"What of your brother, Lord Haslemere? Does he know of it?" Georgiana could feel Lady Clifford's eyes on her, but she kept her own gaze on the duchess. Surely, it was a reasonable question? She only wanted all the facts at her disposal, nothing more.

"He does not, and it must remain that way. Indeed, I insist on having your promise you won't breathe a word about any of this to a soul, and in *particular* not to Lord Haslemere."

"Of course not, Your Grace." Lady Clifford's tone was soothing. "We keep all our business private."

The duchess let out a relieved breath. "Thank you. Fortunately, he's at his country estate in Surrey and intends to remain there for the time being to see to some repairs on the house. It should be easy enough to keep it from him."

Lord Haslemere wasn't returning to London for the season?

Cecilia had told Georgiana that Lord Darlington expected Lord Haslemere in London this week, but of course the duchess must know her brother's intentions better than anyone. The news that he would not in fact be returning to London caused a peculiar pang in Georgiana's chest.

Relief, no doubt.

The *ton* would be in fits of despair over the loss of their favorite, but for Georgiana, it was a stroke of good luck. Yes, that sinking feeling in her belly was *definitely* relief.

"What more can you tell us about Clara Beauchamp, Your Grace?" Lady Clifford asked. "Where she resided last, to start with, as well as the names of anyone acquainted with her who might know where she's gone."

"I mentioned Lady Tilbury already. She'd be the most likely to know where Clara is." The duchess fidgeted with her skirts, her gaze on her hands. "I'm afraid I don't know anything about her whereabouts."

"I see." Lady Clifford went to her desk, withdrew a slip of paper, and dipped her quill. "Is there anything else you think might prove useful?"

"She didn't have many friends, I'm afraid. Her father was landed gentry, but not aristocratic, and well…you know how dismissive the *ton* can be." The duchess's face clouded.

Lady Clifford sat at her desk with her quill poised over her paper. "I do, yes."

"But as I said, Lady Tilbury may know what's become of her." The duchess cast a hesitant glance at Georgiana. "Lady Wylde is hosting a masque ball the day after tomorrow. Lady Tilbury is her neighbor, and will no doubt be there. Perhaps Miss Harley could attend, and see what she can find out from her ladyship."

Georgiana's heart crashed into her slippers at the words "masque ball," and "Lady Wylde."

Lady Clifford didn't bother to write the name down. There was no need. For good or ill, everyone in London knew who Lady Wylde was.

Mostly ill.

Lady Wylde was a voluptuous, red-lipped siren whose wealthy and aged husband, Lord Wylde, had the good grace to expire only three years into their marriage, leaving his lady in possession of a handsome fortune, and her freedom.

She'd made good use of both.

She wasn't the only merry widow in London, of course, but more than one London drawing room buzzed with whispered accounts of Lady Wylde's many dramatic liaisons with the young, handsome, and fashionable gentlemen of the *ton*. If the rumors could be believed, her ladyship was also vain, spiteful, and addicted to wagering and ugly gossip. Despite all this she was, predictably, received by everyone in the *ton*. Her masque ball was likely to be a crush.

"Will you attend the ball, Your Grace?" Lady Clifford asked, setting the quill aside.

The duchess shook her head. "No. The duke doesn't care for Lady Wylde. Perhaps Miss Harley can attend with Lord and Lady Darlington?"

Georgiana said nothing. Privately she agreed with the duke that Lady Wylde was best avoided, and she suspected Cecilia and Lord Darlington did as well. They didn't spend much time in company, and likely had no intention of attending Lady Wylde's masque ball, but they would if Lady Clifford asked them to.

"Yes, I think we can manage something. How fortunate it's a masque ball. It's much better if Miss Harley isn't recognized."

Georgiana smothered a snort. It wasn't likely the *ton* would recognize her, either with or without a masque. Still, she'd just as soon preserve her anonymity, and she couldn't deny a masque ball provided a rare chance to nose about with little risk of being exposed.

She detested balls, but she *did* like to nose about. It was some consolation, at least.

"Very well, then." The duchess rose to her feet. "You'll keep me apprised of Miss Harley's progress?"

"Yes, Your Grace." Lady Clifford rose as well, a reassuring smile on her lips.

But the duchess hesitated, her brow pinched with worry. "You do understand it's of the utmost importance this matter remains between us, Lady Clifford? I have your promise you won't breathe a single word of it to Lord Haslemere, or indeed to anyone?"

Lady Clifford exchanged another speaking glance with Georgiana. "I promise you, Your Grace, that this conversation will not leave this room."

"Very well." The duchess gave a hesitant nod, then turned to Georgiana. "It was a pleasure to make your acquaintance, Miss Harley."

"Thank you, Your Grace." Georgiana curtsied, then dropped onto the settee again as Lady Clifford showed the duchess out. Her head was spinning with conjectures, but so far, she was certain of only one thing.

The duchess had lied to them.

Or, at the very least, hadn't told the entire truth. There was a great deal more to this than just a missing friend. Whether that mattered or not remained to be seen, but one thing was certain. If the Duchess of Kenilworth had been anyone else, Lady Clifford would have demanded the entire truth from her before she took this business on.

As it was, however, she *was* the Duchess of Kenilworth, and whatever it was she was up to, it was worth it to them to do just as she bid them. Even if that meant attending a dreadful masque ball at dreadful Lady Wylde's, of all cursed things.

Georgiana cradled her chin in her hand with a glum sigh. There was, alas, no help for it, even if the very thought of such an entertainment made her shudder, and even though she was the least suited to such a task than any of Lady Clifford's other students.

"What a strange encounter," Lady Clifford murmured when she came back into the room. She wandered over to her desk, picked up the paper she'd laid there, and stared at it for a moment. "It's not much to start with, I'm afraid."

"No. Lady Tilbury is unobjectionable enough, but how in the world am I meant to manage Lady Wylde?"

"I daresay you won't have to speak to her much. You might also want to see what you can find out about the Duchess of Kenilworth while you're at the ball, my love. Balls are wonderful for gathering gossip, and I think we both can agree there are a few gaps in the duchess's story."

"Yes." Georgiana slumped on the settee. "That's easily done, my lady, but Lady Wylde! How does one even approach such a woman?"

Lady Clifford chuckled. "Why, just as you would a rabid dog, my love. *Carefully*."

Chapter Four

Benedict sprawled on the silk settee in Lady Wylde's dressing room, one leg balanced on his knee and his arm flung over the back, watching as she dabbed powder on her décolletage.

Her eyes found his in the looking glass, and she cast him a flirtatious glance, eyelashes batting over her sleepy dark eyes. "Such an intense gaze, my lord. Do you see something that pleases you?"

She shifted, turning toward him, and the lace sleeve of her dressing gown slipped obligingly off her shoulder, exposing her smooth, creamy skin. Benedict's gaze roved over her, lingering on the luscious curves of her breasts. "Quite fetching indeed, my lady."

She *was* fetching. No doubt she'd invited him to her boudoir hoping he'd fall upon her like a ravaging animal, but despite all that lovely skin she was flaunting, he couldn't conjure even a twitch of interest from his nether regions.

"If I'm so fetching, then come here, my lord, and lay claim to me." Lady Wylde's red lips curved as she beckoned to him with one delicate finger, the other trailing from the hollow of her throat down to the bare skin between her breasts.

Benedict stifled a sigh. It was a damnable time for his cock to be so stubborn, but it did tend to be right about these sorts of things. "There's no time, I'm afraid. Your guests have arrived and await your presence in the ballroom."

But Lady Wylde wasn't one to easily relinquish her prey. "My guests?" She threw her head back in a throaty laugh. "Let them wait."

Benedict arched an eyebrow as she rose from her chair. She sauntered toward the settee, pushed his leg aside, and sank down onto his lap.

No. Still nary a twitch.

Lady Wylde wasn't the first woman who'd attempted to ensnare him with her seductive wiles. Benedict had been chased many times, and it had never dampened his arousal before. Quite the opposite. He was an indolent creature, and he'd always been rather grateful to his paramours for saving him the effort of a pursuit.

She wriggled her round bottom against him, her warm breath caressing his cheek. His hand landed her thigh, more from habit than anything else. He gave it a hopeful squeeze—he was a *man*, after all—and eyed the pale, full globes of her breasts spilling from her bodice.

Nothing. His cock was staging a rebellion.

He couldn't make sense of it. He hadn't come to London for a dalliance with Lady Wylde, but he'd been eager enough to bed her last season. At the moment, however, he couldn't recall why she'd caught his attention in the first place.

Troubling, really. He hadn't bedded a woman in months. Now here he was with an obliging lady perched on his lap, and she was just the sort of lush, dark beauty he favored. If his cock refused to stand for a siren like Lady Wylde, he might as well give up on being a wicked rake and return to Surrey now—take up angling, or bird watching, or whatever it was gentlemen did when they declined into their dotage.

"May I offer you more wine, my lord?"

Benedict turned his attention to his wine glass, which had remained untouched since he'd arrived. "Later, perhaps."

"You're somber this evening. Is there nothing I can do to cheer you?" Lady Wylde's red lips curved in an inviting smile, and one slim hand landed on his knee. "There must be *something* that will restore you to your customary good humor."

Her hand inched up Benedict's thigh. Given how determined she was to lift his, er...*spirits*, she'd take a refusal on his part as a grievous insult, indeed, but he couldn't make himself give a damn.

"No, thank you, my lady." Benedict caught her wrist and removed her hand from his thigh. "I believe I'll make an appearance in the ballroom, and leave you to complete your toilette. Perhaps you'll favor me with your first dance tonight?"

Lady Wylde wasn't accustomed to being rejected. Her cheeks reddened with anger, and her full, pouting lips pressed into a tight line. "No, I'm afraid not. I've promised my first dance to Lord Harrington."

She tossed her head, but she didn't relinquish her place on his lap. Instead she clung to him like a burr, as if she were expecting him to leap to his feet in a fit of jealous rage at the mention of Lord Harrington.

Benedict remained where he was. The idea of such a scene exhausted him, and before he knew what he was doing, he raised his fingers to his mouth to hide a yawn.

"Am I *boring* you, Lord Haslemere?" Lady Wylde had been toying with his hair, but now she sank her claws into the back of his neck.

"Ouch! Er, I mean, no, of course not." He winced as he traced a finger over the long, deep scratch she'd carved into his flesh. "You're uniformly charming—"

But it was too late to soothe her ruffled feelings. She leapt free of his lap and flounced back to her dressing table. Her face was mottled with fury, and the eyes that met his in the glass glittered with temper.

Well, that was it, then. Benedict got to his feet with far less regret than he should have felt at being doomed to God knew how many more weeks of celibacy. He turned toward the door, reasoning that the least he could do was save her the trouble of tossing him out of her dressing room, but before he could escape, she stopped him.

"Will your sister, the Duchess of Kenilworth, be attending my ball this evening, my lord?"

Benedict turned back to her with a shrug. "I've no idea. If you recall, I've just arrived in London. I haven't yet spoken to my sister, but as I'm sure you're aware, the duchess doesn't attend many entertainments during the season."

Particularly not any entertainment hosted by Lady Wylde. The *ton* might receive her ladyship without batting an eye, but the Duke of Kenilworth was a high stickler, and he was particularly protective of his wife. Benedict doubted he'd consider Lady Wylde a proper companion for Jane.

Lady Wylde went back to her toilette with a shrug, but there was a spiteful glimmer in her eyes. "Oh, I understand completely, my lord. I don't blame the duchess at all for wishing to avoid company just now, but her favorite is meant to attend tonight, and I thought perhaps she longed to see him."

"Her favorite?" Benedict's eyes narrowed. He didn't care for Lady Wylde's tone, or her insinuation. "I don't have the pleasure of understanding you, madam."

"Oh, I'm certain it's just idle gossip. You know how the *ton* is, my lord. There's likely not a grain of truth to it." Lady Wylde's crimson lips curled in a smirk. "Still, perhaps it's not so surprising the duke won't let her out of his sight."

Benedict took up the coat he'd draped over the back of the settee and offered Lady Wylde a polite bow. Whatever the latest rumor was, he'd be damned if he'd give her the satisfaction of telling it to him. "I'm certain the duke isn't so foolish as to credit whatever damnable lie is on the tip of London's wagging tongues this time. I wish you a pleasant evening, my lady."

But Lady Wylde had no intention of letting him go without spilling her secret. "Oh, but how silly of me! Of course, you wouldn't have heard of it, rusticating in Surrey as you've been. I beg you'll forgive me for repeating something so ugly, my lord, but the gossip has it the duchess and Lord Draven are engaged in a scandalous affair."

Benedict paused halfway to the door. Jane, having an affair with *Draven*?

How imaginative. He'd give the gossips that much. Utter bollocks still, of course. Jane had married the Duke of Kenilworth less than six years ago, and the union was a happy one. Even if she was disappointed in her marriage, why should she choose the Earl of Draven as her paramour? The man was practically a hermit—

"You look skeptical, my lord. It might interest you to know Her Grace was spotted leaving Lord Draven's townhouse one night this week, *alone*. But I'm sure it's all perfectly innocent."

Lady Wylde's voice rang with malice, and Benedict let out a weary sigh. Perhaps he should have remained in Surrey. It was as dull as a bloody tomb there, but at least he was spared this sort of foolishness.

"Now, if you'll forgive me, Lord Haslemere, I must dress. Do enjoy the ball tonight, won't you? It's rumored Lord Draven will come out of hiding to attend. Perhaps you should ask him yourself if the rumors about his affair with your sister are true."

Benedict left Lady Wylde's bedchamber without bothering to give her the satisfaction of an answer. Her mocking laugh followed him through her private sitting room, persisting even after he'd escaped into the hallway, but he hardly registered it as he made his way down the stairs to the first floor.

The doors between the large and small drawing rooms and the music room had been thrown open to serve as a ballroom. He came to an abrupt halt as he neared, knocked back a step by the deafening din of music and footsteps pounding across the dance floor.

Good Lord, what a crush. The acrid scent of sweat and the heat were so stifling he might have been standing at the very gates of hell. Half of London's upper ten thousand were stuffed inside cheek to jowl, and ready to burst from the seams, much like Lady Wylde's breasts from her corset. Even if Draven was here, it would be a devil of a business to find him in this crowd.

Benedict stifled another sigh as he took in the familiar sight of London's fashionable set, their jewels flashing and faces flushed with heat and champagne. Didn't anyone *new* ever come to London? These were all the same people who'd been here last season, except for—

Benedict paused, his gaze catching and holding on a tall lady in a bronze-colored gown and masque. She was some distance away from him, tucked into a far corner of the ballroom, removed from the rest of the crush.

Wasn't that…that is, she looked just like—

No, it couldn't be. It was ridiculous, impossible. This was the last place in the world he'd ever expect to find *her*.

No, he'd mistaken another lady for her. Yes, he must have done. There was no way Georgiana Harley, with her scolding tongue and prim gowns, her manners so stiff and proper she put him in mind of a marionette whose strings had been pulled too tight, could be *here*, at Lady Wylde's masque ball.

He peered over the sea of bobbing heads with far more interest than he cared to explain to himself, trying to catch another glimpse of the tall, graceful lady in the dark silk gown.

Ah, just there.

Hell and damnation. There was no mistake. He knew it as soon as his eyes lighted on her once again. She didn't look anything like he'd ever seen her before, but for good or ill, he couldn't forget her face. Georgiana Harley lingered like a bad taste in his mouth, or a stinging slap to his cheek.

It *was* her. There was no confusing her with any other lady in London.

The drab hat and stiff brown cloak were nowhere to be found. Her gown wasn't nearly revealing enough to catch the lascivious gazes of the rakes who frequented this sort of entertainment, but now he'd spotted her, Benedict found it difficult to take his eyes off her.

Her gown and masque were a deep, rich brown. They were both plain, severe even, her only adornment a bronze and black striped ribbon tied around her waist. There wasn't a single feather or frill to be seen, but the ensemble suited her somehow. Her thick, chestnut hair was gathered into a simple knot at the back of her neck, and a length of the same striped ribbon that made up her sash was wound throughout the thick locks.

He gaped at her, struck dumb, feeling as if he were staring at a ghost. A ghost of a different Georgiana Harley, from another place and time—a ghost of a lady who, despite her obvious efforts to avoid notice and blend into the scenery, outshone the gaudier birds that fluttered around her, with her sleek, rich feathers.

Benedict didn't make any move to enter the ballroom, but lingered in the doorway, watching her. What the devil was she *doing* here? Had she come here alone? No, surely not. He turned his gaze toward her companions, expecting to find Lady Clifford, but instead it was Darlington who was standing beside Miss Harley, and on his other side, her hand on his arm, was Lady Darlington.

That was even stranger still. They were meant to be on their way to Darlington Castle in Kent by now. Even when he was in London, Darlington rarely went into company. If he did venture out, it certainly wasn't to attend this sort of chaotic entertainment.

Benedict pulled his masque from his coat pocket, slipped it over his face, and began to push his way through the crush. As Darlington's closest friend, it was his duty to discover if something was amiss. If that meant crossing swords with Miss Harley again, well, it was bad luck, but it wasn't *his* fault. He had an obligation to Darlington, that was all. If he *did* feel a hint of anticipation about dueling with her again, it was only because he was bored, and it was good fun, ruffling her feathers.

He circled around the long way, keeping to the outer edges of the crowd to avoid any acquaintances who might recognize him. He had no patience for meaningless chatter at the moment.

He kept his gaze fixed on Georgiana Harley as he neared her corner of the ballroom. As he got closer, he noticed her jaw was tight, and her shoulders rigid. She hadn't come here for her own pleasure, then. She didn't *want* to be here, yet there she was, in all her ballroom finery, doing her best to go unnoticed.

She seemed distracted as well. Her gaze was moving over the crowd as if she were searching for someone. Who, though? The ballroom was crowded with *ton*, along with a generous sprinkling of scoundrels, rakes, courtesans, and other dubious members of the demimonde who made up Lady Wylde's circle. Miss Harley didn't know a soul here beyond Darlington and his wife.

No matter. He'd have an answer soon enough, even if he had to tease it out of her—

"Lord Darlington!"

Every head turned, the chatter grew louder, and then the crowd parted and Lady Wylde herself appeared, clad in a daring gown of scarlet silk. Lady Tilbury was with her, and Lord Harrington, the fool, was dangling on her arm like a shiny bauble.

The last person Benedict wished to confront at this moment was Lady Wylde, so he ducked behind a boisterous knot of people standing near Miss Harley and did his best not to call attention to himself.

"Lady Darlington!" Lady Wylde, who was well aware the Marquess and Marchioness of Darlington didn't attend many London entertainments, couldn't quite hide her satisfaction that they'd made her masque ball an exception. "Why, how wonderful to see you both here. I confess I didn't expect it."

"My lady." Darlington bowed over Lady Wylde's hand. "It's a pleasure to see you."

"Oh no, my lord, the pleasure is all mine, I assure you," Lady Wylde gushed in her usual dramatic fashion, simpering over Darlington, flattering Lady Darlington, and relishing having every eye upon her.

Every eye, that is, but Benedict's.

He kept his attention on Georgiana Harley, and he saw her reach out and lay a hand on Lady Darlington's arm. She whispered something to her, and Lady Darlington responded by turning to Lady Tilbury with a smile. "Lady Tilbury, and Lord Harrington. How do you do? May I present Miss Georgiana Harley?"

"Lady Wylde, Lord Harrington, Lady Tilbury." Miss Harley curtsied to each in turn, but Lady Tilbury seemed to be of particular interest to her, and soon enough she'd coaxed her a little apart from the others. At first, they seemed to be exchanging the usual pleasantries. All very dull and ordinary, but for one thing.

Their conversation went on, and on, and on...

For two ladies who'd never met before, Miss Harley and Lady Tilbury seemed to have a great deal to discuss, and judging by Miss Harley's eager expression and the rapidity with which her lips were moving, whatever they were discussing was of some importance to her.

Benedict edged closer to them, taking care to keep his head down and his movements unobtrusive. Closer, then closer still, until he was close enough to overhear Lady Tilbury murmur, "...tell you what I told Lord Draven, Miss Harley."

Draven, again? Benedict frowned. Draven's name seemed to be on everyone's lips tonight. Curious, for a man who rarely set foot outside his townhouse.

"...appreciate any information you might give me, Lady Tilbury."

"Despite my friendship with Clara's late mother, I'm afraid I only know what all of London knows, Miss Harley. Clara was last seen at a Christmas ball at Lord Draven's country estate in Oxfordshire. The previous Lord Draven, that is, the current earl's father."

"The estate is near High Wycombe, I believe?"

"Yes. The Beauchamps lived in the same neighborhood as Lord and Lady Draven, and the two families were friends." Lady Tilbury sighed. "Poor, dear Clara hasn't been seen since that night."

Miss Harley raised an eyebrow. "Are you certain? An acquaintance of hers swore to me she saw Miss Beauchamp sitting in a carriage outside your home less than a week ago."

"No, no. I think I would know it if I'd seen Clara after all these years. Her family searched all over England for her without any success. Goodness, it is warm in here." Lady Tilbury murmured, with a vigorous flutter of her fan.

"Miss Beauchamp's tale is a strange one, isn't it? Unless one believes in vanishings." Miss Harley gave Lady Tilbury an appraising look. "Which I don't."

"Quite strange, yes. Mrs. Beauchamp was a great intimate of mine, but she didn't talk to me much about Clara. She couldn't bear to mention Clara's name after she went missing." Lady Tilbury shook her head. "She died within a year of Clara's disappearance, and I don't mind telling you, Miss Harley, I've always thought she died of a broken heart."

Lady Wylde overheard her, and having finished flattering Darlington, turned her attention to Lady Tilbury. "I recall hearing at one time that Clara Beauchamp had married a viscount, though I never did believe it to be true."

Miss Harley frowned. "Why shouldn't you believe it?"

Lady Wylde swept a disparaging glance over Miss Harley, and despite himself, Benedict's lips twitched. Miss Harley wouldn't get far with her ladyship with that forthright tone. As far as Lady Wylde was concerned Miss Harley, in her plain gown and simple ribbons, was hardly worth a second glance. She might not wish to insult the Marquess and Marchioness of Darlington by snubbing their friend, but Lady Wylde's graciousness would only extend so far.

"From what I've heard, Clara Beauchamp was a sweet little thing, but rather insipid, and of course, her family was in trade. She wasn't the sort of young lady to attract the notice of an aristocrat." Lady Wylde gave Miss Harley a condescending smile. "She had a tidy little fortune, but not enough to make up for the deficiencies in her pedigree, you understand."

Miss Harley gave her a blank stare. "Not really, no."

Lady Wylde settled her ruffles with a disdainful sniff. "It's the way of things, my dear. Miss Beauchamp didn't, to my knowledge, ever become a viscountess. She disappeared soon after that rumor started, and there hasn't been a whisper about her since."

Miss Harley didn't seem to realize a lady of inferior rank such as herself was meant to plead humbly for Lady Wylde's exalted attention. "People don't simply vanish into the air like so much mist, Lady Wylde. Someone must have seen *something*."

"Of course, someone knows something about it, but I shouldn't hold my breath waiting for them to speak up. They've remained quiet for this long, haven't they? Clara Beauchamp is likely dead by now. But that's what comes of young ladies getting above themselves." Lady Wylde's lip curled. "The Beauchamps were common, and Lord and Lady Draven are among the most elegant members of London society."

"Ah, well, what's a kidnapping in comparison to aristocratic patronage?" Miss Harley's voice was bright, but her face had gone hard. "As long as Miss Beauchamp was fortunate enough to enjoy the attentions of *the most elegant members of London society*, I suppose she has nothing to complain of, does she?"

Darlington stifled a cough, and Lady Darlington raised a hand to her mouth to hide a smirk, but Lady Wylde only replied without a shred of irony, "Indeed, she doesn't. But I must say, I don't understand this sudden fuss over Clara Beauchamp. Lord Draven, of all people was asking about her just the other day."

"That is curious," Lord Harrington drawled. "But as we learned this week, Draven has a great many secrets. The Duchess of Kenilworth, for one."

Harrington's sneering tone made Benedict's fists clench. Bloody traitor. He had half a mind to call Harrington out—

"The Duchess of Kenilworth?" Miss Harley repeated. "What does the duchess have to do with Lord Draven?"

"My dear Miss Harley, what *doesn't* she have to do with him?" Harrington smirked. "If the gossips are to be believed, the duchess and Lord Draven are...*intimate* friends."

Miss Harley looked Harrington up and down as if he were a bit of muck she'd found on the sole of her slippers. "Are gossips *ever* to be believed, Lord Harrington?"

Harrington's face reddened, but he glared down his nose at her. "You're not out much in society, are you, Miss Harley? If you were, you'd know this isn't the first rumor that's circulated about Draven and the duchess."

Lady Wylde tittered. "Indeed. Given their past escapades, it's not so surprising the duchess and Lord Draven should have fallen into each other's arms again."

"When did they fall into each other's arms the first—"

"Forgive me, but I must see to my other guests. I beg you will excuse me, Lord and Lady Darlington." Lady Wylde offered them each a curtsy, then swept off in a whirl of scarlet skirts without another glance at Miss Harley.

Benedict had heard enough. He backed into the hallway, leaving the ballroom behind. Once he'd rounded the corner, he tore the masque from his face, an uneasy knot in his stomach. He felt rather foolish, creeping about like a spy, but secrets led to spying, and it was beginning to dawn on him his sister might have more secrets that he'd ever suspected.

What did Lady Wylde mean by *past escapades*?

Jane *had* been acting peculiar lately. She'd spent far more time at his country estate this past winter than usual. Benedict had wondered at it, but he'd assumed Jane would confide in him if something was amiss. At eight years her senior, he'd been as much a parent as a brother to Jane. She'd been hardly more than a child when their mother passed, and they'd only grown closer since their father's death three years earlier.

So he hadn't pressed her for an explanation. He'd let it go and simply enjoyed hers and his nephew Freddy's company. But Jane's silence had continued. As the season drew near, she'd grown unaccountably anxious about Benedict's return to London, and encouraged him to remain in Surrey without offering any explanation why.

But an affair, with Lord Draven? Impossible. Jane would *never* betray her husband. It simply wasn't in her character to do something so low and dishonest.

As for this Clara Beauchamp, Benedict had never heard her name before, but she was somehow connected to Lord Draven's family, and Lord Draven was, according to the gossips, somehow connected to Jane.

The whole business was as murky as the Thames, but all hope wasn't yet lost. Draven hadn't put in an appearance, but there was one other person who'd come here tonight to stick her pert little nose into this mysterious business.

Of course, there was no reason to think Miss Harley had turned up here, in the last place one would expect her to be, because of the rumors about Jane and Draven. She might be after something else entirely. God knew there were enough sinners gathered in this ballroom tonight to keep Lady Clifford busy for an eternity.

But Darlington hadn't come tonight because he'd had a sudden yearning for Lady Wylde's company. No, he and Lady Darlington had come as a favor to Miss Harley. Benedict was certain of it. If she *was* here to poke about in Jane's business, who'd put her up to it?

Draven, perhaps, or the Duke of Kenilworth?

There was only one way to find out.

Benedict stuffed his masque into his pocket and made his way to the entrance hall. He collected his hat and walking stick from Lady Wylde's butler and strolled out into the night. A moment later his carriage appeared, and he climbed inside.

"The Clifford School, Grigg," Benedict ordered his coachman as he pulled the door closed behind him. "No. 26 Maddox Street."

It was time he paid a visit to Georgiana Harley.

Chapter Five

"Was your first adventure in the glittering world of the *ton* everything you hoped it would be, Georgiana?"

Georgiana turned from the carriage window to arch an eyebrow at Cecilia. "I hadn't any hopes at all. I expected the ball would be tiresome, and it was."

Cecilia bit her lip to hide a grin. "You weren't entertained, then?"

"Not in the least." Honestly, she didn't see what was so entertaining about spending an entire evening trapped in an airless ballroom in an itchy masque and a gown that squeezed her breathless.

"What is your opinion of Lady Wylde?" Cecilia blinked innocently at her, but Georgiana wasn't fooled. Cecilia knew very well what Georgiana thought of aristocrats like Lady Wylde.

As usual, Georgiana didn't mince words. "My opinion is she's every bit as dreadful as the gossip claims. Her petulance is exceeded only by Lord Harrington's. He's a haughty, smirking thing, and a fool as well, to let a woman of Lady Wylde's ilk lead him about like a lapdog." Georgiana hadn't any patience for fashionable, arrogant countesses, and even less for fashionable, arrogant rakes.

Lord Darlington hadn't said much since they'd climbed into his plush carriage, but now he choked back a laugh. "Dear God. Poor Harrington."

"Don't encourage her, Gideon." Cecilia lay a hand on her husband's arm and turned what she likely meant to be a stern look on Georgiana. "Nonsense. It wasn't as bad as all that."

Georgiana ached an eyebrow at her. "My dear Cecilia, the entire time he was standing there I was searching for his lead."

Lord Darlington didn't try to hold back this time, but gave a shout of laughter, and even Cecilia couldn't prevent a reluctant grin. "Wicked thing. Shame on you, Georgiana."

Georgiana shrugged off the reprimand. Yes, yes, she had a blistering tongue. She'd been scolded for it often enough, but it had a mind of its own, and she'd long since given up trying to tame it. "What do you suppose happened to Lord Draven tonight?"

Cecilia sighed. "I've no idea, but Lord Haslemere is going to be furious when he hears the rumors about Lord Draven and his sister."

"Yes, he will." Lord Darlington's smile faded. "I'll have my hands full, keeping him from calling Draven out."

"Calling him out! Would he really go as far as that?" Georgiana had assumed Lord Haslemere would treat the rumors as he had those footraces in Maiden Lane—as if they were amusing, but nothing more than that.

Lord Darlington looked surprised. "Indeed, he would. He's fiercely protective of his sister and nephew. He's careless of his own reputation, but he considers any insult to Jane an insult to himself."

"He's a devoted brother, and a loyal friend," Cecilia added. "If it hadn't been for Lord Haslemere, half of London would still believe Gideon was a murderer."

Georgiana winced, her conscience pricking at her. Looking at Lord Darlington now, it was difficult to believe only a few months ago most of London had suspected him of murdering his first wife. She herself had believed him guilty, but she'd been wrong about him. As far as she could tell, his only flaw was his steadfast friendship with Lord Haslemere.

A grievous flaw, indeed.

Cecilia, who often guessed Georgiana's thoughts before she even had a chance to think them, frowned at her. "I've told you before, Georgiana. Lord Haslemere is not the feather-brained rake the *ton* supposes him to be."

Yes, Cecilia had said such things before, but Georgiana hadn't seen any evidence of Lord Haslemere's alleged cleverness. She *had* seen plenty of evidence to the contrary, but she kept that opinion to herself. "Perhaps we should have stayed another hour to see if Lord Draven would turn up." She'd have to pay a call on him now, which would be dashed awkward, given they'd never been introduced.

"Not much chance of that." Cecilia shook her head. "Lady Wylde's entertainments inevitably descend into debauched frenzies as the evening wears on. If Lord Draven had intended to come, he would have appeared earlier, with the other respectable guests."

"There were respectable guests there?" Georgiana didn't recall seeing any. It was nothing but rakes and demi-reps as far as the eye could see, clinging to the edges of the ballroom like scandalous wallpaper. She opened her mouth to say so, but then closed it again, biting her tongue. It was late, and they were all tired. Perhaps the less said about Lady Wylde's masque ball, and Lady Wylde herself, the better.

A few minutes later, the carriage rolled to a stop in front of the Clifford School. "We're off to Kent tomorrow, dearest." An anxious frown creased Cecilia's brow as she studied Georgiana's face. "I'll miss you dreadfully, but we'll be back soon."

However soon it was, it wouldn't be soon enough for Georgiana, but she feigned a careless shrug, so as not to worry Cecilia. "Don't hurry back on my account."

Cecilia squeezed Georgiana's hand, but stopped her before she could open the carriage door. "Oh, wait. I nearly forgot. I have something for you." She leaned over, plucked a heavy object from the floor, and held it out. "Sophia asked me to give it to you before we left for Kent."

It was too dim inside the carriage for Georgiana to see what it was, but as soon as she felt the cool, smooth glass against her fingertips she guessed, and a smile lit her face. "Mrs. Beeson's quince preserves! Cecilia, you're an angel."

Cecilia laughed. "I thought you'd like it. Don't have it all at one sitting, mind you, as you did the last jar. I expect you to make it last, so you'll be sweet-tempered when I return."

Georgiana snorted, but pressed a quick kiss on Cecilia's cheek, clutching her jar of preserves the way another lady might clutch a fistful of diamonds. "I make no promises. It was kind of you to indulge me this evening, Lord Darlington," she added, gathering her cloak tight about her chin. "I thank you for it."

Lord Darlington had been peering through the window into the darkness, a crease between his brows, but now he turned to Georgiana with a distracted smile. "It's my pleasure, Miss Harley."

Georgiana doubted any of them had gotten any pleasure from this evening, but she gave Lord Darlington a brisk nod, then threw open the carriage door herself before the coachman could climb from the box, and leapt down to the pavement.

Lord Darlington came down after her and held out his arm with a bow. "Allow me to escort you to the door, Miss Harley."

"There's no need, my lord, truly. I'll be perfectly fine. It's a quick step or two only." Georgiana waved a hand toward the school.

"Ah, but I insist."

She flushed at his gallantry, but allowed him to take her arm and lead her up the stone stairs to the front door. "Thank you, my lord."

He bowed again, his lips curving in a polite smile. "Good night, Miss Harley."

Georgiana paused on the top step, her gaze on Lord Darlington's broad back as he strode back to the carriage, but she didn't really see him as her mind drifted over the events of the evening.

She hadn't learned nearly as much as she'd hoped to about Clara Beauchamp tonight. Lady Tilbury seemed to know surprisingly little for one who'd been on such intimate terms with the Beauchamp family. As far as discovering Clara's whereabouts were concerned, Georgiana might as well have stayed in her bed with her nose buried in her book.

Still, the ball hadn't been an utter waste of time. She'd learned one thing, a thing she'd suspected, but hadn't been certain of until this evening.

The Duchess of Kenilworth wasn't being truthful with her.

Her Grace, that soft-spoken, wide-eyed, ladylike creature had looked directly into Georgiana's and Lady Clifford's faces, and lied to them.

It was a lie of omission, yes, but a lie all the same. Georgiana and Lady Clifford both had enough experience with secrets to know the duchess was hiding something, but the scope of her lie, the depth of it…

Georgiana hadn't expected *that*. It wasn't some harmless little falsehood. The duchess was at the center of a storm of gossip, a scandal being whispered over in every drawing room in London.

Georgiana didn't much care whether the Duchess of Kenilworth was having an affair with Lord Draven or not, but she didn't appreciate being sent into battle with the *ton* without the proper armor.

She'd been thrown off her guard tonight when that intolerable Lord Harrington had spoken of Lord Draven's "secrets" in such a derisive manner, but that was nothing to the shock of discovering the two people rumored to be having a torrid liaison were the same two people who were searching for Clara Beauchamp.

There wasn't the least chance *that* was a coincidence—

"Wandering about in the dark all by yourself, Miss Harley?"

Georgiana startled at the sound of the low, deep voice behind her, her thoughts scattering.

"Such a clever lady, yet so careless with your safety."

That voice, it was familiar. She'd heard it before, but she couldn't quite place—

"You never know who might be lurking in the shadows, waiting for you." Footsteps thudded softly behind her, and when the voice spoke again, it was closer. "Why, it could be anyone."

Georgiana closed her eyes as that husky murmur hit the back of her neck. Sweat broke out on her palms, her fingers went slack, and the next thing she knew, her precious jar of quince preserves slipped from her hand and rolled down the steps. "Oh, no!" She raced after it, but it was already too late. The jar smashed to the ground in a splatter of thick orange syrup and shattered glass. "My preserves!"

"I beg your pardon." The toe of a spotless evening pump nudged a piece of the broken glass aside. "They look delicious, too. Thick, but not too thick, just as preserves should be. Pity."

That drawl, slow and deep, faintly mocking...

She knew that voice, knew the shape and plumpness of the lips from which it emerged, despite her every effort to forget them. Georgiana reminded herself to hold onto her dignity as she raised her eyes to meet his, but when she caught sight of her tormentor's face, only one word seemed appropriate. "*You.*"

"*Me*, indeed. You do remember me, then?"

Remember him? She could sooner forget a fiend on the back of a hound from hell riding straight from one end of London to the other than she could Lord Haslemere. "Vividly."

He grinned. "I'm flattered, Miss Harley."

Georgiana eyed him, her lips going tight. "I don't see why you should be. People remember all sorts of unpleasant things, Lord Haslemere. Breaking a bone, falling down the stairs, having a tooth pulled."

Her irritation only amused him, and his infuriating grin widened. "You seem cross, Miss Harley. If I didn't know better, I might think you aren't pleased to see me."

"What are you doing here, my lord?" The duchess had promised he was safely tucked away at his country estate in Surrey, and would remain there for the season. Why, then, was he hiding in the shadows, leaping out at innocent passersby and smashing their precious preserves to bits?

"Perhaps I came here to see you." He slouched against the wrought iron railing that led to the front door, one arm draped carelessly over the top of it. "Perhaps I missed you, and longed to see your face again—"

Georgiana held up her hand to silence him. "Somehow, I doubt that."

"Why should you doubt it?" He pressed a hand to his chest. "You wound me, Miss Harley."

No, but I'd like to.

Georgiana knew she didn't have the sort of face that inspired surprise visits from handsome earls, and she had no desire to listen to Lord Haslemere's flirtatious nonsense. "It's not my face that's brought you all the way from Surrey."

His dark eyes flicked over her, a frown marring his handsome features. "Your face quite haunts me, I assure you. I even dream of it, on occasion. Fierce brown eyes, pert nose, scolding lips."

Georgiana snorted. He was mocking her, of course. If he was as enamored of her face as he claimed, he'd know her eyes weren't *brown*. "Well, you've seen it now, so do feel free to leave again."

Nothing could possibly interest her less than Lord Haslemere's scandalous comings and goings, of course. She was only surprised she hadn't heard he'd returned to London. The man couldn't stir a step without half of England knowing of it. The *ton* awaited his every move with such breathless anticipation, even *she* couldn't avoid hearing about him.

A slow smile curved his lips. "Oh, I'm not leaving yet, princess."

Princess? Georgiana gave him an incredulous look. "Did you just call me *princess*?"

He paused, as if deciding whether or not the words had come from his lips, then shrugged. "I believe I did, yes."

"*Why?*" It wasn't what she meant to say, or not *all* she meant to say, but for the first time in as long as Georgiana could remember, her sharp tongue failed her.

He let out an impatient sigh. "I haven't the faintest idea, unless it's that you have an untouchable air about you. What does it matter? The point, Miss Harley, is I have some delicate busines that will keep me in London for some time."

Georgiana crossed her arms over her chest. "Delicate business, my lord? Is there a wager that needs laying, or a mistress who requires jewels? The mind boggles at the possibilities."

"Ah, there's that sharp tongue." He straightened from the railing and sauntered closer. "Now I hear it again, I do believe I've missed it even more than I missed your face. I do like a lady who knows how to wield her tongue."

If she didn't know it to be impossible, Georgiana would have sworn he was staring at her mouth. Except, of course, it *was* impossible. "That surprises me, Lord Haslemere. From what I've heard, you've tamed half the tongues in London."

His eyebrows shot up, then he threw his head back in a hearty laugh. "Have you been listening to the gossip about me? Shame on you, Miss Harley. I thought you were above all that."

Georgiana scowled at him. She didn't know why he was wasting his charm on her, but his teasing wouldn't get him anywhere. "One can't avoid hearing the gossip about you, my lord. There's simply too much of it. Now, if you'd be so good as to be on your way—"

"No, I'm afraid I can't leave quite yet." He stepped in front of her when she moved to brush past him. "You see, Miss Harley, I'm curious about something, and I'm hoping you can enlighten me."

"Me?" Ah, now it was starting to make sense. He was flirting with her because he wanted something. She didn't bother to ask what it was. It didn't matter, because she wouldn't give it to him. "Nothing would please me more than to help you, Lord Haslemere, but as enlightenment requires humility, I'm afraid it's hopeless."

She made to sweep past him again, her nose as high in the air as a lady with quince preserves splattered on her hems could manage, but he caught her arm and turned her to face him before she could escape. "Oh, but I have unerring faith in you, Miss Harley. If anyone can command me, it's *you*."

Command him? Georgiana never permitted herself to blush, but to her horror, she felt her cheeks heating. "Very well, my lord, since you insist on it. I command you to leave here at once."

"Not just yet. Not until you answer my questions, Miss Harley."

He stepped closer, close enough that it was impossible to avoid his eyes. Georgiana had been doing her best to keep from looking at him, because looking at Lord Haslemere was rather like looking at the sun. He burned one's retinas long after they'd averted their gaze.

But when she did risk another glance at him, she noticed something she'd overlooked before.

Lord Haslemere affected a certain casualness in dress, a Bohemian flair that was much imitated among the fashionable gentlemen of the *ton*. He even had a cravat knot named after him—the *Haslemere*—which was, as far as Georgiana could tell, a clumsily tied cascade knot, with the fall off-centered.

Not that she cared one whit about Lord Haslemere's fashion choices. Not at all. She'd simply…stumbled across the information somewhere.

Tonight, however, he was in evening dress. Every thick, silky lock of his auburn hair was in place, every fold of his cravat terrifyingly symmetrical, his coat and waistcoat impeccably tailored, his gloves spotless, and…

Her eyes widened. A black masque was dangling from his fingertips.

Had he been at Lady Wylde's ball tonight? If so, why hadn't she seen him there? It seemed impossible she could have missed him. With his height and auburn hair, he wasn't the sort of gentleman who blended into a crowd.

Georgiana cleared her throat. "Have you been, er…at an entertainment this evening, my lord?"

"No. That is, unless you consider Lady Wylde's masque ball entertaining. Personally, I found it unspeakably dull."

He *had* been there, then. Had he seen her? He might have chosen to ignore her if he had, but he surely would have greeted Lord and Lady Darlington. Unless he'd intentionally kept out of their sight? Why should he, though? Lord Darlington was his closest friend.

"Though now you ask, Miss Harley," Lord Haslemere went on. "It wasn't a completely wasted evening. I may have overheard a few things that interested me."

"*Overheard?*" Georgiana's eyes narrowed. "That implies you heard things by accident, my lord. I think the more appropriate word is eavesdropped."

"Let's not quibble over words, Miss Harley. You may call it whatever you like. The point is I was there, just as you were, though I confess I nearly overlooked you."

Georgiana regarded him warily, the strangeness of his sudden appearance here sinking in at last. Not just here in London, where he wasn't meant to be, but at Lady Wylde's ball, and now *here*, in front of the Clifford School? It was almost as if he'd followed—

Dear God, he *had*. There was no other explanation for it.

He'd hidden from her at the ball, eavesdropped on her conversation, then come here and skulked about in the bushes, waiting for her, all with the specific purpose of accosting her!

But *why*? It didn't make any sense. It wasn't as if *she* had any business with him, nor he with her. It was none of her concern what Lord Haslemere got up to, and no reason at all she should be lingering on a dark street with him.

Georgiana blinked, the first question she should have asked dawning on her only now.

Why *was* she lingering on a dark street with him? She didn't owe Lord Haslemere any explanations. "As delightful as it's been to see you, my lord, it's quite late, and I—"

"You look rather different than you did the last time I saw you." He frowned, his gaze sweeping from the ribbons in her hair to the toes of her slippers. "If you hadn't been with Darlington, I'm not certain I would have recognized you."

Georgiana wasn't sure how to take that remark, but given she'd been far more plainly attired than any of the other ladies at the ball tonight, she doubted it was a compliment. "It was a masque ball, my lord. You weren't meant to recognize me."

"It wasn't the masque that threw me off." He eased a little closer to her—not so close as to be threatening, but close enough she could see the gleam of challenge in his eyes. "No, it was that Lady Wylde's masque ball is the last place in the world I'd expect to find *you*. So, you see, I can't help but wonder what you were doing there."

"Doing?" Georgiana forced a laugh. "Why, the same thing as everyone else. I don't see what's so scandalous about my being there. Lady Darlington invited me to go, and so I went. Nothing so amazing in that, is there?"

"Come now, Miss Harley." A grin played about his lips, but his dark eyes roved over her face, scrutinizing every shift in her expression. "We both know that isn't true. Lord and Lady Darlington went as a favor to you, not the other way around."

Georgiana couldn't prevent a nervous swallow. For a worthless rake, Lord Haslemere was proving far too astute for her liking. "I don't see what concern it is of yours what I do."

"No concern at all, under the usual circumstances, but your presence at a *ton* ball isn't usual, is it? You see, Miss Harley, even a careless, feather-brained, arrogant rake like myself occasionally has a moment of illumination. You were there for a reason—likely at Lady Clifford's behest—and I couldn't help but wonder if that reason has anything to do with my sister, the Duchess of Kenilworth."

Georgiana just managed to stop her mouth from falling open. How in the name of heaven had he worked that out? All of a sudden it was becoming uncomfortably clear how much trouble Lord Haslemere's sudden presence in London was going to cause her. That, and how many lies she'd have to tell him if he chose to make a nuisance of himself.

Well, whatever the number, she'd tell them. She'd tell one lie after the next if it meant protecting the duchess's privacy. Her Grace had made herself perfectly clear on the subject of her brother. Under no circumstances was he to know anything about the search for Clara Beauchamp.

So she crossed her arms over her chest, met his gaze, and spit out her first lie. "I've no idea what you mean, my lord. What reason should I have to poke about in the duchess's business?"

But it was no use. Lord Haslemere was like a dog on a scent. "That's not a denial, Miss Harley. Indeed, it almost sounds like a confession."

"I have nothing to confess. Even if I did, I wouldn't confess it to *you*. Now, unless you're such a blackguard you'd keep a lady standing on a dark street against her will, I'll ask you to stand back."

He braced his hand on the railing, blocking her way. "One more question first, if you please. Who is Clara Beauchamp? You had a great many questions about Clara Beauchamp for Lady Tilbury. It aroused my curiosity."

Oh, he'd spent a good, long time eavesdropping on her conversations tonight, hadn't he? She was not, however, obliged to satisfy his curiosity. "Why, Clara Beauchamp could be anyone, my lord. Perhaps I could help you if you could tell me something more about her."

His dark eyes narrowed, his playful humor now gone. "That what I'm waiting for *you* to tell *me*, Miss Harley."

Georgiana shrugged. "Forgive me, my lord, but there must be dozens of ladies named Clara Beauchamp in England. I can't possibly know which one you're referring to."

Without warning, she darted under his arm and scurried toward the stairs, more than a little pleased with herself, but before she could escape, his deep voice brought her to a halt on the steps. "Did Lord Draven ask you to prod into my sister's affairs?"

Georgiana blinked down at him as she turned over his question. Now why should Lord Draven, of all people, want to prod into the duchess's affairs? If what she'd heard tonight was true, there was little about the duchess Lord Draven didn't already know.

Of course, it might not be true. "You said one more question, my lord. That's your second."

"Indulge me, Miss Harley." He arched an eyebrow, waiting.

"Why should Lord Draven ask me to prod into your sister's affairs, Lord Haslemere?" Georgiana asked, thinking quickly. He might know something she didn't. If he did, this might be her only chance to work it out of him.

But he saw at once what she was about. "Very clever, Miss Harley," he murmured, one corner of his lips quirking. "But you know the answer to that question already. You were at Lady Wylde's ball this evening. You heard the gossip about Lord Draven and my sister."

"Not by choice." Georgiana loathed gossip and gossipmongers, and went out of her way to avoid hearing their ugly slurs, but the Duchess of Kenilworth and Lord Draven's names had been on everyone's lips tonight.

Lord Haslemere's dark eyes flashed. "How noble of you. But I'm her *brother*, and even I couldn't stir a step without overhearing some fool or other discussing my sister's torrid affair with the Earl of Draven. It seemed to me you were as interested in the gossip about her as everyone else."

Georgiana's stomach clenched with alarm. Lord Darlington had warned her Lord Haslemere would call out Draven if he thought the man had insulted his sister. She wasn't worried for Lord Haslemere, of course, it was just…well, no one wanted to see a young man sliced open by a sword or felled by a pistol ball in some ridiculous duel, did they?

She might have a wicked tongue, but she didn't have a wicked heart. "It's likely just that, my lord. Gossip, without a drop of truth to it."

Perhaps he saw a softening in her face, because he stepped closer—so close she felt a surge of heat despite the cold, damp air. "Perhaps, but I know my sister, Miss Harley. Something is amiss, and I think you know what it is. If you're truly concerned for her, then you'll tell me all you know so I can help her."

It wasn't that simple, however. Georgiana was concerned for the duchess, but she'd given her word, and she wasn't going to break it, no matter how persuasive Lord Haslemere was. "When your sister wants your help, my lord, surely she'll ask for it."

He looked up at her for a long time without speaking, then he said, "You asked me once if I ever took anything seriously. I do. My sister's and nephew's well-being are of the utmost importance to me. More so than my own. You'd do well to keep that in mind, princess."

It wasn't *quite* a threat, but it was a warning.

Georgiana rushed up the remaining steps and through the door, shivers running up her spine from the heat of his gaze boring into her back. At last she gained the entryway and pulled the door closed, putting the thick slab of wood between herself and Lord Haslemere.

Yet she felt none of the relief she'd anticipated. She rubbed the back of her neck, her fingers brushing over the spray of gooseflesh there, but she could still feel his dark gaze on her as palpably as a touch, as if it were his hand there, instead of her own.

Chapter Six

When Benedict was a boy, his mother once told him his smile would be both the making of him and his destruction. One quick tilt of his lips, and people—ladies, in particular—would wish to please him, and rush to do his bidding. Her prediction had proved to be true for the most part, but his mother hadn't counted on Georgiana Harley.

Neither had Benedict, because here he was, standing on the street outside the Clifford School, peering up at a closed, locked door.

What the devil had just happened? He'd pulled every weapon from his arsenal tonight. His most charming grin, his most sweetly persuasive tone of voice, a flirtatious wink, and a few judiciously applied sweeps of his eyelashes…why, he'd never been more irresistible in his life.

But all he'd gotten for his trouble was an aching jaw from smiling. He'd done so much twitching and grinning that by the time she left him, Miss Harley's expression had turned wary, as if she thought he were having some sort of fit.

His coachman, Grigg, was waiting across the street with his carriage. Benedict waved him on, preferring to turn the mystery of Georgiana Harley over in his mind on a walk back to Berkeley Square.

Half a mile later, he still couldn't understand how it had all gone so terribly wrong, but one thing was certain. It was all Georgiana Harley's fault. The confounded woman had as much sensibility as a block of ice.

It had been a perfect disaster of an evening. He could salvage it still— it was just past midnight now, early by Benedict's standards—but after his humiliation at Georgiana Harley's hands, he wasn't in the mood for a debauch with his friends.

He stormed through the front door of his townhouse and marched down the hallway to his study. He wanted a fire, a glass of brandy, and *silence*, in that order—

"Ah, here you are, Haslemere." A tall, broad-shouldered shape detached itself from the fireplace when he entered. "I thought I was going to have to search all over London for you."

A curse left Benedict's lips. How had he not noticed Darlington's carriage waiting outside his townhouse? If he had, he would have ducked into the mews, gone in through the kitchens, and sneaked upstairs to his bedchamber.

Cowardly, yes, but effective.

But it was too bloody late now. "Well, you've found me, and right here in my own study. Clever of you, Darlington. What do you want?"

Darlington raised an eyebrow. "That's a dark scowl, Haslemere. What's gotten you into such a temper?"

"I'm not in a bloody temper." Benedict *was* in a temper—as foul a temper as he could ever recall, and the worst of it was, he knew he was being absurd. Was he truly falling into fits because he'd found one lady in London who wasn't charmed by him? It wasn't as if *he* was charmed by *her*.

Certainly not. He'd never met a pricklier woman in his life.

Still, Benedict made an effort to hide his scowl. "Forgive me, Darlington. I'm a trifle…out of sorts. Will you have brandy?" He didn't feel much like talking, but if anyone could set him back to rights again, it was Darlington.

"I already have." Darlington sipped from the tumbler in his hand with an appreciative nod. "You're an ill-tempered fellow, Haslemere, but one can't fault your taste in liquor."

Benedict filled a tumbler, then crossed the room and dropped into a chair with a sigh. "I've had a trying evening."

Darlington raised an eyebrow. "I doubt that. You live a charmed life, Haslemere."

Benedict opened his mouth to protest, but closed it again without bothering. In truth, he'd had precious little to vex him in his thirty-two years. Perhaps that was why he'd become such a wastrel. "Not charmed tonight, I'm afraid. I've been to Lady Wylde's, and she—"

"You were at Lady Wylde's masque ball tonight?" Darlington frowned. "I didn't see you there."

"I was, er…I spent a good part of it in Lady Wylde's dressing room." It wasn't a *lie*, exactly, and since Benedict didn't choose to confess to spying and eavesdropping, it would have to do. "She was—"

"Thank you, Haslemere, but I don't want to know what you and Lady Wylde got up to in her dressing room."

"Not a blessed thing—"

"Ah. Well, that explains your scowl. She rejected your advances?"

"For God's sake, Darlington. Listen to me, will you? I never made any advances. In fact, I chose an importune time to yawn and offended her feminine sensibilities. She fell into a temper and threw me out of her dressing room. But that's not why—"

"Just as well. That woman's a viper. I can't think why you'd want to get tangled up in her web."

"Vipers don't have *webs*, Darlington. You're thinking of spiders."

Darlington shrugged. "Nests, then, though I don't see how that's any better."

"If you think Lady Wylde is such a viper, what were you doing at her ball tonight? It's not your sort of entertainment." Darlington's marriage had improved him immeasurably—happiness always did that for a man—but damned if he hadn't developed a tiresome virtuous streak.

Lady Wylde was many things, but virtuous wasn't one of them.

"I've spent most of the evening asking myself the same question. I had no desire to attend, I assure you, but Miss Harley asked Cecilia if we might accompany her there as a special favor."

Ah, ha. So, it *had* been her idea to attend! He'd been right all along. "What does Georgiana Harley want with Lady Wylde?"

"No idea, and I know better than to ask. Cecilia agreed to go as a favor to Miss Harley, so we went." Darlington's voice took on the tender, husky quality it always did when he spoke of his wife. "I was surprised at it, though. Cecilia was, too. Miss Harley despises balls."

As far as Benedict could tell, she despised most things.

"She didn't say a word about why she wanted to go?" Benedict wasn't sure why he bothered to ask. Of course, she hadn't. Miss Harley's tongue might be covered in barbs, but he'd seen for himself how well she held it. The woman was a cipher.

"No. She didn't confide in Cecilia, either. I suspect it's some business of Lady Clifford's, otherwise Miss Harley wouldn't have been so secretive about it."

Secretive. Yes, that was a good word for it. Lady Wylde's ballroom, more than any other in London, was swirling with scandals and gossip and secrets. The question was, which secret was Georgiana Harley chasing?

Or whose?

Benedict sipped at his brandy, then set his tumbler aside. "Did Draven ever appear at the ball, Darlington? Lady Wylde mentioned he planned to attend."

Darlington stared hard at him, then asked abruptly, "This is about Jane, isn't it?"

"Why would you assume it has anything to do with Jane?" Benedict asked, avoiding Darlington's perceptive gaze.

"Because I know you, Haslemere. You wouldn't give up a night of debauchery with Lady Wylde for anyone other than Jane, or Freddy."

Benedict let out a dry laugh. "Is that a polite way of saying I'm a selfish, degenerate sot, Darlington?"

"No. But you've been concerned about Jane all winter, when she and Freddy spent so much time in Surrey. So, what's the trouble, Haslemere?"

Benedict stared at the fire for a moment, watching the embers smolder in the grate. "I don't know that there *is* trouble. Jane hasn't said a word, but the truth is I'm…a trifle concerned." More than a trifle, after hearing the gossip tonight.

"I know you are. You're not as mysterious as you think, Haslemere."

"I can't make sense of it, Darlington. Jane tells me everything, but not a word of complaint has passed her lips about whatever it is that's troubling her. Freddy is subdued, as well." Benedict hesitated before meeting Darlington's eyes. "You heard the rumors tonight, about Jane and Draven."

"I did." Darlington swirled the brandy in his glass. "I don't believe a word of it, and I can't imagine you do, either."

Benedict shook his head. "No, but I know my sister, and she hasn't been herself for months now. She's never kept a secret from me before, and I can't help but think…whatever is amiss, it's bad, Darlington. Bad enough she's afraid to tell me."

Darlington was quiet for a moment, then he asked, "What do you mean to do about it?"

Benedict sighed. He should have known he'd end up confessing the whole of it to Darlington. "I went to the Clifford School tonight. I was there when you dropped Miss Harley off."

Darlington snorted. "I know. I saw your carriage. I told you, Haslemere— you're not nearly as stealthy as you think you are. Next time tell Grigg to wait a few blocks away."

"Well, Darlington, since you know everything, then it must have occurred to you Miss Harley asked you to bring her to Lady Wylde's ball because she and Lady Clifford are prying into Jane's affairs."

"I don't know that that's true, but I admit it did occur to me, yes. If Jane is in any difficulty, Miss Harley will find out what it is. She's a clever lady."

Georgiana Harley's stubborn expression flashed in Benedict's mind. "Clever, yes, but the woman has all the warmth and compassion of a stick of wood." Just thinking of those cool brown eyes was making Benedict's temper spike.

Darlington made a noise that sounded like a smothered laugh. "Casting aspersions on Miss Harley's good name, Haslemere? I will do you the favor of not repeating your ungentlemanly description to Cecilia. Now, I take it you tried to pry some information out of Miss Harley?"

"I did. She refused to say a word." Mulish, bad-tempered, stony-faced chit. Pretty eyes, though. Were they truly brown after all, or—

"You mean to say she said *no*?" Darlington set his tumbler aside with extreme care, as if everything he'd ever believed about the world had just been turned inside out. "To *you*?"

"Yes, damn her." It was just beginning to sink in how little information he'd pried out of her. Not only hadn't she told him who Clara Beauchamp was, but she'd refused to say who'd asked her to delve into Jane's affairs, or if she even *was* delving into them.

Darlington chuckled. "You were bound to stumble across a lady who's immune to your charms sooner or later."

Benedict pounded a fist on his knee. "I tell you, Darlington, nothing I said could move her in my favor. I swear she's got a cold, dead stone where her heart should be."

"There must be some way to persuade her."

"How? I tried everything I could think of. I smiled and flirted and charmed myself to exhaustion. I was bloody adorable, and it didn't do a damn bit of good."

Darlington rolled his eyes. "Flirting won't work with Miss Harley. There isn't a bit of the coquette in the lady. You'll have to think of some other way."

"How am I to know what she wants?" All Benedict knew was she didn't want *him*. Once he'd determined that, he hadn't the faintest idea what to do with her.

"Well, she must want *something*, Haslemere. I haven't yet met a person who didn't."

Benedict was quiet as he wracked his brains for any insight into what a woman like Georgiana Harley might want. A horsewhip, perhaps? A razor-edged blade to match her tongue? He could only think of one thing, and God knew she needed it to sweeten that sour temper of hers. "She's ah...she's fond of preserves."

Darlington's lips twitched. "Preserves?"

"Yes. I startled her when I came upon her this evening, and she dropped the jar of preserves she was carrying." It had looked to Benedict as if the loss of those damned preserves was going to drive her to tears.

Darlington started laughing. "You spoiled her jar of quince preserves? Well, I'm no longer surprised she refused to help you. Cecilia gave them to her tonight, and Miss Harley was delighted with the gift. Apparently, she's mad for sweets, especially those preserves."

Benedict had a hard time imagining Miss Harley mad for anything. "Do you suppose Lady Darlington can get me another jar?"

"I don't think a jar of preserves will work, Haslemere. You'll have to do better than that."

Those bloody preserves. It was the only time she showed any emotion the entire time he was in her company—

No, that wasn't true. He'd seen her show emotion once before—the first time they'd met, that night in Covent Garden all those months ago. She'd been furious when she'd come upon him with Sarah and Susannah, outraged to find a rakish lord was trifling with her girls. Why, if she'd had a blade to hand, he didn't doubt she'd have plunged it into his heart.

Those girls—or *her* girls, as she'd called them that night…

She might not care a fig about his flirtatious winks and insinuating grins, but she wasn't entirely immoveable. "The girls at the Clifford School—her pupils. Miss Harley may be a hard-hearted, unfeeling, pitiless wretch, but she does care about those girls."

"She does. About Lady Clifford, too. I know Cecilia would do anything for her ladyship. I'd wager Miss Harley would, as well."

"Darlington, you're brilliant." Benedict hadn't, in fact, tried everything he could to pry information from Georgiana Harley's stubborn lips. He hadn't tried bribery. "Money, then. How much should I offer her?"

"No, not money—"

"Well, what then?" Benedict threw his hands in the air, exasperated. Flirtation wouldn't do, and neither would bribery? Damned if Georgiana Harley wasn't the most troublesome female in existence.

"I have a better idea—something that will be impossible for her to refuse. It's not really my place to tell you this, but I'm fond of Jane, and if she needs help, then for her sake I—"

Benedict groaned. "For God's sake, Darlington, will you just say it?"

"Lady Clifford wants to expand the Clifford School. She's been looking for a building for the better part of a year, but she can't find one that suits."

Ah. At long last, a glimmer of hope. Benedict leaned forward in his chair. "What *would* suit?"

Darlington shrugged, but his eyes were gleaming. "Something large. They've got girls tucked into every corner of the Maddox Street building."

"You mean, a building like my grandfather's townhouse on Mill Street, only a few blocks east of Maddox Street? That sort of large, empty building?" Benedict had inherited the townhouse as part of the Haslemere earldom, but he preferred his own townhouse in Berkeley Square. He'd never had any bloody idea what to do with the Mill Street building. It had stood empty for years.

"Yes, I think that building would do nicely. Do you suppose you could come to some sort of agreement with Miss Harley?"

Benedict's mouth curved in a broad smile. "You know what, Darlington? I think something could be arranged."

* * * *

Ping.

The first time she heard the noise, Georgiana was certain she'd imagined it. When she heard it the second time—*ping*—she made up her mind to ignore it. But the third, fourth, and fifth times, one *ping* after the next in rapid succession, had her tossing her coverlet aside and dragging herself from her bed.

She paused in the middle of the darkened room, listening, but now that she was fully awake, the noise seemed to have magically ceased.

Because of course, it had.

Dash it, why did these strange noises only plague *her*? For a practical lady, she seemed always to catch the brunt of every imaginary thump and creak—

Ping.

Ah, there it was. It was coming from the window, like...raindrops pattering against the glass? No, it sounded more like small pellets of ice, but it was the middle of April in London, for pity's sake. An ice storm was unlikely at this time of year, but unless someone was tossing pebbles at her window—

Georgiana froze.

Someone was tossing pebbles at her window.

She tiptoed toward it, her heart rushing into her throat, because somehow she thought she knew what she'd find when she looked outside.

Who she'd find...

Georgiana twitched the curtains aside and peeked out, taking care to keep her face hidden with a fold of the linen. At first glance, she didn't see anything but the darkened street below, but as her eyes adjusted a darker shadow began to take shape. Not a shrub, but a bigger, broad-shouldered shape, with impossibly long, sturdy legs.

The shape of a man, a man who looked very much like...

Georgiana let out a soft gasp and darted back behind the curtain. Dash it, it really *was* him! What was he doing, assaulting her window in the middle of the night? No, she must be having a dream—

That is, a nightmare. Not a *dream*, but a nightmare.

Ping.

A nightmare was managed easily enough. She'd simply burrow under her covers and drag her pillow over her head, just as she would with any other nightmare.

Ping, ping, ping.

An earl-shaped nightmare loud enough to wake the dead, or at least to wake Daniel Brixton.

Ping.

It was the thought of Daniel more than anything else that had Georgiana tugging the drapes aside and jerking up the window. "Have you gone mad?" she hissed. "What in the world do you think you're doing, my lord?"

There was a pause, then the absurd man swept his hat from his head, and sketched an extravagant bow. He actually *bowed*, as if he'd met her on the promenade in Hyde Park. "Good evening, Miss Harley."

"There's nothing good about it," Georgiana snapped. "Go away, before Mr. Brixton sees you and fires a pistol ball into your skull."

She ducked back inside, but before she could close the window, his voice drifted back up to her. "I have a business proposition for you. Come down and let me in."

Let him in? Why, he truly had gone mad! She poked her head out the window again. "Do you have any idea what Daniel Brixton will do to you if he catches you here?" And that was to say nothing of Lady Clifford, who could be a great deal more frightening than Daniel when her temper was roused.

"He *will* catch me here if you insist on conducting our negotiations through the window." He tutted, shaking his head as if she were a naughty child.

"We have nothing to negotiate!" Georgiana meant to whisper, but her ire made her voice louder than it should be. She jerked her head back inside and cast a fearful look at Emma's bed before recalling Emma wasn't there.

She was on her own. On her own with a large, persistent earl who—

"Miss Harley? Are you there?"

An earl who didn't have the sense to keep his voice lowered. Georgiana drew in a deep breath and thrust her head back out the window. "I already told you, my lord. I have nothing to say to you."

He was quiet for a moment, then, "Is this about the preserves?"

She stared down at him, baffled. Preserves? What was the man on about now? What pre—

Oh. Her quince preserves. Her sweet, lovely, delicious quince preserves that he'd sent to a syrupy grave with his foolishness. It didn't have to do with the preserves, though if the truth were told, the loss of them hadn't helped his cause any.

Even from up here Georgiana could hear his exasperated sigh. "Answer the question, Miss Harley. Are you holding a grudge against me because of the quince preserves? If you're that put out about it, I'll scour London until I find you something else—"

"Oh, for pity's sake!" Georgiana tugged the window down, lit a candle, then snatched up her cloak and hat and scurried from her bedchamber, muttering furiously to herself as she made her way down the stairs. "...a menace...meddling, arrogant rake...should just let Daniel have him, only...only..."

Only a pistol shot would wake Lady Clifford and the girls. It wasn't because she cared a whit for Lord Haslemere's welfare.

She reached the bottom of the stairs, hurried down the hallway, and opened the front door, wincing as her bare feet landed on the cold stone of the top step. She didn't venture any further, but glared down at Lord Haslemere, who was waiting on the pavement. "*Well?*"

He didn't answer right away, but frowned as he took her in from head to toe. "Do you *sleep* in that cloak and hat?"

"What?" Georgiana glanced down at herself and huffed out a breath. "What kind of absurd question is that?"

"I was just curious. Aside from Lady Wylde's ball tonight, I've hardly ever seen you out of it." He cocked his head to the side, studying her. "The hat doesn't suit you. The cloak either, but the hat is worse by far."

Georgiana raised a self-conscious hand to her head, then jerked it away again, furious with herself. "Is that why you came here in the middle of the night, my lord? To find out what I wear to bed?"

His brow furrowed. "No. Why should I come here for that?"

"I'll give you exactly one minute to explain what you're doing here, Lord Haslemere, and then I'm going to wake Daniel Brixton."

"My, you're cross when you first wake up, aren't you?"

Georgiana stared at him, her heart turning somersaults in her chest. It was a good thing she was immune to his charm, because otherwise she might have felt a little flutter in her belly at the hint of humor in his dark eyes. "Fifty seconds, Lord Haslemere."

He held up his hands. "Yes, yes, all right. I want you to help me untangle these rumors about my sister."

Georgiana's mouth fell open. Dear God, did he not understand the word "no"? This was what happened to a man when his every whim was indulged. "Let me see if I understand you. You came here in the middle of the night to demand something I've already refused you?"

"I wouldn't put it quite like—"

"Does your arrogance know no bounds, Lord Haslemere? You eavesdropped on my conversation this evening, then followed me home, accosted me on a dark street, smashed my preserves to bits—"

"Ah ha! I *knew* you were holding a grudge about the pres—"

"Now you've assaulted my window and dragged me from my bed, and no doubt you think that charming smile of yours excuses it all!"

There was a brief silence, then a slow grin lit his face. "You think my smile is charming?"

Georgiana clenched her teeth. "I've already given you my answer, my lord."

"Yes, but you didn't have all the information then." He braced his hands against the fence railing, his teeth flashing white in the dim light. "I don't think you'll refuse me this time. You see, Miss Harley, I have something you want."

A sigh jerked loose from Georgiana's chest. Even the man's *teeth* were handsome. "That's curious, my lord, because I can't think of a single thing you can offer me."

"I own an empty building on Mill Street." Lord Haslemere was paying close attention to her reaction, and he noticed her indrawn breath. "Might such a thing be of interest to you?"

Without realizing she did it, Georgiana stumbled down one stair, then another, her held breath burning her lungs.

"Struck dumb, Miss Harley? How gratifying." His lips curved into something that wasn't quite a smirk, but close to it. "I understand Lady Clifford is keen to expand the school. Is that the case?"

Georgiana hesitated. She should deny it, refuse to give him such power over her, but the words tumbled out before she could stop them. "I...yes. There aren't many buildings to let at a reasonable price, and most of them are too small for our needs. You'd be amazed at how much room little girls require."

"As much room as little boys, I'd guess. The building has remained empty since my grandfather's death some years ago. It needs a bit of polishing, but it's large, and near here."

Georgiana thought she knew which building he meant, and had never once imaged it could be theirs. After all those troublesome numbers that refused to add up, those uncooperative columns and rows she could still see swimming in front of her eyes, were their prayers really going to be answered as easily as this?

And by a demon like Lord Haslemere?

"Well, Miss Harley? Don't keep me in suspense. Do we have an agreement?"

One word, one small word was all it would take. Georgiana opened her mouth to say it, but the memory of the Duchess of Kenilworth's pale face, the hint of fear there swam before her eyes. She'd made the duchess a promise.

But then she'd made an implicit promise to her girls, too, her motley little group of six. She'd promised she'd take care of them, give them something to hope for, save them from the years of loneliness and misery she'd lived through after…

She shook the thought from her head. It didn't matter now.

Surely, she could help Lord Haslemere while still keeping her promise to the duchess? Lord Draven was somehow connected to both Clara Beauchamp and the Duchess of Kenilworth, so the two matters already overlapped. Surely, she could do both at once?

"You seem undecided, Miss Harley. Perhaps I should take my offer directly to Lady Clifford—"

"No! We have an agreement, Lord Haslemere." Georgiana couldn't let that building slip through their fingers. She simply couldn't do it.

This time there was no mistaking the smirk, or the subtle mockery of his bow. "Good. I believe a call on Lord Draven is in order. I'll fetch you tomorrow morning, just before calling hours. Until then, sweet dreams, Miss Harley."

He stuffed his hands into his pockets and strolled off into the night, whistling, leaving Georgiana nothing to do but watch him go, and wonder how a careless, feather-brained, arrogant rake like Lord Haslemere had gotten the best of her.

Chapter Seven

It was appalling what a lady had to do to get her hands on a decent-sized Mayfair townhouse.

Georgiana eased open the doorway of her bedchamber, poked her head out, and peeked down the hallway. Empty, just as she'd predicted. She crept down the stairs to the entryway, rose to her tiptoes, and peered through the panel of glass fixed into the front door. Weak morning sunlight struggled through the gray layers of smog and clouds above, but just as she'd expected, the steps and the street beyond were empty.

Her lips curled with satisfaction.

Of course, he wasn't waiting for her. It was much too early for a fashionable gentleman like him to have risen for the day. No doubt he was lounging in his bed, and would remain there for, oh, another two or three hours, at the least. By the time he did stumble from his bed, she'd already have settled their business with Lord Draven.

Lord Haslemere might have gotten his way last night, but just because she'd let him coax her into an arrangement didn't mean she'd changed her mind about him. If last night had proved anything, it was that the man was careless, flighty, and unpredictable. It was sheer dumb luck his trick last night hadn't ended with a pistol ball between his eyes.

How could she be expected to work with such a man as that? At best, he was a distraction, and at worst, a liability. Fortunately, there was another way to get this business done, one that didn't involve Lord Haslemere. If it meant she'd have to tell a few harmless falsehoods and sneak about a bit, then so be it.

It wasn't, after all, the first time.

She eased the door open a crack and glanced around, just to be sure he wasn't lurking in the shrubs as he'd done last night, but there wasn't any sign either of him, or anyone else.

Georgiana slipped outside, taking care to close the door quietly behind her. If she didn't feel even a twinge of conscience at dodging Lord Haslemere, she *did* have an uncomfortable pang or two on Lady Clifford's account.

Georgiana didn't make it a habit to sneak, hide, or lie to Lady Clifford. That is, she'd hadn't *lied*, precisely. She'd simply withheld the entire truth, which wasn't nearly as bad.

In any case, she hadn't had a choice. She couldn't tell Lady Clifford about Lord Haslemere's bribe—not when they'd already agreed to take on the duchess's business. Lady Clifford would insist they do the honorable thing, and the Mill Street building would slip through their fingers like so much water through a sieve.

It was a great pity honor should so often be at odds with practicality. Georgiana didn't object to honor, of course. Not until it got in her way, that is.

As far as Lord Haslemere was concerned, it was best for them both if she let him slumber and proceeded on her own, as she was accustomed to doing, then begged everyone's pardon afterward. She'd wrap up this business more quickly that way, and really, wasn't that what she and Lord Haslemere both wanted? Why, by the end of it he'd be thanking her for—

"Going somewhere, princess?"

Oh, no. Georgiana froze mid-step, her eyes slipping shut.

"It's a bit early in the morning for a stroll." Slow, lazy footsteps approached, and Georgiana turned to find Lord Haslemere sauntering toward her.

He didn't look as if he'd just rolled out of bed. He was perfectly respectable this morning in tight, buff-colored breeches, a bottle-green coat, polished black boots, and a snowy cravat tied *à la Haslemere*. His auburn hair was slightly damp, and…she took a cautious sniff of the air.

He smelled like peppermint, as if…

He'd just emerged from his bath.

An unexpected and wholly unwelcome image of Lord Haslemere lounging in his bath, his skin flushed and his damp hair curling against his neck, rose in her mind. She made a desperate attempt to banish it into the dark, cobwebbed corner where she buried such thoughts, but much like the man himself, they weren't easily dismissed.

Lord Haslemere—who was no doubt accustomed to ladies gawking at him—didn't appear to notice her struggles. "I suspected you'd make an attempt of this sort." He tutted, shaking his head. "Is this how you honor your commitments? For a lady with such high principles, you're as wily as a rookeries pickpocket."

"Don't be absurd. I've never picked a pocket in my life." Why bother picking a pocket when it was so little effort to fleece them? "I don't know what you're suggesting, Lord Haslemere, but—"

"We're well past suggestion, Miss Harley. I'm outright accusing you of lying, sneaking, and base treachery."

Georgiana tossed her head. "Treachery is such a theatrical word. You have a flair for the melodramatic, my lord."

"Is that so?" Lord Haslemere pulled out his pocket watch and flipped it open with a careless flick of his finger. "I told you I'd fetch you at calling hours. It's nine o'clock in the morning. If I didn't know subterfuge to be beneath you, Miss Harley, I might think you were sneaking off to Lord Draven's without me."

Georgiana tried to ignore the guilty heat creeping into her cheeks. Keeping the duchess's secrets from a meddlesome lord who insisted on sticking his nose into his sister's business was a delicate thing. It required some…finessing.

"Careful, Miss Harley. That blush is giving you away." Lord Haslemere raised an eyebrow at her. "It's a very pretty one, but an innocent lady has no reason to blush."

Georgiana's cheeks burned even hotter at his teasing, but she drew herself up with a sniff. "I haven't the faintest idea what you mean, my lord. I never blush."

"No? I must be mistaken. Still, I insist you allow me to escort you on your perfectly innocent morning errands. My carriage is just there." He nodded toward the other side of the street, then held out his arm with an infuriating smirk. "Shall we, then?"

"That's, ah…that's not necessary, my lord." Even as the words left her mouth, Georgiana was bracing herself for the inevitable confrontation. Lord Haslemere had risked a midnight skirmish with Daniel Brixton last night. He was hardly going to give up *now*.

"Oh, but I think it is." His dark eyes were narrowed to slits. "Come now, Miss Harley, you insult me with this game. I know you were sneaking off to Lord Draven's on your own, so let's have the truth, if you please."

Georgiana bit her lip. "I fully intended to seek you out later, and tell you every—"

"I slept well last night, Miss Harley. Peacefully, even, secure in the knowledge that whatever my sister's trouble might be I'd soon get to the truth of the matter, with your help."

"We will get to the truth, I promise you, but—"

"I was well satisfied with our bargain, you see," he went on, as if she hadn't spoken. "My building on Mill Street seemed a small enough price to pay to secure my peace of mind."

"Lord Haslemere, I—"

"But my mind *isn't* peaceful, Miss Harley, nor is any other part of me. We made an agreement, yet here you are, not twelve hours later, already breaking it. If I hadn't been lying in wait for you and caught you out, I suspect you would have continued to prove elusive for the rest of the day."

"You admit you were lying in wait, then?"

It was a feeble enough accusation, and predictably, it did nothing to deter Lord Haslemere, who was intent on a lecture. "Let's clarify our positions, shall we? You're my *employee*. That means I issue the commands, and you follow them."

"*Commands!*" Why, the nerve of the man. "I never agreed to follow your every—"

"No more evasions, Miss Harley. No subterfuge, no lies, and no more sneaking about like a child with fistfuls of pilfered sweets. Do I have your word?"

Protestations rose to Georgiana's lips, but one look at him made her bite them back. He'd spoken calmly enough, but his eyes were surprisingly stern, and for the first time since their infamous meeting in Maiden Lane, it occurred to her Cecilia might be right about him.

Perhaps Lord Haslemere wasn't *quite* the reckless, feather-brained rake all the *ton* supposed him to be. Cecilia had warned her he was much cleverer than people gave him credit for being—than even he gave *himself* credit for being.

Georgiana had always assumed Cecilia was exaggerating Lord Haslemere's abilities because he was Lord Darlington's dearest friend, but now...well, she'd been tangling with him for less than a day, and he'd already managed to pin her down, hadn't he?

She blew out a breath and steeled herself for the humiliation of begging Lord Haslemere's pardon. Oh, he'd make it unpleasant enough for her— she hadn't any doubt of that. He'd tease and crow about it, and she'd hold her tongue, dash it, because the truth was, she *was* his employee, and she desperately wanted his building on Mill Street.

The school needed it. The *girls* needed it.

She threw her shoulders back and forced herself to meet those disturbing dark eyes. "You're right, my lord. I did intend to sneak off to Lord Draven's before you arrived, and I beg your pardon for it. It won't happen again."

She waited, but the gloating she dreaded never came. Lord Haslemere studied her, as if he were gauging her sincerity, and then...

"Very well. We'll say no more about it." A smile curved his lips, and it was like the sun emerging from a bank of clouds. Georgiana blinked at him, blindsided. It wasn't just the smile, although now that the sensuous curve of his lips was directed *only* at her, she began to understand why every lady in London swooned over his smile.

Not her, but...other ladies.

But what really surprised her was the swiftness with which his emotions shifted from frustration to forgiveness, and from there to equanimity. It was all right there for anyone to see, playing like quicksilver over his face.

Her own face felt stiff in comparison, immobile, but she didn't have time to dwell on it, because Lord Haslemere took her arm and began half-leading, half-tugging her toward his carriage. "Are you acquainted with Lord Draven, Miss Harley?"

His coachman sprang to the ground to open the door, and Lord Haslemere handed her in, his hand firm and strong. Georgiana was obliged to suppress a shiver at the warm press of them around her fingertips. "No, not at all."

He fell into a sprawl on the bench across from hers. "What made you think he'd see you, then? Draven's a private fellow. He's not the sort who'd welcome a strange lady who appears on his doorstep in the wee hours of the morning. Did you suppose he'd simply let you stroll into his drawing room and begin quizzing him?"

"It's nine o'clock. That's hardly the wee hours of the morning, Lord Haslemere."

"Close enough." He stretched, and the tip of his boot brushed the hem of her skirts.

Georgiana jerked her feet away from his and tucked them under her seat. A sly grin curved his lips, but she refused to give him the satisfaction of commenting on it. "Since you ask, I intended to speak to Lord Draven's housekeeper."

"There's no need for that now. I'm acquainted with Draven. He'll likely agree to see me, even at this ungodly hour."

Georgiana shook her head. "No, we'll do better with his housekeeper."

He frowned. "Why should you bother with his housekeeper when you can speak to the earl himself?"

"Has it occurred to you, Lord Haslemere, the earl might not care for the accusation that he's insulted your sister's honor? We don't need a duel between two foolish noblemen."

Georgiana thought he'd take offense, but instead he barked out a laugh. "Has anyone ever told you, Miss Harley, that you're exceedingly ill-tempered?"

She gave him her sweetest smile. "I suggest you don't try my patience, then. Or better yet, if you don't like my manner, you can leave me to take care of this business by myself."

His grin actually widened, the scoundrel. "I never said I didn't like it. On the contrary, I find it rather refreshing."

If the gossip were to be believed, Lord Haslemere could charm his way into the good graces of any lady in London. "Does it weary you, my lord, always having your way in everything? I suppose it would become tedious."

If he noticed the touch of acid in her tone, he didn't react to it. "It's the truth."

Georgiana searched his face for any sign of mockery, but he appeared sincere. Perhaps it did grow dull, being the *ton*'s favorite rake. "Ladies who don't find you charming and irresistible must be as rare as pearls in oysters."

"Well then, I've found the right lady, haven't I?" A smile twitched at the corners of his lips. "My very own pearl."

His very own pearl? Georgiana's mouth fell open. That had almost sounded like...an *endearment*. A dozen set-downs rose to her lips, but Lord Haslemere looked just as surprised as she did, and not altogether pleased, so perhaps the less said about it, the better.

Still, it was worrying. The last thing she wanted was for him to become endearing. No matter how engaging his smile, no matter how twinkling those eyes, she couldn't allow herself to fall victim to his charms.

She cleared her throat. "Lord Draven doesn't have any reason to reveal the intimate details of his life to you, my lord. In my experience, gentlemen are apt to guard their secrets, and aristocratic gentlemen more so than most. We're far better off bringing this matter to his housekeeper."

Lord Haslemere didn't appear to have heard her. He was lounging against the squabs, his foot jiggling as his gaze roved over her face. "That color flatters you, Miss Harley."

"I...what?" Dear God, was she blushing again?

"The color of your dress. It's difficult to tell with the way that cloak swallows you, but it's looks as if it's nearly the same color as the gown you wore to Lady Wylde's ball last night. Brown, or bronze, or whatever the modistes are calling it this season. Rich colors bring out the threads of gold in your hair." He frowned at her hat. "What I can see of it, anyway."

Georgiana reminded herself she *didn't* find him charming, and pursed her lips. "What does the color of my gown have to do with Lord Draven?"

Lord Haslemere, who was no doubt far more accustomed to paying compliments than she was to receiving them, gave a careless shrug. "Nothing at all. I noticed the color suited you, and so I remarked on it. That's all."

Why, what was to be done with the man? Was it possible he flirted with whatever woman happened to be in his path, without realizing he was doing it? "We're nearly to Curzon Street, Lord Haslemere. Have we agreed we'll bring our business to the earl's housekeeper rather than the earl himself?"

"If you insist on it, I don't see what choice I have. I'm a gentleman, Miss Harley, and therefore yours to command."

Georgiana snorted. "Not half an hour ago you informed me *I* was obliged to follow *your* every command."

"That does sound more enjoyable, doesn't it?"

"For you, perhaps."

The mischievous grin once again quirked the corners of his lips. "Indeed."

Georgiana eyed him warily. She didn't trust Lord Haslemere not to do just as he pleased when they reached the door, but she couldn't see any way to prevent it. They'd come to a stop outside Lord Draven's townhouse. There was nothing for it now but pray he'd hold his tongue.

In the end, neither of them was given a choice.

Georgiana was distracted by Lord Haslemere's antics, otherwise she might have noticed right away that a commotion was unfolding in front of the Earl of Draven's townhouse.

Despite the early hour, there were two vehicles waiting in the drive, one of them a carriage, and the other a traveling coach with Lord Draven's crest emblazoned on the side. There were a great many servants running about as well, their arms full of baskets and boxes and various other packages, and a trunk was waiting on one side of the door, seemingly abandoned.

"My goodness. Do you suppose the earl is leaving London?"

"I don't know." Lord Haslemere frowned at the parade of servants. "We'll find out soon enough."

No one paid them any mind as they approached the entrance, but just inside the door they found a tall, wiry lady standing in the midst of the chaos, directing the servants who were scurrying up and down the stairs. She had gray-streaked hair pulled into a tight knot at the back of her head, and an air of authority that marked her out at once as Lord Draven's housekeeper.

"No, Lizzy." She was lecturing a quivering housemaid who was holding an arm full of blankets. "Not the trunk. Take them to his lordship's coach, in case he—" She broke off when she caught sight of Georgiana and Lord Haslemere hovering in the open door. "Lord Draven isn't at home to visitors."

"I beg your pardon for the intrusion." Georgiana took another step into the entryway. "Are you his lordship's housekeeper?"

The woman brushed a straggling hair away from her forehead. "Aye, I'm Mrs. Bury."

"How do you do, Mrs. Bury? My name is Georgiana Harley, and this gentleman is Lord Haslemere. I wonder if we might have a quick word with you in private."

Before Georgiana even finished speaking Mrs. Bury had opened her mouth to refuse, but when she heard Lord Haslemere's name she went still, a strange expression on her face. "The Earl of Haslemere? Brother to the Duchess of Kenilworth?"

Lord Haslemere exchanged a puzzled glance with Georgiana, then gave the housekeeper a brief nod. "Yes, Mrs. Bury. The same."

She stared at him, then turned abruptly on her heel. "Aye. I suppose we'd best have a word, at that. This way, my lord, Miss Harley."

She led them down the hall to a drawing room. It was beautifully appointed, the furnishings fine, but the grate was cold, and the drapes had been pulled tightly closed against the morning light. "We're in a bit of a frenzy this morning, I'm afraid. I haven't much time, but I'll do what I can for you. Please do have a seat."

Mrs. Bury gestured to a plush settee done up in extravagant yellow silk. Georgiana perched on the edge, and Lord Haslemere took a seat beside her. "As Miss Harley said, we're sorry to trouble you," he began. "But we've come on a matter of some importance—"

"I know why you've come, my lord." Mrs. Bury sank down on a chair opposite the settee with the air of one who was weary to her bones. "You're here because of that nonsense about the duchess and Lord Draven."

Georgiana, who hadn't expected such frankness, was taken aback. "You believe it to be nonsense, then? The rumor that Lord Draven and the duchess are…well, that they've been—"

"Adulterous sinners? I *know* it to be nonsense, Miss Harley. I've been Lord Draven's housekeeper since he inherited the title, and I was his father's housekeeper for fifteen years before that. His father was a decent, God-fearing gentleman, and so is his son, the current earl."

Georgiana studied Mrs. Bury for any signs of deception, but the woman's gaze was steady, and she spoke with utter conviction, as if she hadn't a shadow of doubt. "You, ah…you seem quite certain, Mrs. Bury."

"I've never been more certain of anything in my life. It's nothing but a vicious rumor meant to hurt his lordship and the duchess." Mrs. Bury turned a sharp eye on Lord Haslemere. "I suppose you've come to pry into the business, and take Lord Draven to task. Well, you should be ashamed of yourself for asking, my lord. Lord Draven is a gentleman, and the duchess a respectable lady. They both deserve better."

Lord Haslemere held up his hands. "I didn't come here to accuse Lord Draven of anything, Mrs. Bury. I merely wish to speak to him. Surely, you can understand why I might be concerned for my sister?"

Mrs. Bury's green eyes remained as hard as stone. "And I'm sure *you* can understand my concern for my employer, my lord. I won't sit here and allow his good name to be maligned. Not while I still have breath left in my body, leastways."

Georgiana cleared her throat. Her next question wasn't likely to endear them to Mrs. Bury, but it was one that must be asked. "The gossips claim the duchess was seen leaving this very townhouse, unaccompanied, at night. Did you ever happen to see her here at odd hours, or here alone with Lord Draven?"

"Well, I…I can't say I never did see her, because lying is a despicable sin, but it was once or twice only, and the two of them as innocent of any wrongdoing as two babies. Why, they never left Lord Draven's study!"

Georgiana thought the sins Mrs. Bury was referring to might be committed as easily in a study as a bedchamber, but she kept that opinion to herself. There was no sense in further offending the housekeeper. Mrs. Bury had already given them something useful. The Duchess of Kenilworth *had* been here in Lord Draven's townhouse, alone and at night.

That part of the rumor was true.

"But you see what comes of such ugly, wicked rumors, Miss Harley." Mrs. Bury rose to her feet, her face flushed with emotion. "Someone must have believed them to be true, and now look what's happened to his poor lordship!"

Georgiana glanced from the tightly drawn drapes to Mrs. Bury's grim face, and a cold prickle of dread started at the base of her spine. "Has, ah…has something happened to Lord Draven, Mrs. Bury?"

"You mean you don't know?" All the anger seemed to drain from Mrs. Bury then, and she half sat, half collapsed onto the chair. "Lord Draven was set upon by a half-dozen villains several nights ago, and beaten to within an inch of his life. It's a miracle he's still alive."

"Several nights ago?" Georgiana's voice emerged in a faint whisper as all the breath fled her lungs. "When exactly?"

"Three nights ago." Mrs. Bury let out a broken sigh.

Three nights ago? That meant…

Lord Draven had been attacked the same night the Duchess of Kenilworth came to the Clifford School. If it was a coincidence, it was a strange one. "We didn't know," Georgiana managed, her head spinning.

At least, *she* hadn't. She glanced at Lord Haslemere and saw the same shock she felt reflected on his face.

"Poor Lord Draven was left for dead." Mrs. Bury shot an accusing glare at Lord Haslemere. "Mark my words, my lord. Whoever's responsible for such a wicked, wicked act will be called upon to explain themselves to their Maker sooner or later, no matter how high they might think themselves."

Lord Haslemere went very still. "Are you saying, Mrs. Bury," he asked quietly. "You believe *I'm* responsible for the attack on Lord Draven?"

"Well, someone did it, didn't they? The way I see it, there are only two people in London bound to defend the duchess's honor. One of them is her husband—an honorable man with a spotless character—and the other?" Mrs. Bury forgot her place entirely then, and pointed a shaking finger at Lord Haslemere. "The other's her rakehell brother. Which of the two do you suppose is the most likely to have done such a thing?"

Georgiana stared at Mrs. Bury. Lord Haslemere was a rakehell, to be sure, but a *murderer*? "I beg your pardon, Mrs. Bury, but it's terribly unjust of you to accuse his lordship of such a heinous act."

Mrs. Bury's face went tight. "Mayhap it is, but I know this much. The Duke of Kenilworth never had a hand in it. He and Lord Draven went to school together, and you've never seen two boys who were closer friends than they were. I can't tell you how many times the duke has visited at Draven House. All of London might believe what they like about Lord Draven and the duchess, but His Grace knows better."

Lord Haslemere was silent, and Georgiana, who felt as if she'd tumbled down a dark rabbit hole and was still falling, struggled for a response. "What will become of Lord Draven? Will he…does the doctor expect him to recover?"

"The doctor has ordered him off to his country estate for fresh air and quiet. I warned him his lordship hasn't been to Draven House in years, and most of the old servants are long gone, but the doctor insists on it. So, we've got a housekeeper and housemaid from London to tend him, and another housemaid from Herefordshire who happened along at the right time. As to whether or not his lordship will ever regain his senses…" Mrs. Bury shook her head. "The doctor can't say. So, we pray for Lord Draven, and hope for the best."

Mrs. Bury dragged herself to her feet, looking as if she'd aged a decade since she'd entered the drawing room. She paused when she reached the door and turned back to say, "I beg your pardon if I offended you, Lord Haslemere."

And then she was gone, her weary footsteps echoing down the hallway.

Chapter Eight

I beg your pardon if I offended you, Lord Haslemere.

Offended him. The woman had accused him of setting a half-dozen murdering ruffians on Draven, then she had the gall to beg his pardon for *offending* him?

Benedict closed his eyes and let out a deep sigh, but it did nothing to ease the heaviness pressing down on him. He'd long since accepted that all of London believed him to be a rakehell, but the leap from rakehell to utter villain was a great deal shorter than he'd imagined.

"I hope you're not taking Mrs. Bury's accusations to heart, Lord Haslemere. She was upset, that's all. Once she's had time to reflect, I daresay she'll regret what she said."

These were the first words Miss Harley had uttered since they left Lord Draven's drawing room. Benedict was lost in his own thoughts, and since he'd never known her to hold her tongue for long, he'd nearly forgotten she was there.

He glanced at her now, and his eyebrows flew up. She was wedged into a corner of the carriage, her face troubled. "You look distressed, Miss Harley. Dare I hope it's on my account?"

She darted a glance at him, then looked quickly away, down at her hands clasped in her lap. "Naturally, I'm distressed. I would feel the same for anyone."

Benedict studied her, a trickle of warmth loosening some of the tightness in his chest. For such a flinty woman, her eyes were suspiciously soft. "I confess your distress on *my* behalf surprises me."

Her brows drew together. "I don't know why it should. I don't like to hear of anyone unjustly accused of such an ugly crime, my lord."

Ah, there *was* a beating heart under that tweedy exterior, then. How… disconcerting. Benedict didn't like it, really. He preferred to think of her not so much as a tender woman, but more a bundle of ill temper and thorns wrapped in layers of heavy, coarse brown wool.

It was easier that way.

"That is, not anyone who's innocent," Miss Harley went on. "London is cursed with any number of aristocratic scoundrels. Still, for all your many, *many* flaws, Lord Haslemere, I can't quite convince myself you're a murderer."

Ah, yes. That was much better. That was the stone-hearted Miss Harley he knew and…barely tolerated. Still, she had been quick to defend him to Mrs. Bury. "I think you're fonder of me than you let on."

She rolled her eyes. "I'm *precisely* as fond of you as I let on, my lord, and no more than that."

Benedict started, his gaze lingering on her face.

Hazel. Her eyes weren't brown at all, but *hazel.*

They looked brown in dimmer light, but this morning, with the sun shining through the carriage window, they were light green, rather like late-summer pears.

Her eyes changed color depending on the light.

It shouldn't matter. It *didn't* matter, only he had a bit of a weakness for changeable eyes, and he couldn't help but wonder if her eyes were like so many other hazel eyes he'd seen, with dozens of different shades of green, brown, and gray at once. Looking at them now, he couldn't imagine how he'd ever thought them brown.

Well, what of it? So, she had pretty eyes. Beautiful eyes, if the truth were told, but her tongue was as barbed as it had ever been.

Not that Georgiana Harley's tongue was any concern of *his.*

Benedict pushed the thought from his head and cleared his throat. "All right then, Miss Harley. Let's see what we have, shall we? Rumors of an adulterous affair, a pair of noblemen who were friends at Eton, and an earl who's been beaten into unconsciousness. What do you make of it?"

She sighed. "I think, my lord, that this business has more heads than a Hydra. Sever one of them, and two more grow in its place."

Benedict cocked his head to the side, considering it. "It's not a Hydra so much as an insect bite. The more one scratches at it, the more it oozes."

"Nonsense. My analogy is much more accurate."

"Oozing sores, or severed heads." Benedict shrugged. "Call it whatever you like, Miss Harley. The question is, where do we go from here, now we can't quiz Draven?"

"Lady Wylde mentioned something last night about your sister and Lord Draven having a scandalous past. Given Lady Wylde's preoccupation with gossip it's likely just another rumor, but we'd better make sure. I think we should pay her a call this morning."

Benedict nearly groaned aloud. This day was taking on a truly nightmarish cast.

He'd sooner drop into the deepest pit of hell than pay a call on Lady Wylde. The moment he set a toe over her threshold she'd assume he'd changed his mind about a liaison between them, and she'd swoop down on him like a bird of prey.

Unfortunately, he didn't have any better ideas. "Yes, very well. I'll pay a call on her. Grigg?" Benedict rapped on the roof of his carriage. "Maddox Street first, to drop off Miss Harley, then we'll proceed to Albemarle—"

"Wait! What do you mean, you'll drop me off? I'm coming to Lady Wylde's with you."

"No, you're not." It was bad enough he'd have to fend off Lady Wylde, but to have Georgiana Harley witness the tawdry scene was…far more unbearable than it should be. "Lady Wylde is a predator of the first degree. You have no idea how savage she can be. She'll swallow you up in one bite, then turn her attention to the main course."

Him.

Miss Harley gave him a thin smile. "Cleverer men than *you* have doubted me before, Lord Haslemere."

Despite himself, Benedict chuckled. "I'm not certain that's anything to boast about."

She thrust her chin up. "I can pay a call on Lady Wylde as easily as you can."

"Certainly, you can. Of course, you'll have to get past her butler first. Egerton's a stiff, proud creature, and rather preoccupied with rank. Even if you do manage to get access to her ladyship, I doubt she can be persuaded to spill her secrets to *you.*"

"She'll spill them to you readily enough though, won't she? I suppose you'll charm them loose. Do you ruthlessly manipulate all your paramours, my lord?"

"Why, Miss Harley, are you a romantic? I never would have guessed." Benedict gave her a lazy grin. "There are certain advantages to being a fashionable earl. It's not fair, perhaps, but I'll get far more out of her if the two of us are left alone."

Deep, red color surged into Miss Harley's cheeks. "You mean to say you'd seduce Lady Wylde to get her secrets out of her?"

"Let's hope it doesn't come to that." Benedict's gaze followed the blush sweeping from her cheeks down her neck. The wash of color turned her eyes an unusually bright green, rather like holly leaves set off by their red berries. Remarkable, those eyes of hers. Quite the loveliest eyes he'd ever seen.

Her expression, though. *Good Lord.*

Perhaps he *should* bring her with him, after all. One look at the severe pinch of those otherwise tempting lips should be enough to chase all thoughts of seduction from Lady Wylde's mind.

"Have you no shame, Lord Haslemere?"

Benedict considered it, then shrugged. "Not much, no. How is seducing her secrets out of Lady Wylde any worse than Lady Wylde seducing jewels out of me?"

"*That's* your defense? Each of you is as awful as the other."

"If you recall, Miss Harley, it was *you* who brought up a seduction. All I have in mind is just a bit of harmless flirtation, nothing more."

"Well then, I don't see any reason why I can't come with you. Did you not, Lord Haslemere, just deliver me a lecture this morning about this very thing? No more sneaking about, you said, and now here you are, ready to sneak off to Lady Wylde's without me."

"Well, yes, but of course I meant *you* shouldn't sneak away from *me*. Not so much the other way around. If you recall, I also said as your employer I'll issue the commands, and you'll follow them."

"You'll be disappointed, my lord, if you expect blind obedience from me," she gritted, her eyes flashing dark green with temper.

Benedict raised an eyebrow. He'd do well to remember that as pretty as holly leaves were, they were also sharp, pointy things, and liable to draw blood from any man foolish enough to meddle with them. "That *is* unfortunate. What do you propose we do?"

She eyed him. "Perhaps we might come to some sort of bargain."

"Perhaps we might. What did you have in mind?" Benedict folded his hands on the head of his walking stick.

She let out an exasperated sigh. "For pity's sake. You know very well I want you to take me to Lady Wylde's with you."

"I do, yes, but I'm far more concerned with what *I* want."

She huffed and squirmed a bit, as if she were being forced to strike a bargain with the devil himself, but at last she gave in to the inevitable. "Oh, very well. What do you want *now*? Quickly, if you please. We're wasting time."

What did he want? Ah, now that was an interesting question. Benedict would have liked to hear the word "please" fall from her lips again, but he didn't fancy risking a limb for it. There was one other thing he'd quite enjoy, however. "I want leave to call you Georgiana, and I want you to use my Christian name, as well."

"I couldn't possibly."

"I don't see why not."

She huffed out a breath. "Because I don't *know* your Christian name."

Benedict hid a grin. It was a lie, of course. For better or worse, everyone in London knew his name. "It's Benedict."

She blinked. "It doesn't suit you."

Benedict choked back a laugh. "The six previous Earls of Haslemere, all of them named Benedict Gabriel Alexander Harcourt, might not agree with you."

"But it's quite a pious name, isn't it? There's Saint Benedict, and his Benedictine monks, for a start. Benedict is Latin for *blessed*, and Gabriel is an angel." She gave him a doubtful look. "Blessed angels are not, alas, the first words that come to mind when I think of you, Lord Haslemere."

"Do you think of me, Georgiana? How delicious. But come, enough of this nonsense. Either you agree to my terms, or I'll have Grigg take you back to Maddox Street."

"Oh, for pity's sake. Very well, I agree to your terms, my lord. Can we go now?"

He raised an eyebrow. "Can we go now, *who*?"

Her lips pursed as if she'd tasted something sour. "Can we go now, Benedict?"

"Certainly, Georgiana." It wasn't very gentlemanly of him to enjoy himself at her expense, but Benedict had to struggle to keep the grin from spreading over his lips again. She didn't have any idea how entertaining she was. He couldn't recall the last time he'd been more amused.

Likely the last time he'd sparred with her.

"Albemarle Street, Grigg." Benedict nodded at his coachman, who was pretending not to listen through the vent.

"Yes, my lord." Grigg slid the vent closed.

Neither Benedict nor Georgiana said a word as the carriage made its way toward Mayfair. She kept her gaze on what was passing outside the window, while Benedict lounged in his seat and occupied himself with stealing glances at her, and savoring his victory.

* * * *

It was clear from the moment Lady Wylde swept into her private sitting room that she'd expected to receive Lord Haslemere alone.

"My dear Lord Haslemere. I imagined I'd see you again, but I didn't anticipate it would be so soon." She prowled across the room, so intent on her quarry she didn't even notice Georgiana was also there. She sashayed right past the settee where Georgiana was seated, the long, diaphanous train of her skirts and a fog of scent trailing behind her.

Rose, or vetiver? Whatever it was it descended on Georgiana like a noxious cloud, clogging her throat and burning her nostrils.

"Lady Wylde." Lord Haslemere attempted a polite bow, but he didn't get far before Lady Wylde put both her hands on his chest, and with a little push sent him sprawling back to the settee.

"I beg your pardon, my lady, but—"

He broke off with a grunt when she landed squarely in his lap. "You've no need to beg for anything, my lord."

"Other than mercy." Lord Haslemere held his hands up and away from her, as if she'd pointed a pistol at him.

Lady Wylde was busily unwinding his cravat, and didn't appear to notice his reluctance. "Shhh." The long length of linen fluttered to the floor. She twined her arms around his neck and pressed her painted lips against his bared throat. "I've already forgiven you for your ungentlemanly behavior last night."

Georgiana stared at them in a daze. She did *not* want to witness whatever Lady Wylde would do next, but she found she couldn't look away from the two of them. She gaped, torn between fascination and horror as Lady Wylde writhed sinuously over Lord Haslemere's lap.

"Do, however, feel at liberty to abandon gentlemanly behavior *now.*" Lady Wylde let out a throaty chuckle. "No woman wants a tame lover, but you already know that, don't you, my lord? There is such delicious gossip about you! I've longed to discover for myself if you're as insatiable, as ferocious as rumor claims."

Ferocious? Georgiana's frozen limbs thawed in an instant. She leapt up from her seat, intending to flee from the room straight back to Lord Haslemere's carriage, but his calm voice stopped her before she could reach the door. "Sit down, Miss Harley."

She turned, trembling, and met his gaze over the top of Lady Wylde's head. He didn't look at all like a notorious rake with a seductress in his lap *ought* to look. He wasn't flushed or panting, and his full, sensuous lips were pressed into a straight line.

Instead of expiring with passion, he looked…irritated. "You remember Miss Harley from your masque ball, Lady Wylde?"

He jerked his chin toward Georgiana, and Lady Wylde glanced over her shoulder. "Miss Harley?"

"Yes." Lord Haslemere wrapped his hands around Lady Wylde's waist, lifted her from his lap and deposited her on the settee beside him with an unceremonious plop. "Miss Harley."

"Miss Harley," Lady Wylde repeated in a flat tone. "Of course, I remember her, my lord. The ball was just last night."

If Lady Wylde was embarrassed by her wanton behavior, she gave no sign of it. She rose leisurely to her feet, a pout on her lips, and took her time neatening her hair and smoothing her skirts over her hips.

"How do you do, my…" Georgiana began, but trailed off into silence as she took in her ladyship's ensemble. She was in dishabille, which wasn't terribly suspiring given the hour, but this particular gown wasn't so much dishabille as…

Invisible? Transparent? Less an article of clothing, and more a… *suggestion* of one?

Georgiana stared, her face on fire, but everywhere she looked she found something else that made her cheeks burn. Lady Wylde's rouged cheeks and lips, the carefully arranged curls just brushing the tops of her breasts, and…Georgiana gasped.

Dear God, was that…

It was. Lady Wylde had rouged more than just her cheeks and lips. Georgiana gaped at her bosom, then tore her gaze away.

"Why, how lovely, Miss Harley, to see you again." Lady Wylde regarded Georgiana with hard, glittering blue eyes. "It's curious, though. I'd never heard your name or been introduced to you at any of the entertainments in London before last night, and now you seem to be *everywhere*. Wherever did you find her, my lord?"

It was the sort of veiled attack common among the *ton*, but Georgiana wasn't accustomed to the aristocratic thrust and parry. She had no idea how to respond, but she was saved from having to say anything at all by Lord Haslemere's drawl.

"Oh, here or there. The usual places one finds young ladies."

"What, at Almack's?" Lady Wylde snickered. "I'm afraid the marriage mart must be terribly dull for you, my lord."

"The marriage mart!" Georgiana meant to hold her tongue, but she didn't care for being batted about between Lord Haslemere and Lady Wylde as if she were a shuttlecock. "You're quite mistaken, I assure—"

"We don't wish to waste your time, Lady Wylde." Lord Haslemere shot a quelling look at Georgiana. "Perhaps I should explain why we've come today."

Lady Wylde flounced over to a chair near the fire and fell into it with a dramatic sigh. "Yes, perhaps you'd better. Quickly, if you please, my lord. I've another engagement this morning."

"Yes, I realize you're in great demand." A lazy smile twitched at Lord Haslemere's lips. "You're very good to indulge me. It's about my sister and Lord Draven."

Lady Wylde perked up considerably at mention of the gossip, but she did her best to hide it under a veneer of concern. "Oh, my poor, dear Lord Haslemere. I'm very sorry, but it was inevitable you'd hear of it sooner or later. Everyone in London is whispering about it," she added with relish.

"Yes, London *does* whisper, doesn't it? I don't concern myself much with rumors, my lady, but you said something last night that does interest me. You said it was inevitable my sister and Lord Draven would fall into each other's arms again, given their past. I wondered what you meant by it."

The pleasant smile on Lord Haslemere's face didn't falter, but his jaw had tightened. It was subtle—imperceptible to anyone not watching him closely—but Georgiana was watching him, and all at once she realized that despite his show of indifference, he was very angry.

Lady Wylde didn't appear to notice it, however, and waved a careless hand in the air. "Oh, well, as to that, I'm sure I don't know what I meant. Nothing at all, really. Now, if you'll excuse me—"

"No, I won't. Not yet."

Georgiana's brow rose at his audacity, but Lady Wylde didn't seem at all irked at being ordered about in her own sitting room. Quite the contrary. Her lips parted and she sucked in a breath, her impressive bosom heaving. "Alas, my lord, I know only what everyone else in London knows."

"Come now, Lady Wylde. How long have we been friends?" Lord Haslemere crooned in silky tones, his lips curling in the barest hint of a smile. "You *always* have more information than anyone else."

Lady Wylde preened under Lord Haslemere's sultry half-smile. "But surely you've heard the story yourself?"

"Of course not. A brother is always the last to hear any unflattering gossip about his sister."

"No, my lord, a *husband* is." Lady Wylde smirked. "Very well then, it's just this. The gossips have it that Lord Draven has been in love with your sister for years, ever since they were introduced at his father's house party. It was some years ago, but surely you remember that party?"

"I vaguely recall it. I didn't attend, but one of Jane's schoolfriends who was a distant cousin of Lord Draven's invited her. It was Jane's first house party. She came out the following season, which means...let's see, that must have been about six years ago. Is that your recollection, my lady?"

"Yes, about then, I think. Lord Draven—the current Lord Draven's father at the time—ended the house party with an extravagant Christmas ball. It was said to have been very grand, with all the most elegant members of the *ton* there." Lady Wylde tossed her head. "Most of them, in any case, but of course I was no more than a young girl then."

Georgiana smothered a snort. A young girl of five-and-twenty, perhaps.

"So, Draven fancied himself in love with Jane." Lord Haslemere lifted his shoulder in a shrug. "I don't see what's so scandalous about that. Many gentlemen admired my sister before her marriage to Kenilworth. She was the belle of her season, if you recall. A true Incomparable."

Lady Wylde let out a long, dramatic sigh—her ladyship had a decided talent for theatrics—and shook her head. "I daresay it wouldn't have been a scandal, except your sister—forgive me, my lord—was rumored to return his affections. Rather *ardently*, from what I understand."

"That doesn't make any sense," Georgiana interrupted. "If Lady Jane was enamored of Lord Draven, and he of her, why didn't she simply marry him instead of Kenilworth?"

Lady Wylde shrugged. "No doubt she would have married Draven if Kenilworth had still been a penniless viscount when they met at the Christmas ball, but he'd inherited the dukedom that summer."

Georgiana frowned. "I don't see why that should make a difference, if Lady Jane truly was in love with Lord Draven."

Lady Wylde gave her a pitying look, as if Georgiana were a dim-witted child. "My dear Miss Harley, the *Duke of Kenilworth* offered for her. Why settle for a mere earl when you can have a duke?"

"You just said, did you not, that Lady Jane ardently returned Lord Draven's affections? Mightn't *that* be a reason for her to marry him?"

"Goodness, you *are* naïve. What's affection when weighed against becoming a duchess? You remember, Lord Haslemere, what a sensation it caused when Kenilworth became the duke? Quite extraordinary, that smallpox should have carried off the three cousins standing between him and the title! Rather convenient, really."

"Convenient!" Georgiana gasped, appalled at Lady Wylde's callousness. She hadn't cared for the woman when she'd met her at her masque ball last night, and she cared even less for her now. She was every inch the sort of cold, calculating aristocrat who thought nothing of sacrificing every higher principle to fortune and title.

Lady Wylde gave a disdainful sniff. "Well, it certainly proved so for Kenilworth, didn't it?"

"You'll have to forgive Miss Harley, my lady," Lord Haslemere murmured. "Not many ladies are as…sophisticated as you are."

Georgiana pressed her lips together to prevent herself from screaming. If she had to suffer another moment trapped in this sitting room while Lord Haslemere coaxed and flattered this awful woman, she feared she'd do someone an injury.

"By all accounts, Lord Draven wasn't at all reconciled to losing Lady Jane," Lady Wylde went on, oblivious to Georgiana's glare. "He went quite wild that season. He might have drunk himself into his grave if his father hadn't intervened, and sent him off to the Continent. It's my opinion he never would have returned to England at all if his father hadn't become so ill."

"By the time he did return, Jane had married Kenilworth. Ah, well. Love's a damnable thing, is it not, my lady?" Lord Haslemere spoke as if the story of Lord Draven's broken heart was unimaginably dull.

"Indeed, and best avoided, but passion is another thing entirely. Such a passion as Lord Draven and Lady Jane reportedly had doesn't simply vanish, my lord, and now it looks as if Lord Draven's had his way at last. One can't really blame the duchess, can one? Why settle for a husband when she can have a lover who's mad for her?" Lady Wylde nodded, as if she'd said something exceptionally wise.

Georgiana shook her head, but didn't venture a comment. There was not, it seemed, any room for irony in Lady Wylde's private sitting room.

Lord Haslemere rose to his feet, his full lips curling in yet another enticing smile as he paused and raised Lady Wylde's hand to his lips. "Thank you for seeing us today, my lady. You're an angel."

"Not *all* angel, I assure you, my lord." Lady Wylde eyed him from under her thick, dark lashes.

He gave a soft laugh, and brushed his lips over her bare knuckles. "Is there anything else you can recall that you think might prove useful to us?"

"Not that I can think of, no, but I'll send for you at once if I do." Lady Wylde fluttered her eyelashes at him. "No matter how late at night it is."

Georgiana was obliged to look down at her lap to hide the roll of her eyes, but this time she wasn't quite able to smother her snort.

Lady Wylde turned on her with a huff. "Does something amuse you, Miss Harley?"

Before Georgiana could get a word out, Lord Haslemere took her elbow and hauled her rather unceremoniously to her feet. "You've been most helpful, my lady. We won't keep you any longer, but will leave you to ready yourself for your engagement."

He marched Georgiana to the door, but Lady Wylde called after them. "Oh, my lord? Now you ask, there is one other thing."

Lord Haslemere turned. "Yes?"

"You might want to pay a call on Lady Archer. She and Lord Draven were…well, I don't wish to offend Miss Harley's delicate sensibilities with such lurid gossip, but they were lovers during Lord Draven's year of debauchery in London, before he got himself banished to the Continent. She might be able to tell you a great deal more than I can."

Lord Haslemere bowed. "As I said, my lady, you're an angel."

"So was Lucifer," Georgiana hissed as he tugged her down Lady Wylde's staircase and back to his carriage.

It had begun to rain, fat, wet drops splattering the pavement. Georgiana scrambled into the carriage and was busy shaking the damp from her skirts when Lord Haslemere said, "Do you know why my sister married the Duke of Kenilworth, Georgiana?"

Georgiana's hands stilled. "I assumed it was for the reason Lady Wylde mentioned—because she wished to become a duchess. Don't ladies of the *ton* all marry for titles and fortunes?"

"I've no idea what most ladies of the *ton* do, but Jane never cared about Kenilworth's title. She never aspired to become a duchess, and she didn't need Kenilworth's money. She had a substantial fortune of her own."

"Why did she marry him, then?"

"For love." Lord Haslemere chuckled at her raised eyebrows. "I see you're skeptical, but I assure you, Jane was in love with Kenilworth when she married him."

Georgiana paused, then asked, "And now?"

"Now?" Lord Haslemere's laugh was harsh. "If the rumors are to be believed, Lord Draven is Jane's secret lover, and for all I know, Kenilworth has a mistress tucked away in some townhouse somewhere. It doesn't sound much like love to me."

Georgiana blinked. She wasn't prepared to hear such a quaint notion of marriage from the fashionable, rakish Lord Haslemere. "You don't know that. Even if he does, it isn't uncommon for a gentleman to take a mistress—"

Lord Haslemere brought his walking stick down hard on the floor of the carriage. "No gentleman who loves and respects his wife takes a mistress, damn it."

Georgiana stared at him, speechless. "I-I'm surprised to hear you express such a sentiment, my lord. You've had a number of mistresses of your own—"

"But no *wife*." Lord Haslemere squeezed the head of his walking stick with such force the silver lion looked as if it would snap off in his fist. "I don't deny I've earned my reputation as a rake, but I'm not utterly devoid of principles. If I did have a mistress, which I don't, it wouldn't be at all the same thing as Kenilworth having one."

"No mistress?" Georgiana bit her lip. "I thought you and Lady Wylde—"

"If Lady Wylde were my mistress, I think I'd know it." His lips twitched at her expression. "I did warn you not to listen to the gossip about me, Georgiana. The truth is much less titillating than the rumors."

Did that mean he *wasn't* insatiable or ferocious, as Lady Wylde had said? Georgiana bit down hard on her tongue before she could succumb to the temptation to ask.

Lord Haslemere tore his hat from his head, tossed it onto the seat beside him, and dragged a rough hand through his hair. "The Christmas ball Lady Wylde mentioned, the one that ended the house party Jane attended. That's the same ball Clara Beauchamp attended on the night she disappeared."

"Yes, it's strange, isn't it?" More than strange, that a young lady should vanish out from under the noses of dozens of guests at a Christmas ball without anyone seeing a thing. "Did Jane attend the ball as well?"

"No. She left the house party early, before it took place. As I said, Jane wasn't out yet, and my father didn't think it was proper for her to attend a ball with so many members of the *ton* present. Whatever happened at that ball may have started at the house party. Perhaps Jane can shed some light on the matter."

"What makes you think she'll tell you anything?" Whatever had happened at that house party, the duchess wasn't likely to confess it to her brother, considering she'd made Georgiana swear she'd keep silent about anything having to do with Clara Beauchamp.

He glanced at her, surprised. "Why shouldn't she?"

"Because you're her brother, of course. What if Lady Wylde is right, and the duchess fell in love with Lord Draven at that party? No lady wants her brother nosing into her romantic entanglements. I daresay she won't tell you a thing."

He shrugged, unconcerned. "I can be quite persuasive when I choose to be, Georgiana."

"Yes, I'm aware of that, my lord. I just watched you *persuade* Lady Wylde's every secret out of her. I'm surprised she didn't confess to setting the Great Fire of London."

Lord Haslemere snorted. "That wasn't her every secret, I promise you."

Georgiana bit her lip, an uneasy knot in her stomach. The very last thing she wanted was for Lord Haslemere to begin asking the duchess questions about Clara Beauchamp. "I don't see how the duchess would know what happened, given she wasn't at the ball. There must be someone else we can ask who'd know more."

"Who? If you recall, Lord Draven is unconscious."

"But there were dozens of other people there, my lord. The Duke of Kenilworth, for one. Mrs. Bury said he spent a great deal of time in Oxfordshire with Lord Draven. Surely, he would have been invited to such a grand house party as that?"

Lord Haslemere considered it, but shook his head. "Perhaps, but I'd rather discuss it with Jane first."

Georgiana, who'd begun to grow quite desperate, was casting about for some logical reason they shouldn't bring this matter to the duchess when the carriage slowed. She glanced out the window, expecting to see the Clifford School, but to her surprise, she saw they'd turned down Grosvenor Street.

Grosvenor Street? Why were they—

Oh, no. Dear God, *no.* Georgiana's stomach fell.

The Duke and Duchess of Kenilworth lived in Grosvenor Street.

The duchess had made herself abundantly clear about her wishes regarding her brother. Georgiana was not, under any circumstances, to breath a word about any of this business to Lord Haslemere. Given such a restriction, it seemed…unwise for Georgiana to appear on the duchess's doorstep with him.

She drew in a deep breath to steady her voice, and asked, "Is it too much trouble for your coachman to take me on to Maddox Street, my lord?"

"Certainly, he will. Right after we see Jane."

She grasped his arm, her fingernails sinking into the damp superfine of his coat sleeve. "Do you think it's wise to call on her now, my lord?"

Lord Haslemere stared down at her hand clutching his sleeve, his brows rising. "It's generally safe enough for me to pay a call on my sister."

But it wasn't at all safe for Georgiana. She could *not* appear on the Duchess of Kenilworth's doorstep with Lord Haslemere. She simply couldn't, not without all of her plans toppling over like a house of cards. "I don't think you want your sister to realize you're poking into her secrets, my lord. It's best if she continues to think you're staying in Surrey for the season—"

Georgiana broke off, wishing she could rip her tongue out. She realized how badly she'd fumbled at once, but by then, it was already too late.

Lord Haslemere went oddly still, then without warning he seized hold of her wrist and tugged her across the carriage onto the bench beside him, close enough so she was practically in his lap. He tipped her chin up and stared down at her with blazing dark eyes. "Now, just how would you know I'm meant to be spending the season in Surrey, I wonder?"

"I...Lady Darlington must have mentioned—"

"No, she didn't. Lord and Lady Darlington have been expecting me in London all week. Oh, princess." His fingers tightened on her chin. "I think you're the one who's keeping secrets."

Chapter Nine

Benedict gazed into wide eyes gone a moody golden-brown, like sunlight on autumn leaves, and wondered if that was the color they turned when she lied.

"I insist you take me back to Maddox Street at once, Lord Haslemere." Georgiana tried to jerk free of his grasp, but Benedict held her fast.

"But I'm so enjoying your company, Georgiana." His lips curved in a smirk, but his words were far closer to the truth than he wished they were, even now, when he knew she'd been lying to him.

"Then there's that other small matter of your dishonesty." He raised her chin higher, fascinated by the rich, chocolate brown melting at the outer edges of those gold eyes. "I don't care for liars, Georgiana."

He was angry with her, yes, and not his usual, tepid discontent. This anger was a searing, belly-deep fire that made his fists clench, his skin heat. Yet at the same time he was achingly aware of the soft glide of her skin under his fingertips, her teeth worrying at her trembling lower lip.

"Perhaps Kenilworth isn't as sure of Lord Draven's friendship as Mrs. Bury imagines he is," he murmured, leaning closer so he could read her secrets in her eyes. "Perhaps he did wonder if his dear old friend Draven had betrayed him, and hired *you* to discover the truth."

She swallowed. "You can't truly believe the Duke of Kenilworth would be so wicked as to send a half-dozen blackguards to assault Lord Draven."

Benedict's gaze darted to her long, pale throat, then back to her eyes. They were darker than he'd ever seen them now, opaque. So beautiful still, but they were the color of shadows, of secrets and lies. "Why not? He's a man, just like any other."

"An *honorable* man, my lord. I've never heard a single whisper against him. All of London sings his praises."

Benedict laughed softly. "Ah, but you see, Georgiana, that's just what I'd expect someone who's working for the duke to say. All of Lady Clifford's girls are clever, but *you*—you're the cleverest of them all. Which is either a very good or a very bad thing, depending on whose side you're on. So, tell me, princess. Whose side are you on?"

"My own side, and Lady Clifford's side."

Benedict said nothing as he let his gaze drift over her. How innocent she looked, with those wide, wary eyes. But she was up to her neck in this business of Jane's. He'd suspected it since the first moment he saw her at Lady Wylde's, in her bronze gown and black masque.

Now he had her, and he didn't intend to let her go until she told him everything she knew. "I'll give you one more chance to tell me the truth, Georgiana. If you truly are on Lady Clifford's side, you'll take it. If not, you'll lose the Mill Street building."

He released her then, and she turned her face away from him at once, no doubt to hide her expression. Benedict waited, a chill settling at the base of his spine as the silence dragged on, unbroken but for the cacophony of doubts crashing against the inside of his skull.

Had he pushed her too far? Despite the tension between them, Benedict couldn't make himself believe she'd refuse to tell him the truth—

"The Duke of Kenilworth didn't hire me, Lord Haslemere." Georgiana turned away from the window to face him. "Your sister did."

"*Jane?*" For a moment, Benedict was too stunned to reply. "But…*why?*"

"To find Clara Beauchamp, or so she said." Georgiana sighed. "Things have become quite a bit more complicated since then."

"Draven and Jane are both searching for Clara Beauchamp? But…*why?*" Benedict was aware he sounded like some sort of deranged echo, but no other question made sense. "Clara Beauchamp has been missing for six years! Why should they have resumed the search for her *now?*"

"Because your sister thinks she saw Miss Beauchamp waiting in a carriage outside Lady Tilbury's townhouse. The duchess sent me to Lady Wylde's masque ball to see what information I could get from Lady Tilbury, which turned out to be very little."

Benedict blew out a breath. "Well, there is one bit of good news, at least. The rumor about Draven and Jane has never been anything more than that. Jane's been seen sneaking in and out of Draven's London townhouse because they're both searching for Miss Beauchamp, not because they're engaged in a love affair."

"Or there is an affair, and Miss Beauchamp knows something about it. Lord Draven and Jane could just as easily be looking for her to see to it she keeps their secrets to herself."

Benedict scowled at her. "I prefer my explanation. Do you believe Jane really did see Clara Beauchamp?"

"It's difficult to say." Georgiana hesitated, her teeth once more attacking that vulnerable lower lip. "Whether she did or not, we can't rule out the possibility Lord Draven was attacked because he's been searching for Clara. If that's the case, then—"

"Then Jane may be in danger." Not just Jane, but also Georgiana, who'd made no attempt to hide her interest in Clara Beauchamp's whereabouts at Lady Wylde's masque ball last night. "What else, Georgiana? What haven't you told me?"

She drew in a long breath, then admitted with obvious reluctance, "The duchess came to us at the Clifford School three nights ago, on the same night Lord Draven was attacked."

"Is there anything else?" Benedict's voice was clipped.

"No," she whispered.

He closed his eyes. Between Lady Wylde's tiresome antics, the scene with Georgiana, and his worry for Jane, he felt as if days had passed since he left his home this morning. By the time Grigg brought the carriage to a stop in front of Kenilworth's elegant white brick mansion and Benedict handed Georgiana down, he was in no mood to suffer fools.

That was when he remembered Bagshaw.

As usual, the duke's butler was standing guard in the entryway, and as usual, he frowned when he saw Benedict. "Lord Haslemere."

"Bagshaw." Benedict's lip curled.

Bagshaw *looked* perfectly harmless—rather like a chess piece, in his black hose and severe black coat with the polished silver buttons—but he was a wily old devil, not to mention a shameless gossip. Nothing escaped Bagshaw's notice, and everything he noticed found its way from his lips to the duke's ears.

"My sister is in the drawing room, I trust?" Benedict didn't wait for an answer, but took Georgiana's arm and hurried her toward the stairs.

"I beg your pardon, my lord, but the duke prefers I announce every guest before permitting them—"

"I'm not here to see the duke, Bagshaw, and I'm not a *guest*. I'm the duchess's brother, for God's sake. Must we do this every time?"

Bagshaw drew himself up with a dignified sniff. "Yes, my lord. But the young lady—"

"The young lady is *my* guest, and no concern of yours."

"As you wish, my lord." Bagshaw's tone was cold, his bow stiff.

Benedict didn't spare the man another glance, but gestured to Georgiana to precede him up the massive, carved mahogany staircase. The sooner they got to the bottom of this mess about Jane, Draven, and Clara Beauchamp, the better.

"Benedict?" Jane rose to her feet when they entered the drawing room, her brows drawn together in a frown. "What are you doing here? I didn't expect you to appear in London at all this season."

"Careful, Jane, or I'll think you're not pleased to see me." Benedict crossed the room and dropped a kiss on his sister's cheek.

"Nonsense. I'm always pleased to see you." Jane offered him a bright, false smile. "I hope you haven't come all this way just to quarrel with Bagshaw. Really, Benedict, it's not at all gentlemanly of you to harass His Grace's servants."

"I don't quarrel with him, Jane. *He* quarrels with me. But never mind Bagshaw. I've brought someone to meet you today. This is Miss Georg—"

"Miss Harley." Jane reached out to grip the back of the settee beside her. She fought to keep her face blank, but she went so pale she looked as if she were one pump of her heart away from falling into a swoon.

Benedict froze, his stomach giving an uneasy lurch. Jane was staring at Miss Harley with an expression on her face he'd never seen before. Jane wasn't one to fall into tempers, but her eyes flashed, a quick lightning bolt of anger before her expression shifted into something much, much worse.

Panic, and then...fear.

Benedict took an instinctive step toward her, then froze again, suddenly unsure. Surely, she wasn't afraid of *him*? He glanced between Jane and Georgiana, who looked as if she wished herself anywhere but here. "I didn't realize you were acquainted with Miss Harley, Jane."

Whatever spell Jane had fallen under snapped at his words. "I...yes, of course, I am. The Marchioness of Darlington introduced me to Miss Harley at Lord and Lady Darlington's wedding breakfast. It's a pleasure to see you again, Miss Harley."

Georgiana curtsied. "How do you do, Your Grace?"

"Lady Darlington. Ah, yes. How could I have forgotten?" It was a perfectly truthful explanation. They *had* met at Darlington's wedding breakfast, but it was, at once, both the truth and a lie. It rolled off Jane's tongue with such ease, if Benedict hadn't already known there was some secret bubbling just beneath the surface, he might have been fooled.

"Since you're already acquainted, then you must also know Miss Harley is one of Lady Clifford's pupils, Jane." Benedict led Georgiana to an enormous settee across from his sister, then dropped into a chair beside it.

"I, ah...yes, I suppose I did. We only met for a moment, but the Marchioness speaks of Miss Harley with great affection." Jane turned to Benedict with a wan smile. "But you never answered my question. What brings you to London? The last time we spoke, you told me you were bored with the city and intended to remain at Haslemere House to do some repairs."

Benedict hesitated, recalling once again how Jane had made a point of encouraging him to remain in Surrey. He hadn't been surprised at it at the time—he *did* tend to get into more trouble when he was in London, after all—but now he couldn't help but wonder if she'd known there'd be rumors about her and Draven, and was determined to keep him out of it.

"I might have done, if Surrey hadn't proved to be as dull as a tomb." Benedict offered his sister a careless smile, but it was as false as her bright one. "I imagine I'll grow bored with London soon enough. You'll have to tolerate me until then, I suppose."

"Tolerate you? Nonsense. Freddy will be thrilled to see you. Shall we call him?" Jane didn't wait for an answer, but crossed the room to pull the bell. She tried to hide it, but Benedict noticed her hands were shaking as she reached for it.

"Wait, Jane. Don't call him just yet." Benedict got to his feet, took her hand, and led her back to the settee. He was quiet for a moment, choosing his words carefully. "We've never kept secrets from each other, Jane. Not even when we were children."

Jane shrugged, but she couldn't look at him. "No, but children's secrets are harmless, Benedict."

"The more harmful a secret, the more reason to share it." Benedict pressed her hand gently between his. "I know something is amiss, Jane. I've known it for months, since this winter, when you and Freddy spent so much time in Surrey. I'd hoped you would have confided in me by now. You haven't, and now I must have the truth."

"What truth, Benedict?" Jane laughed, but the sound was as sharp and brittle as shattering glass. "I haven't the vaguest idea what you mean."

"I attended Lady Wylde's masque ball last night." Benedict long fingers swallowed her delicate ones. "I heard the rumors about you and Lord Draven."

Jane stared at him, her throat working. "I—it's gossip, Benedict. Nothing more. Surely you must know there isn't any truth to it?"

Benedict drew in a breath. What he was going to say next would hurt both him and Jane, but it must be said. "I called on Lady Wylde this morning, Jane. She told me quite a tale about you and Lord Draven having a secret past."

"You spoke to Lady Wylde about this? *Lady Wylde*, of all people?" Jane pressed a shaking hand to her forehead. "Dear God, Benedict, what have you *done*?"

"She reminded me you met Draven six years ago, at his father's house party. What happened at that party, Jane? Did you fall in love with Lord Draven?"

"No!" Jane cried. "I can't...I won't talk about this with you."

"You must, Jane. You *will*, before this gets any worse. You know Lord Draven was attacked?" One glance at her face, and Benedict had his answer. "Yes, I see you do."

Jane flinched away from him, as if every word out of his mouth was a blow. Benedict despised hurting her, and wished with all his heart he could let this go and never speak of it again, but the only way he could help her was to have the truth from her. "Listen to me, Jane. Whatever it is, however bad it is, I'll help you. You must know that. I'd do anything for you."

"Benedict, please. You don't know what you're...you'll only make it worse. We're not children anymore. You can't solve my problems by bloodying noses, or pushing my tormentors in the fishpond."

"The devil I can't." It might take a pistol or sword this time, but he'd do what he must.

"No, Benedict." Jane snatched her hand from his, leapt to her feet, and crossed to the window. "You can't help me with this."

"Draven was beaten to within an inch of his life, Jane, just days after a rumor began to circulate that you and he are having an affair." Benedict's voice was quiet. "An affair that began six years ago, at the same house party where a young lady named Clara Beauchamp disappeared. Something happened at that party, and six years later, people are still being hurt over it. What if you're next?"

At mention of Clara Beauchamp, Jane's entire body stiffened. She turned from the window to face him, her voice pleading. "*Please*, Benedict. I'm begging you to let this go."

He let out a harsh laugh. "I can't do that. You know better than to even ask it."

Georgiana hadn't said a single word during this exchange, but now she scrambled up from the settee and reached a hesitant hand out to Jane.

"Please, Your Grace. Your brother doesn't wish to force confidences from you, but—"

Benedict turned on Georgiana, incredulous. "Yes, I *do*."

* * * *

Georgiana bit her lip as she glanced from Benedict's angry face to Jane's agonized one.

This wasn't going well at all, and it was all Lord Haslemere's fault.

He was making an utter mess of things. He'd barreled forward without any caution or sense, like a child who upends a chess board, obliterating any chance they might have had at making rational, precise moves. Then with every word out of his mouth, he'd made things progressively worse.

Georgiana had feared this visit would end in disaster, but *this*—it was worse than she'd imagined. The duchess had buried her face in her hands, her slender shoulders shaking, and Lord Haslemere was pacing from one end of the enormous drawing room to the other, eying his sister much as he had Lady Wylde, right before he set about squeezing her until drops of information trickled from her lips like rain from a gray winter sky.

That dark, intense gaze wasn't even directed at *her*, but it sent a shiver up Georgiana's spine nonetheless. No one who looked at Lord Haslemere right now could possibly think he was nothing more than a charming rake.

His lean body was rigid, his lips pressed into a tight line, and his eyes were glittering with anger and worry, and...something else, something forged in fire, and edged in ice.

Determination.

None of them spoke, and the silence stretched until it swelled into every corner of the cavernous room. Georgiana's gaze moved over the fine furnishings, the enormous blue silk settee the duchess had been seated on when they first came in, so large and overstuffed it looked as if it might swallow her whole. For all her wealth and her exalted title and the magnificence that surrounded her, the duchess seemed oddly lost here in this grand house.

Or perhaps it was because of the magnificence, rather than in spite of it. It emphasized how small the duchess was, how slight. The massive marble fireplace, the extravagant gold pier glasses, the glittering chandeliers and oceans of blue silk—it overwhelmed her. She put Georgiana in mind of a tiny, fragile bird, its wings fluttering nervously, as if it were on the verge of flying away.

"Come here, Jane." Lord Haslemere's face softened as his sister struggled to regain her composure, and he reached for her and gathered her into his arms.

Georgiana stared at him, a strange flutter in her chest. She never would have imagined Lord Haslemere could wear such an expression as that. His handsome face was tight with pain, his dark eyes bleak.

This wasn't the same man who'd strolled into Lady Wylde's drawing room and ruthlessly manipulated her as if he were a virtuoso strumming an instrument, nor was he the arrogant earl who'd caught Georgiana's chin in his hard fingers and demanded answers.

This man held his sister tenderly, a fond brother who, like so many fond brothers before him, was rendered helpless by the sight of her tears. Anyone could see he was desperate to protect her, and Jane clung to his coat until her hitching breaths calmed, as if he'd soothed her in just this way dozens of times before.

When Lord Haslemere released her at last, Jane's face was pale but composed. "I'll summon Freddy now, shall I?"

He nodded, and made an attempt at a smile. "Yes. I've missed him. The remainder of the winter dragged without the two of you at Haslemere House."

The duchess crossed the room to pull the bell, and a few moments later a maidservant entered the drawing room. "Fetch Freddy, won't you, Betsy? His uncle is here, and wishes to see him. He's in the library with Mr. Chilcote, I believe."

"Yes, Your Grace." Betsy went off to do the duchess's bidding, and a little while later quick, light footsteps echoed in the hallway. They got closer and closer until at last a small boy of about five with a shock of wild, dark red curls ran into the room.

"Uncle Benedict!" The boy's face lit up with a sweet, guileless smile as he hurried across the room. He was carrying a flat wooden puzzle, which he pushed into Lord Haslemere's hands. "See, Uncle?"

"A new dissected puzzle, Freddy?" Lord Haslemere turned the puzzle right side up and balanced it on his lap. "'Europe Divided into Its Kingdoms.' That's a very good one. But before you show it to me you must make your bow to Miss Harley." He turned Freddy toward Georgiana with his hands on the boy's shoulders.

The boy's cheeks flushed as he gave Georgiana an awkward bow. "How do you do?"

Georgiana smiled. The boy had very pretty dark eyes, and an expressive, endearing face. She liked him right away. "Is that one of Madame Beaumont's dissected maps, or one of John Spilsbury's?"

The boy flushed again, this time with pleasure. "Mr. Spilsbury's, ma'am."

"I always wanted a dissected map when I was a girl, particularly Madame Beaumont's dissected map of Europe." She'd never gotten one, of course, or even seen one before. They were very dear, some of them as much as two guineas.

"Here, Freddy. Take the map to Miss Harley, so she may see it." Lord Haslemere handed the wooden frame back to Freddy. "Mind you don't jostle the pieces, or we'll see how familiar Miss Harley is with the borders of the European Kingdoms."

Freddy approached Georgiana somewhat bashfully, but like most children he could tell the difference between an adult who was simply humoring him and one who was sincerely interested, and Georgiana truly was fascinated with the map. "I like the British Isles best. See?" Freddy plucked the piece up and offered it to Georgiana.

Georgiana turned it in her hand, admiring it. "It's wonderful, isn't it? The British Isles is the best, of course, but I've always been fond of Italy, because of its curious shape." Well, that and because so many of her favorite Gothic romances were set there. "See this bit here?" She traced a finger around the southern edge of Italy. "It looks like a pointing finger, doesn't it?"

"Yes." Freddy darted a look at her from under his eyelashes, his plump cheeks once again blooming with color. "I thought girls didn't like things like geography and maps."

Lord Haslemere chuckled. Georgiana darted a glance at him, half-expecting him to claim most ladies *didn't* like such things, and that it was just as well because they didn't have the analytical brains to appreciate them, but all he said was, "Who gave you that idea, Freddy? Not Mr. Chilcote, I hope."

Freddy shook his curly red head. "No, Uncle Benedict. It was Father who said so."

A brief, awkward silence fell before Georgiana broke it. "I daresay *some* ladies don't like maps and such things, but many do, and many other things not considered strictly ladylike besides."

Freddy's dark eyes, which were very much like his uncle's, sharpened with interest. "What things?"

"Maths, for one. It appeals to analytical minds because numbers are rational, dependable things, unlike, for example, poetry."

Or people.

"Are you good at maths?" Freddy asked doubtfully.

"Very good. So good I teach it."

"You mean you're like Mr. Chilcote?" Freddy looked quite impressed.

"Yes, though I teach young ladies."

"Freddy," the duchess interrupted gently. "It's impertinent to ask so many questions."

"Thank you for sharing this with me." Georgiana handed the British Isles back to the boy.

Freddy took the piece, then hesitated. "You will come back again, won't you, ma'am?"

Before Georgiana could reply, the duchess said, "Freddy. You're keeping Mr. Chilcote waiting."

"Yes, Mama." Freddy offered Georgiana one last grin, showing off the gaps in his gums, then shoved the British Isles in his pocket, trotted to the door, and darted through it. A moment later, however, he peeked back around the corner again. "I'll see you again very soon, won't I, Uncle Benedict?"

"Yes, Freddy, you will. I have some business in London, and I don't intend to leave until it's completed." But Benedict wasn't looking at Freddy. He was looking at his sister. "I'll start by paying a visit to Lady Archer this evening."

The duchess, who could hardly fail to understand him, shook her head. "You'd be much better off returning to Surrey, Benedict." She didn't give him a chance to reply, but shifted her attention to Georgiana. "It was kind of you to visit, Miss Harley. I daresay it will be some time before I can return the courtesy."

It was plain to see the duchess wasn't pleased with her, and no wonder, what with Lord Haslemere storming into her drawing room and demanding answers after Georgiana had sworn to keep this business a secret from him.

She bit her lip. How had she managed to bungle this so badly? Now she'd have to confess to Lady Clifford that she'd angered the Duchess of Kenilworth. Lady Clifford would know how to repair the rift, but until then, there was only one thing Georgiana could do.

She dropped into a curtsy. "As you wish, Your Grace."

Chapter Ten

"Will this do?" Georgiana peeked around the door leading into Lady Clifford's private parlor. "I hope so, because it's the best I can do."

Lady Clifford was tucked into an overstuffed chair near the fire, her fat pug dog, Gussie, snoring in her lap. "Come closer, so I can get a better look at you."

Georgiana didn't *want* anyone to look at her—not Lady Clifford, and certainly not Lord Haslemere—but as there wasn't any help for it, she moved into the middle of the room, caught a fold of the dark red silk gown she was wearing, and dipped into a mocking curtsy. "Well?"

Lady Clifford cocked her head to the side. "Is that the gown Emma wore to Sophia and Lord Gray's holiday party?"

"It is, yes, which explains why it's too big in the bosom and waist, and several inches too short." Georgiana plucked at the gaping neckline where her bosom was meant to be overflowing her stays. She felt like an utter fool already, and she hadn't even left the house yet.

No doubt she looked a fool, too. Finery didn't flatter her the way it did other ladies. Silk gowns and corsets only seemed to emphasize her tall, gangly form, and she ended up looking like an awkward giraffe. It didn't bode well for an evening surrounded by the most fashionable members of the *ton* at Lady Archer's faro table.

Lady Clifford rose to her feet, set Gussie down in her place, and drew closer, her critical gaze sweeping over Georgiana. "Hmmm."

Georgiana plucked nervously at her skirt. "Lady Archer and her ilk are very…I don't have the right…everyone will know at a glance I don't belong there."

"Hmmm."

"It's very bad, I know, but I haven't anything else that's suitable." There was a shocking lack of party gowns in her wardrobe. "If this won't do, I suppose I can wear the bronze gown again."

Rich colors bring out the threads of gold in your hair...

Georgiana flushed right up to the roots of said hair. Threads of gold, indeed. Her hair was brown. It had never been anything other than brown, and never would be anything other than brown, no matter what color she wore. Lord Haslemere was so accustomed to flattering ladies the compliments flew from his lips without a second thought—

"Are you too warm, dearest? You look flushed."

"No, I'm just..." Georgiana trailed off, and threw herself into the chair across from Lady Clifford's. The back of her gown would be all wrinkles by the time she got up, but her legs felt wobbly. "I detest parties, and I'm terrible at them. I'm bound to make a mess of it tonight. If only Emma were here! She'd do the thing splendidly, and the gown fits *her*."

"Actually, my dear, I was just thinking that gown looks very well on you. The fit isn't as bad as you imagine, and the color flatters your—"

"Hair?" If Lady Clifford said one word about gold threads, Georgiana was going to scream.

Lady Clifford smiled. "I was going to say your skin, but it looks very well with your hair, too. You've such an elegant figure, Georgiana. Perhaps we should dress you in silk gowns more often."

"Heaven forbid it." Georgiana forgot the weakness in her legs and leapt up from her chair to check her reflection in the pier glass on the wall opposite the fire. A pale-faced lady stared back at her, her lips tight, and her ordinary—and not at all gold-threaded—brown hair piled on top of her head in a mockery of a fashionable chignon.

She looked like a spinster playing at being a debutante.

"I don't think I...that is, perhaps it would be best if Lord Haslemere went to Lady Archer's by himself, after all." He'd tried to discourage her from attending, but Georgiana had been determined to do her duty by the duchess after that dreadful call this afternoon. But now, with her stomach in knots and her bosom threatening to vanish into her ill-fitting bodice, she couldn't recall why she'd been so insistent.

"You made a commitment to the duchess, Georgiana."

Lady Clifford's tone was mild, but a glance at her reflection in the mirror revealed her eyebrow was inching up. That quirked eyebrow was a sure sign her ladyship disapproved.

Well, of course she did. When Georgiana returned from Grosvenor Street this afternoon, she'd confessed to Lady Clifford she'd let Lord Haslemere insinuate himself into his sister's business, with disastrous results. They'd agreed the best way for Georgiana to make amends was to continue on with the task the duchess had assigned her—finding Clara Beauchamp.

Now here she was, trying to take the coward's way out. She turned away from the mirror with a sigh. "It's just that no one will be surprised to see *him* there. He won't attract any undue attention, whereas I—"

The sound of a carriage pulling up outside interrupted her. Lady Clifford stepped to the window, pulled back the drapes, and peeked outside. "It's too late." She let the drape drop back into place and turned to Georgiana with a calm smile. "He's here."

Every one of Georgiana's instincts urged her to flee up the stairs and not come back down until Lord Haslemere was gone, but her knees had gone all wobbly again, and she could already hear heavy footsteps thudding up the steps toward the door.

"Oh, dear. Quickly, Georgiana. I forgot to tell Daniel Lord Haslemere was coming to fetch you, and it sounds as if he's answered the—"

"What do ye want, Haslemere?"

"Ah, Brixton. Always a pleasure to see you. I've come to fetch—"

"It's the middle of the night. Whatever ye want, it can wait until morning."

If Lord Haslemere was cowed by Daniel's threatening tone, one couldn't tell it from his provoking drawl. "No, I'm afraid it can't, Brixton. I want Miss Harley."

I want Miss Harley? Scorching heat flooded Georgiana's cheeks at those words, and she felt a strange tug deep in her belly.

"Fetch her for me, will you?" Lord Haslemere added in a careless tone. "There's a good fellow."

There was a brief, frozen silence, then Daniel growled, "Nay, my lord. Yer business with the lass can wait until morning."

"On the contrary, Brixton. The business I have with Miss Harley is much better conducted at night."

The sounds of a scuffle followed this shocking announcement, as if Daniel were trying to shove Lord Haslemere out the door, and Lord Haslemere was shoving back.

Lady Clifford gave Georgiana a little push. "You'd better go now, my love, before they come to blows, or one of them tosses the other down the steps."

Georgiana didn't move. Not because she wanted to see Lord Haslemere thrown down the stairs, precisely, but then again, it might be preferable to an evening at Lady Archer's—

"Shame on you, Georgiana." Lady Clifford took Georgiana's arm and tugged her toward the entryway. "Come with me this instant, before Daniel cracks open his lordship's skull."

Lord Haslemere didn't appear to be worried about his skull, or any other part of himself. He and Daniel were standing nose to nose—well, nose to neck, as Daniel was the size of a barouche—each holding the other's gaze without blinking.

Lord Haslemere was either very foolish or very brave. In this case, there wasn't much difference between the two. "Good evening, my lord." Georgiana insinuated herself between the men before fists could start flying. "Shall we go?"

"Ah, Miss Harley. Here you are." Lord Haslemere's gaze drifted over her, taking her in from the top of her head to the hem of her skirts. "You look ravishing this evening." He took her hand and raised it to his lips, his mouth curving in a sensuous smile. "Don't bother to wait up for us, Brixton. I imagine we'll be *very* late."

Georgiana's mouth fell open. Lady Clifford smothered what sounded like a laugh, but Daniel's fists clenched, as if he were preparing to wring Lord Haslemere's neck. "Oh, I'll be waiting for the lass, my lord. Ye can be sure of that. If I find a single hair on her head out of place, ye'll be answering to me for it."

"Not to worry, Brixton." Lord Haslemere gave him an infuriating grin. "Miss Harley's hair is safe with me. As for the rest of her—"

Another ominous growl rumbled in Daniel's chest, but before he could strangle Lord Haslemere with his own cravat, Georgiana snatched Lord Haslemere's arm and dragged him from the entryway. "For pity's sake," she hissed, when the door between the two men was safely closed. "Why must you bait him?"

Lord Haslemere shrugged. "Entertainment, primarily."

"I daresay you won't find it entertaining when he tosses you down the stairs. Have you no sense at all? You don't want to anger Daniel, my lord. I've seen him knock a man unconscious with a single blow."

Lord Haslemere shot her a dark look, his mouth tight. "He's too possessive of you. I don't like it."

Georgiana turned to him in surprise. It almost sounded as if he were…jealous? No, surely not. "He's not *possessive*. He's protective, but perfectly harmless."

"You just told me he wouldn't hesitate to throw me down the stairs, and now you say he's perfectly harmless. Which is it, Georgiana?"

"He's perfectly harmless to *me*. He'd certainly throw *you* down the stairs."

"I'll take my chances."

He reached for her arm to escort her to the carriage, but Georgiana tugged away from him. "I can make my own way to the carriage. Keep your hands to yourself, my lord, before Daniel tears them loose from the rest of your body."

Lord Haslemere snorted. "I'm not afraid of Daniel Brixton."

"I begin to think, my lord, you don't have the sense to be afraid of anyone."

"Yet for all my recklessness, as you can see, I'm still in one piece." He gestured to himself with a wave of his hand.

Georgiana darted a glance at him as they waited for Grigg to set the step and open the carriage door. She looked away again quickly, but it was already too late.

Once glance was all it took.

He *was* still in one piece. One gloriously handsome, disturbingly masculine piece. His dark evening clothes were impeccable, flawlessly fitted to his broad shoulders and lean body, and his spotless white gloves emphasized the long-fingered elegance of his hands.

But despite this, he was still Lord Haslemere, with his unruly auburn curls escaping from under his hat, and his cravat just slightly askew. Georgiana didn't care for affectations in dress, but there was no denying that crooked cravat suited him.

Lord Haslemere handed her into the carriage, climbed in after her and seated himself on the opposite bench. "It occurred to me after I left you this afternoon to check White's betting book for mention of either Lord Draven or my sister. Scandal and rumors turn into wagers quickly enough."

"That was a good thought. Did you discover anything?"

"Apart from my sister's name penned onto every page?" Lord Haslemere's laugh was bitter. "Every lord in London is wagering on her torrid affair with Draven."

"Oh, dear." The poor duchess! It was this sort of thing that made Georgiana despise the *ton*. "Did Lord Draven take part in any of these wagers?"

"No. He doesn't wager at all, it seems. His name doesn't appear even once in the betting book. I suppose he may have squandered a fortune at Lady Archer's faro bank, just like half the noblemen in London, but somehow I don't think so. Draven's rather a recluse."

"Now you mention the faro bank, my lord, there's something I don't understand. Lady Wylde said Lord Draven was once an, er...intimate friend of Lady Archer's, so—"

"No, that isn't what she said. She said they were *lovers.*" Lord Haslemere raised a mocking eyebrow at her, his lips twitching. "Surely you can say the word 'lovers,' Georgiana?"

Lovers, indeed. Why, the odious, teasing man.

She would *not* give him the satisfaction of a blush. "Whatever you wish to call it, the point is that Lady Archer may still have tender feelings toward Lord Draven, and may refuse to divulge his secrets to us."

"Tender feelings? Lady Archer doesn't have *tender feelings* for anything other than the fistfuls of coins her faro bank takes in every night."

Georgiana pursed her lips. "Such cynicism, my lord, does you no credit at all. All I mean to say is, she has more reason to be loyal to Lord Draven than she does to help us."

"And more reason to help herself than any of us. Lady Archer is a businesswoman, Georgiana. She'll help Draven only as long it suits her purse to do so. I intend to make it worth her while to transfer her loyalty to *me.*"

Georgiana fell silent. It was dim inside the carriage, and she took the opportunity to study him as she turned his words over in her mind. His features were more perfect than any man she'd ever seen. He was every bit the devastating gentleman the *ton* thought he was. Given his extraordinarily handsome face and the shallowness of London's fashionable set, perhaps it wasn't so surprising they'd drastically underestimated him.

After all, she'd done the same thing herself.

But she'd been wrong about him, just as nearly everyone else in London was. Lord Haslemere wasn't frivolous, nor was he dim-witted, or vain. Reckless? Yes, at least on occasion. No man with any sense of self-preservation provoked Daniel Brixton. Careless? Of himself, perhaps, but not of his sister or his nephew, and not of his friend Lord Darlington.

Not even of *her*, though he hardly knew her, and would be justified in thinking of her more as his foe than his friend.

But one thing was certain. Lord Haslemere was no fool, and Georgiana didn't doubt he'd have Lady Archer right where he wanted her within moments of crossing her threshold.

There was a certain brilliance to the way he handled people. He knew how to read them, how to see what they tried to hide. It wasn't the sort of brilliance Georgiana had ever admired—at least, not until this afternoon, when she'd watched him draw one confession after another from Lady Wylde, as easily as if he were pulling fish out of a pond on the end of a hook.

Perhaps it hadn't been wise of her to spend so much time locked away with her numbers, avoiding people as she did. The trouble was, people were complicated. Unpredictable. One never knew what they would do, when they'd lash out, or the numerous different ways they'd find to hurt you—

"We're here. Welcome to Lady Archer's notorious faro bank, Georgiana."

The carriage rolled to a stop, and Georgiana peered out the window. They'd arrived in St. James's Street and stopped outside an elegant townhouse of cream-colored brick, with a pair of soaring columns flanking the entrance. Light poured from the large bow windows on the ground and first floors, and Georgiana could see scores of fashionably attired guests moving behind the glass.

A shaft of light splashed onto the street, illuminating her face, and Georgiana instinctively drew back to a darkened corner of the carriage. A spray of gooseflesh rose on her neck, and a shiver wracked her body.

All at once, she felt cold down to her bones.

"Are you chilled? Here, take this." Lord Haslemere took up the wrap that had slipped from her shoulders and tucked it back around her before hopping from the carriage to the pavement and holding out his hand to assist her to alight.

Georgiana shrank away from him, deeper into the safety of the carriage.

She didn't want to go in there. The fine people inside would take one look at her and know at once she wasn't meant to be there, that she wasn't like them, and they'd stare at her, and snicker behind their fans, and there'd be nowhere for her to go, nowhere to hide.

Lord Haslemere let out an impatient sigh. "The sooner we go in, Georgiana, the sooner we can come back out again."

Georgiana tried to make herself reach for his hand, but instead she found her cold fingers gripping the sleeve of his coat. She pressed the fingers of her other hand hard against her lips and closed her eyes, dreading the moment when he'd demand to know what the matter was. She'd have to tell him, and he'd laugh at her...

"Georgiana?" He stuck his head back inside the carriage. "Are you coming?"

"I-I think I've made a mistake, my lord. I-I can't go in there. I don't know how to...I beg your pardon, but I just...I can't go in there."

She didn't realize she'd made a small, choked sound until the carriage tilted under Lord Haslemere's weight. The next thing she knew he was beside her on the bench, his long, warm fingers wrapped around hers.

* * * *

He didn't mean to touch her. Her hand was in his before he realized he'd moved, and words were falling from his lips before he realized he'd opened his mouth.

So strange that, somehow, he knew just how to speak to her, where to touch her. Every word, every movement was somehow exactly the right one, flowing from him like water in a stream cascading over smooth, damp rocks, or wisps of cottony clouds across a clear, blue sky.

"Perhaps you're right, and we have made a mistake coming here. Let's consider it, shall we?"

She didn't answer him, but her fingers curled around his.

He glanced out the window at Lady Archer's townhouse, and tried to see it as Georgiana must. "Grand, isn't it? Far too bright, of course. Every time I attend one of Lady Archer's faro parties, I always end up with a headache from the glare."

She peeked over his shoulder to the townhouse on the other side of the carriage window, then asked hesitantly, "How…why is it so bright?"

"There are pier glasses crammed onto every available bit of wall. The *ton* does like to admire itself, you know, but unfortunately it throws the light about until you feel as if you've stumbled into the sun itself."

Benedict waited. Georgiana remained silent, but he knew she was listening. "The marble in the entryway is the ugliest I've ever seen. Black, with blotches of beige, done in a trompe l'oeil. Lady Archer has the worst taste imaginable."

Still nothing from Georgiana, but her eyes—wide, and very green this time—were fixed on him. Benedict went on, hardly knowing what he said. Just bits of nonsense he'd picked up here and there—but all of it was meant to show Georgiana there was nothing inside that townhouse that could hurt her.

"As for the faro, there will be a great number of green baize tables, a great scattering of cards, and a great many fashionable ladies with towering feathers in their hair and too much rouge on their cheeks."

"Rouge?" Sudden color flooded into Georgiana's face. "Lady Wylde was, ah…she was wearing rouge this morning."

"She was, yes. Lady Wylde is a devotee of rouge, and of Lady Archer's faro tables. She's likely to be here tonight, no doubt dangling Harrington on her arm. I doubt you'll have to speak to them. Her ladyship rarely moves once she's seated at a table, and Harrington, being a proper lapdog, won't stir a step without her."

Ah, a smile, at last! It was a tiny one, but there was a perceptible upward curve at the right corner of Georgiana's pink lips. Pleasure rushed over

Benedict, far more pleasure than he should feel at a mere smile, but before he could chastise himself for being so foolishly, absurdly gratified by it, he was speaking again, trying to earn another one.

"Lady Trowbridge will be here. Lady Trowbridge is *always* here, usually lurking in the entryway so she can see who comes in. She's far more interested in the company than she is in playing faro, a circumstance that drives Lady Archer mad."

"Why does it drive her mad?"

And there it was, the spark of interest Benedict had hoped to see in her eyes. "Because Lady Trowbridge is rumored to have a fortune in gold coins stuffed into every corner of her townhouse. Lady Archer is desperate to relieve her of them."

"Is…is Lady Archer perfectly awful?" The high, panicked note had left Georgiana's voice, and her slender body, so rigid only moments before, had relaxed.

Benedict smiled. "Not really, no. She's a product of the fashionable world, certainly, but no worse than the rest of them. Lady Trowbridge is among the best of the lot. Oh, she's as foolish as any of them, but she's got a kind heart, and she's amusing."

"An aristocrat with a kind heart, my lord?" Georgiana shook her head. "I've never heard of such a thing."

Benedict had never been happier to hear that sharp tongue than he was right now, and relief swept over him. "It's rare enough. Of course, not everyone is agreeable, the guests being mostly *ton*, and the *ton* being mostly rather awful people."

Georgiana still hadn't withdrawn her hand from his. "Why do you say they're awful?"

"Why? Well, consider the Marquess of Templeton, for instance. Dreadfully high in the instep. He takes great pleasure in lording it over everyone, but he's squandered a substantial fortune at faro, and left his elderly mother and three younger sisters without two farthings to rub together."

"That's dreadful." Georgiana's voice was soft.

"It is, yes. Not uncommon, though, sadly." Benedict lowered his gaze to their hands as he played with her fingers, then raised his head and looked directly into her eyes. "The point, Georgiana, is that Lady Archer's guests might be *ton*, but under their rouge and feathers and jewels, they're people with the same faults and flaws as anyone else in London."

She let out a shaky laugh. "Most people don't bother to look beneath the rouge and feathers and jewels, my lord."

"Perhaps not, but that doesn't change a thing. None of them are any better than you, Georgiana," Benedict murmured, with a squeeze of her fingers. "And most of them are a great deal worse."

"I daresay *they* think they're better than me." But even as she said it, the hint of a smile was back, the curve of her lips tugging the most fetching dimple into her cheek.

How have I never noticed that dimple before?

"They're wrong. But if you don't want to come inside, then you don't have to. You can wait here for me in the carriage. I'll go in, have a quick word with Lady Archer, then come back out at once and take you back to Maddox Street." A slight grin curved his lips. "Daniel Brixton will be very relieved to have you back so soon."

They were both quiet for a long moment. He wasn't aware he was stroking her knuckles with his thumb and tracing her fingertips until he heard her breath catch. When he turned to her, he found she was watching him under cover of her thick, dark lashes, and her face...

Her pallor had fled, leaving a soft, pink blush on her cheeks. Her lips were parted, her mouth soft. She was still hiding her eyes under her lashes. It was shyness, not flirtation, but Benedict's body didn't give a damn. His blood began to stir, and within seconds, his heart was thundering in his chest. "If you do decide to come in, there is one thing you should be aware of."

"Oh?" She sounded as breathless as he felt. "What's that, Lord Haslemere?"

"Benedict." He continued his stroking, back and forth over her fingers. "You promised you'd call me Benedict, Georgiana."

Her eyes seemed enormous, and such a vivid green in her flushed face. "Benedict."

A thrill shot through him at his name on her lips, and he was obliged to clear his throat before he spoke. "Lady Archer's faro tables are infamous for attracting adventurers and scoundrels. Rakes and rogues will be lounging against every wall and crowded into every table, all of them on the hunt for deep pockets, or a pretty face."

This time when Benedict reached for her, he knew precisely what he was going to do, where he was going to touch her. Softly, gentle as a whisper, he dragged the back of his gloved fingers down her cheek.

Georgiana sucked in a quick breath. "But...how will I know one when I see him? A rogue, I mean."

Benedict stared at her, heat flooding through him, all the desire he hadn't felt for Lady Wylde—for *anyone*—gathering in his lower belly and burning hotter until it released in a heady rush into his groin. His cock hardened in an instant, leaving him dizzy and panting.

Dear God, he wanted her mouth open under his, wanted it with such visceral hunger he could already taste her, sweet and warm on his tongue, quince preserves and something else, something unexpected, a hint of tartness, just enough to drive him mad.

But if he took her mouth now, he'd never let her go. So, instead he caught her fingers in his, lifted them to his lips, and met her gaze over their clasped hands.

Her black pupils had swallowed the warm hazel irises of her eyes. They stared at each other for a long moment, the space between them crackling with tension. "What...what will a rogue do?"

"A rogue won't be satisfied with kissing your glove." His voice was deep and husky, his fingers shaking as he turned her palm up, and with a gentle tug, peeled her glove back to bare her wrist. "He'll kiss you here."

He brought her hand up to his mouth and pressed his lips over the beating pulse point there, grazing the delicate blue vein. She let out a soft cry, and Benedict's eyes fell closed at the feel of her skin against his lips, the warm rush of her blood under the tip of his tongue.

Chapter Eleven

The moment Benedict's lips touched her skin, every thought fled Georgiana's head. The fear, the anxiety and panic that had tried to swallow her when they'd arrived at Lady Archer's vanished into mist, chased away by a rush of desire so sweet it left her dizzy, breathless.

Those dark emotions were no match for a kiss from a rake.

No match for *him*.

The warm clasp of his fingers around hers, his tentative smile and the gentleness of his touch, the soft murmur of his voice…somehow, he'd known just what to say, just how to reassure her.

She gazed down at the dark head bent over her bare wrist and her lips parted, her heart thrumming madly in her chest as his mouth grazed her pulse, his kiss both comforting and devastating at once. Once she did manage to withdraw her hand from his she was dazed, her head spinning and her pulse beating wildly under the tingling skin of her wrist.

Could he even be called a rake at all?

Georgiana hardly knew how to think of him now, but she knew she *would* think of him, long after he'd taken her home tonight. She'd lie in her bed and remember his whispers, the hot brush of his lips against her skin.

If Benedict noticed her agitation, he didn't remark on it. His hand was warm and firm around hers as he handed her from the carriage, his arm reassuringly steady under her trembling fingertips as he escorted her to the entrance of Lady Archer's townhouse.

"Good evening, Lord Haslemere." Lady Archer's butler, a somber-looking fellow in a royal blue coat with sumptuous gold-braiding on the cuffs, ushered them into a grand entryway with black marble floors and blazing chandeliers hanging in matched pairs from the ceiling.

No soft, comforting glow for Lady Archer, but a hard, bright light pouring down onto the unsuspecting heads below until it was absorbed into the pit of black marble under their feet.

Oh, dear. Lord Haslemere was right. It was quite the ugliest marble Georgiana had ever seen, and no matter which way she turned, she caught a glimpse of her own reflection in a gilt pier glass.

She looked...strange. Pale, but with burning eyes and bright spots of color in her cheeks. Was she feverish? She started to lift her hand to her cheek, but Lord Haslemere caught it and lowered it to his forearm.

"I can feel you trembling." His voice was low, and his warm breath stirred the tendrils of hair at her temple. "I thought we agreed there's no need for you to be nervous."

"I'm not nervous." It wasn't a lie. Whatever nerves still lingered after those moments alone in the carriage with him were gone, but the delicate blue vein at her wrist was still throbbing, as if clamoring for his mouth. "What makes you think I'm nervous?"

Nerves weren't the reason her knees were weak, or tiny shivers were chasing each other over her skin. It wasn't *nerves* causing the warm, melting sensation in her lower belly, or the dizzying flutter of her heart against her ribs.

It was *him*, and he'd only kissed her wrist. If he ever kissed her mouth, she'd likely swoon. Georgiana couldn't tell if she found the thought titillating, or terrifying.

"If you're not nervous, why are you squeezing my arm so tightly you're about to tear my coat sleeve to shreds?" He smiled down at her.

"Oh." Georgiana glanced down, saw her knuckles had turned white, and loosened her fingers. "I beg your par—"

"Lord Haslemere, you naughty thing!"

Georgiana turned, her eyes widening as a plump lady in a bright green satin gown bore down on them, her hands outstretched. She was half-smothered in diamonds and emeralds, and she wore such enormously tall blue and green peacock feathers they threatened to touch the candles set into the chandelier and set the whole arrangement ablaze.

"My dear Lord Haslemere!" the lady gushed. "Why, what extraordinary luck, to find you here this evening. It's been an age, has it not?"

"Good evening, Lady Trowbridge." Lord Haslemere took the lady's hand and raised it to his lips in a gesture so gallant Lady Trowbridge, who couldn't be a day under sixty years of age, succumbed to a girlish giggle.

"Ah, charming as ever, I see, you wicked man. Have you come for Lady Wylde? I saw her just a moment ago, at a table with your friend, the

Earl of Harrington." Lady Trowbridge's merry brown eyes sparkled with mischief. "He's caught you out there, I'm afraid."

Lord Haslemere chuckled. "Not as much as you might imagine, my lady. May I introduce you to my friend, Miss Georgiana?"

He didn't give her last name, but Lady Trowbridge didn't seem to notice. "How do you do, my dear?" Her shrewd gaze swept over Georgiana with undisguised interest. "Friend, is she? She's not in your usual style, Haslemere. Pretty all the same, though."

Not in his usual style? Dear God, did Lady Trowbridge think she was—

"Do you play, my dear?" Lady Trowbridge waved her fan toward the back of the house, setting her peacock feathers quivering.

Georgiana glanced over Lady Trowbridge's shoulder and saw the doors between the rooms had been thrown open and crowded with tables and dainty gilt chairs upholstered in red satin. Aristocrats of every age, size, and description were perched atop them, chattering like monkeys and flirting, gossiping, and tossing cards about with wild abandon.

Goodness, what a spectacle. Even from here, the din was deafening. It put Georgiana in mind of one of the battle reenactments at Astley's Amphitheater, but less entertaining, and with a greater likelihood of bloodshed.

"You look positively terrified, you poor thing." Lady Trowbridge tapped Georgiana's arm with her fan. "It is a bit of a crush tonight, but I daresay we can squeeze you in somewhere."

"I, ah…I'm afraid I don't know how to play, my lady."

Lady Trowbridge gave her a blank look, as if Georgiana were speaking in another language. "You mean to say you've never played faro?"

Georgiana shook her head. "No, I'm afraid not."

Lady Trowbridge's eyes went wide. "What, *never*? Why, how perfectly charming you are! Wherever did you find such a sweet little thing, Haslemere? I'm quite mad for her already."

Lord Haslemere gave an indulgent laugh, and Georgiana glanced up at him to find him looking down at her with a fond expression that must surely be feigned. "You can't expect me to tell my secrets, my lady, but perhaps you'd like to join us at a table? You can tutor Miss Georgiana on the play."

"I shall, indeed. *Someone* must take care of her, and you're a shamelessly negligent attendant. Come along, my dear." Lady Trowbridge linked arms with Georgiana. "You're sure to enjoy yourself. What could be more delightful than squandering Lord Haslemere's money?"

Georgiana didn't quite know what to say to that, but she let herself be led toward the back of the house. The air grew thicker and the buzz of conversation louder as they neared the drawing room. It was disorienting.

Georgiana, who'd never been fond of crowds, stumbled a bit, but Lord Haslemere pressed a strong, reassuring hand to the middle of her back to steady her as they made their way toward a table in the corner.

"It's terribly warm, is it not, my dear? I'm parched." Lady Trowbridge plopped herself down in one of the gilt chairs and fluttered her fan vigorously in front of her face. "Fetch us some champagne, won't you, Haslemere? There's a dear boy."

Georgiana perched on the edge of the red satin chair Lord Haslemere secured for her. Directly across from her a gentleman presided over a green baize board with two rows of cards arranged by suit spread across the top, some with neat piles of chips placed in front of them.

"That gentleman there is the banker. You, my dear, are a *punter*, or more simply put, a player." Lady Trowbridge twittered on, pointing out different aspects of the game and explaining how to place a wager. Georgiana nodded politely, but one sharp glance had been enough for her not only to see how the game was played, but to calculate the odds of winning or losing on each turn of the cards.

She hadn't lied to Lady Trowbridge—she'd never played faro before—but it was a game of numbers, much like every other card game. It was not, however, a particularly complicated game, nor was it a game of chance.

Not for anyone who could count, that is.

"Your chips, my dear." Lord Haslemere reached over Georgiana's shoulder, placed a tall pile of chips to one side of her place and a sparkling glass of champagne on the other, and took the opportunity to murmur in her ear. "I'll keep an eye out for Lady Archer while you play. Do make an effort not to lose my fortune, won't you?"

Georgiana heard the smile in his voice, and her own lips curved in response. "I make no promises, my lord."

He straightened, chuckling, and said little from that point on, leaving her to the tender ministrations of Lady Trowbridge, but he never stirred from behind her chair, and she was acutely aware of him there, very close, the heat from his long, lean body teasing her senses.

Georgiana didn't anticipate getting much pleasure from the game, but between Lord Haslemere's strong, tantalizing presence at her back, Lady Trowbridge's endless stream of entertaining nonsense, and the cool, delicious tickle of the champagne on her tongue, it wasn't long before she was having a perfectly lovely time.

And then, of course, there were the cards.

She didn't have fond memories of her time spent on the London streets, yet Georgiana couldn't deny playing at cards was a bit like seeing an old friend again—a friend as accommodating now as it had ever been.

The trouble was, once one knew how to count cards, one couldn't *not* count them, particularly when the banker was marking each card off on an abacus it was played. Georgiana couldn't understand it. It was almost as if they were *inviting* her to cheat.

How was it that aristocrats lost entire fortunes at this game?

"My goodness, Miss Georgiana, you're doing very well for yourself," Lady Trowbridge exclaimed as the chips on the table in front of Georgiana continued to grow. "How lucky you are!"

"It isn't luck, is it?" Lord Haslemere whispered the words directly into her ear, his voice low and dark and amused. Georgiana went still but for a deep shiver at that seductive whisper, the faint, intoxicating scent of peppermint lingering on his skin.

She'd always had a weakness for peppermints.

"No one would ever guess how wicked you are, would they? Not with those innocent eyes of yours." His soft laugh wasn't so much a sound as a breath, the warm rush of it against her ear making her quiver. "But I know your secret, Georgiana."

Georgiana gripped the edge of the table to steady herself, dazed at the powerful tug of desire in her lower belly. Dear God, he wasn't even *touching* her, but his seductive whisper made her nerve endings spark, made the fine hairs on her neck rise, made her as dizzy as if she'd drank a half-dozen glasses of champagne.

"So clever, aren't you, princess?" He crooned, a silken whisper in her ear. "Such a clever, wicked lady."

* * * *

He didn't touch her. He wanted to—wanted it more than he'd ever wanted anything—but he didn't dare.

He imagined it as he stood there behind her, inhaling her scent, taking it inside himself in one rough breath after the next, his gaze on her hands, the fingertips of her gloves damp with condensation as she toyed with the stem of her champagne glass.

Imagined touching her...

In some strange, fevered dream he saw himself leaning over her, opening his mouth against her smooth, pale neck, teasing the loose tendrils there with his tongue, sinking his hands into her hair, plucking out her pins one by one until the soft, thick locks spilled into his palms, and he drew her head gently back so he could take her lips...

A low, frustrated groan rumbled in his chest. Good Lord, what was happening to him? He hadn't even touched her, but he'd never been more aroused in his life.

He was *shaking* with desire, drowning in it—

"Well, Lord Haslemere, here you are at last. I'd begun to believe you'd remain in Surrey forever. What a delight to have you back in London again."

Benedict tore his gaze from the back of Georgiana's neck to find Lady Archer at his elbow, an amused smile on her lips. "How do you do, Lady Archer? It's a pleasure to see you."

She pouted as he raised her hand to his lips. "Is it really, my lord? If I hadn't spoken to you, I doubt you would have noticed me at all."

Benedict let his lips linger just a touch too long on her glove. "That would be impossible, my lady. Why would I have come tonight at all, except to see you?"

"You're a shameless creature, Haslemere, but I'm inclined to look favorably upon you, as you seem to have done the impossible." Lady Archer nodded at Lady Trowbridge. "I can't conceive how you managed to get her to the tables. I've been trying for an age, with no success."

Benedict shrugged. "My masculine wiles, of course."

Lady Archer let out a trill of laughter. "If it was anyone other than *you*, Lord Haslemere, I'd say that was utter nonsense, but you've always been far too charming for your own good. Still, I'm not inclined to question my good fortune. Lady Trowbridge has plenty of money to waste, and she's dreadful at faro."

Benedict hesitated. He didn't like to leave Georgiana, but she was safe enough with Lady Trowbridge, and he wanted to seize his chance to pry information out of Lady Archer while she was pleased with him. "You could return the favor, my lady."

"Oh?" Her eyebrows rose. "Is there something I can do for you, my lord?"

"A quick word or two in private, nothing more."

"Private? You intrigue me. But of course, I'm pleased to indulge you. No lady would ever refuse Lord Haslemere a favor. Will you come to my private sitting room?"

"Thank you, my lady." Benedict rested a hand on Georgiana's shoulder to get her attention, then leaned down to whisper in her ear. "Stay with Lady Trowbridge, and don't stir from your seat. I'm off to have a word with Lady Archer. Once I'm finished, I'll return to fetch you."

Georgiana nodded. "Yes, all right."

She sounded slightly breathless, and Benedict just had time to wonder if she was as affected by him as he was by her before he was obliged to leave her, and follow Lady Archer.

"Now, Lord Haslemere." Lady Archer closed the sitting room door behind her and gestured Benedict to a chair. "How can I help?"

"I have a few questions about Lord Draven I thought you might be able to answer." Benedict didn't mention the rumor he'd heard from Lady Wylde about Draven having been Lady Archer's lover. Lady Archer was a worldly woman, and would likely understand right away why he'd chosen to come to her.

"Poor Lord Draven. You did hear about his, ah…accident, did you not?"

"Are we pretending it was an accident, my lady?"

Lady Archer sighed. "I don't suppose there's much point in that, is there? I won't insult you by asking if you had a hand in it, though I've heard whispers to that end."

"Whispers? Is that all? I've had accusations hurled directly in my face," Benedict said, thinking of Mrs. Bury. "London does love their rumors, and the *ton* must have their gossip, regardless of whether there's any truth to it."

"Indeed. But I've known you long enough to know there's not a morsel of truth in this case. You may be a rake, Haslemere, but you've never been a villain."

"I thank you for that, my lady." Benedict paused for a moment over his next words, but there was no delicate way to say it. "I suppose you've also heard Draven's meant to be having an affair with my sister, the Duchess of Kenilworth."

"Ah. That rumor is not, I'm afraid, quite as easily brushed aside. The *ton* has long believed Lord Draven is nursing a desperate passion for the duchess. That rumor has endured these six years or more, and is so entrenched people regard it as fact."

"I don't trouble myself much with what the *ton* does or doesn't believe, but I think you, Lady Archer, may have more insight into the business than most."

Lady Archer was quiet for a moment, then she crossed the room and took the chair opposite Benedict's. "I might. What would you like to know?"

Benedict blew out a breath, relief rushing over him. Lady Archer would have been well within her rights to toss him out onto St. James Street for his impertinence. "That house party—the one hosted by Lord Draven's father. The trouble seems to have started there."

"Yes, I believe that's right. Unfortunately, I didn't attend that party, my lord, so anything I tell you about it is merely what I've heard secondhand."

"I'd be grateful to hear it, just the same." Lady Archer might know something without realizing she did.

"Very well. The duchess—well, she was Lady Jane then—attended the previous Lord Draven's house party, and the current Lord Draven was said to have fallen madly in love with her then. More than one gentleman sighed after Lady Jane, but I don't need to tell you that, my lord."

It was on the tip of Benedict's tongue to ask about Clara Beauchamp, but he decided against it. Miss Beauchamp was never introduced in society, and she wasn't *ton*, or even aristocracy. Hence, no one in London seemed to know a thing about her.

"Alas for poor Lord Draven, the Duke of Kenilworth also attended that house party. He and Lord Draven were good friends, you know. But Kenilworth fell in love with Lady Jane as well, and she with him, if the gossips have the right of it. It was a tragic love triangle, I'm afraid."

A love triangle, of all absurd things. Benedict would have said Jane was far too sensible to involve herself in such nonsense, but what insight did a brother have into the secret depths of his sister's heart?

None, and nor did she wish him to. If nothing else, Jane had made that clear to him this afternoon.

"You likely know the rest of it, Lord Haslemere. Lord Draven, Kenilworth, and Lady Jane met in London after that doomed house party. Lady Jane came out that season, and Kenilworth immediately began courting her. Well, Lord Draven never really had a chance, did he? Kenilworth inherited an enormous fortune, as you know, and he didn't hesitate to spend it. He purchased the Grosvenor Street house the previous winter, and every belle in London that season was wild to become mistress of it. By the end of it, Lady Jane was the Duchess of Kenilworth. Poor Draven was out, and has spent the past six years trying to get back in."

"And now, according to the gossips, he's succeeded."

Lady Archer shrugged. "Some think so, yes, but no one really knows the truth. Unfortunately for Lady Jane, it's far more exciting to believe she's succumbed to a years' long passion for Lord Draven than otherwise. Fidelity to one's husband is, alas, a dull business."

Every fool in London might believe what they liked. Benedict didn't give a damn. All that mattered was what the Duke of Kenilworth believed. If he thought he had reason to doubt his duchess, wasn't it possible he'd taken his wrath out on Lord Draven?

Benedict rose to his feet and began to pace the small room. "Yet for all those rumors of a rekindled love affair between Lord Draven and Jane, no one seems to think the Duke of Kenilworth had a hand in Lord Draven's… mishap, though it seems far more likely a husband would be driven to violence over it than a brother would."

"I beg your pardon, Lord Haslemere, but it is *not* the case that everyone in London believes the Duke of Kenilworth is innocent of the attack on Lord Draven."

Benedict froze mid-step and turned a sharp look on Lady Archer. "Is that so?"

"It is, indeed."

He marched back across the room and resumed his seat. "Do you mean to say, Lady Archer, that *you* don't believe it?"

Lady Archer eyed him for a long moment, an expression Benedict couldn't read on her face. She looked…wary. Fearful, even.

"I understand Lord Draven and the Duke of Kenilworth were great friends." Benedict paused, but Lady Archer remained silent. "Perhaps the friendship between them is such that the duke would never suspect—"

"There *was* a friendship between them, Lord Haslemere. It ended years ago at that house party, presumably because of the rivalry over Lady Jane. The friendship between the duke and Lord Draven cooled after that."

Benedict leaned forward, his gaze rivetted on Lady Archer. "Just how cool did it become?"

"Cool enough that by the time Kenilworth and Lord Draven returned to London for the season, they couldn't stand the sight of each other."

"My God." Rivalry for a lady's affections did tend to sour a friendship, but this was the first Benedict had heard about such deep animosity between Draven and Kenilworth. "How is it possible there was no gossip in London about their falling out?"

"There was some gossip, but the *ton* never became aware of the, ah… extent of their disagreement. I only know of it because Lord Draven and I became…friends of a sort when he came to London that year." Lady Archer shook her head. "He was in a dreadful state. I've never seen a man more devastated. It's fortunate his father intervened and sent him away to the Continent. I don't exaggerate, Lord Haslemere, when I say I believe it saved his life."

Benedict nodded. Lady Wylde had told him the same thing.

Lady Archer hesitated, then murmured, "Lord Draven's and Kenilworth's falling out was far worse than anyone realizes, Lord Haslemere. After the house party was over and they returned to London for the season, they, ah...they fought a duel."

"A *duel*? Was it...were they fighting over—"

"Lady Jane?" Lady Archer gave him a pitying look. "Lord Draven never said, but I imagine it must have been."

Benedict was hardly able to believe what he was hearing. No one had ever whispered even a breath about a duel before. This thing grew worse with every word out of Lady Archer's mouth.

But Lady Archer wasn't finished. "There is one other thing, Lord Haslemere."

Something in her voice made Benedict's blood run cold.

"I...forgive me, but Lady Jane and Lord Draven were in London together that season, and there are some who say Lord Draven was still pursuing her, even after Kenilworth started courting her. I'll leave you to make of that what you will, but it did occur to me it might be the sort of thing that would lead to a duel."

Benedict stared at her. No, it was impossible. Jane would *never* encourage one man's affections while accepting the courtship of another.

"There's only one thing that doesn't make sense." Lady Archer frowned. "If the duel was over Draven's continued attentions to Lady Jane, one would think it would be Kenilworth who challenged Lord Draven. It was the other way around. It was Lord Draven who challenged Kenilworth."

"Draven may have challenged Kenilworth for stealing away the lady he loved." Benedict might have done the same, had he been in Draven's position.

"Perhaps, though that seems a drastic measure for Lord Draven to take. It wasn't as if a duel would change anything. By then he'd already lost Lady Jane's heart to Kenilworth." Lady Archer shook her head. "Lord Draven may have been madly in love with Lady Jane, but he's never been a fool."

"Every man in love is a fool, my lady."

"Perhaps." Lady Archer's rose from her chair with a sigh. "Or perhaps there's a great deal more to this business between Lord Draven, Lady Jane, and the Duke of Kenilworth than anyone suspects."

Chapter Twelve

"Well, Miss Georgiana, as delightful as your company is, I believe I've had enough faro for one evening." Lady Trowbridge placed spotted hands heavy with jewels flat on the baize, and heaved herself up from her chair. "I'm not in luck tonight, and I do so hate to lose."

Georgiana glanced uneasily toward the drawing room door. Benedict had disappeared with Lady Archer some time ago. She'd expected him back by now, but there wasn't a sign of him yet.

"Oh, but you can't leave me alone, my lady!" Georgiana grasped Lady Trowbridge's hand to stop her. "Faro is dreadfully confusing, and I don't like to lose all of Lord Haslemere's money."

"My dear girl, I doubt you've ever been confused about anything in your life." Lady Trowbridge nodded at the tall pile of chips in front of Georgiana. "As for Haslemere, I daresay he wouldn't bat an eye if you emptied every blessed coin from his coffers. Anyone can see he's besotted with you."

Besotted? It was the last thing Georgiana expected Lady Trowbridge to say, and she couldn't think of a single word to say in reply until she recalled the way Benedict had looked at Lady Wylde this morning. Anyone who'd seen him then would have thought he was besotted with *her*. He was, above all, a consummate performer. He could make anyone believe whatever he wished them to believe.

"But it can't be proper for me to sit here alone…" Georgiana trailed off, biting her lip. Not many mistresses worried about propriety, did they?

Lady Trowbridge blinked in surprise, but then she offered Georgiana a kind smile. "You, Miss Georgiana, are quite a breath of fresh air. I do hope I have the pleasure of seeing you again."

She patted Georgiana's hand, and then she hobbled off, feathers waving and her bright green silk skirts trailing behind her. Georgiana was half-tempted to follow Lady Trowbridge, but Benedict had asked her to wait here, and in any case, she didn't like to attract attention to herself by leaving the room.

So, there she sat, the skin of her neck prickling with self-consciousness, feeling as if every eye in the room was upon her. They weren't, of course—no one paid her any attention—yet the longer she waited, the more uncomfortable she became.

What in the world was keeping Benedict? He'd been gone for ages. Georgiana reached for her flute of champagne and downed the contents in one swallow before reaching for Lady Trowbridge's glass, and with a shrug, finishing it as well.

Lovely stuff, champagne, so pleasantly refreshing and...*bubbly?* Yes, that was a good word for it. Georgiana had only ever had it once before, but as the cool liquid flowed down her parched throat, she couldn't think why.

"More champagne, Miss Georgiana?"

Georgiana had been watching the doorway of the drawing room, trying to conjure Benedict through the sheer force of her will. She didn't notice someone had approached until he spoke.

Georgiana turned. "Oh, no thank you. I—" She broke off, gooseflesh prickling her skin.

The Duke of Kenilworth was standing beside her chair.

He placed the flute of champagne in his hand on the table before her, as if she hadn't just refused it, then, without an invitation, seated himself in Lady Trowbridge's vacant chair. "I insist. This room is very warm, and you appear flushed."

His voice was deep and smooth, his address flawlessly polite, but his eyes...

Gray, narrowed, and pure ice.

Georgiana drew back, instinctively putting more space between them. "H-have we been introduced, Your Grace?"

"Not formally, no. I am the Duke of Kenilworth." The duke smiled, baring a mouthful of gleaming white teeth. "And you are Miss Georgiana, friend of my brother-in-law, Lord Haslemere. I don't believe I was told your surname."

Georgiana hesitated. It wasn't at all likely the duke would recognize her surname. She shunned social engagements, and rarely ventured past the bounds of the Clifford School. She was a no one in London, even to those who were familiar with Lady Clifford. She was certainly far beneath the Duke of Kenilworth's notice.

Still, Benedict had made a point of withholding her full name, and now she thought of it, why should the duke be interested in knowing it? As far as Kenilworth knew, she was simply Benedict's latest mistress. Her name should be of no consequence to him.

So, she acted as if she didn't understand his hint, and instead offered him a vacant smile. "Do you play faro, Your Grace?"

"Not much, no. Certainly not as well as you do."

He lifted a shoulder in a casual shrug, but Georgiana could see by the slight tightening of his lips he'd noticed she'd dodged his question, and he didn't like it.

The Duke of Kenilworth was, not surprisingly, accustomed to having his way.

"Won't you drink your champagne?" He slid the crystal flute closer to her hand. "As I said before, you look flushed. Haslemere will be angry if I allow you to become overheated."

"It's kind of you to be so concerned for me, Your Grace." Any more champagne, and Georgiana's wits would be well and truly addled, and she couldn't help wondering if that was what the duke intended. Still, she didn't think it wise to refuse him a second time, so she clasped the thin crystal stem in her fingers, lifted the flute to her lips, and took the smallest sip imaginable. "Very refreshing, indeed."

The duke plucked up one of her chips and turned it lazily between his fingers, his intent gaze focused on her face. "Now I think of it, where has Haslemere gone? It's bad form for him to leave you here all alone, at the mercy of whatever blackguard chooses to accost you. Perhaps you don't know it, Miss Georgiana, but every coxcomb and villain in London attends Lady Archer's faro parties."

Georgiana watched the chip moving between his gloved fingers and a tremor darted up her spine. Again, his manner was courteous, solicitous even, but she couldn't shake the feeling he'd just threatened her.

She swallowed. "Lord Haslemere stepped out for a moment only to bid Lady Archer a pleasant evening. He should return at any moment, Your Grace."

"Not quite any moment, Miss Georgiana. He's been gone for half an hour already."

Georgiana blinked. Had he been *watching* her, and waiting until she was alone before he approached?

"Where did you and Haslemere happen to meet, Miss Georgiana? It's curious, the way you appeared in London seemingly out of nowhere."

"Not *nowhere*, Your Grace." Georgiana let out a gay laugh, but even she could hear the brittle note in it, and the duke's eyes narrowed. "Lord Haslemere and I were introduced at…that is, we met at—"

"I beg your pardon for keeping you waiting, my dear," a deep voice said, just as a warm hand landed in the middle of Georgiana's back. "Good evening, Kenilworth. What a pleasant surprise to see you here. I've never known you to frequent Lady Archer's faro parties before."

Georgiana jerked her head up, nearly sagging with relief when Lord Haslemere's dark eyes met hers.

"Ah, Haslemere. Here you are at last." The duke tossed the chip in his hand back on the table. "I thought perhaps you'd gone."

"Gone? Come, Kenilworth. Do you think I'd leave without collecting my treasure?" Benedict nodded at the table in front of Georgiana, but the way he curled a proprietary hand around her waist made it clear he wasn't referring to the wager.

"Quite a treasure, indeed. I admire you, Haslemere. You've accomplished a great deal in just a few short days. You've only just arrived in London, and here you are with a pile of coins in front of you and a new *chère amie* on your arm."

"No sense in wasting time, is there?" Benedict shrugged, but his fingers tightened in warning on Georgiana's waist.

"No, indeed. But I'm sure your sister told me you intended to remain in Surrey for the season. What brings you to London?"

"Boredom, primarily. There's only so much rusticating a man can do before he goes mad, Kenilworth. I confess I didn't have much hope for London, either, but I find myself pleasantly surprised at the company this season."

"I see that. How odd, though, that I don't recall ever having seen Miss Georgiana's face before."

The duke was smiling as his gaze swept over Georgiana, but his tone wasn't quite friendly, and Georgiana couldn't suppress a shudder at the shard of ice in his voice. Those cold, narrowed gray eyes seemed to see everything, to peel away everything one wished to hide, their secrets and lies and sins, like peeling flesh from the bone.

"My dear, may I present the Duke of Kenilworth?"

If Kenilworth heard the reluctance in Benedict's voice, he did an admirable job of pretending he hadn't. "Oh, we've met already, much to my pleasure." The duke seized Georgiana's hand and bowed over it.

"Your Grace." Georgiana fixed a smile on her lips, but the duke's grip was tighter than it needed to be, and it was an effort not to snatch her hand away.

In a thousand years, Georgiana could never have predicted what would happen next, and it passed so quickly it was over before she realized it had begun. She felt Benedict go rigid beside her, and the next thing she knew his long fingers closed around her wrist, and he tugged her toward him until she was nearly sprawled in his lap.

"A trifle possessive, are we, Haslemere?" The duke released her hand and turned his attention to Benedict, Georgiana wholly forgotten. "She's lovely. Wherever did you find her?"

"Lady Wylde's masque ball." He raised Georgiana's hand to his lips and pressed a fervent kiss to her gloved knuckles. "Quite a successful evening all around."

"For everyone but Lady Wylde, yes." The duke studied Benedict for another moment, his gaze speculative, then his lips stretched in a cool smile. "But she has a new admirer in Lord Harrington, so it seems she's landed on her feet, as all cats do."

Benedict didn't appear to have anything to say in reply to that, and a heavy silence fell between them until the duke rose to his feet and offered Georgiana a bow. "Have a pleasant evening, Miss Georgiana. I trust I'll see you again very soon."

The duke nodded at them, then turned and made his way across the room, pausing once or twice to greet acquaintances. They waited until the duke had disappeared into another room before Benedict caught Georgiana's hand and tugged her away from the faro table. "Collect your winnings, Georgiana. We're leaving."

"No. Not yet." Georgiana spoke through gritted teeth, that frozen smile still pasted to her lips. "He's likely still watching us. It will look suspicious if we flee the moment he's out of sight. Another game, and then we'll go."

Benedict dropped into the chair beside her without a word, but all Georgiana's pleasure in the play had evaporated. Her chest was tight, and she was no longer able to concentrate on the cards. The pile of coins in front of her shrank as she lost one hand, then another, until Benedict lost patience, and with a low grumble snatched her hand and hurried her through the crowded rooms and out to the pavement, where Grigg was waiting for them.

* * * *

Benedict handed Georgiana into the carriage, threw himself onto the bench beside her, and slammed his fist against the roof with enough violence to make her jump.

Damn it. He never should have agreed to let Georgiana accompany him to Lady Archer's this evening. He'd been a fool to let her talk him into it. He didn't like the way Kenilworth had looked at her, and he didn't like the way he'd touched her. The second the duke lay a hand on her, Benedict had envisioned, in lurid and realistic detail, ripping the man's arm from his body.

Until tonight, he would have said he knew Kenilworth well, but the man they'd left just now—the man who'd grabbed Georgiana, and seemed to take pleasure in frightening her—he didn't know *that* man at all.

London was overflowing with scoundrels, but Benedict had never heard any ugly rumors about the duke. His Grace didn't engage in any of the usual aristocratic sins and foibles that characterized so many gentlemen of the *ton*. He didn't drink, wager, or keep mistresses. There'd never been as much as a whisper against him, and this was London, where everyone was always whispering about everyone else. The man had a spotless reputation.

Too spotless.

Every single aristocrat in London had felt the sharp edge of the gossip's tongues. Everyone, that is, but Kenilworth. Benedict had never thought it suspicious before, but after his conversation with Lady Archer and that disturbing scene with Georgiana, he couldn't help but wonder if he ever truly knew the duke at all.

"Do you think he believed we're...do you suppose the duke believes I'm your mistress?" Georgiana asked, once Grigg closed the door and they were tucked into the carriage and waiting in the queue to turn onto St. James's Street.

"No." Benedict didn't see any point in pretending. Kenilworth's suspicion had been plain enough.

Georgiana was quiet for a moment, then she muttered, "No. I don't imagine he did. Lady Trowbridge seemed to accept it readily enough, but she's an elderly lady. The duke is too worldly to believe such an unlikely story."

Benedict was peering out the window, but the strange inflection in her voice made him abandon his watch and turn toward her. "What do you mean? Why shouldn't he believe it?"

She frowned at him. "You just said yourself he didn't believe it."

He had said so, but not, he suspected, for the same reason she did. "I know why *I* think he wouldn't believe it. I want to know why *you* think so."

"Well, why do *you* think he didn't believe it?"

"Because Kenilworth was likely suspicious of us before he arrived at Lady Archer's tonight. Bagshaw will have told him all about our visit to Jane this morning, and Bagshaw, curse him, has a talent for embellishment. After Bagshaw bent his ear, Kenilworth was bound to be skeptical of anything we said. Why do *you* think it?"

"Well, because I'm not...I don't look..." Georgiana waved her hand over herself, as if it clarified everything. "I don't look like a mistress."

What the devil did that mean? "Just what do you suppose a mistress looks like, Georgiana?"

She blinked. "Well, I don't know, exactly. I'm not sure I've ever seen one before. I just mean I don't look like the sort of lady who'd have a protector."

Benedict made an impatient noise in his throat. "I don't see why not."

She laughed, but there was no amusement in the sound. "Oh, come now, my lord. I'm nothing like Lady Wylde, am I?"

Lady Wylde? What did Lady Wylde have to do with anything?

After struggling through an hour of the woman's tiresome company this morning, Benedict could no longer recall why he'd ever considered making her his mistress. The red lips, the fluttering eyelashes, the exposed bosom—it was like hanging thick wallpaper over flaking, cracked plaster. Cracks tended to make themselves known, sooner or later.

Sooner, in Lady Wylde's case.

"No, you're nothing at all like Lady Wylde." And thank God for it. Lady Wylde's voice alone was enough to curdle the blood of a saint, and Benedict was no saint.

"Well, then." Georgiana straightened her shoulders, her tone brisk. "We're in agreement. Only a certain type of lady stirs a gentleman's amorous inclinations, and I'm—"

"Amorous inclinations?" Where had he heard that phrase before? It sounded familiar, but he couldn't quite recall where he'd...

Damn it. The first pangs of anger flickered in Benedict's belly as it dawned on him what she meant.

Those ladies who don't excite your amorous inclinations must be governesses.

"Are you saying, Georgiana," he asked through clenched teeth, "that you think you're the sort of lady a gentleman wouldn't want for his mistress?"

Her eyes widened at his tone. "Are you *angry*?"

"That depends," Benedict gritted, his jaws grinding together. "Are you, or are you not, saying you think you couldn't attract a protector?"

She drew herself up with a sniff. "I don't see why you're falling into a temper over it. After all, *you* mistook me for a governess the first time we—"

"No, I didn't. You said I looked like the sort of gentleman who thought every woman I didn't want to bed must be a governess, and *I* said—"

Georgiana gasped. "You're mad! I never said a word about anyone *bedding* anyone else!"

"And *I* said there was nothing wrong with governesses, and you said the fault didn't lie with the governesses, but with me, and then I asked why you thought I wouldn't want to make you my mistress!"

She blinked. "I think I've lost the thread of this conversation."

"Damn it, Georgiana. How much champagne did you have? I asked why you think Kenilworth wouldn't believe you're my mistress, and the next I know you're spouting some nonsense about Lady Wylde!"

She jerked her head toward him, startled by his vehemence. "There's no need to become so agitated, my lord. I only meant there are a great many beautiful faces and figures for the gentlemen of London to choose from. Lady Wylde, for instance—"

"Devil take Lady Wylde! A man can't walk down a street in London without stumbling over a dozen women just like her. There's nothing special in Lady Wylde, whereas you, you're..."

What? Benedict trailed off into silence as he struggled to come up with words that might encompass the entirety of who she was, and found he couldn't do it. Georgiana Harley was so many things, each one more surprising than the last, and all of it wrapped up in the most brilliant, alluring package.

Clever? Yes, she was clever, but it wasn't only that. He'd known clever women before. Ill-tempered? Yes, she was that, too. An unwilling smile tugged at his lips at the thought of her sharp tongue, but there was more to it than that. There must be, otherwise he wouldn't find her so endearing.

As for her appearance...Benedict stared at her, the desire simmering in his belly rushing to the surface, stealing his breath, and sending a surge of hot blood to his cock.

The intelligence in her eyes, the way they couldn't decide if they were green or gray or brown, but changed with her moods and the light and the colors she wore. Her hair, those strands of gold hidden like buried treasure in the thick waves, and the smooth, creamy skin she didn't seem to realize was a temptation, luring his fingertips, making him ache to touch her, and her mouth, those sweet, plump pink lips hiding that tart tongue...

She was right about one thing—she was nothing like Lady Wylde, who was interchangeable with every other dark-haired London beauty. No,

Georgiana was far more tempting, with a unique beauty that was wrapped up in everything else about her, and wholly her own.

She was gaping at him, her eyes wide with shock. "I don't understand why you're arguing the point with me, Benedict. You just said yourself the duke knew we were lying about my being your mistress, so I don't see what—"

"Yes, but not because a man wouldn't want to bed you!" Benedict's anger was flaring to life again. "That's bloody nonsense."

Georgiana crossed her arms over her chest with a huff. "Is this your idea of flattery, my lord? Because I assure you, I don't need your empty praise, or—"

"Not another word," Benedict hissed through tight lips. "I'm warning you, Georgiana."

"How *dare*—"

That was as far as she got, because Benedict seized her wrists, tugged her against his chest, and took her mouth with his.

For the first few seconds, the kiss wasn't so much an expression of desire as a battle of wills, with Georgiana determined to have her say, and Benedict just as determined to silence her.

But then…then, somehow, her mouth softened under his, and his tongue found its way between those irresistible pink lips, and the kiss became something else entirely.

Wild, passionate, a tiny spark busting into flames. He'd had a taste of it earlier, when he'd pressed his lips to the soft skin of her wrist and felt the wild flutter of her pulse under his tongue, but *this*…nothing could have prepared him for this.

The seductive heat of her mouth, her plump lower lip caught between his teeth, and her breathy little moan as he sucked and nibbled her there. Her hands on his cheeks burned his skin, the scent of her hair dizzied him, the sensual stroke of her lips against his maddened him.

In an instant he was hard for her, every inch of him aching to get closer, to have more of her. Her mouth was eager but hesitant, her tongue stroking his before darting shyly away again, and the tease only served to arouse him further. "Georgiana," he whispered through strangled breaths, sinking his hands into her hair to still her for his mouth. "Let me…give me your mouth."

He'd felt the tug of desire in his belly before, had kissed dozens of women before her, had taken them to his bed, but no woman had ever affected him as she did. He couldn't get close enough to her, couldn't take her mouth deeply enough, and passion made him desperate.

"Come here, princess." He wrapped his hands around her waist and lifted her into his lap, a strangled groan escaping his lips when she sank against him without a moment's hesitation. She was trembling in his arms, but not from fear.

For *him*. She was trembling for him.

"Put your arms around my neck," he whispered against her lips. "Yes, like that. Dear God, Georgiana, you feel so…"

Perfect.

The slender curves of her hips in his hands, the soft swell of her breasts against his chest, her hair spilling from its pins, the wayward strands teasing the narrow strip of bare flesh between his gloves and his coat sleeves—such a tiny, fleeting caress—but enough to drag a helpless moan from him.

Dear God, if another part of their bare bodies ever touched, it might kill him.

"Is this what a mistress does? Shamelessly kisses her protector in his carriage?"

Benedict could hear the smile in her voice, and his own lips curved in response. "It's a start."

Her fingernails stroked lightly over the back of his neck. "What else does she do?"

"Ngh," Benedict said, his eyes sliding shut. How did she know just how to touch him? She was an innocent, he was certain of it, but her shy, eager caresses were driving him mad. He arched his neck, begging without words for more of those tiny kisses. "Nughh."

She drew back, a shaky laugh slipping from her lips. "I didn't quite understand you."

"Are you teasing me, princess?" Benedict breathed, regaining his wits with an effort. God, he loved this playful side to her, all the more delicious because he'd never expected it. She was so serious most of the time, and kept such tight control over her emotions, but now she'd let herself go, she was reveling in her freedom.

He wanted to see her like this always, with that little smile on her lips, and desire turning her eyes a warm golden brown.

Benedict cupped her hips and dragged her closer, but resisted the temptation to thrust against her. He was as hard as iron, and he didn't want to frighten her, but he kissed her everywhere. Her lips, over and over again. He pressed a tender kiss to her temple, then ran his tongue around the shell of her ear before sliding lower to nip and tease her earlobe, smiling when she gasped. Her hands twisted in his hair when he suckled at the tender skin of her throat, and she let out a soft cry when he buried his face between her neck and shoulder, sliding his lips over the sensitive arch there.

By the time they came to a stop, they were both panting. Grigg, bless him, had turned down a side street instead of pulling directly in front of the school, likely in an effort to keep Brixton from tearing Benedict limb from limb if he happened to look out a window.

Still, he had to stop now, before he gave into the temptation to take her back to his townhouse and take her to his bed. Benedict forced himself to release her and set her back in her seat, then he had to resist the urge to drag her right back again. "I think you'd better go, Georgiana."

She caught his hand in hers when he reached for the carriage door. "No, there's no need to escort me."

He frowned. "I'm not going to drop you off on the street, Georgiana."

"It's best this way. If Daniel sees you looking so disheveled, he'll have your head."

"Humph. I told you before. I'm not worried about Brixton."

"Well, you should be."

Benedict tweaked one of her loose curls. "What about you? You look disheveled, as well."

"Yes, but my head is safe from Daniel." She pressed one last quick kiss on his lips, then slid across the bench toward the door. Grigg was waiting to hand her out, but Benedict caught her elbow before she could slip away.

"Wait." He held her gaze as he raised her hand to his lips and pressed a fervent kiss into her palm. Even in the dim moonlight, he could see a surge of color rush into her cheeks. "Goodnight, Georgiana."

"Goodnight, my lord."

Benedict waited until she reached the corner, then he leapt from the carriage to the street. "We can't let a young lady wander about in the dark alone, can we, Grigg?"

Grigg grinned. "No, my lord."

"No, no matter how stubborn she is about it. Wait for me here, Grigg. I'll return in a moment, once I see Miss Harley makes it safely into the house."

Chapter Thirteen

The trouble with kissing a rake was that one became so distracted *during* the kiss they didn't consider what might happen once it was *over*.

Georgiana had never kissed a rake before. She'd never kissed anyone, so she hadn't understood how heady a kiss could be until Benedict's lips took hers. She hadn't known she could lose herself in a man's scent, his touch, or that a simple kiss could steal her thoughts, her breath—even her reason.

But by the time she reached the top of the steps the haze of passion had receded, and doubts were already crowding into its place. By the time she gained the entryway, it occurred to her it might not have been wise of her to kiss Benedict, and by the time she closed the door behind her, she was convinced the kiss had been a dreadful mistake.

Not the *during* part. No, that had been…delightful? It seemed too stiff a word to describe it. Splendid? No, that was the sort of word one used to describe a particularly delicious slice of tea cake. Benedict's kiss had been something else entirely, something out of her experience.

He'd seemed to enjoy it, but according to Sophia and Cecilia, a man's passions were easily aroused. To hear them tell it, a mere touch to a man's hand was enough to stir his lust.

Benedict was lustier than most, but what worried her wasn't that *he'd* enjoyed it. It was that *she* had. It was shocking enough a man had even kissed her at all. She'd never imagined such a thing would happen, much less that she'd tumble headlong into it.

She leaned back against the door, closed her eyes and raised her hand to her lips. They felt tender, swollen, the memory of his kiss lingering like a warm caress.

Dangerous. That's what his kiss had been—

A step in the hallway made her look up. Lady Clifford was standing there, watching her. "My lady—"

"I think it's time we had a chat, dearest." Lady Clifford disappeared into the drawing room, and Georgiana, who knew a summons when she heard one, followed after her.

"Sit down, Georgiana." Lady Clifford nodded at a chair. She seated herself on the settee across from it, and Gussie crawled into her lap, turning in a circle before settling down with a contented snort.

Georgiana perched on the edge of her chair, her heart pounding. Had Lady Clifford seen her in the carriage with Benedict? If she had, what must she be thinking right now?

"There. Isn't this cozy?" Lady Clifford stroked her hand rhythmically over Gussie's sandy head. "Now, let's get right to it, yes? Suppose you tell me all about Lord Haslemere."

Georgiana twisted her fingers together, eyes downcast. "I already told you everything, my lady. Lord Haslemere has proven to be far more… persistent than I imagined, and he's managed to wriggle his way into the middle of our business with the duchess."

"Wriggled, has he? My dear child, I've never known you to let anyone wriggle their way around you. But I'm not asking for details about the Duchess of Kenilworth's business. You've already told me about all that. I want you to tell me what's happening between *you* and Lord Haslemere."

Oh, no. "I—there's nothing to tell, my lady." Georgiana winced at this feeble reply. She was quite an accomplished liar, but Lady Clifford—and strangely enough, Benedict—seemed able to see through her every falsehood.

"No?" Lady Clifford raised a slim, blonde eyebrow. "Well, if you insist, dearest. I suppose there's a perfectly innocent, rational explanation why you were dallying with him in the carriage just now, then."

Dallying? Oh, dear God. Heat flooded into Georgiana's cheeks, and she buried her face in her hands with a groan, all of her defenses collapsing at once. "That's just it, my lady! Nothing about this is rational. If it were, I'd know just how to proceed, but it's messy and confusing and…and now he's gone and kissed me, and I don't know what to do!"

Lady Clifford didn't look at all shocked at this confession. She continued stroking Gussie's head, her face calm. "Ah, I see. Well, kisses do tend to complicate things. Perhaps you'd better start there. Lord Haslemere kissed you, and what did you do?"

"Nothing at all!" Georgiana's words were too quick, however, and too vehement. It was a pathetic attempt at a denial, and Lady Clifford, predictably, saw through it at once.

"Well, you must have done *something*, dear, to put such a blush on your cheeks." Lady Clifford chuckled. "Now isn't the time to be secretive, Georgiana. A kiss is nothing to be ashamed of, you know. Lord Haslemere is exceedingly handsome and charming."

"Yes, he is. It's quite provoking of him." But the real trouble was that Georgiana wasn't as immune to those charms as she should be. She still had no idea how he'd managed to sneak under her defenses. It wasn't as if he'd *tried* to charm her. Indeed, when he had been trying, she hadn't had the least trouble resisting him. It was this blasted sincerity that was doing her in.

As for the kiss…well, it meant nothing. Less than nothing. It had simply *happened*. No doubt Benedict had already forgotten it, and she'd do well to do the same. Nothing would come of it, and she didn't want Lady Clifford to know what a fool she'd been.

"I kissed him back!" she blurted, then slapped a hand over her mouth, horrified. She hadn't meant to confess to it, but since this business with Benedict began, her natural reticence seemed to have fled. She was like a cracked teapot now, with hot tea leaking from every fissure.

To Lady Clifford's credit, she didn't squeal or fall over in shock. "And?"

"And what? And nothing. He kissed me, and I kissed him back, and that was it." That *had* been it, too, unless one counted the flood of emotions and confusion that had followed that kiss. Georgiana *didn't* count them, so there was no reason to mention them, was there?

"You mean to say, my dear, that Lord Haslemere—the same Lord Haslemere every lady in London either wants to seduce or marry, *that* Lord Haslemere kissed you, and that was it?"

Georgiana fussed with the folds of her skirt, studying them as if they were the most fascinating folds she'd ever seen. "Yes, that's it."

Lady Clifford reached over and plucked the fabric from Georgiana's fingers. "Look at me, Georgiana. Lord Haslemere kissed you, and you kissed him back. None of that sounds terribly shocking, so what has you so upset?"

Georgiana stole a look at her. Lady Clifford didn't appear perturbed, but then she knew a great deal more about this sort of thing than Georgiana did. That is, about gentlemen, and attraction, and…things of that nature.

She drew in a deep breath. "I kissed him back, yes, but after it was over, I thought perhaps he…"

"Yes? What did you think, dearest?" Lady Clifford asked, her tone gentle.

It was the gentleness that undid Georgiana. "I thought perhaps he only kissed me because he…he pitied me."

No sooner were those words out of Georgiana's mouth than the pressure behind her eyes started to burn. She didn't cry—she *never* cried—but there was no denying the troubling stinging sensation in her nose.

This, this right here, was the reason she didn't let anyone trifle with her, particularly not handsome gentlemen. Because it led to emotions, and tears and regrets, and it was dreadful, truly dreadful the way it all got so tangled up inside her, and pulled so tight she couldn't breathe anymore.

Oh, why had she ventured out to Lady Wylde's ball in the first place? As if that weren't reckless enough, why had she insisted Benedict take her to Lady Archer's? She should have stayed safely behind the closed doors of the school with her account books. This sort of thing didn't happen with numbers. Numbers were tidy, sequential, predictable, not like people, who were messy and chaotic and confusing—

"No," Lady Clifford said.

Georgiana's spinning thoughts ground to a halt. "*No*? What do you mean, no?"

"Lord Haslemere didn't kiss you because he pitied you. That's utter nonsense. Gentlemen don't kiss ladies because they pity them, and in any case, why should Lord Haslemere pity you? I can't think of a single reason. No, Georgiana. Lord Haslemere kissed you for one reason, and one reason only. Because he *wanted* to kiss you."

"You don't understand, Lady Clifford. He was...we were...I said a gentleman wouldn't choose to make me his mistress because I don't look anything like Lady Wylde, and then he asked what Lady Wylde had to do with it, and I said Lady Wylde was the sort of lady gentlemen lost their heads over, or something like that, I can't quite recall—I had several glasses of champagne, you see—but then he got angry and asked if I was saying I couldn't entice a protector, and then he kissed me to prove a point."

Somehow, Lady Clifford managed to sort through this convoluted explanation. "A man doesn't kiss a lady to prove a point any more than he kisses her because he pities her."

"Well, Lord Haslemere did."

Lady Clifford only smiled. "No, he didn't. Men are transparent creatures, Georgiana, especially when it comes to their passions—"

"Passions! There was no passion on either of our parts." That was a scandalous lie, of course, but it was bad enough she'd already admitted to the kiss. Admitting to passions on top of that was out of the question.

Lady Clifford ignored her, and went blithely on. "But let's put aside Lord Haslemere for a moment, shall we? The more important question is, how did *you* feel about this kiss?"

Georgiana opened her mouth to deny she'd felt any way at all, but she couldn't quite force the lie past her lips. The truth was, she felt a dozen different ways about it at once, and not one of those feelings made any sense to her.

"I don't know." She gave Lady Clifford a helpless look. "I don't know what I think about it."

"Ah. It was one of *those* sorts of kisses." Lady Clifford patted her knee. "Why don't you sit here and have a little think about the kiss. You'll feel better afterward, I promise it."

Georgiana nodded reluctantly. "All right, but do I have to tell you what I'm thinking about?"

"Not if you don't like it. What matters is *you* understand it, not that I do."

Georgiana squirmed about for a bit, wrestling with herself, but eventually she closed her eyes, stilled, and let her thoughts start to untangle themselves in her head. "I liked it while it was happening, but then afterwards I felt…frightened."

She opened her eyes, surprised. Why should she be afraid of a kiss?

Fear wasn't a rational emotion in this situation, and how had emotion crept into this again, anyway? She'd agreed to sit here and *think* about the kiss, not *feel* it.

But the feelings were always sneaking back into it somehow, weren't they? She couldn't seem to separate the two, and feelings were even messier than people were. The trouble with feelings was once you'd had one, others inevitably followed, and soon enough they took over, overwhelming any chance at rational deliberation.

That was why they were best avoided, or shoved deep down inside where they couldn't trouble her. That wasn't going to work this time, however, because Lady Clifford wasn't going to let her hide from it.

"So, Lord Haslemere's kiss frightened you, Georgiana? Well, I imagine he, ah…knows what he's doing. It's not surprising you enjoyed it."

Georgiana's eyes widened. "I never said…how do you know I enjoyed it?"

"It wouldn't have frightened you otherwise. Dull, insipid kisses don't inspire any passionate feelings."

"But there *was* no passion—"

"It sounds to me as if there was. Lord Haslemere kissed you, there was an explosion of passion between you, and it frightened you. Now *that* makes perfect sense, dearest."

Perfect sense! None of this made the least bit of sense to Georgiana.

"Once the kiss had ended, did you wish he might kiss you again?"

Wish for it? She'd done more than that. She'd allowed—no, *encouraged*—him to kiss her again.

Again, and again, and again...

What would it be like, to believe he was kissing her because he desired her, wanted *her?*

But that was what had frightened her. It hadn't been the kiss itself. Benedict had been gentle and sweet, tender even. But his kiss had lured to the surface all the dreams and wishes she'd long since given up on, long since buried. It was better that way—better if dreams destined to go unfulfilled remained buried.

She didn't want them back.

Did she?

Oh, she didn't know! The only thing she was sure of was her head was once again spinning with questions that had no answers, and now long forgotten hopes had rushed to the surface along with a miasma of wretched *feelings.*

Georgiana sagged against the chair, suddenly exhausted. "May I go to my bed now, my lady? I-I think I'd better rest."

"Of course, my dear." Lady Clifford gave her a reassuring smile, but before Georgiana could escape the drawing room, she stopped her. "Georgiana?"

Georgiana turned at the door, waited.

"Not everyone is like your mother, my love," Lady Clifford said quietly. "There are those you can trust, and those you can't."

And no way to tell the difference between them.

Georgiana had learned that lesson young, and she'd learned it well.

She'd trusted her mother, all those years ago, and look where it had gotten her. Left on the London streets like so many children before her, discarded by a desperate mother who could hardly care for herself, much less her young daughter. But what was the use of sniveling over it? She wasn't the first to be abandoned thus, and God knew she wouldn't be the last.

"Go on, then, and go to your bed, Georgiana." There was a hint of sadness in Lady Clifford's eyes. "But think about what I said, won't you?"

Words tangled in Georgiana's throat, so she only nodded.

Lady Clifford smiled. "Good. Sweet dreams, dearest."

* * * *

It wasn't until Georgiana had disappeared behind the doors of the Clifford School and he was returning to Grigg that Benedict saw the carriage.

If he hadn't followed her to her door, he would have missed it entirely, as it had emerged from the mews on the opposite side of the school.

He recognized it at once.

That particular shade of bottle green, the handsome brass fittings, and the black and gold crest emblazoned on the door...only one man in London drove a carriage like that.

If the Duke of Kenilworth wanted to sneak about unnoticed, he should have chosen a less conspicuous vehicle. Benedict ducked behind one of Lady Clifford's thick shrubs and waited until the carriage pulled smoothly out of the mews. Once it had disappeared down the street, he hurried around the corner to where Grigg was waiting.

When Grigg caught sight of him, his brows shot up. "My lord?"

"Kenilworth had us followed from Lady Archer's." Whoever was driving had been damn sly about it, too, or else Benedict would have noticed them sooner, when it still might have done some good.

Before he led them right to the Clifford School. If the duke hadn't known who Georgiana was, he did now.

Benedict's fingers curled around the walking stick in his hand. It was an act of pure instinct—a need to grab onto something solid as the world tilted under his feet.

Kenilworth had complete control over Jane and Freddy, and now that he knew who Georgiana was, it would be the easiest thing in the world for him to target her, as well. Benedict had to warn her, *now*, before she took it into her head to wake at dawn and call on Jane, or send her a note that would hardly have a chance to graze Bagshaw's palm before he handed it over to the duke.

Whether Georgiana liked it or not, she was done chasing after Clara Beauchamp, and the sooner she understood that, the better. Benedict didn't want her anywhere near Kenilworth.

"Listen to me carefully, Grigg. I need to have a word with Miss Harley. I want you to leave me here and go to Kenilworth's mansion on Grosvenor Street. Keep out of sight, and keep your wits about you. If you see *anything* amiss—if Kenilworth's eye so much as twitches—come fetch me at once."

"Aye, my lord."

"Good man." Benedict waited until Grigg had taken off down the street, then he was on the doorstep of the Clifford School, pounding with the brass knocker.

Heavy footsteps approached, and the door burst open with such violence it threatened to fly off its hinges. "What the devil do you want, Haslemere?"

Damn it. Benedict let out a silent groan. Why must Daniel Brixton be the one to come to the door? "Let me pass, Brixton. I need a word with Georgiana."

Brixton's answer was a scowl. "Come back tomorrow if ye want to talk to Miss Georgiana. Or don't. Makes no difference to me."

He attempted to close the door, but Benedict shoved his foot between the door and the frame. "No. *Now.* Damn it, Brixton, it's urgent."

"Urgent for *you,* mayhap, but not for Miss Georgiana. Get back, Haslemere." Brixton glared at Benedict's foot as if he'd be more than happy to crush it against the door frame.

Benedict peered over Brixton's massive shoulders into the inner sanctum of the Clifford School. He fancied he'd have more luck with Lady Clifford, but the hallway was empty of everything but shadows. "Look, Brixton. I realize this is irregular, but—"

"Go home, Haslemere. Whatever your business is, it can wait until tomorrow."

"No, it *can't.* Look here, Brixton—"

Benedict didn't get any further before Brixton gave him a shove. Benedict wasn't a small man, but he was obliged to shift his foot from the doorway in order to keep himself from toppling backward down the steps. By the time he caught his balance and righted himself, Brixton had slammed the door in his face.

"Bloody savage." Very well. If he couldn't get past Brixton, he'd go around him.

Benedict ran back down the steps and rounded the side of the school, pausing to pluck up a few pebbles from the ground as he went.

The entire house was dark, including Georgiana's window. Benedict winced as the first pebble hit the side of the building with a crack that sounded much louder than he'd anticipated. He waited, but there was no sign of either Brixton or his pistol, so he tried again. This one didn't strike the window either, but hit the brick about a foot below it.

Surely, he could do better than that. He'd been one of the best bowlers on his cricket team at Eton, damn it.

He closed one eye, focused on the window with the other, and let another pebble fly. This one hit the dead center of one of the panes. A moment later he saw the drapes twitch, heard the window slide open, and then Georgiana's head poked out.

"Lord Haslemere? What are you doing down there?"

In spite of his worry, Benedict's lips curved in a helpless smile. "I'm standing outside your window like some sort of demented Romeo, Georgiana. Under the circumstances, one would think you could see your way clear to calling me Benedict."

"Is that why you've come? To tease me once again about calling you by your Christian name?"

Even from down here, Benedict could see the prim pinch of her lips, and his grin widened. If she thought that severe frown would scare him off, she was very much mistaken. All it did was make him want to kiss her. "No, but I thought I'd just mention it, since I'm here."

She glared down at him. "Why *are* you here? For pity's sake, I would have thought you learned your lesson the last time you tried this."

"I *did* learn my lesson. If you recall, the last time I threw pebbles at your window you came downstairs to scold me, and I coaxed you into helping me with Jane. Even better, I got to see you in your night rail."

"No, you didn't. I was wearing my cloak and a hat, and I distinctly remember you saying neither flattered me. Now, will you listen to reason this time, or will I need to come down there again and make you go before Daniel catches you?"

"No, don't come down." If she did, Benedict wasn't sure he could let her return to her bedchamber without begging her to take him with her. Better not to risk it. "I only want to tell you something."

"You do realize you can tell me things during the day, don't you?"

"This couldn't wait. Kenilworth followed us here from Lady Archer's tonight. I saw his carriage sneaking out of the mews behind the school. He knows where you live and that you're associated with Lady Clifford, and very likely knows who you are."

Georgiana hesitated, then shrugged. "Well, it was inevitable he'd find it out sooner or later. I don't see that there's anything we can do except inform Lady Clifford and Daniel, and carry on as we have been."

"Carry on? No, Georgiana. Do you have any idea how much power a man like the Duke of Kenilworth has at his command? Now that he knows who you are, I don't want you anywhere near him. It's no longer safe for you."

"What? You can't mean you expect me to simply drop it! What about Clara Beauchamp? We still haven't figured out how she fits into this, and what of your sister, and your nephew? I can't just walk away—"

"You can, and you will! Do you understand me, Georgiana? You're no longer my employee—"

Benedict broke off as a light suddenly illuminated one of the rooms on the ground floor.

"Now you've done it," Georgiana hissed, her head so far out the window she was an inch from toppling to the street below. "You've woken Daniel with your shouting."

"Get back inside, Georgiana. I'll deal with Brixton."

As usual, she ignored him. "I'm coming down. Someone has to keep Daniel from shooting you." With that, her head disappeared, and a moment later the dull glow of candlelight lit the window.

"Damn it. That woman is going to drive me straight to Bedlam." He had half a mind to climb up the trellis that led to her bedchamber window to stop her coming down, but before he could execute that ill-conceived plan, he heard the clop of horses' hooves, and the rattle of carriage wheels drawing near.

Georgiana's head appeared at the window again. "Who's that?"

Whoever it was, they were moving quickly. Benedict waited, and a moment later, his own carriage came around the corner and shuddered to a sudden stop on Maddox Street.

"Lord Haslemere!" Grigg shouted as soon as he caught sight of Benedict. "Something's afoot with the duchess and the little lad. You must come at once!"

Chapter Fourteen

Georgiana was shouting out the window at Lord Haslemere. Lord Haslemere was shouting at the coachman, who was babbling incoherently in reply, and Daniel was standing on the pavement in his shirtsleeves, his pistol stuffed into his waistband and one enormous fist cocked and aimed at Lord Haslemere's head.

This was the scene waiting for Lady Clifford when the commotion at last drove her from her bedchamber to the doorway of the Clifford School. She took one look at the chaos, planted her hands on her hips, and started barking orders. "Daniel, kindly refrain from assaulting Lord Haslemere. Georgiana, it is not at all ladylike to shout into the street from your bedchamber window. You, young man." She pointed at the coachman. "Silence, if you please. As for you, Lord Haslemere, this is hardly the proper time for a call. What are you doing on my doorstep in the middle of the night?"

"Georgiana…Kenilworth…my sister and nephew…" Benedict began, but when he tried to explain himself to Lady Clifford, he realized he hadn't any bloody idea what was going on. "Explain yourself, Grigg," he demanded, tugging poor Grigg into the midst of the melee.

Grigg stumbled forward, his wide-eyed gaze moving between Benedict, Lady Clifford, and Daniel Brixton's pistol. "Erm, well, I went off to the duke's like ye told me to, my lord, and what do ye suppose I found?"

"That's what we're waiting to find out, Grigg."

"Right. Well, the duke's house was all lit up, an' servants all scattering this way and that, and there was a traveling coach waiting outside."

Benedict's blood went cold. "What's Kenilworth want with a traveling coach at midnight? Was there anyone inside it?"

"Nay, my lord, but someone was going somewhere, right enough, because the servants were shoving all sort of packages and bundles and whatnot inside."

"Jane and Freddy." Benedict's frantic gaze met Lady Clifford's. "He's sending them away from London."

"We don't know that, Lord Haslemere, but he's certainly sending someone somewhere." Lady Clifford tapped her lip, thinking. "Is the duke likely to hurt either the duchess or their son?"

"A week ago, I would have said no. Now?" Benedict's hands clenched into fists. He'd never felt so helpless in his life. "I think it's possible, yes. At the very least, he has the means to hide them. He has dozens of homes in England, and several more in remote parts of Scotland. If he succeeds in getting them out of London, we'll never find them."

That was enough for Lady Clifford. "Daniel, ready yourself while I fetch Georgiana."

"No!" Benedict's voice was harsh. "I don't want Georgiana involved in this any more than she already is."

"Does the duke know who Miss Georgiana is?" Brixton's face was like stone. "He knows she works with Lady Clifford?"

"Yes. He had us followed from Lady Archer's. I saw the carriage hidden in the mews. I came back here to warn her, but thanks to you, Brixton, we've wasted precious time." But as much as Benedict wanted to blame this whole mess on Brixton, he knew this was all his own fault.

He'd endangered Jane, Freddy, and Georgiana when he'd insisted on paying that call at Grosvenor Street this morning. That devil Bagshaw must have eavesdropped on their conversation, then wasted no time telling the duke all about it. There was no other explanation for why Kenilworth had turned up at Lady Archer's when he never wagered. He'd never appeared at any of her entertainments before.

The duke had come to Lady Archer's tonight specifically to find out who Georgiana was, and he'd succeeded. Once he discovered she was part of the Clifford School, it would be easy enough for him to deduce she was prodding into secrets he'd prefer remain buried.

There were discreet rumors about the school, and rumors about Lady Clifford. There were *always* rumors, but only those people who had reasons to hide their behavior knew precisely what she did. Benedict had made a grave error assuming Kenilworth wasn't one of them.

How much would his inattention cost him? How much would it cost Georgiana, Jane, and Freddy? What was Kenilworth hiding? Whatever it was, he was going to great lengths to keep anyone from discovering it. First

Draven, and now Jane and Freddy. The thought of his sweet, gentle sister and young nephew at the mercy of such a man made Benedict shudder.

"What's happened?" Georgiana was hurrying down the stairs. "It's not the duchess, is it?"

Benedict gave her a grim nod. "Both Jane and Freddy. Grigg saw a traveling coach waiting outside the Grosvenor Street mansion. Kenilworth's sending them away from London. I know it."

"Dear God. Quickly, then. They'll have a start on us."

"I want you to go with them, Daniel," Lady Clifford said. "Do whatever you must to prevent their leaving London. Once you've recovered them, bring them back here. I'll make arrangements to keep them safe while we decide what to do."

Georgiana was halfway out the door, but Benedict caught her arm. "No, Georgiana. You're staying here. Brixton and I will go."

"No. I'm going with you." Georgiana jerked her arm free. "The duchess came to me for my help, my lord. I'm not going to abandon her now when she needs it more than ever."

"For God's sake, Georgiana, will you listen to reason? It's not *safe*. How can I focus on Jane and Freddy if I'm trying to keep an eye on you?"

"You don't need to keep an eye on me. I'm perfectly able to take care of myself."

Benedict glanced at Lady Clifford, hoping she'd support him, but she was looking at Georgiana with an unmistakable look of pride on her face. He threw up his hands in frustration. "You're all mad, every last one of you."

"Benedict, please. I can't just stay here, waiting and worrying. I promise you I can take care of myself." Georgiana touched his arm, a wry twist to her lips. "I may even be able to help."

"We're wasting time, Haslemere," Brixton growled. "Let the lass come."

"It doesn't look as if I have any choice." Benedict was far from reconciled to the idea, but for once, Brixton was right. There was no time to argue about it.

They didn't speak as they hurried into Benedict's carriage and Grigg drove them to Grosvenor Square. Benedict could hardly think as they rattled through London. What would they do if Jane and Freddy were already gone? It had been nearly half an hour since Grigg appeared in Maddox Street. How would they find them then? Even if they did have the good luck to catch up to them, how would they get them away from the duke—

"Look," Georgiana said softly, laying her hand on Benedict's arm. "Just there."

Grigg, who knew to be cautious, had stopped the carriage on the corner of North Audley and Brook Street, out of sight of the Kenilworth mansion, but close enough so they could see what was happening on the other end of Grosvenor Street.

Brixton grunted. "If the duke wanted to hide 'em, he should have had 'em taken out through the mews. Fool."

Benedict had gone still, anger rushing like poison through his veins. Just as Grigg had said, a traveling coach was waiting in front of the house. It was luxuriously appointed, but black, and unmarked.

"It looks as if the duke intends for them to take a lengthy journey." Georgiana watched out the window as two servants dragged out a heavy trunk and loaded it onto the coach.

"A lengthy, *secret* journey," Benedict said. "There's no crest on the door. That's a hired coach."

There was no sign of Kenilworth, but a burly footman was hurrying a petite lady down the front steps to the open carriage door. A veiled hat covered her face, but it was certainly Jane. A second footman followed, half-dragging a little boy behind him. The boy was similarly disguised with a cap pulled low over his face, but Benedict would know Freddy anywhere.

"That *villain*." Benedict scrabbled for the door, half-crazed with fury and fear. "I'm going to bloody kill him—"

Brixton stopped him. "Nay, my lord. Stay where ye are, and let them go."

"Let them *go*? Damnation, man, you're mad if you think I'm going to let that blackguard kidnap my sister and nephew!"

"Nothing ye can do about it, Haslemere. Kenilworth's her husband. He wants her to go, she goes, no matter if ye like it or not. You try and stop it, the duke will have ye taken up, and then what?"

Georgiana squeezed his arm. "Daniel's right, Benedict. There's nothing you can do just now."

Benedict sucked in a breath, struggling to get control of himself. Brixton was right, damn him. He'd only make it worse if he charged into the middle of it. "What do you suggest then, Brixton? Because I'll be damned if I let that scoundrel take my family."

"They won't get far. We'll let 'em get out of London. It's dark, ye see?" Brixton's mouth stretched into a bloodthirsty grin. "It's not safe, traveling in the dark. Anything can happen once ye get onto a deserted country road, eh?"

Benedict blinked. He'd never seen Brixton smile before. It was… disturbing, but what the man said made sense. It would be much better to follow the black carriage at a discreet distance, and strike when there were no witnesses about. There were only two footmen and the coachman, and they wouldn't be expecting an attack.

Even so, it took every shred of Benedict's control to sit still while Jane and Freddy were shoved into the carriage. The footmen climbed in after them, and a second later the coachman brought the ribbons down on the horse's backs.

The black carriage headed southeast out of London, and from there further south, toward Bromley. Mile after mile they went, the black coach rumbling ahead of them. They didn't seem to be in much of a hurry, nor did they give any indication they were aware they were being followed.

One of the benefits of being a duke, Benedict thought, bitter anger flooding his chest. It would never occur to Kenilworth he couldn't do precisely as he wished, no matter how heinous it was. It made Benedict's stomach roil to think about how many times Kenilworth must have done something as fiendish as this, all while Benedict was oblivious to his perfidy, and all of London was singing his praises.

"There's a bend in the road up ahead," Brixton said, startling Benedict from his thoughts. "It's narrow—too narrow for both carriages to stay on the road."

"You're thinking we should come along beside them, and force them into the ditch?" Georgiana peered out the window. "I don't know, Daniel. That ditch looks deep. The coach may overturn."

"Nay, we won't run 'em off. We can't risk hurting the duchess and the lad. We'll get in front of 'em and force 'em to stop once we get to the bend. They can't get around us there. We're lighter and quicker than the coach, so it won't be any trouble to get by 'em, but if they hit us, your carriage may not escape without a battering, Haslemere."

"I don't give a damn about the carriage." All Benedict cared about was keeping Georgiana in one piece, and getting Jane and Freddy safely out of the duke's hands.

"What about Grigg?" Georgiana asked. "Do you suppose he can manage it? As soon as he gets the carriage into position he'll need to leap down from the box, just in case they do hit us."

Benedict stared at her, amazed to hear her discussing a coaching accident with such sangfroid. But then, she was one of Lady Clifford's girls, and had likely seen things not many young ladies her age had seen.

Ugly things.

He watched the dim shafts of moonlight moving across her face. It was peculiar to him, how she was so experienced in some ways, yet so innocent in others. He'd never known a woman like her—doubted there *was* another woman like her. His chest pinched at the thought, and for a moment he couldn't catch a breath.

"Benedict?" Georgiana's brows drew together. "Are you all right?"

Benedict jerked his attention back to the matter at hand. "Yes, I'm fine, and Grigg is capable." He and Grigg had been in a few scrapes during their time together, and Grigg had more than proved his skill with the ribbons. Benedict trusted him implicitly. "How far along is the bend?"

"Just up ahead. We need to warn yer man."

Benedict slid the panel open and called to Grigg, who listened to Brixton's instructions with unmistakable relish. Grigg was fond of a good dustup now and again, and nodded his agreement.

"Once he's stopped the carriage, everyone gets out. Lass, you get to the side of the road while Haslemere and I get into the coach and—"

"I won't be of any use to anyone standing on the side of the road, Daniel. No, I'll follow you to the coach, and see if I can get the duchess and Freddy out of—"

"No!" Benedict's voice was louder than he'd intended it to be. Georgiana jumped, and even Brixton, whom Benedict had never seen caught off guard before, jerked his head toward Benedict in surprise. "You'll stay out of the way, just as Brixton says."

For the first time ever, Brixton gave him an approving look. "Aye. It's best that way, lass."

Georgiana didn't appear to hear him. She was staring at Benedict, her lips tight. "Is that so, my lord? I beg your pardon, but the duchess engaged my services, not *you*. My loyalty is to her. As fond as you are at issuing commands, I don't recall ever agreeing to follow them."

"Then *don't* follow my commands. Follow Brixton's. It makes no difference to me, as long as you keep to the side where you're less likely to be trampled by a horse or caught beneath the coach's wheels."

"This may surprise you, Lord Haslemere, but I'm perfectly capable of—"

"I don't care what you think you're capable of, Miss Harley." On some distant level, Benedict realized he'd lost control, but he was becoming more agitated with every word out of her mouth. He couldn't stop himself from picturing her bloody, mangled body under the horses' massive hooves, or worse, with one of Kenilworth's savage footmen with his hands around her neck.

She didn't answer, but the expression on her face didn't inspire confidence. Her lips were tight, and that incredulous eyebrow remained arched, but Benedict refused to give in.

Grigg was urging the horses forward, and they were closing in on the black coach. "They've seen us, my lord!" he shouted through the open panel. "Hold on tight, now. I'll have to speed up to catch them at the bend, and it'll be a hard stop."

"Do what you must, Grigg, but see that you catch them." Benedict braced his feet against the floor, then reached for Georgiana. She squeaked in surprise as he slid her across the bench and tucked her as tightly against the length of his body as he could, to protect her if the coach did hit them.

"Lord Haslemere!" She made an attempt to squirm away from him.

"Quiet," Benedict hissed, holding her fast. "All right there, Brixton?"

Brixton snorted. "Don't worry about me, Haslemere. This won't be the first time I've been knocked about. Just mind ye take care of that lass."

The sky had gone an ominous black above them. The road was dark, and they were moving at such a brisk pace the view outside the window was an indistinct blur, but Benedict caught a glimpse of the coach as they careened past, a bulky shadow in the darkness. The duke's horses let out a frightened screech as the carriage sped by them. There was a shout—Grigg, Benedict thought—an answering curse, then a jolt as Grigg wrenched the horses to the left, bringing them broadside across the road.

There was another shout, this one edged with panic. The carriage shuddered around them, every seam creaking as they tipped to the right, listing dangerously until Benedict was sure they'd go over. He closed his eyes and tightened his arms around Georgiana, but just as he'd braced himself for a crash into the ditch, the carriage fell back onto its wheels again with a wrench, sending them all crashing to the floor.

And then...pandemonium, as everyone scrambled from their vehicles at once.

"Don't move, Georgiana." Benedict swept her off to the side of the road, away from a battle that was already shaping up to be an ugly one. Kenilworth's coachman scrambled down from the box, and the two footmen erupted from the carriage, shouting and cursing. "Promise me!"

Georgiana *didn't* promise, but they were already in the midst of the frenzy by then, and there was no time for Benedict to do anything but dart for the coach. A child's terrified cries rose from inside, swelling above the commotion. "Freddy!"

"Mind the coachman's pistol, Haslemere!"

Before Benedict could react to Brixton's warning a sharp crack echoed in the night, and a pistol ball flew past his head, a mere fraction away from striking his temple.

"Benedict!"

The night tried to steal Georgiana's scream. Benedict heard her, but when he turned back, she was no longer there. He whirled around, his heart rushing into his throat when he caught a glimpse of her dark red skirts rounding the side of Kenilworth's carriage.

"Georgiana!" He started to go after her, but one of Kenilworth's footmen charged at him and knocked him to the ground. He rolled and was up again in a flash, his fists clenched and a snarl on his lips, but Grigg, who was small and wiry, had leapt onto the man's back and was pressing his forearm into his windpipe.

"Good man, Grigg." Benedict wiped his eyes to clear the dust, then seized ahold of the footman. "Let him go. I've got him. Go after Miss Harley."

Grigg dropped nimbly to the ground and darted around the side of the carriage while Benedict dragged the footman, who was still choking and coughing, to the side of the road and, with one powerful shove, heaved him into the ditch.

Benedict whirled around again to find Brixton making quick and brutal work of the other footman. The man's hand was pressed to his nose, blood spurting through his fingers and gushing down his chin. "Here, Brixton!"

Brixton turned, and Benedict jerked his head toward the ditch. "Over the side. Neither of them is climbing up from that hole anytime soon."

A ferocious grin spread over Brixton's face as he dragged the man through the dirt to the edge of the embankment and tossed him gleefully over the edge. "Yer smarter than ye look, Haslemere."

"I'm just glad we're on the same side," Benedict muttered as he charged back toward the coach with Brixton on his heels. The only one of Kenilworth's men who was unaccounted for was the coachman, but he was the one who had the pistol, and Georgiana…

Georgiana was nowhere to be seen.

"The lass?" Brixton shouted. "Where's the—"

They caught sight of her at the same time, hurrying around the back of the coach, Freddy in her arms. Waiting for her on the other side, just out of her sight, was the coachman, his pistol drawn.

A sound tore from Benedict's throat, a cry of warning, deep and raw and painful, and then he was running, his boots sliding over the loose dirt, his heart pounding, his gaze fixed on the muzzle of the pistol as it lifted, aimed…and then, incredibly he was there, seizing the man's wrist and wrenching it into the air, a blast ripping through the night as Benedict slammed the man into the side of the coach.

Brixton was on them the next second. "Into Haslemere's carriage," he shouted to Georgiana as he snatched the pistol from the coachman's hand. "Both of you. Hurry, lass."

Georgiana hardly spared them a glance as she darted past them, but instead of doing as Brixton bid her, she shoved Freddy into Grigg's arms, then turned and rushed back toward the coach.

"*Georgiana!*" Benedict roared. "Get back—"

"Some help, Haslemere?" Brixton was pressing the coachman's face into the dirt, grunting as the man howled and cursed and thrashed to get free.

Benedict grabbed the man by the collar and hauled him to his feet. "Quiet, you bloody villain," he snarled as he dragged him across the road, and without the slightest hesitation, tossed him into the ditch. To his shock, Brixton scrambled after the man, skidding and slipping down the side of the ditch, the coachman's pistol still in his hand. "Brixton, what the *devil* are you doing?"

"Never mind me. Fetch the lass, Haslemere."

"Don't shoot them," Benedict warned before he turned and flew back to the coach. Georgiana was just emerging from the thick cloud of dust raised by the scuffle, her arm around Jane's shoulders as she helped her toward his carriage. "Jane!"

Jane's head jerked up. "Benedict!" She rushed toward him.

Benedict gathered her into his chest, his eyes closing. "Jane, thank God. You're not hurt?"

"N-no, but you have to listen to me, Benedict." Jane clutched at his coat with frantic fingers, struggling to catch her breath. "You *must* leave this alone! Promise me, Benedict—swear to me you won't dig any further into the duke's secrets."

"I can't do that, Jane. I *won't*." Benedict's heart broke to see her in such distress, but Kenilworth had tried to kidnap her and Freddy, damn him. There was no going back from that. "Tell me what Kenilworth has done, Jane. Why are you so frightened of him?"

"You have no idea what he's capable of, Benedict. He...he'll make you pay, just like..." Jane trailed off, her face crumpling.

"Let me worry about Kenilworth—"

"No! Benedict, wait." Jane clung to his hands with icy cold fingers. "You should know what you're risking. The duke isn't the only one with secrets. Freddy is...h-he's not Kenilworth's heir."

"Not his heir?" Benedict stared at her, numb with shock, unable to believe what he was hearing. "Jane—"

"Time to move on, Haslemere." Brixton had climbed out of the ditch and was approaching the carriage, clutching three pairs of boots in his hands. "I took their boots. It'll slow 'em down, but they'll find their way out of that ditch sooner or later. We'd best be gone before then."

"No! Where are you going?" Jane's eyes were wild as she clawed at Benedict's coat. "Don't go! Benedict, please. He'll come after you. He'll *hurt* you—"

"It's all right, Jane." Benedict cupped her head and eased it down to his chest, but over her head, he met Brixton's gaze. "Take Freddy and Jane in my carriage, and Brixton? You and Lady Clifford will take care of them?"

"Aye. We'll keep 'em safe."

Benedict nodded, but his throat was tight as he led Jane to his carriage and handed her up. "Go with Mr. Brixton, Jane. He'll take you to Lady Clifford. All right there, Freddy?" He leaned into the door, a false, reassuring smile on his face, but as soon as he got a look at his nephew, it vanished.

Freddy's eye was swollen closed, and his cheek shadowed with ugly black and purple bruises. Benedict stared at the boy's injury, rage and grief swelling in his chest until he was gasping for breath.

He held out his arms to his nephew, and Freddy dove into them with a strangled sob. Benedict gathered him tightly against his chest, stroked his hair, and murmured soothingly to him until the boy's trembling eased. "I'll see you soon, all right, my boy?" Benedict forced a smile, and chucked Freddy gently under the chin. "You'll take care of your mama for me, won't you?"

"Yes, Uncle," Freddy whispered.

"Good boy."

Benedict gave Freddy a gentle squeeze and set him back in his seat, but before he could close the carriage door, Jane grabbed his arm. "Benedict, I'm begging you to leave it be. I can't…if something should happen to you…I can't lose you."

"You won't lose me, Jane." Benedict pressed a kiss to her forehead. "I promise it."

"Close the door, Haslemere," Brixton called down from the coachman's box. "Well, lass? Are you coming, or not?"

Benedict turned to find Georgiana standing behind him, her dark red gown streaked with dirt, her face white. She was silent as she watched him close the carriage door, an expression he couldn't read in her eyes.

"No," she said at last, shifting her gaze to Brixton. "I'm going with Lord Haslemere. You'll tell Lady Clifford, Daniel?"

"Aye, lass. I'll tell her." Daniel brought the ribbons down, and the horses started with a nervous jerk.

Within moments the carriage was off, swallowed into the darkness.

Chapter Fifteen

Georgiana didn't know where they were going, but wherever it was, Grigg was wasting no time getting them there. Or perhaps he was just in a great hurry to get them away from *here*.

She gazed out the window, but she didn't see anything. She didn't hear anything, and she didn't say a word, just sat dumbly on the seat, thinking about…nothing. Such a thing had never happened to her before, but it was as if her head had been pumped full of fog, and every coherent thought was lost in the mist.

Was this what it felt like to be in shock? Yes, that was likely what was happening. Her brain, bombarded with too many appalling things to consider at once, had chosen not to consider any of them. It was rather comforting, really, to think about nothing.

She might have stayed in her blessed fog forever if Benedict hadn't cleared his throat. "I've never objected to speechlessness in a lady before, but right now, it's making me nervous. Say something, would you?"

Georgiana turned to find a pair of dark eyes fixed on her face. She opened her mouth to speak, but closed it again without uttering a single word.

Say something, say something…

But where did she even begin? With the coachman and two footmen they'd left bootless at the bottom of a ditch? The traveling coach they'd just stolen? Snatching a duchess out from underneath her husband's nose? The pistol ball that had nearly left Benedict facedown on the road, his life's blood draining into the dirt beneath him?

Now she'd allowed herself to think, one terrifying image after another whirled through her head, each one more awful than the last. But as the disturbing scenes chased each other across her eyelids, one stood out from the rest, and made her blood run cold. "Did you...did you see Freddy's face?"

Benedict didn't reply right away. He seemed to be struggling with his emotions. At last he gritted out, "I saw it."

Georgiana shuddered, a chill deeper and colder than any she'd ever felt before seizing her and shaking her like a ragdoll. She'd never forget the sight of the boy's face when she'd flung open the coach's door and held out her arms to him. He'd been white as a ghost, his mouth twisted with fear, his eye blackened and swollen closed, the tender skin underneath it purple, and an angry red gash across his cheekbone. The wound was the same size and shape as...

A man's fist.

The duke wasn't a good man. Georgiana knew that, but what she hadn't known was that he was a monster. A sob caught in her throat as she recalled the way Freddy had crawled into her arms without hesitation when she'd held them out to him. Such trust from a child who had been on the other end of a blow tonight.

But she fought back the tears before they could spill over. She didn't cry. Ever.

"This ends tonight. Whatever I have to do, wherever we have to go, I'll make certain the duke never sees either Jane or Freddy again." Benedict's hands were opening and closing into fists.

Without thinking, Georgiana lay her own hand over his, stilling them. "What can we do?" The duke was wealthy, titled, and possessed of a spotless—if false—reputation. Jane was his *wife*. As unfair as it was, he could do whatever he liked with her.

"We can get to the truth of the secret between Kenilworth and the Earl of Draven."

Georgiana's brows drew together. "What secret? As far as we know, the secret is between Lord Draven and Jane, not Draven and Kenilworth."

"Not according to Lady Archer."

Benedict was half-hidden in darkness, but the moonlight illuminated enough of his face to reveal his expression, and dread washed over Georgiana at what she saw there. "W-What do you mean? What did Lady Archer tell you?"

"It seems Kenilworth and Draven aren't quite the *dear* friends Mrs. Bury made them out to be." Benedict dragged a hand through his hair. "They fought a duel when they returned to London after that house party."

Georgiana gasped. "A duel! Were they fighting over Jane?"

His face was bleak. "Lady Archer thinks so. She also said she believes Kenilworth is responsible for the attack on Draven. They're sworn enemies, Georgiana, and that's not the worst of it."

Georgiana clutched his hand. "What do you mean?"

Benedict's cold fingers wrapped around hers. "Tonight, Jane told me Freddy isn't Kenilworth's heir."

"Not his heir? Does that mean he's Lord Draven's…" Georgiana fell back against the seat, too stunned to force the word from her lips.

"I'm not sure what it means, but whatever happened between Kenilworth and Draven must reveal the duke to be the monster he is, otherwise he wouldn't be going to such great lengths to keep it a secret. I intend to find out what he's hiding."

Georgiana was quiet as she turned Benedict's words over in her mind. Some mysterious disagreement between the duke and Draven had led to a duel. Lord Draven and Jane had a murky past that might or might not include a long-standing love affair, and both of them were searching for Clara Beauchamp—a search that had led to Lord Draven lying unconscious in his bed, his skull cracked open by a gang of ruffians, and an attempt by the duke to spirit his wife and son out of London in the dark of night.

It was like one of Freddy's dissected puzzles, but with half the pieces lost six years ago, and the other half scattered across England.

What did any of this have to do with Clara Beauchamp? Was she the only one who knew the truth about Freddy? If Freddy truly wasn't the duke's son and Clara knew it, mightn't that be a reason Draven and Jane were searching for her?

"Clara Beauchamp is at the crux of this, Benedict. If we can find Clara, we'll find the truth, but where do we begin? Your sister claims she saw Clara in London a week or so ago, but no one else seems to have seen her, not even Lady Trowbridge."

"We won't find what we're looking for in London, but we might find it at Draven's estate in High Wycombe. Clara Beauchamp vanished that night. Someone there knows something about it. If not Draven's servants, then his neighbors. There are as many gossips in the country as in London. You can be sure someone will be overjoyed to tell us all about it."

Georgiana nodded slowly. It was their best hope, but it wasn't without its own risks. "The duke will send his men after us."

"Yes. It'll be a bit more complicated than simply strolling up to Draven's front door and questioning his servants. It's going to be dangerous, Georgiana." Benedict paused, then went on in a softer voice, "Back there, you told Brixton you wanted to come with me, but it's not too late to change your—"

"No." The word was out of Georgiana's mouth before she'd even considered the question. "I…that is, the duchess hired me to find Clara Beauchamp. I told her I would do so, and I don't intend to go back on my word. Do we go to Oxfordshire tonight?"

"No. We need to get rid of this coach. The duke's men will be looking for it, and we need fresh horses. I know of a place outside London we can spend the night where no one will think to look for us. Grigg is taking us there now."

He hadn't meant they'd spend the night *together*, so there was no reason her heart should have given that ridiculous, pathetic thump. Georgiana withdrew her hand from his, and kept her nose pressed to the window after that, watching the darkness fly past.

They seemed to drive on for such an interminable length of time she thought they must be halfway to Oxfordshire when the carriage came to a stop at last. "We're here," Benedict murmured. Grigg appeared at the coach's door, and Benedict jumped down, muttering a few words to his coachman before turning to help Georgiana.

"What is this place?" Georgiana took the hand he offered and stepped down onto the drive, glancing around. If it was an inn, it was a particularly grand one, faced with cream-colored stone and a series of pretty balconies under each enormous bow window. "It looks like a private home. Is it an inn?"

"Er…not exactly." Benedict didn't elaborate, but took her arm and led her toward a pair of tall, handsome double doors protected by a generous portico and gently illuminated by an ornate gas lantern suspended from the ceiling. He reached for the heavy brass door knocker, but before he could knock a distinguished-looking butler in smart, dark blue livery appeared, and with a formal bow, ushered them into a lavish entryway with green and gilt paper on the walls.

"Lord Haslemere, for Madame Célestine."

"Very good, my lord." The butler offered another smooth bow, then disappeared down a hallway.

Georgiana watched him go, then turned to Benedict, her confusion growing by the minute. "Madame Célestine? That name almost sounds like…" She trailed off as the painting over Benedict's shoulder caught her attention. "Is that a…" Her eyes widened, and she stepped closer to get a better look. No, surely not—

"It's nothing of any import." Benedict stepped in front of her, blocking the painting. "There's a settee behind you. Will you have a seat? You must be fatigued."

"Dear God, it *is*." Some sort of noise leapt to Georgiana's lips. She couldn't say whether it was a gasp or a laugh, but she slapped a hand over her mouth to stifle it.

Benedict braced his hands on her shoulders and tried to urge her away from the painting, but she'd seen too much, and by now she'd also noticed there were another half dozen of the same sort of paintings in the entryway alone.

He might prod her all he liked, but he couldn't prevent her from seeing all of them.

She let him guide her to the settee, but once he thought he'd gotten his way and relaxed his grip, she twisted away from him and hurried to the other side of the room where another one of the paintings was hanging.

"God in heaven." Georgiana gaped at it with rounded eyes.

A pair of heavily lashed painted dark eyes stared back at her from the canvas. Whoever the lady was, she was beautiful, with masses of loose dark hair falling around her white shoulders and the most alluring, inviting smile on her red, red lips.

But it wasn't her hair, her smile, or her eyes that caught Georgiana's attention. It was her breasts.

Not because Georgiana was particularly enamored of breasts, but because this lady's breasts were…well, they weren't bare, precisely, but it was a near thing. Her unlaced corset dangled from her delicate fingertips, leaving her clad in only a transparent chemise, which—if one could judge by the playful glint in her eyes—was a mere breath from being ripped from her body by some unknown gentleman and flung unceremoniously to the floor.

The other painted ladies were in similarly provocative poses. Fair, dark, and red-haired beauties; blue, brown, or green-eyed; each with those same red lips, that same inviting smile. One was clad only in a petticoat, her arms crossed over her bare breasts. Another stood in her chemise, a full-length looking glass behind her, one stockinged leg balanced on a chair. She appeared to be, ah…removing her garters?

"How curious," Georgiana murmured, glancing over her shoulder at Benedict, who was shifting awkwardly from one foot to the other. "I remove my own shoes and stockings *before* I take off my gown, and I've never needed a chair to remove my garters. Do you suppose I've been doing it wrong all these years?"

He seemed to be casting about for a reply, but just as he opened his mouth, footsteps tripped down the hallway, and with a grand swish of silk skirts, a fair-haired lady entered the room, a brilliant smile on her full lips. "Lord Haslemere." She took both of Benedict's hands in hers and rose to her tiptoes to kiss one of his cheeks, then the other. "Shame on you, my lord. It's been much too long since you came to see me, *n'est-ce pas?*"

Georgiana watched this effusive welcome with raised eyebrows.

Benedict shot her an uneasy glance, but he bowed graciously over the lady's hand. "Madame Célestine. It has indeed been a long time, but you remain as lovely as ever."

Madame Célestine threw her head back in a merry laugh. "Such flattery! You have not changed either, *monsieur*. Do I dare hope you've come to see me, or will one of my young ladies be so fortunate as to enjoy your attentions this evening?"

Despite Georgiana's vow not to show any reaction to the scenes playing out in front of her, her jaw dropped open, and another noise escaped her lips. Not a snort—certainly not something so unladylike as *that*—but, well…a noise that sounded rather like it.

Madame Célestine turned then, and seemed to notice for the first time that Georgiana was standing behind her. Her eyes widened in surprise, but then a wicked grin curved her lips. "Or have you brought your own entertainment, my lord?"

Benedict glanced from Madame Célestine to Georgiana, looking as if he wished himself at the bottom of the Thames. "I brought my own—"

"Lord Haslemere!" Georgiana gaped at him, her cheeks on fire.

"I mean to say, I brought a friend," Benedict hastened to clarify. "That is, not a friend, at least, not in the, er…very *friendly* sense of the word. Not a *chère amie*, you understand, but rather a young lady. A pure, spotless, innocent young lady."

Madame Célestine arched an eyebrow, but her lips were twitching, as if she were greatly enjoying Benedict's discomfiture. "You brought a pure, spotless, innocent young lady to a brothel, my lord?"

"This *is* a brothel, then?" Georgiana shot Benedict an accusing look. "I thought it must be. I can't think why I'm surprised, my lord, but this is taking it a bit far, even for *you*."

"Indeed, *mon chère*, I'm afraid I must agree with your friend. My establishment is of the highest quality, as you know, but even so, it's not a proper place for an innocent girl—"

"If you'd both do me the favor of ceasing your infernal chatter for one blessed moment," Benedict huffed, "I'd be delighted to explain myself."

"But of course, my lord." Madame Célestine smiled sweetly at him, then shot Georgiana a mischievous wink.

Benedict turned to Georgiana. "I wouldn't have brought you here if I'd had another choice, but Madame Célestine is an…an old friend, and her, er…this establishment is out of the way, and known only to a few select gentlemen in London. We may rely on Madame's discretion to keep our visit utterly private, may we not, Madame?"

Madame Célestine inclined her head. "Of course, you may, my lord."

"We need a room for the night. Just tonight, preferably overlooking the front drive, so I can keep an eye on the gentlemen coming and going. Can you provide us with that, Madame?"

Madame Célestine inclined her elegant blonde head again. "I can provide you with whatever you wish, Lord Haslemere."

Oh, there was little doubt of that. Georgiana snorted, and this time there was, alas, no denying it *was* indeed a snort.

"Thank you, Madame." Benedict offered her a polite bow, then turned an impatient look on Georgiana. "You had a chance to return with Brixton, but you chose to come with me instead. I assumed that meant you trusted me to look out for you. If you've changed your mind, I'll send a note to Lady Clifford at once, and have her send a carriage to fetch you."

Had she changed her mind? Less than a week ago she'd been the sort of sane, rational being who would have changed her mind the moment some arrogant lord escorted her over the threshold of a brothel, but it seemed it took less than a week for Benedict Harcourt to scatter her wits.

Because the truth was, she *hadn't* changed her mind.

She told herself it was because of the building on Mill Street—that she was doing it for her girls and Lady Clifford. That she'd come this far, and wouldn't let it slip through her fingers now. But somehow, even in her own head, it sounded like a lie.

Still, she raised her chin. Perhaps she hadn't quite figured out why she'd decided to come with Benedict, but she *had* decided it, and she had no intention of changing her mind now. "No, there's no need to bother Lady Clifford. I'm perfectly happy to remain where I am, in…a brothel."

With a rakish, irresistibly handsome earl. What could possibly go wrong?

"Very well." A small smile played at the corner of Madame Célestine's lips. "If you'll be so good as to follow me, I'll take you to your bedchamber for the night."

They followed her to an extravagantly appointed anteroom, which boasted another handful of those salacious paintings. Georgiana promised herself she'd find a chance to get a closer look at them as she followed

Madame Célestine up two flights of stairs to a spacious bedchamber tucked into the end of a hallway.

"Here we are. I'll send hot water up with one of the housemaids." Madame Célestine stood back and let them pass, then turned and left them alone, closing the door behind her.

The bedchamber was lovely and warm, with a handsome gold embroidered coverlet and matching bed hangings, and dozens of royal blue pillows scattered across the bed. The one enormous bed was placed in the dead center of the bedchamber, as if it were the only piece of furniture that mattered.

Which, this being a brothel, it *was*.

It was on the tip of Georgiana's tongue to banish Benedict to the floor for the night, but one look at his exhausted face made the words freeze on her lips. She sighed, impatient with herself. She was alone in a sumptuous bedchamber with a massive bed and a wicked rake, and *this* was the moment she'd chosen to indulge her tender feelings?

It seemed so. She strode over to the bed, grabbed an armful of the pillows, and began arranging them down the middle. Once she'd finished the first layer, she added another until there was a wall of colorful silk pillows down the center of the bed.

Benedict watched these proceedings with a bemused expression. "What are you—"

"That's your side." Georgiana pointed to the side of the bed farthest from her. "This is mine. You will *not*, Lord Haslemere, venture to put so much as a single toe over the barrier. Is that understood?"

Benedict's lips curved in a wicked grin. "Only my toes are forbidden? Does that mean other parts of me might be welcome?"

Georgiana eyed him. He blinked innocently at her, but that grin of his was...worrying. She couldn't be certain he was teasing, so she snatched up another handful of pillows and piled them on top of the others.

He raised an eyebrow. "You do realize, princess, that if I'm seized with an uncontrollable urge to venture over the line, a dozen pillows won't stop me?"

Georgiana ignored him, finished stacking her pillows, then stepped back to survey her handiwork. It wasn't a very sturdy barrier, but short of rolling up the carpet and dragging it onto the bed, there wasn't much else she could do. "Keep your uncontrollable urges to yourself, Lord Haslemere."

To Georgiana's surprise, he burst into a laugh. "That's not nearly as much fun, but it won't be the first time I've done so where you're concerned, Miss Harley."

She scowled at him. "I don't see what's so amusing about it, but I'll have your word, Lord Haslemere."

Benedict choked back his laughter and gave her a mocking salute. "Yes, ma'am. Not a single toe."

Chapter Sixteen

The next morning Benedict woke to something soft tickling his chin.

He cracked an eye open and a drowsy smile curved his lips. He couldn't have said what the soft thing was, but it smelled lovely, and it was attached to something warm, the weight of it pleasant against his chest.

It felt like…a woman.

Benedict's brow furrowed as he considered that possibility. For all the rumors about his insatiability, he'd spent a long, lonely winter in Surrey without a woman to grace his bed.

A dream, then? No, it felt too warm, too real to be a dream.

He cracked open the other eye and let his blurry gaze rove over the room. A marble fireplace, embers still glowing, a plush Aubusson carpet on the floor, heavily embroidered gold silk bed hangings, and—

Gold silk bed hangings?

His bedchamber in Surrey was done in shades of blue. He wasn't in Surrey, nor was he in his bedchamber in Berkeley Square. Where the devil had he slept last night, then? More importantly, who had he slept *with*?

Lady Wylde? No, it couldn't be. In a rare display of good sense, he'd decided against that entanglement. Who, then? Because there was most definitely a lady in his arms, one hand curled on his stomach and her long legs tangled with his.

Her body felt divine snuggled against him, and so utterly right he was tempted to close his eyes and lose himself in the sleep that still lingered, but instead he pulled his head back to get a better look at the delectable creature sprawled over his chest.

All he could make out was a mess of mahogany brown waves with dozens of useless hairpins scattered among the heavy tresses. He studied the wayward curls, his eyes narrowing. They looked familiar, but he was sure he'd never before seen them spread across his chest in such wild abandon before. He reached for one and let his fingers caress the long strands. The only lady he knew with hair like this was—

Benedict froze, the last vestiges of sleep falling away with a vengeance. *Georgiana Harley.*

He threw his arm over his eyes, a low groan leaving his lips as the events of the night before came flooding back to him. Chasing after the coach, rescuing Jane and Freddy, then turning them over to Brixton. Their escape in the duke's hired coach, and their arrival at Madame Célestine's last night.

But none of this explained how Georgiana Harley came to be nestled in his arms. For God's sake, she'd barricaded herself behind two dozen pillows in order to ensure not a single part of his body touched hers last night. If she'd had a suit of armor to hand, no doubt she would have donned it before allowing him to join her in the bed.

How, then, had she ended up with her head on his chest, her hair tickling his chin, her hand burrowed under his shirt and pressed against the bare skin of his stomach?

Her hand was pressed against the bare skin of his stomach....

Another pitiful groan escaped Benedict's lips as arousal flooded him, and his cock did what they tended to do when they discovered a warm female anywhere in their vicinity.

It rose to the occasion.

Benedict lay there, afraid to move lest he wake her. Georgiana would go mad if she woke and found herself in his arms with his cock pressing insistently against his falls.

He was still dressed, at least, and so was she. Thank bloody heaven for that.

But how had this happened? Had he tossed aside the dozens of pillows between them while he'd been asleep, like some sort of savage intent on ravishing an innocent virgin? Had he rolled over to her side of the bed until she'd had no choice but to cling to him to keep herself from falling over the edge?

Christ, he was almost afraid to look, but this was no time to turn coward. He shifted cautiously onto one elbow and cast a wary glance over the bed.

The barrier Georgiana had erected between them had disappeared. He peered over the side, expecting to find confirmation of his guilt in a pile of pillows on the floor, but there was nothing there. Not a single pillow to be seen. Not only that, but he was right at the edge.

He hadn't wriggled his way over to her side of the bed at all.

She'd wriggled *her* way over to *his*.

Well, that was…unexpected. But did this make his situation better or worse? Benedict eased himself back down onto the pillows and tried to decide. On the one hand, he hadn't done anything wrong aside from open his arms to her, but on the other, she was an inexperienced virgin, and he was a known rake and debaucher. Everyone knew the rakish debaucher was always at fault in such situations, no matter the circumstances.

Yes, he was certain to be blamed for this, and since that was the case, the only rational solution was to enjoy the warm, drowsy body pressed against his while he had the chance. So, Benedict tightened his arms around her and closed his eyes, a contented sigh leaving his lips.

He didn't fall back asleep, but lay quietly, dragging his fingertips over her back and breathing in her scent. They were safe enough for the moment, as well-hidden as they were, but he couldn't let her sleep much longer. They needed to be on their way to Oxfordshire before the duke's men began searching for them.

But if that threat hadn't been there, if he'd had the luxury of holding her in his arms as long as he wished…what would that be like?

He dipped his head lower and let her silky hair tickle his nose and cheeks. Georgiana made a soft sound in her throat, and stirred against him. He knew the precise moment when she awoke and realized where she was, and who was holding her.

She went utterly still, not even drawing a breath. Benedict waited, hardly daring to breathe himself as he braced for an explosion.

It never came.

Instead, her fingers curled against his stomach. He felt her back move in a deep breath, and then…then she raised her head from his chest and tilted her face up to his. Her hazel eyes were sleepy, and she had the most adorably shy half-smile on her lips. "I, ah…beg your pardon, Lord Haslemere. I seem to have fallen asleep on top of you."

Benedict stifled the groan that threatened to break free, but he couldn't prevent his shiver of desire as he gazed into those sleepy hazel eyes. He itched to pull the pins from her hair until it spread like a fan over him, and he might run his fingers through it, and bring a long lock of those silken threads to his lips.

Neither of them said a word as their gazes held. Benedict expected her to squirm away from him at every moment—to leap from the bed and bolt to the other side of the room, far enough away from him that he couldn't touch her.

God in heaven, don't touch her.

But it was too late. His fingers were already inching closer to her, and then the next thing he knew he was sliding his knuckles down the soft, warm skin of her cheek, his gaze holding hers.

She didn't pull away. She didn't shriek or slap his hand, and she didn't attack him with a pillow. Benedict curved his fingers under her chin and studied her expression, searching for any sign of distress or hesitation, but all he found was those hazel eyes glittering from between heavy eyelids.

He dragged his thumb over her bottom lip. "Come here, princess."

Her eyes darkened as she did as he bid her, sliding up the bed until her hair caressed his shoulder, and he felt her gentle exhalations against his lips. "Like this?" she asked, her soft, husky voice dragging goosebumps to the surface of his skin.

"Closer," he whispered, toying with a lock of her hair, unable to stop the smile that curved his lips when her eyes widened. Not his wicked, seductive smile, but a real one that started deep down in his chest. "Closer, Georgiana," he crooned, cupping the back of her head and urging her closer, until her lips hovered over his.

"I can't get any closer than this, my lord."

Benedict was dying to prove her wrong. "Oh, but you can, sweetheart."

Then he was kissing her, gently at first, the merest brush of his mouth over hers, his breath catching at the softness he found there, and then a little deeper, a groan on his lips as he caught a hint of damp heat on the tip of his tongue. Dear God, she tasted so good he couldn't stop himself from delving deeper into her temping mouth. He teased his tongue lightly against the seam of her lips, another groan tearing from him as she parted so sweetly under the tender pressure.

Benedict struggled to remember they were in a dim bedchamber, in a large, soft bed with no one here to stop them, no one to recall him to his senses before he took it too far. Already their bodies were pressing eagerly together, her arms wrapping around his neck as his tongue became bolder still, dancing along the inside of her bottom lip, and there was nowhere to go from here but deeper, harder, wetter…

All the reasons Benedict needed to let her go drifted from his mind as his lips clung desperately to hers. God, it was so easy, here in this moment, in this quiet bedchamber to forget everything but her taste, her scent, her soft whimpers in his ears.

She was intoxicating, and not in a way Benedict had ever known before. Georgiana was nothing like Lady Wylde, or Madame Célestine, or any of his other lovers. Holding her felt different and new, profound in a way he didn't yet understand. He wanted her, yes—his stiff cock was proof enough of that—but what he felt for her wasn't simple lust.

If it had been, surely holding her like this wouldn't cause this strange tightness in his chest, or the quick, pounding beat of his heart. Lust wouldn't make him want to pull her closer, hold her tighter, and not only because he desired her, but because he…wanted to protect her?

As soon as the thought wound its way through his consciousness, the truth of it overwhelmed him, and with it, a wild surge of fear.

Jane, and Freddy…he hadn't protected *them*. He hadn't seen who—what—Kenilworth really was. He'd tied his sister's and nephew's fate to a man who treated them as if they were his possessions, no more important than his fine, bottle-green carriages or his gold-tipped walking stick.

Because of *him*, Jane was at the mercy of a monster, and Freddy…

Kenilworth had *put his hands* on Freddy. He'd blackened his eye, cut open his cheek. A man like that, a man who'd hurt a child—would he hesitate to do the same to his wife?

Benedict already knew the answer. The only reason Jane's eye wasn't as black as Freddy's was because Kenilworth could control her easily by threatening their son. Jane would do whatever Kenilworth said to protect those she loved, including *him*.

Now Benedict had involved Georgiana in this mess, called her to Kenilworth's attention. Jesus, what had he been thinking, allowing her to come with him on this mad chase to Oxfordshire, in search of God knew what? The duke's buried secrets and sins? For Clara Beauchamp, a woman who seemed to have somehow dropped off the face of the earth?

Benedict had long since grown accustomed to having his own way. He'd been born to doting parents, the heir to an enormous fortune. The *ton* had turned a blind eye to his worst behavior because of his wealth, with predictable results. He'd been indulged so often and for so long he'd become selfish with others, and worthless to himself.

But this? *No.* He'd failed Jane and Freddy, but he still had a chance to do the right thing with Georgiana. She'd fight him, but he had to send her back to Lady Clifford, where she'd be safe.

He didn't realize his entire body had gone rigid until Georgiana stilled on top of him. "Benedict?"

His gaze moved between her eyes and her lips, his stomach aching with want. His worries about Kenilworth, his concern for Georgiana's safety—all of it threatened to disappear like so many seeds in the wind as long as he was touching her and inhaling her scent with every breath.

So, Benedict did the only thing he could think to do. He leapt from the bed, out of Georgiana's arms and raced to the window, as far away from her as possible, praying the throb of desire in his belly would subside before he gave into his weakness, and made her his.

* * * *

Georgiana fell face first into the bed as the warm body stretched underneath hers vanished, leaving her with nothing but a mouthful of sheets.

"This isn't…we can't…we have a problem."

Georgiana rolled over, gaping at Benedict. He'd retreated to the window and was looking down into the courtyard below, his muscular arms braced on the windowsill and his back tense.

"A problem," she echoed faintly, pressing her fingers to her parted lips. His taste lingered there, like sweet summer berries on her tongue. Her head was still spinning, her knees still shaking from his kiss, but if he was at all affected by it, he was doing an excellent job of hiding it.

But then he'd kissed dozens of women, hadn't he? Had she really thought this kiss meant any more to him than the kisses he shared with the others? He was London's favorite rake, after all. It was ridiculous of her to suppose it meant anything to him, and even more so for her to allow it to mean anything to *her*.

She raised her chin, determined to ignore the butterflies even now fluttering against her ribs. "We have a number of problems, Lord Haslemere. Which one are you referring to?"

"*Lord Haslemere?*" Benedict turned to face her, leaning against the windowsill and crossing his arms over his chest. "Are we back to that, *Miss Harley?*"

Georgiana frowned. There was a hint of a curve at the corner of his lips, but it wasn't a smile. In fact, he sounded almost angry. She opened her mouth to answer him, but he interrupted before she could get a word out. "Never mind. It doesn't matter now, because I'm sending you back to Lady Clifford this morning."

She scrambled upright in bed, the seductive languor in her limbs dissipating in an instant. "No, you're not. I told you once before, my lord. I don't follow your commands. My loyalty is to your sister."

His mouth tightened. "Ah, but my sister isn't here, Miss Harley. *I* am, and I've just informed you of my decision. Ready yourself. You leave for London in the next hour, whether you like it or not."

"I *don't* like it."

He shrugged, as if what she wanted didn't matter one way or the other to him. "I've made up my mind."

Georgiana stared at him, baffled. Less than five minutes ago they'd been wrapped around each other in bed, and now he was looking at her as if he'd never seen her before. What had happened between now and then? She hadn't the vaguest idea what she'd done, and…oh, dear God, was her lower lip wobbling?

"Are you…*crying?*" Benedict stumbled toward her, his face a mask of horror. "Georgiana, *please* don't—"

"Don't be absurd," Georgiana snapped. "I *never* cry."

Benedict had shouted at her, yes, and nearly tossed her over the side of the bed in his haste to get away from her, but she absolutely refused to collapse into a flood of tears over it.

No, just…*no*. She might not have any experience with men, least of all rakes, but she had her pride. She imitated Benedict's—that is, *Lord Haslemere's*—shrug, and looked him in the eye. "Very well, my lord. If you wish for me to return to Lady Clifford, then I'll go."

Benedict's eyes narrowed in suspicion. "If I wish it? That's it?"

"Well, it's a bit of an inconvenience. It would be much easier for me to leave for Oxfordshire from here rather than London, but since you *command* it, I suppose I haven't any choice."

He stared at her for a moment in frozen silence, then without a word he was across the room, his hands grasping her shoulders. "What the devil do you mean by that, Georgiana—"

She wrenched herself free of his grasp. "That's *Miss Harley*, my lord. I think it's best if we keep our distance from this point on, don't you?"

"If you think you're going to wander off to Oxfordshire on your own, straight into Kenilworth's clutches, you've very much mis—"

"Don't be silly. I won't be on my own. Daniel will come with me."

"No, he won't. Kenilworth will have sent men after Jane and Freddy. Brixton will remain with them as long as they need his protection."

Georgiana tapped her lip, as if considering that. "Lady Clifford, then. Of course, Kenilworth's men are likely watching the Clifford School, so there's a chance we won't even make it out of London before he realizes we've—"

"Damn it, Georgiana. For such a clever lady, you don't have any bloody sense at all. Kenilworth is *dangerous*. He hurt Freddy, tried to kidnap Jane, and nearly killed Draven." Benedict seized her again, eyes wild, his hands biting into her upper arms. "What do you suppose he'll do to *you* if he catches up with you?"

Georgiana's eyes widened. This was *not* the same man she'd met months ago in Maiden Lane, the rake who treated everything as if it were an amusing lark. "I don't intend to find out."

Benedict snatched his hands away from her, a frustrated grunt leaving his throat. "I doubt Draven intended to find himself beaten half to death, either. You have no idea how clever the duke is, or how sinister."

There was no question the duke was clever. After all, he'd kept his secrets this long. Nor was Georgiana under any illusions about how dangerous he was. But she was clever, too. She eyed Benedict, considering her next words carefully. "Is Lord Draven's Oxfordshire estate a large one, Lord Haslemere?"

He blinked at her. "I don't see how that matters, but yes, it's a good-sized estate."

"You mean to say it's one of those sprawling, untidy places, with dozens of outbuildings spread out over the grounds in every direction?"

"Most large estates are."

"It's not an easy place to spy upon, then?"

He blew out an impatient breath. "Easy enough if one has a regiment at their disposal. What are you getting at?"

"Oh, nothing of any import, I'm sure, but it occurs to me that Lord Gray—are you familiar with Lord Gray, my lord? He's married to my dear friend Sophia. No? Well, that doesn't signify. The point is—"

"Yes, please do get to the point, if you would. We're wasting time."

Georgiana gave him a sweet smile. "Why, of course, my lord. I beg your pardon. The point is, Lord Gray happens to have a hunting box in Burham, in Buckinghamshire."

Benedict went still. "Burnham? That's less than—"

"Less than an hour's ride on horseback from Lord Draven's estate in High Wycombe, yes. One might get about quite easily between them. Stealthily, too, and the duke isn't apt to go poking about Lord Gray's hunting box, is he?"

"No. I don't suppose he is," Benedict allowed, grudgingly enough, in Georgiana's opinion. "But I doubt Lord Gray will appreciate your poking about there."

Georgiana waved this objection aside. "We needn't go anywhere near the hunting box. The gamekeeper's cottage is adequate for our purposes."

"Gamekeeper's cottages generally come equipped with a gamekeeper, Miss Harley. What do you intend to do with him? Toss him out the window?"

"Don't be absurd, Lord Haslemere. Lord Gray rarely uses the hunting box now. He pensioned the gamekeeper off long ago."

He lifted an eyebrow. "And how would you know that?"

"Why, from Lady Gray, of course." Georgiana looked down her nose at him. "It may surprise you to know this, Lord Haslemere, but not all ladies are preoccupied with fashions and gossip. We do occasionally talk of other things."

"*Gamekeepers?* That's what you talk of?"

Georgiana shrugged. "Among other things, but I fear you're missing the point, my lord. I can either accompany you to Burham, or you can *command* me to return to Lady Clifford, and she and I will go to Burham together, and you may do as you wish."

Benedict gave a humorless laugh. "It seems you've thought of everything. I suppose we're off to Burham, then."

He was still angry with her—she could tell by the edge to his voice—but he didn't offer any more arguments, and Georgiana let out a silent breath of relief. If they could get along with each other, the next few days would be far easier for both of them. "Very good, Lord Haslemere. I'm ready to leave when you are."

There. If she could be cordial, then so could he. Cordiality meant no more arguing, and no more raising their voices.

And no more kissing. That was entirely *too* cordial.

Certainly, no more kiss—

"I'll leave you to, er..." His gaze roved slowly over her. "Tidy yourself, while I go and see Madame Célestine about getting a carriage for us. Wait here until my return, if you please, Miss Harley."

He strode to the door and vanished into the hallway, leaving Georgiana choking on the ill-tempered retort that rose to her lips. Why, the consummate arrogance of the man! She'd just solved their most pressing problem, and still he presumed to order her about, as if she were a hunting dog he'd commanded to heel.

With an irritable whirl of her skirts, Georgiana abandoned her place beside the bed and marched to the window. It was early still. The carriage drive below was deserted, and the rooms that had been filled with laughter and the low murmur of conversation last night had gone silent. No doubt Madame Célestine and her ladies were exhausted from their efforts the night before, and had tumbled into their beds at first light.

That thought gave rise to another, this one far less welcome. Had Benedict gone to consult with Madame Célestine in that lady's bedchamber? Georgiana's shoulders moved in a quick shrug before the thought could take root. What did it matter to her where he'd gone? Lord Haslemere might do as he wished, and he had said he and Madame Célestine were...

How had he put it? *Old friends.*

Georgiana snorted. Friends, indeed. Madame Célestine wasn't the sort of lady a man chose to make his friend. It was far more likely she'd been his mistress, and that they were renewing their intimate acquaintance even now.

If the only emotion surging through her body had been anger, Georgiana might have managed it easily enough. But this stinging ache, this sharp, pointed thing lodged under her breastbone was a great deal more complicated than just anger.

She sank down onto the edge of the windowsill.

He'd rejected her. He'd kissed her passionately, stroked her face, and begged her to come closer, then he'd fled the bed as if the devil were after him, and gone off to frolic with his *old friend.*

It was...not humiliating, no. Not hurtful, either. It might have been both of those things if she cared whether or not Lord Haslemere desired her, but she *didn't*, and she'd wasted quite enough time thinking about it.

She rose and crossed the room to the basin, making use of the cold water to wash, then did what she could to tidy her limp, soiled dress. A wasted effort, as it happened, as the dress hadn't taken kindly to being slept in the night before. She donned her stockings and shoes, then sat down on the side of the bed to await Lord Haslemere's return.

And wait, and wait, and wait...

It was coming up on nine in the morning according to the small clock on the mantel, and still Benedict didn't return. Georgiana tried to distract herself, first by straightening the coverlet, then by arranging the dozens of small pillows into a neat row against the headboard. What might a courtesan need with so many pillows?

Five more minutes passed, ten, half an hour...

By ten o'clock, the walls of the bedchamber seemed to be closing around her. She paced from one end of the room to the other like a caged animal before finally coming to a halt by the window again, bracing her hands on the sill as she tried to calm her breathing.

For pity's sake, where was he? It was a wonder the duke hadn't found them here by now, given he'd had enough time to check every other place in London while she sat about up here like a discarded handkerchief while Lord Haslemere...did whatever it was he was doing with his *friend.*

She huffed and fretted through another fifteen minutes. Benedict had told her to wait here, but Georgiana couldn't bear to remain in this bedchamber a moment longer. Who did he think he was, ordering her about? Well, she hadn't obeyed any of his other commands, and she saw no reason to start now.

Georgiana slipped through the door and made her way down the hallway toward the staircase. Either she'd see Benedict on his way up, or else she'd find him downstairs.

But he wasn't downstairs. The parlor they'd been taken to the night before was empty, and there wasn't any sign of the butler who'd attended them last night.

There wasn't any sign of anybody. Not Madame Célestine, not Benedict, and not any of the dozen young ladies who'd been entertaining the gentlemen last night.

Georgiana crept down the hallway and peeked around the door into a formal drawing room, but it was empty as well, so she turned with a huff and made her way through the elaborate entryway back toward the parlor. Perhaps there was a bell there to summon a servant, or—

A soft gasp rose to her lips as she paused in the anteroom, all thoughts of Benedict, and servants and bell pulls flying from her head as her gaze caught on one of the scandalous paintings she'd seen the night before.

She glanced around, but no one was about. The entire house was as silent as a tomb. So she tiptoed closer, seizing her chance to examine the paintings without Benedict gaping over her shoulder. Why these paintings should fascinate her so, she couldn't say. Perhaps it was simply that such things were so far out of her experience, and…well, she'd always been fond of learning new things.

Georgiana stepped up to the first painting, blinked, then stepped closer, and closer still, until her nose was nearly touching the canvas. "Oh, my goodness, that looks like…"

It *was*. A fair-haired lady with an impressively large bosom was reclining on a gold silk settee, her skirts thrown up over her waist, and she wasn't alone. A gentleman was on his knees beside the settee, his hands resting on the inside of her thighs, and his face was—

Georgiana slapped a hand over her mouth, her face bursting into flames. She whirled around, turning her back on the painting, but in the next instant she turned back again for another peek.

She cocked her head to the side, her brow furrowing. How did the lady get her leg to bend at such an unusual angle? And was the man missing a hand?

No. There it was, on his…oh, dear God.

Perhaps she'd better wait for Benedict upstairs, after all.

But that wasn't what Georgiana did. She moved on to the next painting, then the next, heart pounding, eyes wide, and her palm pressed to her lips.

Chapter Seventeen

"Miss Harley is an intriguing creature, *mon ami*. Not your usual sort though, is she? Wherever did you find her?"

Benedict rolled his eyes. Why did people keep asking him that? "In my wardrobe, of course. She was hanging next to my waistcoats. My valet was appalled." A rude answer, to be sure, especially to as devoted a friend as Célestine, but Georgiana wasn't an errant shoe or a missing cravat, for God's sake.

She was a woman. An infuriating, distracting, incomprehensible woman with the most alluring lips he'd ever kissed.

Damn her.

Célestine was far from being offended, however. She let out a delighted laugh, and placed a hand on his arm. "Such a sharp tongue, *mon chère*! It's not like you, but love makes fools of us all, *n'est-ce pas?*"

"*Love?*" Benedict shot her an incredulous look. "Have you gone mad, Célestine? She's the most uppity, sharp-tongued chit I've ever come across. I'd sooner fall in love with a hissing cat than I would Georgiana Harley."

Much to his annoyance, Célestine let out another merry laugh. "Ah, so she is severe with you. But maybe she has reason to hiss. What did you do to earn her ire?"

"Not a thing." Benedict's lips twisted in a sullen pout. "Well, that's not quite true. I did sneak up on her once and make her drop her jar of preserves."

Célestine's brow furrowed. "Preserves? I don't understand."

"I…well, it's foolish, really, but it was dark, and she didn't see me, and when I spoke it startled her, and the next thing I knew the jar rolled down the steps and smashed on the pavement. I also threw pebbles at her window to make her come down and talk to me, and I may have stolen a kiss."

Or two. Or two dozen.

Christ, it sounded rather bad, all taken together. He hadn't meant any harm, though. He'd just—

"You want to have your way in all things, my friend, and you're accustomed to getting it, except, it seems, from Mademoiselle Harley. *Oui?*" Célestine, who was making no attempt to hide her enjoyment, gave him a sly grin.

"You don't have to look so happy about it," Benedict grumbled.

"Ah, but I am happy, *mon chère*, because you need a...a firm hand, shall we say? Mademoiselle Harley will be the making of you, if you allow it."

Benedict huffed out a breath. There wasn't any question he would allow it—*had been* allowing it since that first day he'd met Georgiana in Maiden Lane, all those months ago. Now he looked back on it, he could see his surrender had been inevitable from the start.

But his capitulation wasn't what bothered him.

A mental image of Freddy's bruised and battered face rose to his mind, and his hands clenched into fists.

"*Mon ami?*" Célestine's smile faded. "What is it? You look *désolé.*"

Benedict shook his head.

"Come, my lord. We are friends, *oui?*" Célestine took his chin in her hand and forced him to look at her. "We are no longer *les amoureux*, but you are still dear to me. You may confide in me."

"Georgiana Harley is..." Bright. Clever, brave, and beautiful, and he...he was a rake and a flirt and London's most entertaining scandal. He wasn't a bad man, no, but he was a reckless, selfish one. He couldn't think of any reason Georgiana should bother with him. "She'd do better to save her firm hand for a gentleman worthy of her efforts." He dragged his fingers through his hair. "It would be foolish of her to put her faith in me, and Georgiana Harley is no fool."

"But my dear friend, your Miss Harley does not agree. She has already put her faith in you. If she had not, she would not be here with you now. Indeed, *mon ami*, you are more deserving than you imagine. Behave as a gentleman does with your Miss Harley, and all will be well."

"A gentleman?" Surely, he could manage that much?

"*Oui.*" Célestine patted his cheek, then gave him a gentle push toward the door before crossing the room to ring the bell for a servant. "Now, go and fetch your mademoiselle while I see to your carriage, hmmm?"

"Yes, all right." Benedict pressed a grateful kiss to Célestine's cheek, left her small private parlor, and went around the corner and up the back staircase.

But when he entered the bedchamber, he found it empty.

Georgiana was gone.

He strode toward the window, but she wasn't on the drive below. Had she decided to return to Lady Clifford, after all? Benedict dropped his forehead against the glass, a strange tightness in his chest. It was what he'd told her he wanted, but he'd never believed she'd actually *leave*.

It would be just like her to choose *this* command to obey.

But if she had gone, she couldn't have gotten far. He rushed back down the stairs, but stopped on the bottom step, not sure where to look next. Had she gone to the drawing room in search of him? Or should he go back to Célestine's private parlor, and see if she—

Huff.

Benedict stilled, his head jerking toward the entryway. What the devil was that? The noise was too soft for him to make it out for certain, but it almost sounded like...a muffled gasp.

The skin on his neck prickled with warning.

Maybe Georgiana hadn't *chosen* to leave at all. Maybe the duke had discovered where they were hiding and sent one of his villains to snatch her up. Even now some blackguard might be dragging her outside, his paw clamped over her mouth, stifling her desperate screams. Benedict hadn't seen a carriage in the drive, but that didn't mean the duke's men weren't prowling about.

He didn't pause, but charged down the hallway toward the front door. He couldn't have explained what it was about that sound, but his heart had rushed into his throat when he heard it, and it was lodged there now, pulsing with dread.

When he reached the anteroom off the entryway, it stopped altogether.

Georgiana wasn't being attacked. She wasn't being dragged across the floor, or kidnapped, or silenced with a paw over her mouth. There wasn't a villain to be seen.

She was alone, standing in front of one of Célestine's paintings, her hand over her mouth and her eyes as wide as tea saucers.

Ah. No wonder she'd gasped.

Benedict knew the paintings well. They were titillating, but any pleasure he'd gotten from them paled in comparison to the pleasure of watching Georgiana gape at them. She looked like a naughty schoolgirl caught hiding an erotic novel under her pillow. "Do you see something that intrigues you, princess?"

"Oh!" Georgiana jumped, then whirled on him, her hand pressed to her chest. "For pity's sake, you nearly scared the life out of me!"

"Only because you know you're doing something wicked," he drawled, leaning a hip against the doorframe.

"Nonsense. I'm merely looking at the, ah..." Georgiana drew herself up with a prim frown. "The art."

"Ah, yes. The art. Forgive me, Miss Harley. I didn't realize you were such an aesthete." Benedict sauntered across the room to stand beside her. "Which one is your favorite?"

"I don't have a favorite," she muttered, her cheeks flaming.

"No?" He gestured to the painting in front of her. "You seem preoccupied with this one. It is impressive, isn't it? The lines, the colors, the, er... position of the subjects."

"I don't...I wasn't...I have no opinion on the painting at all, Lord Haslemere."

Benedict couldn't help smiling at that. "That's a vivid blush for a lady who has no opinion."

She lowered her gaze to the floor, guiltily biting her lip.

"No, that won't do. Look at me." Benedict caught her chin in his fingers and raised her face to his. "Arousal is nothing to be ashamed of, Georgiana."

She glanced at the painting, then back at him, her expression hesitant. She looked as if she were unsure whether to trust him, and Benedict cursed himself. The last thing he'd meant to do was make her believe her desire was shameful.

"Shall I show you my favorite?" He took her hand and led her to the other side of the room, stopping in front of another painting. This one depicted a gentleman on his back on a settee, his lover atop him, her skirts hiked up and her legs on either side of his hips. He was gripping her waist, and her head was thrown back, her mouth open in a silent scream.

"Look at her expression." Benedict drew closer, his lips mere inches from Georgiana's ear. "She's taking her pleasure."

She said nothing, but a shiver swept her slender frame as she stared at the painting.

He turned her face back to his and stroked his thumb gently over her lower lip. "Do you understand what it means to take your pleasure, Georgiana?"

Georgiana stole a look at him from under her lashes. "I-I think so."

Benedict smothered a groan. "Can you guess why this painting is my favorite?"

She shook her head, swallowing. Benedict caressed her throat with his thumb, fighting the urge to close his eyes at the glide of her warm skin against his fingertips. "Because it's about *her* pleasure."

She gazed up at him as if mesmerized, her eyes a deep, dark green—darker than he'd ever seen them, and glimmering like emeralds.

"A gentleman always makes certain his lover takes her pleasure first. A gentleman takes as much of *his* pleasure from her release as he does from his own." A hot, deep ache unfurled in Benedict's lower belly as he hovered his lips over hers.

"Are...are you a gentleman, Lord Haslemere?" Georgiana's voice was soft, hesitant, but her eyes held his, and her lips parted.

Was he? Benedict hardly knew who he was anymore. He knew only that he wanted her—yearned for her with a longing that stole his breath away. He settled his hands on her hips, squeezing gently as he urged her closer, and his lips took hers.

* * * *

"I told you to behave as a *gentleman* does, Lord Haslemere. Is this how you follow my advice?"

Georgiana and Benedict sprang apart as if someone had lit a fire between then, and turned to find Madame Célestine standing in the doorway, watching them. She tutted, shaking her head. "Come, my lord. You and Mademoiselle Harley must go. Take my curricle. It won't be recognized."

Georgiana gathered her wits with an effort, and shook her head in protest. "We can't take your curricle."

"Hush. You can, and you will." Madame Célestine took Georgiana's hands in hers. "Not to worry, Mademoiselle Harley. Your *chère ami* is my old friend, and one does not turn one's back on an old friend."

Georgiana searched Madame's Célestine's blue eyes, and saw only friendliness and concern there. "You're very kind."

"*Mais oui,* of course I am." Madame Célestine gave her a sly wink. "And in return, you will take good care of my friend, Mademoiselle?"

Georgiana glanced at Benedict. His auburn hair was standing on end, his clothing was wrinkled and soiled from his brawl with the coachman the night before, there was a livid cut on his forehead from the scuffle with Kenilworth's footman, and still...she'd never seen a man more handsome than he.

The thought made Georgiana's heart lurch in her chest, and she swallowed as she turned back to Madame Célestine. "I'll do my best."

"Ah, Mademoiselle, that is all any of us can do." To Georgiana's surprise, Madame Célestine leaned forward and pressed an affectionate kiss to her cheek. "And you, my lord. You will behave like a proper gentleman, yes?"

Benedict cleared his throat. "I'll do my best, madame."

A tiny smirk rose to Madame Célestine's lips. "Hmmm. You will have an exciting trip then, I think. Goodbye!"

With that, Madame Célestine sashayed across the room and disappeared through the door. Georgiana waited until the sound of her footsteps had faded before turning to murmur to Benedict, "She's rather remarkable, isn't she?"

He nodded, but his gaze remained fixed on Georgiana, his eyes dark and compelling. "She is, yes. I have a weakness for remarkable ladies."

Georgiana's cheeks heated once again, but she didn't know quite what to say in answer, so they waited in silence until Madame Célestine's coachman brought her curricle into the drive. The top was pulled up, to prevent their being recognized.

"Shall we, Miss Harley?" Benedict offered her his hand.

She took it, and he led her out to the drive and helped her into her seat, then climbed into his own seat and took up the ribbons. A moment later they were off in a shower of gravel, with Madame Célestine's house retreating from sight behind them.

Georgiana didn't expect she'd fall asleep, but between last night's excitement and the drama of her confrontation with Benedict this morning, they were only an hour or so into their journey before her eyelids grew heavy and she drifted off.

She woke with a start when the curricle hit a rough patch of road.

"All right there?" Benedict glanced down at her, a tentative smile on his lips. "There was no avoiding that jolt, I'm afraid."

Georgiana blinked up at him. He was very close, nearly on top of her, and—

No. Oh, dear God, he *wasn't* nearly on top of her. *She* was nearly on top of *him.*

Again.

Her head rested on the warm, solid curve of his shoulder, where she must have slumped against him when she grew drowsy. Judging by the afternoon light, she'd been asleep for at least an hour, and lounging on him the entire time.

She scrambled upright and rubbed the sleep from her eyes. "I beg your pardon, Lord Haslemere. I shouldn't have been...why didn't you wake me, or at least nudge me over to my own side of the bench?"

He shrugged. "I didn't mind it."

She cast him a wary look. My, he was being awfully gentlemanly about this, wasn't he? Her lapse in propriety gave him the perfect opportunity to tease her, but aside from the satisfied grin hovering at the corners of his mouth, he held his tongue. He *had* promised Madame Célestine he'd behave himself. Perhaps he'd meant it.

There was no reason that thought should make her heart sink, but there was a heaviness in her chest she'd never felt before. She couldn't explain it, but it felt like…disappointment? No, something deeper than disappointment, sharper than that. Something that had sunk into the edges of her heart and was dragging it down into her belly.

"If you look to your right, you can see glimpses of Cliveden House through the trees. The Duke of Buckingham built it for his mistress, the Countess of Shrewsbury."

Georgiana turned to look, curious to see the house, and also relieved to have an excuse to look away from Lord Haslemere, who was being altogether too charming for her liking. They were traveling down a rutted country road lined on both sides with a hedge so thick it was difficult to see beyond it, but after a moment she caught a fleeting glimpse of a corner of a stone manor house. "Yes, I think I see…"

She trailed off with a gasp as they came to a slight gap in the hedge, and the whole of Cliveden House in all its breathtaking splendor appeared in the valley below them, like a warm, honey-colored jewel set into endless rolling acres of verdant green. "Oh," she breathed, raising her hand to her mouth. "It's magnificent."

Indeed, Georgiana found it difficult to tear her gaze away from it. She'd never seen a house so grand as this one. It was enormous, seeming to sprawl from one end of the valley to the other, and even from here she could see a patchwork of formal gardens and walkways branching out from the main house.

"Is your own estate anything like it?" She knew, of course, that gentlemen of rank had handsome country estates—everyone in England knew that— but it had never occurred to her to wonder what one might be like.

"Haslemere House is a monstrous old pile of rocks." Benedict chuckled. "Damp, and the eastern roof leaks every winter, at least half a dozen of the fireplaces bellow smoke, and the glazing seems to require constant repair. But I'm rather fond of it, despite its many quirks. I find I spend more time there than London these days. I imagine I'll give up on London entirely at some point, and spend all my time in Surrey, rusticating."

"You'd give up all your London frolics in favor of country living? You shock me, my lord. Whatever will London do without you?" Georgiana smiled to take any sting out of her words, but in truth, she really was shocked.

He laughed. "There are only so many footraces a man can run before he becomes bored of them, Georgiana."

"But you're..." Georgiana found she had no idea how to explain what she wished to say, and lapsed into silence.

Benedict raised an expectant eyebrow at her. "Yes? What am I?"

"You're...you're Lord Haslemere," Georgiana replied, then immediately felt foolish. He *knew* he was Lord Haslemere, for pity's sake. What she meant was, he was a darling of the *ton*, the upper ten thousand's most beloved rake, pursued by the most beautiful belles in the city, and flattered by everyone else. "I would think it would be quite satisfying, to be you."

She hadn't really given much thought to it before, but over the last few days she'd begun to consider the enormous power a man like Lord Haslemere commanded. She'd been in the habit of thinking of fashionable rogues like him as rather useless people, but...

She glanced back down at Cliveden House. An estate of this size would have hundreds of tenant farmers working the land, all of whom depended on the lord to ensure their livelihood. It was a staggering level of responsibility.

"I think Haslemere House must be lovely, my lord." She hesitated as she sneaked a glance at him. "But perhaps rather lonely."

He'd been looking past her at Cliveden House nestled into the valley below, but now his gaze shifted to her face. His eyes held hers as he murmured, "I confess I don't fancy rusticating on my own, but perhaps someday I can persuade someone to come live at Haslemere House with me."

Long, silent moments passed, then Benedict cleared his throat and looked away. "High Wycombe isn't far now. We'll have a warm fire and a bed soon enough."

He said no more, but turned his attention back to the road, leaving Georgiana to attempt to hide her blush as she contemplated his singular use of the word *bed.*

She'd never been to Lord Gray's hunting box, never mind the gamekeeper's cottage, but Sophia had mentioned once the hunting box was at the western edge of the property, and the cottage nearby, half-hidden among a forest of towering old trees. Once they arrived it took a bit of poking about to find it, but they stumbled across it eventually.

"We'll be safe here from the duke's men, that much is certain." Benedict leapt down from the curricle and offered her his hand. "No one will think to look for us here."

Georgiana let him help her down and surveyed the cottage, her hands on her hips. It was square and small, made of dark stone with a thatched roof, and with a thick chimney made of the same stone. "It's not the sort of place you'd come across by accident, is it?"

"No. One would have to know it was here to find it." Benedict peered through the window, then turned back to her with a shrug. "I hope you're fond of rusticating. It appears sound enough, but not extravagant."

"I don't need extravagances."

"I'm pleased to hear it, Miss Harley, because you won't find any." His dark eyes twinkled at her. "What it lacks in charm, it makes up for in dust. I saw a cobweb in there bigger than my fist."

Georgiana marched to the door. "I'm not afraid of spiders, Lord Haslemere."

"Good, then you can protect me from them. I detest the things."

Georgiana couldn't help but smile at his exaggerated shudder. Really, he was the most teasing man she'd ever come across. Endearing, though, with that boyish grin on his lips. "How shall we get inside?"

Benedict strode across the narrow dirt drive, put his shoulder to the door, and gave it a good shove. It opened with a creaky groan, and he turned to Georgiana with an elegant bow. "After you, madam."

Georgiana peeked through the doorway. The air inside was stale and musty, and there were a shocking number of cobwebs, just as Lord Haslemere had said, but it was a cozy space for all that, with a massive stone fireplace at one end, flagstone floors covered with a threadbare carpet, and low, beamed ceilings. A few thick logs rested on the hearth, and several chairs were scattered about. A rough-hewn wood table stood near a grimy window, and a bed with a patchwork quilt was pushed against one wall.

Only one bed, but to Georgiana's relief, she spotted a set of narrow wooden stairs leading to a second floor. The bedchambers must be up there. "I'll just have a look upstairs."

She crossed the room, pausing at the bottom of the staircase. The first step appeared sound. The second and third steps let out protesting squeaks when she put her weight on them, but they were steady enough. The real trouble began when she ventured onto the fourth step, which let out a menacing crack under her foot.

That was when she realized her mistake.

"Georgiana, wait."

She froze, but by then it was too late. The step shuddered and then splintered under her foot, upsetting her balance. "Oh!" Her arms pinwheeled as she struggled to stay upright, but between her skirts and the disintegrating steps, it was hopeless. She squeezed her eyes shut as she fell backward and braced herself for a bone-rattling thud.

But it never came.

She heard Benedict shout her name, then there was an explosion of movement behind her, and instead of the flagstone floor rushing up to meet her backside, his muscular arms closed around her, and his hard chest appeared under her palms.

"It's all right. I've got you." He was short of breath, not from exertion but from alarm, for he lifted her easily, carrying her down the stairs and depositing her carefully on the edge of the bed. He crouched in front of her, his concerned eyes on her face. "Are you all right?"

Georgiana stared into those lovely, melting dark eyes, so close to her own, and for a single, breathtaking moment she wanted nothing more than to tuck herself against him and feel his arms around her again. "I...yes. Quite all right. Thank you, my lord."

"Perhaps we'd better not venture upstairs again."

Georgiana nodded, her heart still pounding, though she couldn't have said whether it was from the near fall, or from those few brief, glorious moments she'd been in his arms.

"That, ah...that leaves us with only one bed." Benedict glanced around the room, as if he could conjure another bed simply by force of will alone, then returned his gaze to hers, his throat moving in a swallow. "I'll sleep in one of the chairs."

Georgiana opened her mouth to tell him they could each take a side and share the bed, but then she closed it again without a word. Sharing a bed had seemed like a harmless enough idea last night, but he'd nearly broken his neck to get away from her this morning.

No, she couldn't go through that again. So, she swallowed her words and nodded. "Yes, I think that's a good idea, Lord Haslemere."

From now on, it was best if they kept their distance.

Chapter Eighteen

When Benedict woke the following day, his neck was stiff and his back cramped from sleeping on the chair all night. If it hadn't been for that—well, that and the Duke of bloody Kenilworth trying to kill them—it would have been the most pleasurable morning of his life.

He opened his eyes to the soft sound of Georgiana's deep, even breaths, and raised himself up onto his elbow, hoping to steal a peek at her face before she awoke. He was treated to a delicious glimpse of her long eyelashes resting on her flushed cheeks, and her loose, mahogany-brown waves spread in wild disarray across the pillow.

Benedict let out a sigh and flopped dramatically onto his back, like every lovelorn fool before him. It wasn't the first morning he'd woken with a lovely lady in his bedchamber, but it was the first time his chest pinched with longing and despair as it did now.

He'd never felt about any of the others the way he did about Georgiana Harley.

She wasn't a distraction, nor was his attraction to her a passing thing, sure to pall with familiarity. When they'd paused to look down on Cliveden House yesterday, he'd pictured Haslemere House in his head. He'd imagined bringing Georgiana there with him, leading her from room to room, and showing her all the private corners and nooks he'd taken such delight in when he'd wandered those halls as a child.

That had never happened before. He'd never even considered bringing a lady to Haslemere House, but kept his liaisons confined to the London townhouse. Now here he was, wishing he could fling open the front doors of his most sacred place and reveal everything about himself to her.

And there wasn't a damn thing he could do about it. Or about *her*. He couldn't have her. Even if they did find Clara Beauchamp and learned the duke's secret, there was no way of knowing how the discovery would affect Freddy and Jane. As long as they remained in England, the duke had complete control over them. If the only way to keep them out of Kenilworth's clutches was to leave England, then that's what he would do.

North America perhaps, or—

"Benedict?"

He turned his head, warmth flooding through him at her soft murmur, his Christian name on her lips. "I'm here."

The coverlet rustled as she shifted in the bed. "What time is it?"

He fumbled for his pocket watch and flipped open the lid. "Early still. Go back to sleep, sweet—go back to sleep, Georg—er, Miss Harley."

She let out a little sigh that went straight to his cock. "It's not yet calling hours?"

Benedict chuckled. "Are we observing calling hours? Given we're sneaking through the forest to pay a secret visit to Draven, I thought we might dispense with the proprieties."

"Well, let's see." Georgiana rolled from her back to her side to face him. "We've kidnapped a duchess and her son, stolen a duke's carriage, and you've assaulted his coachman and footmen. So yes, I suppose there's no point in fussing over a call."

"No, especially since we may be forced to break down Draven's door to gain admittance to him. Something tells me he won't be pleased to find us on his doorstep. If he's even conscious, that is."

"Poor Lord Draven." She was quiet for a moment. "What if he isn't conscious, or is, but sends us away without speaking to us? I suppose we'll have to quiz the servants then, though I don't know how far that will get us, as most of them have only been in Lord Draven's service since the attack."

"Not far. We'll just have to hope Draven has regained consciousness and is willing to talk to us. I've no doubt he knows Kenilworth's secrets. If we want to find them out, we have to move quickly, before Kenilworth has a chance to organize his men." Benedict heaved himself up from the chair, wincing as he stretched his cramped muscles, then padded across the cold flagstone floors to the door of the cottage. "Are you hungry?"

As if on cue, her stomach let out an insistent growl that made him grin, and her cheeks flush. "Why, are you preparing breakfast, my lord?"

"Certainly not. I haven't the first idea how to do so. I did, however, have the foresight to request provisions from Madame Célestine." He disappeared through the front door, and returned a few moments later bearing a large hamper. "Here we are."

Georgiana blinked at it, then struggled upright in the bed. "My goodness. I'm impressed, my lord."

"I don't fancy starving in the woods." Benedict was busy unloading the hamper as he spoke, but he watched from the corner of his eye as Georgiana swung her legs over the side of the bed and approached the table. She'd slept in her dress again the previous night, and her long hair was tumbling over her shoulders in a ripple of unruly waves. "What shall I serve you?"

"Hmmm. If you're offering to serve me my breakfast in bed, Lord Haslemere, perhaps I'll return to it."

A shy smile crossed her delectable lips, and Benedict was assailed with a vivid image of the two of them lying in bed together while he fed her the choicest morsels from the hamper. It was too tempting to resist. "If you wish me to serve you in bed, princess, I will. What will you have first?"

"Hmm. Fresh strawberries? Warm scones with clotted cream? Hot tea, or…no, I think I prefer chocolate." Her lips curved in a teasing smile. "Surely you have all that there, my lord?"

Benedict swallowed, and returned to rummaging through the hamper to keep himself from staring at her mouth. "No, but I did ask for…ah, here it is. I believe I owe you a jar of preserves, Miss Harley?" He held the jar aloft triumphantly, quite pleased with himself, but to his surprise she looked taken aback. "Is something wrong?"

"No, no. I'm just…amazed you thought of the debacle with the preserves." She flushed, then looked away.

"How could I not? My valet was in despair over the sticky mess it left on my evening shoes. He grumbles every time he looks at them." Benedict spoke lightly, but when Georgiana still avoided his gaze, he lowered the jar of preserves to the table with a defeated thud. "I don't understand, Georgiana. I thought you'd be pleased, but you seem upset."

"No, no. That is, I *am* pleased. Indeed, it's a kind gesture on your part. I just didn't think…"

"Didn't think I was kind?" He gave her a half smile even as he hoped that wasn't what she'd been about to say. He had dozens of flaws, but he'd never been accused of unkindness before.

She shook her head. "No, that's not what I mean. I just never imagined you'd paid much mind to the…preserves."

She said "preserves," but it wasn't what she meant. This wasn't about the bloody preserves. What she meant was she hadn't imagined he'd paid much mind to *her*. How incredible she should think so, when he'd thought of nothing *but* her since he'd returned to London—

No, that wasn't true. His preoccupation with Georgiana Harley had started before that.

She'd haunted him since he'd first laid eyes on her.

The truth was, it had started in Maiden Lane, when she'd emerged from the darkness like an avenging angel, her tongue sharpened to a fine edge and wearing that damned brown cloak and the ridiculous hat she used to hide under. Only it hadn't been enough, that hat. He'd seen beyond her disguise, had noticed the vulnerable curve of her lower lip, the slight shake of her hands when she'd delivered him a set-down he wouldn't soon forget.

He'd seen *her*. Once he had, he couldn't *unsee* her, and now...now he could see nothing *but* her. The smooth, creamy skin that made his mouth water to kiss, to taste, and the rich brown tresses his fingertips itched to caress. Her slender curves, so sweet, that fit into his hands so perfectly, as if she were made just for him, and her hazel eyes, that flicker of temper in their depths he'd grown to crave, replaced now with a softness he'd never seen in them before.

Benedict cleared his throat. "Yes, well, I'm fond of...preserves. Perhaps you didn't realize how fond I am of...preserves."

Christ, was he talking to her about *preserves*?

If Georgiana thought it odd, she didn't say so. "Oh, yes. Preserves are..." Her teeth sank into her lower lip. "Irresistible. The sweetness, you know, and the, ah...the pleasing thickness on one's tongue."

Her husky murmur, the unbearable eroticism of hearing the word *tongue* on her lips—Benedict's eyes slid closed as he prayed for strength. When he opened them again, her gaze had dropped to his mouth.

A groan tore from his chest, but he didn't kiss her lips. He wanted to—God, how he wanted to—but they were alone in a cottage half-buried among the trees. It was a great deal of privacy for an amorous gentleman like himself. One kiss would lead to another, then another, and then...

No. He wouldn't think about it.

He leaned toward her, and pressed as chaste a kiss as he could manage on her forehead. Then he stepped back, and busied himself with unpacking the remainder of their provisions from the hamper. "Since we both dote on preserves, shall we have some?"

* * * *

Georgiana had expected they'd leave for Lord Draven's estate as soon as they'd finished their breakfast, but Benedict kept them in the cottage until the bright morning light had waned, so there was less of a chance they'd be detected moving through the forest.

There wasn't much to do in the gamekeeper's cottage while they waited for the light to change. Georgiana felt inexplicably shy around Benedict, and he didn't seem to be much more comfortable than she was. She did notice him staring at her a good deal, but each time their gazes chanced to meet his darted away, as if he'd been caught doing something he shouldn't.

After their encounter with Kenilworth's scoundrels, she was as jumpy as a cat at the thought of the duke's men pouncing on them when they left the cottage, but she was relieved when they were on their way at last, riding the two horses that had been hitched to Madame Célestine's curricle. Either Benedict's cautiousness had paid off, or luck was on their side at last, but they made it through the forest without encountering anyone.

But as soon as she got her first glimpse at Lord Draven's estate, her heart sank. "It looks as if the house is closed." There wasn't a soul to be seen, not even a stray gardener, and all the shutters were drawn tight. "It's sealed up like a tomb."

"There has to be someone here. Remember, Draven was being taken to his country estate the day we spoke to Mrs. Bury." Benedict's brow furrowed as he frowned up at the house. "No, this way, Georgiana," he added when she set her horse's head in the direction of the main entrance. "We'll go in the back way."

Georgiana followed him along the western edge of the tree line to the stables, which were clean and well-provisioned, but deserted. Benedict led their horses to two empty stalls, then they made their way across the back drive on foot to a door she suspected must lead into the kitchen. Benedict strode up to it and gave it a firm knock, as if he traipsed through the woods to this door every day, and hadn't any doubt he'd be welcome.

It was some time before anyone answered the knock, long enough so Georgiana's heart had begun to sink again, but when Benedict knocked a second time, she heard footsteps approach, and a moment later a stout, dark-haired woman with a kindly face answered the door. Her tidy gray dress and the ring of keys at her waist marked her as the housekeeper.

Her eyebrows flew up when she saw them. "My goodness. Where did you two come from?"

"Lord Haslemere, to see Lord Draven." Benedict stepped up to the door, every inch the distinguished earl who couldn't imagine he'd be turned away.

"Oh, my lord, I beg your pardon. We've been here a week, and not set eyes on a single soul aside from the staff. It startled me, it did, finding you here on the doorstep." The woman's hands fluttered nervously. "But I'm afraid Lord Draven isn't well, and isn't able to see visitors."

Benedict raised a haughty eyebrow. "I'm the Earl of Haslemere, and an acquaintance of Lord Draven's. I'm aware his lordship has had an... unfortunate accident. I've come to see how I might help him."

The woman dropped into a hasty curtsy. "That's kind of you, my lord, but there's no help for poor Lord Draven. Not now, leastways, and perhaps not ever again."

An anxious lump rose in Georgiana's throat, and she pressed closer to the door. "Perhaps not ever again? Is...is the earl not expected to recover?"

The housekeeper gave a sad shake of her head. "I can't say for sure, Lady Haslemere."

Georgiana glanced at Benedict and found him staring back at her with the oddest look on his face, but he didn't correct the woman, and by the time Georgiana gathered her wits to do so, the moment had passed.

"His poor lordship hasn't regained consciousness since he was brought here from London several days ago," the housekeeper went on, oblivious to the sudden tension. "He just lies in that bed, he does, as still as death. The doctor says his injury is severe, and he may not wake up again."

Without thinking, Georgiana took the woman's hand. "We're very sorry to hear of Lord Draven's misfortune, Mrs...."

"Mrs. Ellery, Lord Draven's housekeeper. Cook too, if truth be told, but we do what we must, don't we, my lady? It's no fuss, really, what with there being just the four of us here aside from Lord Draven." She leaned forward confidingly. "All of Lord Draven's previous servants scattered to the winds when his lordship settled in London, you understand."

Georgiana did understand—far more than Mrs. Ellery imagined she did. "We've just come from a long ride, Mrs. Ellery. Might we come inside for a cup of tea?"

Mrs. Ellery blinked. "I beg your pardon, Lady Haslemere. You must think me an utter savage. Please do come inside."

"Thank you." Benedict took Georgiana's arm, and the two of them followed Mrs. Ellery into the kitchen.

"Oh, dear. I didn't think...the drawing room fire hasn't been laid. There isn't much call for it, there being no visitors—"

"That's perfectly all right, Mrs. Ellery. Lord Haslemere and I are happy to sit in the kitchen." Georgiana pulled out a chair and seated herself at the massive table in the center of the room. "Aren't we, my lord?"

"Whatever suits you, my dear." Benedict gave her a sly wink, then seated himself beside her. "Please don't go to any trouble on our account, Mrs. Ellery."

Mrs. Ellery was pouring hot water into the teapot and arranging some biscuits and tea things on a tray. "It's no trouble, my lord, and you must have your tea, mustn't you?" She bustled over, placed the tray on the table, and helped them each to a cup of tea.

"You mentioned there are four of you here, Mrs. Ellery." Georgiana accepted the teacup Mrs. Ellery passed her and helped herself to several lumps of sugar.

"Yes, that's right. It's just me and two housemaids, and I don't mind telling you, my lady, we lose track of each other in this big, grand house."

"It looks as if someone's taking care of the stables, as well. I hope you don't mind that we left our horses in two of the stalls, Mrs. Ellery," Benedict said.

"Not at all, my lord. Peter, the stable boy, will see to them. He's but a young one, Peter, but he's a good lad, and a hard worker. Has a way with the horses, too." Mrs. Ellery sipped at her tea. "He's from High Wycombe, is Peter. His family has lived here for years."

Georgiana glanced at Benedict. "You don't hail from Oxfordshire yourself, Mrs. Ellery?"

"Oh, heavens no, my lady. I'm here from London. Mrs. Bury, Lord Draven's London housekeeper, hired me and Martha—she's one of the housemaids—in London. High Wycombe's a pretty place, Lady Haslemere, but a bit quiet for my tastes."

Georgiana gave Mrs. Ellery a polite nod, but her heart was sinking once again. Mrs. Ellery and Martha weren't familiar with the neighborhood, and wouldn't be able to tell them anything about Lord Draven, Kenilworth, Clara Beauchamp, or the duel. That left Peter, and the other housemaid.

"Is the other housemaid from High Wycombe?" Benedict asked, stirring his tea with a distracted air, as if he were merely making conversation and the answer was of little consequence to him.

If Mrs. Ellery thought their curiosity strange, she didn't remark on it. "Rachel? Well, I don't rightly know where Rachel hails from, now you ask, my lord. She's…oh, here she is now. Is it time to try Lord Draven's broth again already, dear?"

"Yes, ma'am."

Georgiana turned to find a housemaid who looked to be about four or five years older than she was standing in the doorway. She was rather pretty, with a smooth, pale face and dark hair tucked under a lace cap.

"Lord and Lady Haslemere were just asking where you're from, Rachel. Not Oxfordshire, is it?" Mrs. Ellery bustled about the kitchen, preparing another tray with a bowl of broth.

"No, ma'am. Herefordshire. Thank you, ma'am," she added when Mrs. Ellery handed her the tray, then she turned and left the kitchen without another word.

"She doesn't talk much, that one," Mrs. Ellery said, once the housemaid was gone. "But she's a good girl, for all that, and an excellent nurse to Lord Draven. She takes such good care of his poor lordship there's nothing left for Martha or me to do for him."

Georgiana and Benedict chatted with Mrs. Ellery for a while as they finished their tea, then Georgiana rose from the table. "Thank you for your hospitality, Mrs. Ellery. We'll be on our way now, and let you get back to your work."

Benedict rose, as well. "Our best hopes for Lord Draven's recovery, Mrs. Ellery."

Mrs. Ellery's face fell at the reminder of Lord Draven's pitiable state. "You're very kind, my lord. That's the best we can do for him now. Hope, and pray."

"Indeed," Georgiana murmured. "No, no need to escort us to the front door, Mrs. Ellery. We'll just nip out the back."

"Hope, pray, and catch the scoundrels who did this to him and make them pay for it," Benedict muttered as they bid Mrs. Ellery a final farewell and made their way back across the carriage drive toward the stables. "Despicable villains, beating a man so brutally."

"Not as despicable as whoever ordered them to do it." Georgiana thought of Kenilworth's icy gray eyes and a shudder ran over her.

They entered the stables then, and found a lad of twelve or thirteen years of age brushing one of Madame Célestine's horses. The other horse had already been rubbed down and brushed and was in a clean stall, munching contentedly on some hay.

"Peter, is it? Good job with the horses, lad." Benedict strode forward and dropped a coin into the young man's hand.

Peter's eyes widened at the guinea resting on his palm. "Thank you, my lord."

"Mrs. Ellery mentioned you're from High Wycombe, Peter. Do you know Lord Draven's family at all?" Benedict asked, stroking an affectionate hand down the horse's nose.

"Not much, my lord. I don't remember the earl as was, and this earl," Peter jerked his head toward the house. "Don't remember him much, either. He doesn't come here."

"You couldn't have been much more than a child the last time Lord Draven was here," Benedict said, more to himself than Peter. "Did you ever hear any talk in the neighborhood about Lord Draven fighting a duel?"

"What, ye mean the duel with the duke?" Duels were rare enough, and a duel between a duke and their lordly neighbor a thrilling occurrence in a small village like High Wycombe. Peter brightened considerably at mention of it. "Aye, I heard of it. People say as it was over a young lady."

"Yes, I believe it was. Do you know what occasioned the disagreement?"

"The way I heard it, both the duke and Lord Draven was in love with the lady. That's what duels are always about, innit? Nobles fighting over women or money? Begging yer pardon, my lord," Peter added, flushing.

Georgiana stepped forward as Benedict waved the apology off. "What about the Beauchamp family, Peter? They lived in this neighborhood too, didn't they?"

"Aye, my lady, but the Beauchamps are all dead and gone now."

"Do you remember them at all? There was a daughter in the family— Clara Beauchamp. Do you remember her?"

Peter shook his head. "Nay, except I know she were lost somehow, and never found, and the family right sorrowful about it, my lady. My grandmother was housekeeper for the Beauchamps back then, and she used to say as Mrs. Beauchamp died of grief over it."

"Your grandmother? Does your grandmother still live in High Wycombe, Peter?" Georgiana clasped her hands together, sending up a quick prayer that Peter's grandmother was still alive, and had an excellent memory.

"Aye, my lady. She's got a little cottage down Crescent Road way."

Georgiana looked at Benedict, hope surging in her chest. "Do you suppose she'd mind if we paid a call on her?"

Peter gave them a doubtful look, as if he couldn't imagine what a lord and lady would want with his grandmother, but then he shrugged, and his face split in a boyish grin. "Well now, I think she'd like that just fine, my lady. I can tell ye where she lives, if ye like."

"We would, Peter." Benedict dug into his coat pocket and produced another coin. "We'd like it very much."

Chapter Nineteen

Mrs. Payne, a tiny, white-haired lady of near seventy years of age, lived in a little white cottage at the end of a rutted road just outside of High Wycombe. Benedict doubted Mrs. Payne received many visitors, but she welcomed them with perfect composure, as if aristocratic strangers appeared on her doorstep every day.

Once they were settled in Mrs. Payne's tiny parlor with refreshments, Benedict got straight to the point. He and Georgiana had very little time left to get to the heart of the duke's secret, and Mrs. Payne was their best chance of uncovering it.

"We hoped you'd be willing to talk to us about the Beauchamp family, Mrs. Payne. Your grandson Peter told Miss Har—that is, Lady Haslemere that you served as Mrs. Beauchamp's housekeeper at one time."

"That I did, my lord, that I did. She was a dear, sweet lady, never had a cross word to say to anyone. I don't mind telling you I shed many a tear when she died."

Benedict gave her a sympathetic nod. "The Beauchamps' story is a tragic one. Were you attached to the family when their daughter Clara disappeared?"

"I was, and afterwards, too, up until Mrs. Beauchamp's death. We didn't talk about Clara after she went missing. Mrs. Beauchamp couldn't hear Clara's name without breaking down, and then she became so frail. The poor lady died of a broken heart, Lord Haslemere, and make no mistake."

"I'm very sorry for it, Mrs. Payne. Mrs. Beauchamp's grief must have been terrible to witness. Clara vanished the night of Lord Draven's Christmas ball, I believe?"

"Aye. She was dressed all in white that night. Pretty as an angel, she was, and in such high spirits! It never occurred to any of us we'd never see her again after she left that evening." Mrs. Payne's pale, wrinkled hands shook as she sipped from her teacup.

"No, I'm sure it didn't." Benedict paused, choosing his next words carefully. "It was a strange evening. From what I understand, something transpired that night that led to a duel between Lord Draven and the Duke of Kenilworth."

"There was a duel, aye, and a shameful thing two noblemen should behave so disgracefully." Mrs. Payne sniffed. "But then that's what happens when two proud, stubborn gentlemen fancy themselves in love with the same lady, isn't it, my lord?"

The same lady.

Benedict had assumed, along with the rest of London, that the lady in question must be Jane, but what if they'd all been mistaken, and Jane wasn't at the center of this mystery? What if it was another lady altogether?

What if, all this time, it had always been about Clara Beauchamp?

His heart was pounding as he turned his attention back to Mrs. Payne. "I understand the Beauchamps were close friends of Lord Draven and his family. Were Clara and Lord Draven friends?"

"Friends? Why yes, my lord. I've never seen two children more devoted to each other. One couldn't separate those two for anything. It did my heart good to see them, such dear friends as they were."

"I didn't realize Lord Draven and Miss Beauchamp were such…close companions." Georgiana's keen hazel eyes were fixed on Mrs. Payne.

"Oh my, yes, and a good thing, too. Clara was a sweet little thing, Lady Haslemere, but innocent as a lamb. Lord Draven took care of her, watched out for her, especially when she became a young lady and the gentlemen started sniffing after her fortune. The Beauchamps had a good deal of money, and every scoundrel keen to get their hands on it."

Benedict's eyebrows rose. If Clara was prey to fortune hunters, then the Beauchamps must have had more money than he'd realized.

Mrs. Payne let out a mournful sigh. "It's a great pity, what happened to Clara. Broke all our hearts, it did, but no one's so much as Lord Draven's. He was out of his head over it. He searched everywhere for her, even after all the rest of us had lost hope. He gave up at last, poor soul, but he's never got over the loss of her. That's why he doesn't come to High Wycombe now. The poor man can't bear to be here without her."

"I beg your pardon, Mrs. Payne, but let me make sure I understand you." Georgiana's voice was faint. "You're saying Lord Draven was *in love* with Clara Beauchamp?"

Mrs. Payne looked surprised. "Why yes, my lady, since he was a boy. He was maddened with grief when she disappeared. Went off to London and got himself into enough trouble there his father fetched him home, then ordered him off to the Continent. Saved his son's life, I daresay. He would have destroyed himself otherwise. That's how heartbroken he was over Clara."

"*Clara.*" Benedict met Georgiana's eyes. "All this time, it was never Jane, but *Clara.*"

Mrs. Payne looked from one to the other of them, baffled. "Jane? I don't know of any Jane, my lord. It was always Clara for Lord Draven. She was a kind young lady, and a beauty, too, with that white-gold hair and those big blue eyes of hers. She caught the attention of more than one gentleman. But beauty is both a blessing and a curse, and so it proved for poor Clara."

Benedict placed his teacup carefully in the saucer, his heart still racing. "I'm not sure I understand you, Mrs. Payne."

"Why, I mean that dreadful business with the Duke of Kenilworth, my lord. Beauty like Clara's tempts wicked men as surely as it does good ones, though I always thought the duke was more tempted by her money than he was by her face. He didn't have any back then, you know. He was still a viscount when he first set his sights on Clara."

Benedict frowned. "I beg your pardon, Mrs. Payne, but Kenilworth had already become the duke by the time of Lord Draven's Christmas ball." He'd inherited the dukedom the previous summer.

"Aye, he was duke by *then*, but he set his sights on Clara well before that, my lord. He and Lord Draven were friends, you know. Kenilworth had been to High Wycombe a half dozen times before that party. He took up with Clara...oh, let me think now. She was seventeen, so...yes, it was nearly a year before that Christmas ball."

Benedict didn't realize his fingers had gone tight until the delicate handle of his teacup actually snapped. "Damn—that is, I beg your pardon, Mrs. Payne. I believe I've ruined your teacup."

"Oh, you mustn't think of it, my lord."

Mrs. Payne made an attempt to rise and collect the pieces, but Georgiana got there first. "Here, it's all right. Give it to me, my lord." She took the pieces from Benedict's slack hand, and pressed her napkin into his fist. "Here, hold this to the cut." Benedict looked down, and to his surprise saw one of his fingers was bleeding.

"You mean to say, Mrs. Payne, that on one of his visits to Draven House, the Duke of Kenilworth seduced Clara Beauchamp?" Georgiana rested her hand on Benedict's shoulder, as if steadying herself. "He seduced and ruined the woman Lord Draven—his *close friend*, Lord Draven— was in love with?"

Mrs. Payne's mouth twisted in a sad smile. "Aye, Lady Haslemere, and such a pity it was. He seduced Clara, ruined her, then abandoned her after he became duke. I suppose he thought he could do better than an obscure lady with no title, and he'd squandered most of her fortune by then."

Do better...

Benedict went still, his body frozen to the chair in Mrs. Payne's tiny parlor. Kenilworth *had* done better, hadn't he? He'd met Jane at Lord Draven's house party, then courted her the following season. Jane was just the sort of beautiful, accomplished young lady a duke would want for his duchess, and she came with a dowry that matched her father's fortune.

"You look shocked, Lady Haslemere, as well you might be." Mrs. Payne reached out to pat Georgiana's hand. "It's dreadful what Kenilworth did, both to Clara and to Lord Draven. He betrayed a friend, and broke a lovely, innocent young lady's heart."

Benedict clenched his hands into fists. Kenilworth had done much worse than that. Betrayal, heartbreak...those were the least of his sins. He'd lied and coldly manipulated everyone unlucky enough to cross his path. He'd trapped Jane in his web of deceit, involved her and Freddy in his treachery—

Mrs. Payne sighed, shaking her head. "Lord Draven knew nothing about Clara's downfall at first, but you never can hide such things, can you, my lady? He found out what Kenilworth had done the night of the Christmas ball, and challenged him to a duel. Lord Draven's father put a stop to it, but there's not a doubt in my mind Lord Draven would have shot Kenilworth if given the chance."

But Lord Draven's father *hadn't* put a stop to it. The duel had gone forward after Kenilworth and Draven returned to London.

"Clara fancied herself in love with Kenilworth, of course. I knew it would end in disaster, but Mrs. Beauchamp allowed the duke's attentions. Oh, she never meant any harm, but she was a simple lady, my lord, and in awe of the aristocracy. I think she hoped Clara would one day become the Duchess of Kenilworth."

But she hadn't. *Jane* had, and Clara...what had become of Clara? Benedict rose abruptly, suddenly desperate to leave this tiny parlor and this tiny cottage and speak to Georgiana alone.

Mrs. Payne startled. "Are you all right, Lord Haslemere?"

"Forgive me, Mrs. Payne." Benedict's hand shook as he placed his bloodied napkin on the tea tray. "I didn't realize how late it had become. You've been a tremendous help to us. Lady Haslemere and I are grateful. Shall we, my lady?"

Georgiana took Mrs. Payne's hand and pressed it between hers. "Thank you for your hospitality, Mrs. Payne."

"You're welcome, my lady. I don't know that there's anything you or Lord Haslemere can do, and poor Clara is, I fear, beyond our help, but it would bring me a measure of peace if the Duke of Kenilworth were made to pay for the misery he's caused."

"I promise you, Mrs. Payne, that Lord Haslemere and I will do whatever lies in our power to do." Georgiana released Mrs. Payne's hand, bid her a last goodbye and followed Benedict out.

He waited until they'd left the cottage before the fury and anguish that had been building in his chest burst forth in a flood of angry words. "That *blackguard*. I'll see Kenilworth swing for what he's done, not just to Jane and Freddy, but to Clara and Draven."

"Benedict, listen—"

"The Duke of Kenilworth," Benedict spat, bitterness swelling in every word. "Such a proper, distinguished gentleman, so admired and revered in London, a man of such impeccable honor. He's a *murderer*, Georgiana."

"We know only that he *attempted* a murder. Lord Draven is still alive, and Clara might not be as far beyond our help as Mrs. Payne supposes she is. Remember, Benedict, that Jane swears she saw Clara in a carriage outside Lady Tilbury's townhouse."

"But how could Clara have hidden herself for all this time? Mrs. Payne said Draven searched all over England for her. How could she have disappeared so thoroughly even the man who loved her couldn't find her?"

"I don't know, but I've seen stranger things. Lady Tilbury may know more than she pretends to. Jane and Lord Draven must believe she's still alive, or they wouldn't be searching for her."

Benedict dragged his hands down his face, guilt pressing in on him. "I should have seen what Kenilworth was from the start. Instead I allowed my only sister to marry a villain. I failed her and Freddy—"

"No." Georgiana tugged his hands away from his face, her grip fierce. "You couldn't have known, Benedict. The duke is an accomplished liar. You can't be blamed for believing what everyone else in London did."

"But why didn't Jane just tell me the truth about Kenilworth?" He was the elder of the two of them, and Jane had always trusted him. "How could she not have trusted me to help her and Freddy?"

"It's not a matter of her not trusting you. Don't you see? Jane is terrified of the duke. He had Lord Draven attacked. He blacked Freddy's eye—a *child*, Benedict. Any man who'd hurt a child must be a monster. Do you believe for one second Kenilworth didn't threaten you? Jane didn't want you to know because she wanted to protect you, not because she didn't trust you."

Benedict stood with his head down and let her words wash over him. He couldn't excuse his own actions as easily as Georgiana did, but it meant a great deal to him that she believed him to be blameless, even if he didn't.

"There's one other thing, Benedict. Mrs. Payne said Kenilworth was more tempted by Clara's fortune than he was by her face, but there's only one way he could have gotten his hands on Clara's fortune."

Benedict's head came up.

Marriage.

Was there a possibility Kenilworth had actually *married* Clara Beauchamp?

Benedict's mind was racing. Clara was an heiress, and Kenilworth a greedy, grasping man who at the time had no money, and three cousins standing between him and his uncle's dukedom.

Cold dread dropped from Benedict's chest to the pit of his stomach. "A vulnerable, naïve young lady with a tidy fortune might not have tempted a duke, but Clara might have proved irresistible to a penniless viscount."

"A viscount, Benedict. A *viscount.*"

Georgiana's voice was heavy with meaning, and Benedict recalled he had heard someone say something about Clara Beauchamp and a viscount, but he couldn't quite remember…

Lady Wylde. Of course. At her masque ball she'd told Georgiana there'd been a rumor floating about that Clara Beauchamp had married a viscount. *Married* a viscount. Not that she'd been betrothed to a viscount, or ruined by one, but *married* one.

Something Lady Archer had said drifted back to him then, something he hadn't remarked on at the time. "Kenilworth didn't inherit the dukedom until the summer before the Christmas ball, but he purchased his Grosvenor Street mansion much earlier that year, in January. *Before* he inherited."

Georgiana grasped his coat, understanding dawning on her face. "That was *Clara's* money. He'd married her by then, and he was spending her money!"

Benedict could hardly believe it, but it made perfect sense. "Kenilworth's an utter villain, Georgiana. A cold-hearted debaucher who ruthlessly betrayed a friend and ruined a young lady's hopes. How far do you think he'd go to keep his secrets?"

Benedict hardly had a chance to think the question before the answer was there.

As far as he must.

He stared at Georgiana, bile crawling up his throat. "He's already tried to drag Jane and Freddy out of London, to bury them in some remote part of England, away from all their friends and family, and he sent a half-dozen blackguards to beat Lord Draven to death."

Georgiana's face had gone pale. "My God, Benedict. You don't think... could Kenilworth be so depraved he'd actually do his young wife an injury once she became an inconvenience to him?"

"He did *something* to her, that much is certain." Benedict's voice was grim. "Whatever it was, he must have been *very* sure she'd never turn up again, or he never would have dared to marry Jane."

"Benedict, do you know what this means? If Kenilworth and Clara did marry, and Clara is still alive, that would make the Duke of Kenilworth—"

"A bigamist."

If they could prove Kenilworth was a bigamist, his marriage to Jane would be declared invalid, and Jane would be free of him forever. There was still Freddy to consider—no matter what, he was still Kenilworth's son—but they might find Kenilworth willing to negotiate once Benedict held the power to destroy him in his hand.

Hope surged, but Benedict pushed it away. Until they could prove their suspicions, there was nothing to celebrate. "What are the chances Clara Beauchamp is still alive, Georgiana?"

She gave a helpless shrug. "I don't know, but Jane seemed very sure of it. Lord Draven must have believed it as well, but bigamy is merely speculation unless we can prove a marriage between Clara and Kenilworth actually occurred."

"We need the vicar who performed it, or another witness, or Kenilworth's and Clara's names recorded in a marriage register."

Even if they were fortunate enough to find proof of the marriage, they still had to determine if Clara Beauchamp yet lived. Finding a lady who'd been glimpsed only once in the past six years seemed an impossible task, but if there was the least chance Clara was alive, Benedict would tear England apart piece by piece to find her.

He glanced at the sky. It was still early afternoon, but dusk would be upon them soon enough, and they weren't likely to find the proof they needed in the first place they looked.

"We'll begin with the parishes closest to High Wycombe." He clasped Georgiana's hand in his and led her toward their horses. "They couldn't have gone farther than a day's journey from here without Clara spending a night away from home."

They'd have to move quickly, and pray Kenilworth hadn't buried his secrets so deeply they could never be uncovered.

Chapter Twenty

Georgiana had never given much thought to the number of parishes there might be in Oxfordshire. One didn't tend to think of such things until they were obliged to scour their marriage registers.

They hadn't turned up anything of interest at St. Michael's and All Saints in High Wycombe. Neither of them had expected to, the duke being far too wily to marry Clara in her home parish, but the parishes in Chinnor and Princes Risborough proved equally fruitless.

It was well into midafternoon by the time they left All Saints Church in Little Kimble and started on their way to Great Missenden. It was nine miles to the southeast, and from there it was an additional three-hour ride back to High Wycombe, and on to the gamekeeper's cottage in Burham.

This time, no matter how she looked at it—miles or hours—the numbers were not in Georgiana's favor. She tried to banish the hateful things from her mind, but it insisted on busily calculating, just as it always did, until her head was as sore as her backside.

She wasn't a skilled horsewoman. She was doing her best to hide that fact, but it didn't take long for Benedict to notice it. "You look fatigued, Georgiana."

Fatigued? Yes, that was one way to describe it. Another was that her bottom was screaming in protest with every step as if they'd ridden across the entire county of Oxfordshire and back. But there was no help for it, and thus no sense in complaining. Neither of them wanted to risk waiting until the following day. There simply wasn't time. Georgiana was stunned they hadn't yet come across any of Kenilworth's men. Their luck wouldn't hold out forever.

Georgiana glanced at Benedict, then quickly looked away. She *was* fatigued. Her arms ached from holding the reins and her thighs were completely numb, but there was no way she'd admit to it him when he looked as if he'd been born on his horse, with his broad shoulders relaxed, his back straight, and his hands easy on the reins.

"I'm perfectly fine," she said through gritted teeth.

He gave her a skeptical look, but he said no more until they rode into the courtyard of an establishment called the Silver Stagg an hour or so later. He brought his horse to a halt, leapt nimbly from the saddle—no numbness in *those* legs—and strode over to Georgiana, who was still mounted. "Enough of this."

"Enough? Are we in Great Missenden, then?" Georgiana made an effort to keep the desperation from her voice.

"No, we're in Dunsmore. Great Missenden is another five miles south of here."

"Five miles!" Dear God, she'd never make it. Already her body felt as if it had sustained irreparable damage. Any more time spent in the saddle and she might never walk again.

Benedict's gaze roved over her, his lips tightening. "It's not even an hour's ride for an experienced horsewoman, Georgiana. Two hours, for you. Perhaps three."

He was right, of course, but that didn't stop Georgiana's cheeks from heating with humiliation. "I beg your pardon if my riding doesn't meet with your approval, Lord Haslemere." She was aware of how petty she sounded, how like a whining child, but her pride was stung, and worse, well…she felt almost as if she might burst into tears, which was so ridiculous as to be intolerable.

She didn't burst into floods of tears, *ever*, and she wouldn't start now. Tears were absolutely out of the question.

"If I'd grown up on a grand estate with a stable full of horses at my disposal, perhaps I'd ride like the cavalry as you do," she said resentfully. "But as it is—"

"Hang the cavalry. Come down from there."

He reached up to wrap his hands around her waist, but Georgiana squirmed away from him. "I can't get down on my—" She broke off at the sound of a low, angry rumble coming from his chest. "Did you just…*growl* at me?"

Benedict, however, had evidently run out of patience, because instead of dignifying her question with a reply, he reached up, grasped her waist in his strong hands and jerked her from the saddle.

"Lord Haslemere! How dare—"

"I said, *enough*." He set her on her feet, but kept his hands on her waist, keeping her body close to his.

Georgiana would have died before she'd admit it, but as the blood rushed back into her limbs, her knees threatened to buckle, and she clung to his muscled forearms, grateful for those commanding hands and the solid, steady strength of him. She glanced up into his face, and was puzzled to find him staring down at her with wrathful dark eyes. "You, ah...you look angry."

His fingers tightened around her waist. "That's because I am angry, Georgiana."

Oh, that was unmistakably a growl.

"Because I can't ride?" But of course, that was the reason. He was an *earl*, for pity's sake, and accustomed to ladies who rode as well as they walked. It must be tedious in the extreme for him to be stuck with *her*. The thought was unexpectedly painful, and when she spoke, her voice wasn't quite steady. "Well, I beg your pardon if I can't—"

"I don't give a bloody damn if you can ride or not. I'm angry because you didn't simply tell me you couldn't make it this far on horseback. I thought we were past this sort of nonsense, Georgiana."

Georgiana had trained her gaze on her feet in order to avoid looking at him, but his words made her eyes snap back to his, and she was stunned to see a shadow of hurt cross his face. He wasn't angry because he was disappointed in her. He was angry because he'd wanted to take care of her, and she'd deprived him of that chance.

That was *not* the sting of tears in her eyes, no matter how much it felt like it was.

His arm muscles tightened as if he were going to pull away, but before she could reason herself out of it, Georgiana clutched at the fabric of his coat to keep him with her. "I...you're right. It was foolish of me. I'm sorry, Benedict."

She offered him a tentative smile, and though he didn't quite return it, his face softened. "We'll continue the journey in a hired carriage, as I have an aversion to dragging an exhausted lady across a half-dozen counties in England. Madame Célestine's horses need a rest, in any case. We can fetch them on the way back."

"Won't that take too much time?" If they didn't reach Great Missenden soon, they wouldn't be able to visit the parish church until tomorrow.

"No." He pressed a finger to her lips. "No arguments. Go inside and order us luncheon while I arrange for a carriage. I've no wish to starve you, either."

He didn't wait for an answer, but turned and strode off in the direction of the stables. Georgiana watched him go, his broad shoulders straight, his long legs eating up the ground at his feet, and an odd breathlessness overtook her, born of both tenderness and panic. If he'd been the frivolous, selfish lord she'd expected him to be, all this would have been so much easier, but Benedict Harcourt was nothing like she'd imagined.

She tore her gaze away and turned toward the entrance of the inn, but she couldn't shake the feeling Jane and Freddy weren't the only ones at risk.

Now, it was also her heart, and every moment she spent with Benedict Harcourt, the greater the risk she'd lose it to him.

* * * *

Great Missenden proved to be a typical English village, sleepy despite its proximity to the larger town of Wendover. Lee Old Church was a small building of pale gold stone with arched, whitewashed windows, rather pretty but not remarkable, and situated at the end of a narrow, tree-lined lane.

"Remote, isn't it?" Benedict gazed out the carriage window. "Difficult to find, if one doesn't know it's here."

It was deserted at the moment, the only sound the soft sloughing of wind drifting through the gravestones in the tiny churchyard to one side of the building. No one appeared as Benedict brought the carriage to a stop in the drive, but there was a small house of the same pale stone just behind the church that was presumably the vicar's house.

Georgiana took in the small building, shading her eyes from the late afternoon sun reflecting off the windows. "Yes. It's the ideal place for a clandestine marriage."

So ideal, in fact, there was some chance the duke might have believed his secret marriage to Clara Beauchamp would never be discovered, and so hadn't bothered to cover his tracks.

She had a feeling about this place…

She'd never much relied on *feelings*. That was more Cecilia's realm. Georgiana was enamored of facts, not fancies, but there was a strange exhilaration in her belly, a certainty that they'd find something in this humble place.

It seemed incredible it could be as simple as that. After all the mystery surrounding Kenilworth's sins and his efforts to keep his secret, she could hardly believe a mere scrap of paper might be the means of exposing him, but neither would she have predicted everything that had happened over these last few days.

A dastardly duke, a kidnapped duchess, faro, masque balls, scandalous gossip and a notorious rake with the handsomest dark eyes she'd ever seen—

But she wouldn't think about that now. It would only distract her. Now was the time for action, not mooning over a rakish earl.

"Shall we?" Benedict took her arm and led her to the entrance of the church.

Georgiana grasped the heavy iron latch and turned it. A draft of cool air wafted over them as the door opened with a gentle creak of its hinges. It was dim inside, but she could see it was as humble a place as it appeared from the outside, with plain whitewashed walls, the arched windows lined in the same stone, and the simple altar illuminated by a leaded glass window behind it, dust motes lingering in the pale light that shone through the diamond-shaped panes.

"It's a simple little place. Not quite what you'd imagine for a man like Kenilworth." There was a dark thread of bitterness in Benedict's voice. "He always insists on everything being as magnificent as possible, as befits a grand duke."

There was nothing grand about Lee Old Church—no stately altar here, and no stained glass. It was the last place in the world one would expect a duke to be married, but then Kenilworth hadn't been a duke then, nor had he had any expectation of becoming one.

So he'd found his heiress, seduced and then married her, gained control of her fortune, and then once he became a duke he left her behind, as if she were no more significant than a bit of mud on his boots.

For such treachery as that, one church did as well as another.

"And a grand wife who befits a grand duke as well. Not that I blame Jane, but Clara Beauchamp—God in heaven, Benedict. What do you suppose happened to her that night?" There was a reason Kenilworth had been so certain Clara would never return to expose his perfidy.

It made Georgiana shudder to think about it.

The odds were against Clara still being alive, despite Jane's certainty that she'd seen her outside Lady Tilbury's London townhouse. It seemed impossible a man as cold and calculating as the duke would have been as careless as to leave a witness behind.

Another shudder raced down Georgiana's spine. As awful as the duke was, surely, he wouldn't have...he couldn't have been so wicked as to—

"I don't know, but once we have Jane and Freddy settled, I intend to find out." Benedict's jaw tightened. "Kenilworth won't get away with what he's done, Georgiana. I promise it."

"Good afternoon," a voice called, and Georgiana turned to find a diminutive man dressed in the somber black suit and white cravat of a vicar stroll through a doorway at the back of the church. "I beg your pardon for keeping you waiting. I didn't realize anyone was here. I'm Martin Henshawe, the vicar. May I help you?"

"Good afternoon, Vicar Henshawe. You may be able to help us, yes. This young lady and I have come to inquire about a marriage—"

"Ah, yes. I thought it must be that. Such a lovely young couple." Vicar Henshawe beamed at them. "You need only give me your names. Once I've called the banns over three successive Sundays—"

"Banns?" Benedict cleared his throat. "No, that's not...we're not here about calling banns."

"A special license, is it? We don't get many of those here, but of course I'm pleased to assist you. I just need to see the—"

"Er, no, Vicar Henshawe. We, ah...this young lady and I aren't betrothed. We're acquaintances only, or...well, more friends, really, but not...we're not here about our own marriage, but about someone else's."

Benedict's cheeks turned pink as he fumbled through this explanation.

A rake, blushing? Georgiana had never seen such a thing before, and she couldn't help but find it...well, an oddity, really. Peculiar, but nothing more. It wasn't fetching, or charming, or singularly adorable.

The vicar blinked at them. "Indeed? I beg your pardon. The two of you look rather...that is, I assumed you were...well, no matter. You've come to ask about another marriage, you say?"

"Yes, Vicar Henshawe." Georgiana gave him her most gracious smile. "A dear friend of mine, a lady by the name of Clara Beauchamp, may have been married here, but it would have been some time ago. Seven years or more. Perhaps her name sounds familiar to you?"

Vicar Henshawe shook his head. "No, I'm afraid it wouldn't. I came to this parish just two years ago, after the previous vicar, Vicar Smithfield, passed away. Of course, I know the names of the members of the parish, but I don't recognize the name Clara Beauchamp."

Georgiana glanced at Benedict, and saw her own disappointment reflected in his face. If Clara Beauchamp and the duke's name weren't in this register, there'd be no one to verify their marriage had taken place with the previous vicar dead.

But if they *had* married here, their names would be in the register. They *had* to be. "Perhaps we might have a look at the register, Vicar Henshawe? It's a matter of some urgency, you see." Georgiana lowered her voice. "A dispute about the legality of the marriage, I'm afraid, and some disagreement over an inheritance. A rather unpleasant business, you understand."

"Oh, dear. Yes, I imagine so." Vicar Henshawe looked mildly scandalized. "I'll just fetch the register for you so you might have a peek, shall I?"

"That's very kind of you. Thank you." Georgiana waited until the vicar shuffled off in the direction he'd come before turning to Benedict. To her surprise, she found him smirking at her. "What?"

"Lying to a vicar, and in a church, too. I noticed the falsehood rolled rather easily off your tongue. Shame on you, Georgiana. I think you must be far more wicked than I initially suspected."

Georgiana noticed the teasing glint in his eyes, and her lips quirked. "Well, someone had to tell him something. If I'd left it to you, the poor man would be calling our wedding banns this Sunday."

She'd expected him to laugh out loud at such a preposterous idea, but he didn't. Instead, his eyes met hers, and he gazed at her with such intensity heat climbed into her cheeks, and she had to force herself to look away before she was tempted to give in to foolish flights of fancy.

Fortunately, the sound of a door closing broke the silence between them. Vicar Henshawe came down the center aisle, a thick, heavy book in his hands. "Here we are. I have some business to attend to in the back, so I'll just leave this here with you for a bit. Do let me know if I can be of any assistance, however." He handed the book to Benedict, then toddled off back down the aisle and vanished through the door again.

"Well, that was easier than I imagined it would be." Benedict gestured Georgiana toward a seat in one of the pews, then slid in beside her and spread the book open over both their laps.

It was on the tip of Georgiana's tongue to say it was *too* easy, and disappointment would be sure to follow, but she bit the words back. There was no reason to infect him with her gloomy portents, and after all, perhaps it *would* be that easy. If not, they'd find it out soon enough without her dire predictions.

She opened the book to the middle and bent over it, squinting down at the dates. "Let me see. If Mrs. Payne had the right of it, Clara and Kenilworth would have been married sometime between seventeen-ninety and ninety-one."

"Start a year earlier, just to be safe." Benedict held the book steady while Georgiana turned the thin pages until she'd reached January of seventeen eighty-nine.

"Here we are. My goodness, either the previous vicar had dreadful handwriting, or he was very old when he died." The letters were uneven and shaky, and the ink faint, as if the writer had trouble managing a quill. "It looks as if a bird hopped across the page. It'll be quite a task, making sense of this."

"Here." Benedict moved closer, so the length of his thigh was tucked against hers. "I'll read this page, and you read the other. It will go more quickly that way."

No, it wouldn't, because now she was distracted by the sensation of his warm, muscled thigh. She couldn't say so, however, so she drew in a deep breath and ran her finger down the page, reading off the names in her head as she went down the row.

It wasn't a long list, Lee Old Church being a small church in a small parish, but the ink was so faded by the time she reached the end of her row the names were swimming across the page. One thing was certain, however. "No Clara Beauchamp."

"Not on my side, either. Go on to the following year."

She turned the page, and they both fell silent as they each read through their list of names. October, November, December…Georgiana's heart sank as she read the names of the last couple married in December of seventeen ninety. "She's not here either."

"No." Benedict let out a sigh, and rubbed his fingers over his forehead, as if he had a headache. "Keep going."

Georgiana did as she was bid, but even as she began reading down the row of names, her hopes were fading. There were dozens of churches in Oxfordshire alone, and dozens more of them close to here, in Buckinghamshire and in Kent. Kenilworth could have taken Clara to any one of them—

Georgiana paused, her finger stopping partway down the page. "Benedict, look." She pointed to the first name on the top. "The date here is February of seventeen ninety-two. What happened to the previous year?"

Benedict slid the book onto his lap to get a closer look, then flipped back to the previous page. "It's missing. The dates go from December of seventeen ninety to February of seventeen ninety-two. Seventeen ninety-one is missing!"

Georgiana stared down at the book spread across Benedict's lap, and that was when she saw it, pushed deeply into the inside of the spine.

The ragged edge of a missing page.

Someone had been here before them. Someone who had something to hide. And they'd torn the page out of the marriage register.

Chapter Twenty-one

Neither Benedict nor Georgiana spoke on the carriage ride from Great Missenden back to Dunsmore. They collected Madame Célestine's horses at the Silver Stagg, but Benedict insisted they ride together and bring the second horse on a lead. "I can't promise we'll be comfortable, but at least we'll be…"

Together.

"Warm." He took her hand and raised it to his lips, his gaze holding hers as he pressed a lingering, open-mouthed kiss on her palm. "Your throne, princess," he said with a courtly bow, sweeping his arm toward the horse.

He half-expected her to protest, but instead she dipped into a dainty curtsy. "Why, how gentlemanly, my lord."

He chuckled. "You're too kind. It's rather a poor throne, I'm afraid. Not a single cushion."

"I'll just have to recline on you, then. I daresay you'll make a proper cushion." A blush stained her cheeks, but she offered him a smile that went straight to the most secret depths of Benedict's heart.

He removed his coat, draped it over her shoulders, then handed her up and swung into the saddle behind her. "Lean back on me." He drew her into the space between his legs and shifted so she could rest her back against his chest. "Yes, just like that," he whispered, wrapping an arm around her waist.

He urged the horse into a brisk walk, pressing Georgiana tightly against his chest. He glanced up at the first few faint stars studding the night sky before resting his cheek on the top of her head. He wouldn't wish himself anywhere but here. If he could, he'd stay here with her forever.

They didn't speak much. Neither of them said aloud that their investigation into the Duke of Kenilworth was over, that his ugly secrets seemed destined to stay buried. There was no need to say it. The marriage register had been their last hope, and even proof of a marriage between Clara and Kenilworth wouldn't have been enough to save Jane and Freddy.

They needed Clara Beauchamp. Not just a glimpse of her in a carriage on a darkened street, but Clara in the flesh, her skin warm and her heart beating.

In the eyes of the courts, Kenilworth was no bigamist unless they could prove Clara was still alive, and they were as far from being able to do that as they'd been when this business first began. Now there was nowhere left to go except back to London, and for Benedict, from there to North America, to give Jane and Freddy a chance at a new life.

Benedict wished for a new life, too, but not the life he'd find in North America.

Not any life that didn't include Georgiana Harley.

He wanted to tell her, but there was too much to say, and too little time left in which to say it. Neither of them tried to fill their last moments with frantic words. Instead she let her body melt against his, and he held her close.

This was the most he'd ever have of her. These fleeting moments, with her nestled against him in the saddle, her slender back pressed to his chest, his arms resting against her sides. He leaned forward so his face was mere inches from the back of her neck and inhaled a deep breath of a scent that had breathed new life into him—a scent he'd never forget, no matter how many miles came between them.

He was in love with her—had been in love with her for months now—and it didn't make a damn bit of difference.

"Sleep, Georgiana," he whispered, his lips close to her ear. "It's late."

Too late to be making the long ride back to the gamekeeper's cottage, but they'd decided not to remain at the Silver Stagg. If Benedict thought they'd come across the duke's men on the darkened road he wouldn't have risked it, but the duke hadn't sent his men after them at all.

He hadn't needed to. Any evidence of his marriage to Clara Beauchamp had long since been obliterated. Kenilworth had covered his tracks too well to believe they'd find anything they could use against him.

Benedict leaned closer to Georgiana, his eyes falling closed as the stray locks of hair that had come loose from her hat brushed against his cheek. "It's all right to rest, Georgiana. I've got you."

He waited for her to insist she wasn't fatigued, and didn't need to sleep, but the words never came. She drifted to sleep in his arms in such an unexpected show of trust it brought an ache to his throat.

The ride back to Burham was both too long and too short.

When they arrived at the cottage, he eased himself from the saddle and then reached up for her, taking care not to wake her as he lifted her down and gathered her into his arms. He nudged the cottage door open with his foot, strode inside with her cradled against his chest, and carried her to the bed in the corner.

She stirred when he lay her down, made a low, protesting noise in her throat, and caught his sleeve when he tried to draw away. "Don't go, Benedict."

He caught her wrist between gentle fingers and tried to free himself. "Shhh. You need to sleep, Georgiana. We have a long ride back to London tomorrow."

A small frown crossed her lips, and she held him fast. "You need to sleep, too. Lie down here, next to me."

A rueful smile drifted over Benedict's lips as he shook his head. "You're inviting a notorious rake into your bed?" He thought of how it would feel to hold her in his arms, their bodies pressed together, his every breath an echo of hers, the firelight playing over them and her lips mere inches from his. "I don't think that's a good idea, princess."

She opened her eyes, and her answering smile was…Good Lord, he'd never seen such an inviting smile grace any woman's lips before. It was innocent and sultry at once, the slight pout of her lower lip making him hard in an instant, all the blood rushing from his head to his cock in one thunderous surge, leaving him dizzy with arousal.

"I do." Her fingers tightened on his sleeve. "I think it's a wonderful idea."

Benedict gazed down at her, his best intentions warring with a desire that grew stronger with every flutter of her eyelashes, each of her quickening breaths. She didn't know what she was saying, didn't realize how dangerous it was to tempt a man like him to lie beside her in a bed in a darkened cottage. How could she? She was inexperienced, an innocent.

But Benedict knew better, and so it was up to him to deny her, to pull away—

"Just for a little while, until I fall asleep," she whispered, tugging him closer.

That whisper brushed across his skin like a caress, sparking across his nerve endings, and Benedict cursed himself for a fool as all thought of denial fled and he crawled across the bed to lie down next to her. He was careful to leave an ocean of empty bed between them, a thousand warnings not to touch her, not to lay a single finger on her whirling through his head even as his cock pressed eagerly against his falls.

When he didn't make any move to take her into his arms, Georgiana raised herself onto her elbow and peered down at him. "You don't look terribly comfortable, Benedict."

"Nonsense. I'm as snug as a kitten in a basket." A bald-faced lie, of course. He'd be more comfortable lying on a bed of iron spikes than he was lying here beside her, knowing he couldn't touch her. "Go to sleep," he added, squeezing his eyes shut and resigning himself to a night of torture.

"Don't you want to take off your coat? Your waistcoat too, I think, and your cravat."

Benedict nearly whimpered. "No. I prefer to sleep in my clothes. Go to sleep."

He lay there with his arms at his sides, his entire body as rigid as a stick of wood, and prayed she'd leave it there, fall asleep, and leave him alone in his misery.

She was quiet for a moment, but then she stirred again, and he felt her fingertips brush his chin. He gasped, nearly jumping out of his skin. "What are you doing?"

"Helping you remove your cravat. I can't sleep if I think you're uncomfortable, and it's crooked, anyway." Her knuckles brushed against the sensitive skin of his throat as her nimble fingers worked on the folds. Finally, she got it unwound and slid it from his neck. "There, that's one knot *à la Haslemere* undone. Now your coat."

Benedict wasn't usually slow to catch on when a woman wanted him, nor was he usually slow to take advantage of such a fortunate occurrence. Tonight, his brain was befuddled with love and desire, but at last it dawned on him what Georgiana was doing. "Are you...are you trying to take my clothes off?"

She let out a soft chuckle. "Yes. I confess I didn't think it would take so much effort. Perhaps you'd be willing to help me?"

"No! That is, I mean..." Benedict shook his head to clear it. "You do realize what's much more likely to happen between us if you strip off my clothing, don't you?"

"I have some idea, yes." She'd been trying to tug his arm out of his sleeve, but now she paused. "If you don't want me—"

She let out a little squeal of surprise as Benedict heaved himself up and with one quick move rolled her onto her back and stretched out on top of her, his chest heaving with emotion. "Don't you dare say I don't want you. I *do* want you. I have since I first laid eyes on you, and you called me a selfish, useless rake."

Georgiana's lips quirked. "I never called you a rake that first night. I called you a scoundrel."

"Ah, yes. I remember now." Benedict stroked a fingertip over her lips so he might memorize that sly little smile. "Yet in spite of your cruelty, I want you more than any woman I've ever known."

Her eyes went wide. "You want me more than Lady Wylde?"

"*Lady Wylde!*" Benedict gave her an incredulous look. "Why does Lady Wylde keep coming into it? I haven't given her a single thought since the day after her masque ball, whereas your face haunts me no matter where I am, or what I'm doing. How can you even imagine she compares to you?"

"But she's very...and I'm just—"

Another rumble tore from his chest, and he silenced her by pressing his fingers to her lips. "Not another word about Lady Wylde, Georgiana. Do you understand me? She's of no importance to me at all."

Georgiana peeked up at him and gave a quick nod.

"Good." Benedict reluctantly pulled his fingers away from her soft, warm lips, and dragged a hand through his hair. "This isn't about my not wanting you, Georgiana. Far from it."

She twisted one of the buttons on his coat. "This is our only chance, Benedict," Georgiana whispered, the ache in her throat unbearable. How could she let him go without spending a night in his arms?

Benedict's breath caught. "Do you want me, Georgiana?"

She nodded, still avoiding his gaze, but that wasn't enough for Benedict. He tipped her chin up with his fingers. "Look at me. When you tell a man you want him, you say it aloud, Georgiana, and you look him in the eyes."

Her eyes met his, and the faint embers still glowing in the grate were reflected in their golden-brown depths. "I-I want you, Benedict. I can no longer remember a time I didn't want you."

Her words flowed through him, touching every place inside him, then settling in his heart. He brought her hand to his lips and pressed a tender kiss into her palm, but he was already shaking his head. "You shouldn't want me, sweetheart. Nothing but heartbreak will come from it."

"Please don't say you'll break my heart because you're a rake or a rogue or a blackguard who cares for no one, because it's not true. I may have thought that of you once, but that was before..." Her throat moved in a rough swallow. "Before I knew you. You're a loving, caring brother and uncle, and...and a good man, Benedict."

Benedict's eyes drifted closed at her words. He loved her, and to hear her say she believed he was a good man meant everything to him. All he could do, the best he could do was be worthy of her faith in him. "Listen to me, love. I...I'm taking Jane and Freddy away, Georgiana. The only way I can be sure they'll be safe from Kenilworth is if we leave England."

For a brief moment, Georgiana's dark eyelashes swept down to hide her eyes. They were glistening when she opened them again. "Where will you go?"

"North America. I don't think...I don't know if we'll ever be able to return, Georgiana. Do you think I'd steal your innocence only to abandon you?"

He shifted to move away from the temptation of her, but she twined her arms around his neck, stopping him. "You can't steal something I'm offering to give you, Benedict."

"You think so now, Georgiana, but later, after I'm gone, you'll regret—"

"No. My only regret will be not giving myself to the man I love." She slid her hands from the back of his neck to his face, cupping his cheeks in her palms. She could only give the gift of her innocence to one man, and she would give it to the man who already held her heart. "If it isn't you, Benedict, it won't be anyone."

* * * *

It was nothing but the truth, and a truth that came from the very depths of her, from a place so deep in her soul no one had ever touched it before. She'd thought no one ever would.

Until him.

With that realization came the feelings she'd evaded for so long, a raging flood of them, one wave after the next, so strong, so relentless nothing could hold them back, nothing could stop them.

There was nothing left for her to do but *feel* them, and it was as frightening as she'd always imagined it would be to be at their mercy. Yet at the same time it was glorious to feel them unfurling like a clenched fist opening inside her.

Benedict didn't speak, but the emotions running wild inside her must have shown on her face, because he made a choked sound, and then...

Then he was kissing her, his hands buried in her hair and his lips tender and demanding at once. "Open for me, Georgiana," he whispered against her lips, and she did as he commanded, her lips yielding to his hot, coaxing tongue.

"You taste so sweet, like Mrs....Mrs....confound it, what's Gray's cook's name again? The one who makes the quince preserves?"

She blinked up at him. "Are you talking to me about Lord Gray's cook while you're kissing me, Lord Haslemere?"

Benedict dropped a kiss on the end of her nose. "Hush. I'm trying to be romantic by telling you that you taste sweeter than the sweetest fruits, and you're ruining it."

"I beg your pardon." Georgiana tucked her face against his neck to smother a laugh. "It's Mrs. Beeson."

"Right. Mrs. Beeson." His lips curved in a smile against her temple. "Unfortunately, I think the moment has passed, so I'll just say you've cursed me with your sweet tooth, and now I can't get enough of you."

Georgiana thought that quite romantic indeed, and urged his face down to hers, eager for his lips. He crooned to her as he took her mouth again and again, jumbled words of passion and tenderness, his whispers hot against her mouth and the tender skin of her throat and neck. She couldn't make sense of everything he said, but it didn't matter, it didn't matter, because she could feel it in the brush of his lips against hers, each dizzying stroke of his tongue in her mouth.

He murmured to her as he nibbled and licked his way from her lips to her jaw, and from there to her throat, the lobe of her ear. She cried out when his teeth closed over that sensitive flesh, her body arching under his. "Oh, that's…"

"Yes? What is it, princess? Tell me." His wicked lips danced over her skin, nuzzling into the secret place behind her ear before suckling at her lobe again, a quiet laugh escaping him when she arched under him a second time.

"It's…it makes me shiver." Georgiana sank her fingers into his thick hair and gave it a quick, sharp tug that made him moan. A bolt of pure, feminine pride shot through her at his obvious pleasure, and all at once she was desperate to get closer to him, to feel his warm skin against hers. "Take this off." She gave the hem of his waistcoat a fruitless tug, then her restless fingers tugged open the buttons of his coat and tried to drag it over his broad shoulders. "It's too tight!"

He nipped at the hollow of her throat. "I'll have you know that's a perfectly tailored Weston coat."

Georgiana ceased her struggles with the tight sleeves and raised an eyebrow at him. "Does that mean you wish to leave it on?"

"God, no." A grin crossed his lips as he wrestled his way out of his coat and waistcoat, threw them on the floor, then eased himself back on top of her, taking care not to crush her. "There. Are you satisfied, madam?"

Georgiana hardly heard him, she was so distracted by the smooth expanse of his bare throat and the hard chest revealed by the open neckline of his shirt. "This is very nice, right here." She traced the hollow of his throat, then fanned her fingers over the length of his collarbones.

He seemed to hold his breath as her fingers wandered over the muscles of his shoulders and arms and his taut, straining biceps, then let it out in a low moan as she scored her fingernails lightly over the warm flesh of his back. "You're driving me mad, Georgiana."

"I am?" She paused in her caresses. "But dozens of ladies must have touched you here before me."

The corners of her mouth turned down in a frown at the thought, but he swooped down and kissed it from her lips. "No ladies who matter the way you do."

"Oh." She gave him a shy smile. "I think I like driving you mad."

He pulled back to gaze down at her. "You always drive me mad, without even trying to. Your sharp tongue, the occasional flash of temper in your eyes, your smile, that enticing way you bite your bottom lip—everything about you drives me mad, Georgiana. I've been on the verge of ravishing you from the moment I met you that night in Maiden Lane."

Georgiana's mouth fell open. "But I was horrible to you that night!"

"I *know*." He grinned, obviously relishing the memory. "No lady has ever dared to scold me like that before. It was...stirring."

Georgiana fingered the neckline of his shirt, peeking up at him from under her eyelashes. "What do you suppose would happen if I *tried* to drive you mad?"

He let out a strained laugh. "You'd find yourself with a deeply aroused earl in your bed, and you might regret it. Aroused earls are demanding creatures."

"Hmmm. I think I'd like to see for myself." Georgiana tugged on the hem of Benedict's shirt. "Take this off."

Benedict didn't need any more coaxing. He rose to his knees, tore his shirt over his head and tossed it on the floor behind him. "As you wish, Miss Harley. May I remove anything else for your pleasure?"

Georgiana was vaguely aware he'd asked her a question, but she was so distracted by the sight of his bare chest she didn't reply. He was...dear God, the long, lean lines of him, his broad shoulders and muscled arms and the hair-roughened expanse of his hard chest...

He was magnificent. She didn't think she'd ever be able to tear her eyes away from him. Until he moaned, that is, and her gaze flew to his face. "Is...is something wrong?"

"The way you're looking at me." His voice was hoarse, his dark eyes burning with heat. "It feels like my skin is on fire."

Georgiana's tongue crept out to touch the corner of her mouth as she reached out her hand and lay her palm flat against his ridged stomach. "You, ah, you do feel rather warm."

Benedict took her wrist in his hand and slid her palm up his torso to the center of his chest. "Touch me, Georgiana."

Georgiana dragged her hand slowly over his heated skin, caressing his shoulders, the strong column of his neck and his bare chest, mesmerized by the smooth skin under the sprinkling of dark red hair, the tickle of it against her palms.

He kept his gaze on her face as she stroked him, his lips parted, his burning eyes watching every shift in her expression until the edge of her thumb grazed his nipple. He sucked in a breath at her touch, his eyes squeezing closed.

"Benedict?" Georgiana snatched her hand away. "Did I do something wrong?"

"No." He caught her hand in his and dragged it back to his chest. "Touch me there again."

Georgiana did as he bid her, stroking her thumb lightly over his nipple once, then again. He let out a ragged moan, his throat and chest flushing and his nipple stiffening under the pad of her finger. She went on stroking him with both her hands on his chest, her thumbs tracing circles around each of his nipples.

"*Yes*," he hissed when she scraped her fingernail over the rigid peak. "Again."

She hesitated, then did it again, catching her bottom lip in her teeth when his body jerked under her hands. Was this what he meant by driving him mad? "Does it...does it feel good?"

Benedict's eyes had gone dark and sleepy under heavy eyelids. "Let me show you."

Georgiana gave a tiny nod, a soft sigh rising to her lips when Benedict caught her wrists and raised her arms over her head, then settled his big, warm hands on her sides, close to her breasts, but not yet touching.

"It feels like you're pulling a string inside me here." He lay a heavy palm on her lower belly. "It pulls tighter with every touch, an unbearable tension building inside you, so deliciously tight, Georgiana, until you become desperate to release it."

He began touching her then, just a light stroke of his thumbs against her sides. Just that soft, simple touch was enough to make her breath catch, but then his thumbs were edging closer to her nipples, closer still, and they were already stiffening for him, aching for his touch...

She cried out when it came at last, a quick caress, as light as a breath. Georgiana opened her mouth to beg for more, but before she could get the word out, Benedict's hands were on her again, stroking and teasing, gentle at first, but relentless, and then firmer as she began to squirm under him. He circled and pinched her tender nipples until her back was arching to get closer to those wicked fingers. More, she needed more...

"Do you feel it, Georgiana? That knot, deep inside you?" His dark eyes glittered down at her. "So tight. It's maddening, isn't it? That's why you're squirming for me, princess—because you want me to soothe that ache."

Georgiana was so lost in his touch and his wicked words she didn't notice his hands had moved to the back of her gown to release her buttons until she felt the tantalizing slide of cool air across her skin and realized the bodice of her gown was now bunched around her waist.

Benedict drew back a little, sitting on his heels as he stared down at her, his gaze moving from her stiff nipples to her lips, then back to her eyes. "I've dreamed about you like this, Georgiana. I can see your nipples through your chemise. Such a dusky pink, and so hard for me." He tweaked one, then squeezed it gently between his forefinger and thumb.

"Oh." Georgiana gave a soft gasp as he did it again, pinching the turgid peak until she couldn't lie still anymore.

"Yes," he whispered when her head fell back. "You need more."

It wasn't a question, and he didn't wait for an answer before he brought his mouth down to her breast, his lips closing around one stiff peak. Georgiana gasped again, her hands sinking into his hair as he licked at her nipple, quick, hard strokes with his tongue, his hot breath turning ragged as a moan broke from her lips.

She whimpered when he lifted his head, her fingers tightening in his hair to bring him back to her breasts.

"Shhh." Benedict brushed a curl back from her forehead. "I want to make you feel good, Georgiana. Will you let me touch you?"

Georgiana, who'd nearly started weeping when he *stopped* touching her, gave him a dazed nod. "Yes. Please, Benedict."

He brushed his lips over hers, then kissed his way down her neck, pausing to taste the hollow of her throat before he moved lower, his lips grazing her breasts. He sucked a tender peak into his mouth as he trailed his fingertips up her leg, dragging her skirts up as he went.

Georgiana gasped when he touched the soft tuft of hair between her thighs. For long moments he simply stroked her there, letting his fingers drift through her curls until she grew restless for more of his touch, her legs parting as she squirmed against him. She caught her breath when he slipped a finger between her damp folds, delving gently, rolling his fingertip over the swollen nub and making her cry out.

"So wet. So hungry for me, Georgiana. You feel like warm silk." A harsh moan fell from Benedict's lips as he rubbed and circled and teased until she was slick from his wicked caresses. "Open your legs for me."

In that moment, Georgiana couldn't have refused him anything. She let her knees slide apart, arching her neck when he eased a long finger gently inside her as he continued to stroke her throbbing center. "Here, princess? Is this where you ache for me?"

"Yes." Georgiana gripped his wrist, desperate to keep his teasing fingers where they were, the word nearly lost in her gasping breaths. "I... oh, *please*, Benedict."

"Shhh. I'm going to take care of you, Georgiana," he rasped before leaning down again to torment her breasts with slow, wicked strokes of his tongue. Her taut nipples strained for his lips and the pleasure swelled until it all blurred together into a throbbing ache inside her. Benedict was merciless, pinning her hips to the bed and stroking her, his fingers quickening until the pleasure built to a sharp edge, pushing her higher and higher until at last the tight heat unfurled in long pulses of bliss. They seemed to go on and on until at last she collapsed against the sheets, damp and trembling and breathless.

Long, quiet moments passed, their panting breaths the only sound until at last Georgiana opened her eyes.

Benedict was kneeling between her legs, his chest heaving. His lips were red and swollen, his hair mussed and falling over his forehead as he stared down at her with wild dark eyes.

"Benedict." She reached for him, a drowsy smile curving her lips.

He caught her hand and brought it to his mouth, his lips grazing her knuckles. "I've never seen anything more breathtaking than you taking your pleasure, Georgiana. Nothing is more beautiful to me than you."

A spasm of pain twisted his face, and Georgiana knew he was thinking of their parting tomorrow. For an instant her own heart felt heavy, but she made herself push the sadness away. These were the last hours she had with Benedict, and she wouldn't waste them wishing for something that could never be. She'd love him now, and be grateful for the brief time they had together.

"You know, I wasn't done teasing you before." She traced a pattern over his thighs with her fingertips, her gaze fixed on the hard ridge straining against his breeches. Her eyes met his as she toyed with the buttons on his falls.

Benedict caught his breath, but he didn't move as she twisted the buttons loose and pushed the fabric aside. "Oh." Her eyes widened when his long, stiff length sprang free from the tight confines of his clothing.

She gazed at his erection, curious and baffled at once. It seemed impossible such a large thing could fit...well, where Sophia and Cecilia insisted it was meant to go, but Benedict had reduced her to a quivering, moaning heap of flesh with just the touch of his mouth and fingers alone, so perhaps this was like that had been.

Inexplicable, but wondrous.

It didn't occur to her she'd been staring for quite a long time until she noticed Benedict had gone strangely still. Her eyes flicked to his face, and her heart clenched at his anxious expression.

He thinks I'm frightened.

She wasn't. Not of it, and not of *him*—especially not of him, and she wouldn't let him think otherwise. So, before he could say a word or draw away from her, she reached out her hand and touched him.

"Warm," she murmured. "And your skin here is so soft."

There was nothing else soft about him, though. Under the smooth, sleek skin he was as rigid as an ebony walking stick. She slid her hand experimentally over him, marveling at the smooth slide of that impossibly delicate skin over the hardness beneath, and the bead of moisture that rose on the blunt head.

She ran her thumb gently over the tip and a low moan broke from Benedict's chest. Her gaze snapped to his face to find his eyes closed and his jaw clenched. She snatched her hand away at once, afraid she'd hurt him. "I'm sorry, Benedict. I didn't mean to—"

"No. Touch me." He grabbed her hand and pressed it against himself, letting out another desperate groan when she wrapped her fingers around him.

"It sounds as if I'm torturing you."

A hoarse laugh broke from his lips. "You are. The only thing worse than your teasing strokes is not having your hand on me."

Georgiana touched her tongue to her bottom lip. "Show me."

He covered her hand with his and closed her fingers around his length. He gripped himself much more tightly than she ever would have dared, but any anxiety she might have felt about hurting him fled when his mouth went slack, and his eyelids fluttered closed.

"Yes, sweetheart. Just like that. Now stroke me, like...ah, *yes*." His head fell back as he guided her hand up and down his shaft. Georgiana stared, fascinated as the rigid length in her hand grew impossibly harder. The swollen head flushed and wept, turning the tip a dark, glossy red.

"So good, Georgiana. Harder, sweetheart, please…please, ah, *ah*…" He seemed to grow more desperate with every caress, broken pleas breaking from his lips and his hips jerking as he thrust his hot, straining length into her fist.

Georgiana bit her lip, an intoxicating sense of triumph sweeping through her as her gaze darted from his face to the twitching length in her palm. *She* was giving him this pleasure—*she* who'd always thought of herself as the perennial virgin spinster—was making this beautiful man shudder and moan and plead for her.

It was…heady, touching him like this, so much so she wanted to get closer, touch him everywhere. Georgiana rose to her knees, her hand still moving up and down his length, and pressed her open mouth to his.

He let out a helpless groan as she darted her tongue out to lick at his bottom lip, and a hard, muscular arm wrapped around her waist, his hand settling low on her back to press her harder against him. "Are you teasing me, princess?"

Was she? All Georgiana knew was that she wanted to wring more of those delicious pleas from him. "Perhaps I am, a little."

"Teasing a rake?" His hand slid lower to cup her bottom. "Do you think that's wise, Miss Harley?"

Georgiana's lips curled against his. "Well, it's been delightful so far."

He nuzzled her neck before catching her earlobe in his teeth, his tiny bite making her shiver. "Oh, princess. We haven't even begun."

"You mean, there's more?" Georgiana knew there *was* more. Cecilia and Sophia had, for better or worse, shared every breathless detail of their experiences with her, but she hadn't understood until this moment that no one could explain what it would mean, or how it would feel to her to be with the man she loved.

She wanted Benedict. Desire pooled in her lower belly, and every inch of her skin burned for his touch, but her heart, the swell of tenderness there…no one had told her about that.

Because they couldn't. This moment belonged to her and Benedict alone.

She met his heavy-lidded dark eyes, saw the softness in them as he gazed down at her, and her heart flailed in her chest, its frantic rhythm both exquisite and painful at once.

Slowly, she began to stroke him again, pressing the weeping head against the soft skin of her belly, her mouth opening when she felt a streak of dampness there.

Benedict sucked in a sharp breath, then caught her wrist to still her hand. "Stop."

Georgiana didn't want to stop. She wanted to press her lips to his and make him fall apart for her. "No, I want...Benedict!" She squealed and threw her arms around his neck as he tumbled her onto her back in the bed.

"I know what you want, sweetheart." Benedict buried his face in the curve of her neck, nuzzling her there as he eased her legs open and settled himself between them.

Georgiana sank her hands into his hair as he dropped a string of tender kisses from her neck to the hollow of her throat.

"Do you trust me to take care of you, Georgiana?" He brushed her hair from her forehead, his dark eyes serious as they held hers.

He even had to ask? A small smile drifted over Georgiana's lips and she opened her legs wider, cradling his hips between her thighs. "Yes."

He drew in a deep, shaky breathy and reached between them to stroke her, teasing and pinching her tiny bud until she was slick with arousal, and gasping and arching against him. "I—I need—"

"Sshh. I've got you, princess," he whispered, shifting his hips so the tip of his cock nudged against her throbbing center. He didn't thrust inside her, but remained still, caressing her damp folds and suckling and licking her nipples as he let her get used to the sensation of him between her legs.

Soon that slight heaviness there wasn't enough, and she was writhing against him, soft whimpers on her lips. She wanted...she wanted...

"Oh!" Georgiana's back arched as he sank one long finger inside her.

Benedict gazed down at her, his lips parting. "Does that feel good, sweetheart?"

Georgiana's reply was lost in a strangled moan as he shifted his hips again, dragging the head of his cock over her center at the same time as he stroked his finger inside her, taking up an easy rhythm, his glittering dark eyes on her face. He kept up the slow, steady thrusts until her hips began to move to the pulses of his finger inside her.

Then he added a second finger, groaning as her legs fell open to welcome him inside. "God, look at you. So beautiful, and so wet for me. Do you want me, Georgiana?"

"Yes!" She clawed at the sheets beneath her, desperate. "Please..."

She cried out in protest when he suddenly withdrew his fingers, her head thrashing on the pillow at being left empty and aching, but he caught her chin in his hand to still her. "Look at me, Georgiana."

She stilled, meeting his hot, dark gaze.

"I need to see your face when I take you," he gritted out, his voice hoarse. "Do you feel me, sweetheart? Do you feel how much I want you?"

As he spoke, he was pressing into her, at once impossibly large and hard inside her and somehow necessary at the same time.

Then he gave a quick, hard thrust and a sharp pain exploded inside Georgiana. She sucked in a breath, stunned, but Benedict was there, stroking her damp hair back from her face and murmuring to her, tender words of praise mixed with regret at having hurt her, until at last the burning pain receded, and her body relaxed around his.

He began to move then, slow, gentle strokes at first, crooning to her as he kissed her lips and neck and teased his tongue into the hollow of her throat, and she was so lost in his kisses, so lost in *him* she wasn't aware she'd wrapped her legs around his waist and was urging him on, her body and her words begging him for more.

"Benedict, please, *please…*"

He threw his head back with a groan when she sank her nails into the sweat-slick muscles of his back, the cords of his neck straining as he worked his hips to give her what she needed. "Come for me, princess. I need to feel you come…"

Georgiana didn't understand what he meant, but her body cooperated instinctively, pulling tighter with each snap of his hips, pushing her closer and closer to the edge of the peak, then holding her there for a breathless instant until the tension inside her began to unravel in warm waves of bliss, and she clutched at Benedict, lost in pleasure as she cried out his name.

She clung to him as he went rigid above her, a hoarse groan tearing from his chest as he took his pleasure. She held him tightly against her as the final spasms rocked him, a dazed smile on her lips as damp heat rushed between her legs.

Then his lips were in her hair, and his whispered words in her ears, and she was falling, falling into a dark, soft place where no one had to go away, and she and Benedict might stay here forever, with his arms wrapped around her and his heart beating against her cheek.

Chapter Twenty-two

It was strange how the night could drag on endlessly when one wished for it to be over, but pass in the blink of an eye when one wished it might linger forever.

Benedict was still asleep when Georgiana woke. His warm chest was pressed closely to her back and his arms were wrapped snugly around her. His soft exhalations tickled her skin and stirred the loose hairs at the back of her neck, and she squeezed her eyes closed to savor the sensation.

If she could have remained here like this with him forever, she would have everything she ever wanted. Something had woken her, though—a log falling to pieces in the fireplace. Despite the darkness, real life was already stirring, already prying into the private cocoon they'd woven around themselves.

London loomed large on the horizon, but she wouldn't think of it now. Not yet. Not while she was still here with him. Their time together was nearly over, but right now this was her world, the only one that existed.

Everything else could wait.

Georgiana slid from his arms and raised herself onto an elbow, a delicious flutter in her chest as she gazed down at his sleeping face. His sensuous lips were parted, his hair tousled, and a faint flush stained his cheekbones. His cravat and shirt, his waistcoat and coat were on the floor beside the settee where he'd tossed them when he stripped them off last night, and her fond gaze lingered on his bare skin, the smattering of dark red hair on his chest.

He looked like a different man when he was asleep. More powerful somehow, without the layers of clothing covering his body and hiding the hard, tight muscles of his shoulders and arms. Those arms had been wrapped around her, and those long fingers had tangled in her hair, and her own hands had stroked the hard planes of his chest.

Georgiana gave into the urge to brush the wayward lock of dark red hair from his forehead. Benedict stirred at her touch and opened his eyes. His lips curled in a smile the moment he saw her face. "Good morning, Miss Harley."

"Good morning, Lord Haslemere." She returned his drowsy smile even as her heart gave a painful throb in her chest.

He pressed a sleepy kiss behind her ear before stretching with a contented groan. "Are you hungry, princess?" He rose from the bed, and Georgiana curled into the warm spot he left behind, pressing her face into the sheets to inhale his scent.

"I'm famished."

Georgiana peeked over the edge of the coverlet to find Benedict standing by the table, peering into the hamper. His thick hair was mussed, his chest bare, and his breeches hanging low on his lean hips. Despite the heaviness of her heart, her breath caught in her chest. If this was how he looked freshly tumbled from the bed, it was no wonder every lady in London wanted him.

But he wasn't with any of those ladies. He was with *her*, and she intended to take advantage of the little time they had left together. "Are there any quince preserves left?"

"We finished them yesterday." He rummaged through the hamper. "Bread with butter, sliced ham, boiled eggs and...ah, here we are." He held up a jar with a triumphant air. "Another jar of preserves. Strawberry, this time."

"I suppose the strawberry will have to do." Georgiana attempted a pout, but a grin rose to her lips instead. "May I have bread with some butter and preserves, please?"

Benedict's gaze roved over her, lingering on her lower lip caught between her teeth, and an answering grin tugged at the corner of his lips. "You, Miss Harley, may have anything you wish for."

Not anything. I can't have you.

She pushed the thought away, unwilling to say it aloud and break the spell between them. Instead, she arched a coy eyebrow at him. "Anything?"

Benedict was arranging the rolls he'd found in the hamper on a cloth, but at her suggestive drawl, he raised half-lidded eyes to her face. "Anything, Georgiana. Everything."

"There *is* one thing I'd like." She beckoned to him with a quirk of her finger.

He took in the long waves of her hair tumbling over her bare shoulders, and the strong column of his throat moved in a swallow. "I'm at your command." He paused at the fireplace, coaxing it back into a blaze before settling himself on the edge of the bed. He gazed at her for a moment, then held a piece of bread generously slathered with butter and preserves to her lips.

Georgiana opened, sighing with pleasure as he fed her.

"The strawberry preserves meet with your approval, then?" Benedict asked, his voice husky.

"They do, indeed." She licked her lips. "They're lovely and sweet."

He watched her with hot, dark eyes as the tip of her tongue darted out to lick daintily at the corner of her mouth. "Are they? May I have a taste?"

"Of course." She held the piece of bread out to him.

He took it, but instead of biting it he leaned forward and ran his tongue over her lower lip. "Mmm. That *is* sweet. I don't think I've ever tasted any sweeter, but just to be sure..."

He held the bread to her lips. Georgiana took an obedient nibble, the sweet flavor rolling over her tongue before the bread was gone again, abandoned on the table, and his mouth was there, hot and tart with strawberries, nibbling on her parted lips before he teased his tongue between them and plunged inside. He devoured her with a seemingly endless hunger until she was moaning, her lips swollen from his kisses and her fingers clutching desperately at his hair. "Benedict—"

"Lie down, back against the pillows." His voice was strained, his touch urgent as he eased her onto her back with a gentle tug on her hips. "Yes, like that." He lay on top of her, settling his hips between her legs and pressing his open lips to her throat.

Georgiana arched her neck, offering it to him. "I thought you were hungry."

"Oh, I am." He buried his face in the crook of her neck and inhaled deeply before dropping a chain of wet, open-mouthed kisses down her throat to the tops of her breasts. "Starving."

She sank her fingers into his hair, tugging hard to urge him lower.

"Beautiful." He slid his hand down her throat and over the center of her chest before cupping a breast in his palm. Georgiana let out a helpless groan when he dragged his thumb over her nipple.

That soft, breathless groan seemed to madden him. He became merciless, wringing helpless moans and gasps from her as he toyed with the reddened peaks, circling and teasing until Georgiana was writhing beneath him, and she pressed the back of her hand over her mouth to smother her incoherent whimpers.

But Benedict wouldn't allow that. "Don't. I want to hear how much you want me." He took her wrists in a firm grip, dragged them over her head, and held them there with one hand as his mouth hovered over her breasts, his hot breath caressing the enflamed peaks. He pinched one lightly between his fingertips, making Georgiana quiver in his arms. "God, you're so beautiful like this, so responsive. Would you beg me, Georgiana?" he crooned wickedly in her ear. "Beg me to suckle you?"

Georgiana arched up into the warm weight of his body over hers, ready to do whatever he demanded, but despite his roguish teasing, Benedict didn't make her beg. He settled his hot mouth over one nipple and sucked gently on the tender bud. "Let go, princess. Let me hear you cry out for me."

There was nothing Georgiana could do but succumb to his sensuous demands and give voice to the sighs and moans building in her throat as he slowly—so slowly—took her closer and closer to the edge of the precipice she'd tumbled over the night before with his sinful, beautiful mouth.

And all the while he was murmuring to her, whispered words of praise and passion, tenderness, and arousal, and…love? Georgiana didn't know, she couldn't think, couldn't hear his breathy words above the thunderous pounding of her own heart, but as his lips slid over her skin, his whispered words like a prayer, she told herself she could feel his love in every breath, every touch.

Was this what it felt like to let go, to let her emotions flow through her like cool water between her fingers? This was the thing she'd spent all those years fighting against, running from? So many years of fear, and in the end, it had been the easiest thing in the world to simply let go.

To let herself fall in love…

Or was it only easy because it was him? Benedict Harcourt, London's most desirable rogue—a man she'd thought of as having no principles, no true feeling—had been the one who taught her how to love.

A quiet sob left her throat at what she'd almost lost, and what she still had to lose.

Benedict had reduced her to a quivering, sobbing mass of aching flesh by the time he ceased his sensual assault and finally lifted his mouth from her breasts. His dark, glittering eyes met hers. "Do you trust me, Georgiana?"

How could he even ask? Didn't he know, didn't he see she'd given him everything? She cupped his face in her hands, smiling at the tickle of his bristles against her palm. "I do."

His answering smile was both tender and wicked at once. "Then you'll let me kiss you?"

"I…of course, I will. You *have* been kissing me, haven't you?"

Benedict slid his warm hand slowly down her side and settled it on the slight swell of her belly. "This is a different kind of kiss."

A different kind of kiss? As far as Georgiana knew, there was only one kind. "How is it—"

"Do you remember the painting in Madame Célestine's entryway? The one I caught you staring at, where the gentleman's face was here?" He parted her thighs with his knee and cupped her between her legs, one long finger sinking inside to stroke her.

Georgiana fell back against the bed with a gasp. Oh, she remembered it. How could she forget it? The man on his knees beside the settee, the lady's legs parted, and the rapturous expression on her face, her head thrown back in ecstasy—

"That's how I'm going to kiss you, Georgiana," Benedict crooned, opening her legs and moving down the bed. "This kiss will be unlike any you've felt before. I'm going to make you cry out for me."

"I—" That was as far as Georgiana got before Benedict settled between her legs. She sucked in a breath as his soft lips delved into the nest of darker brown hair between her thighs. "Oh!"

For a moment, she was too shocked to move, and a moment was all it took for Benedict to render her utterly speechless with the sinful, delicious strokes of his tongue against her swollen, hungry core. He seemed to know just what to do, just how to kiss and lick and nibble on that tender flesh to make her gasp and squirm in his grasp.

Not because she wanted to get away from him, but because she wanted *more*. "Benedict, please…"

"Shhh. I've got you." He did, and he was utterly ruthless when it came to giving her pleasure. He pinned her hips to the bed, nudged his broad shoulders between her legs to keep them open, and just…devoured her.

And she…she writhed and whimpered and cried out for him, just as he said she would.

One low, harsh moan after another tore from his chest with every drag of his tongue over her core, spurred on by her hoarse cries and her wild tugging on his hair. She couldn't be still, couldn't be silent as he edged her slowly, inexorably toward the edge she'd balanced on the night before, when he'd been inside her and every thrust of his hips had brought her closer, closer, warmth gathering in her belly and between her legs until it pulled so tight and hot there was nothing else for it to do but explode—

"Benedict!" Georgiana arched closer to his teasing lips as she unraveled. He stayed with her, his strokes gentling as he coaxed her down the other side.

He didn't stop until he'd wrung the last shudder from her, and she was lying in a boneless heap in the middle of the bed. Then he pressed a sweet kiss to the inside of her thigh before crawling up the bed and dropping another kiss onto her forehead. "You look pleased," he murmured, grinning down at her.

Georgiana gazed up at him. His cheeks were flushed, his lips glossy and his hair standing on end from her frantic fingers, and she thought she'd never seen a more beautiful sight in her life. "Nearly as pleased as you do," she said, with a teasing tap on his chin.

Another one of the wicked grins Georgiana had come to love drifted over his lips. "If I could, I'd spend every morning with you in just this way, making you squirm and cry out for me."

But he couldn't spend every morning thus, and neither could she, no matter how much she might want to. The thought cast a dim cloud over her pleasure, but Georgiana pushed it aside before it obliterated all the beauty of their time together.

Instead, she let her teeth sink into her lower lip as she slid her hands down his muscular back toward the tempting curves of his arse. "I like making *you* cry out for me, too."

"Oh?" A grin quirked his lips. "Is that so, Miss Harley?"

"It is." Georgiana let her fingers wander under the waistband of his breeches and squeeze.

He gave her a scandalized look. "Did you just *pinch* my arse?"

A very uncharacteristic giggle slipped from her lips. "If I did, it's your own fault."

"I beg your pardon, madam. How it is *my* fault?"

"If you didn't wear such tight breeches your, er…the back of you wouldn't be as likely to catch a lady's attention."

He stared down at her for a moment, mouth hanging open, then threw his head back in a laugh. "Are you saying you've been sneaking peeks at my arse?"

"Well, not *just* that." Georgiana moved her hands to the front of his breeches and slipped loose one of the buttons of his falls. "Your legs, too."

His eyes widened as she slid the other button free. "That's not very… ladylike of you."

"Is that a complaint, my lord?" Georgiana stroked her palm over the hard plane of his stomach, inching lower with every caress.

His breath caught, and he swallowed. "No."

"No, I rather thought not." She might not know much about a gentleman's anatomy still, but she knew a great deal more than she had last night, and she knew he was aroused, both by the flush of color high on his cheekbones, and, more importantly, the hard length rising from the crumpled fabric of his falls.

Georgiana teased her fingertips around the waistband of his breeches. They slipped off easily when she gave them a little tug. "There. That's better."

"Better for what? Do you intend to ravish me, Miss Harley?"

"It crossed my mind, yes." Georgiana let her fingers drift over the narrow trail of dark hair low on his belly.

"I was hoping you'd say that." Without warning Benedict grabbed her around the waist, tumbled onto his back and dragged her on top of him. His fingers closed on the hem of her shift, and with a quick flick of his wrist he tugged it over her head. "Come here, love, your thighs on either side of my...*yes*," he hissed, when he had her straddling his hips.

Georgiana squirmed on top of him, already breathless. He'd hardly touched her yet, but the delicious pressure was already building in her belly again. "Benedict, I—"

She broke off with a choked gasp as he reached between her thighs to stroke the eager bud hidden in her damp folds. His dark gaze never left her face as he circled and teased, harsh breaths tearing from his chest. "God, look at you. Your hair wild, lips swollen, that flush on your cheeks. I could watch you like this..."

Forever.

He didn't say it, and Georgiana pretended the word didn't echo in her heart, all the louder for remaining unspoken. Instead she ran her hands over his shoulders and chest, a small smile curling her lips when a stroke of her fingertip around his nipple made him suck in a breath. "Take my cock in your hand, Georgiana."

Georgiana lifted his rigid length from his taut stomach and gave him a leisurely stroke, her fingers caressing his shaft and cupping the head.

"*Ah.*" He jerked beneath her and grasped her hips. "Put it inside you."

She raised herself to her knees and pressed the dripping head to her core. "I don't know what—"

"Sink down onto me, love. Slowly. Yes...God, yes."

Benedict was panting as she lowered herself onto him, her eyes widening as his stiff length eased inside her. "Oh, I...Benedict, I want..."

"You want to come, princess?" Benedict was trying not to move, to let her take him in as slowly as she needed, but he was biting his lip, his hips twitching with the effort to remain still. "Just a little more. Slowly... you're so wet, Georgiana. I can feel how much you want me."

Oh, she did. She *did* want him, so much her knees were shaking as she took him in, her body softening around him as he filled the empty place inside her until at last, at last she'd taken all of him.

Benedict groaned, his neck arching as his head fell back against the pillow. "You're so perfect, Georgiana." His hips jerked helplessly against hers, nudging his cock deeper. "Ride me, sweetheart."

Georgiana could deny him nothing. She did as he commanded, whimpering when he reached between her thighs to rub a tormenting finger against her aching nub as he thrust up into her. She let the pleasure seize her, suck her into the vortex until everything blurred around her, and she knew only Benedict, his big, warm hands clutching her hips, his hoarse cries as he nudged her closer, closer...

She cried out when the pleasure rolled over her. She braced her hands on his chest and threw her head back, her thighs trembling, tears she wouldn't let fall swimming in her eyes. Her name was on Benedict's lips and his hands tangled in her hair as he took her with him, over the edge and into bliss.

* * * *

The room was quiet, the only sound the faint hiss of the fire as it burned low in the grate.

They'd have to leave soon. London was waiting.

Georgiana was sprawled across Benedict's chest, her hair wild and her skin damp. He'd gathered her against him as their breathing calmed, and she'd drifted into a doze.

He pressed a tender kiss to her temple, twining one of her curls around his finger. He'd opened his mouth more than a dozen times to beg her to come to North America with him, but closed it a dozen more without uttering a single word.

She had a life here—a home, friends, and a purpose that gave meaning to that life. What did he have to offer her that could compete with that? A treacherous ocean journey, and an uncertain future. There wasn't even time for him to marry her before he sailed for North America.

He'd be asking her to risk everything for him, and he couldn't even promise he'd be able to make her happy. No. He might not be as selfless a man as he should be, but there was no way he'd ever ask her to give up everything for him.

But there was one thing he could give her, something that would make her happy. Once he was gone, thousands of miles away, if he could think of her as happy, he might be able to grab and hold onto just a tiny bit of happiness for himself without her.

"Tell me about your plans for the Mill Street building. What are your hopes for the next Clifford School?" She'd been dreaming of her school for years now, putting all of her energy into it, and he couldn't imagine a better way to spend the little time they had left than to hear her talk about it.

She woke from her doze, and let her head roll against his chest with a sigh. "I didn't find Clara Beauchamp, Benedict. I didn't help Jane. I didn't fulfill my promise, and I can't accept the Mill Street—"

"Don't, Georgiana." Benedict's arms tightened around her to hush her. "You *can* take it, and you will. If you don't, it will sit there empty, of no use to anyone. I trust you to use it wisely. Don't deprive me of the chance to do something worthwhile."

She remained quiet for a time, drawing patterns over the backs of his hands with her fingertips. "If you truly wish for it, I'll do as you ask."

Benedict pressed a soft kiss to her temple. "I do wish it."

Silence fell between them, but Georgiana broke it before it became too heavy by laying a tentative hand on his chest. "What of you, Benedict? Your home here, your servants, all your things. Will you just leave it all behind?"

"Yes. Darlington will look after my interests here, and I have trustworthy servants. They'll take care of things until I..." He'd been about to say *until I return*, but he broke off without speaking the words. The truth was, he'd likely never return to England, and it was best if he didn't hold out any hope this journey would be temporary. He and Jane and Freddy needed to build a new life, and there was no way he could do that if he was constantly longing to return home.

To return to Georgiana.

"I suppose they don't matter, do they?" Georgiana's voice wasn't quite steady. "Clothing, carriages, horses—I used to think you cared about those things, but I was wrong."

"Georgiana Harley, *wrong*?" Benedict attempted a teasing tone, but his throat was too tight for mirth, and it was a dismal failure. "What do I care about, then?"

"People." Georgiana's voice was quiet. "Your sister and nephew, your friends. They all mean more to you than anything else."

You mean more to me, Georgiana. You mean everything.

He wanted to say the words aloud, to tell her it was killing him to leave her—tell her that he loved her. Holding it back was tearing his heart to shreds, but he couldn't speak to her of love when he'd be gone by this time tomorrow.

So he said nothing, just lay quietly with her cradled in his arms, burying his face in her hair and breathing in her scent so he might recall it, and lose himself in the memory of her once he was gone.

Georgiana was quiet as well, but she stirred when he dropped a kiss on her forehead. "It won't end here."

Benedict couldn't have said why, but her softly spoken words made him stiffen. "What do you mean? What won't end here?"

"My pursuit of Kenilworth." She looked up at him, surprise crossing her face at his expression. "Surely, you didn't think Lady Clifford and I would just drop it, and let Kenilworth get away with what he's done?"

That was precisely what Benedict had thought, fool that he was. He should have known better. "Georgiana—"

She struggled upright and pulled free of his arms. "He had Lord Draven *attacked*, Benedict. He hurt Clara Beauchamp, and Jane and Freddy—"

Benedict tugged her back into his arms and trapped her against his chest. "Do you think he won't do the same to you? Kenilworth is a monster, Georgiana. He'll hurt you if you keep up your pursuit!"

"And he'll hurt someone else if I don't! I know he's dangerous, Benedict, but I have Lady Clifford and Daniel to help—"

"*No!*" Benedict grabbed her chin and forced her to look at him. "I forbid it, Georgiana."

She jerked her chin free. "I beg your pardon, Lord Haslemere, but you don't have the right to forbid me anything. As long as there's a chance Clara Beauchamp is still alive—"

"There *isn't* a chance! Damn it, Georgiana, she vanished six years ago, and not a single person has seen her since."

"That's not true! Jane said—"

"Jane got a fleeting glimpse of a fair-haired lady in a darkened carriage, nothing more. Lady Tilbury said she hadn't seen Clara since she disappeared." Benedict clutched at his hair, torn between anger and panic. "Even you and Lady Clifford thought Jane made a mistake."

"Lady Tilbury denied it, yes, and I believed her at first, but I've changed my mind. She lied to me about something else, so she wouldn't hesitate to lie about this, as well."

"What do you mean? What did she lie about?"

"She never said a word to me about a liaison between Clara and Kenilworth. Given she was a great intimate of Clara's mother, I find it difficult to believe Lady Tilbury didn't know about it. It puts her denial in doubt."

Benedict's head was spinning. Could Clara Beauchamp really still be alive, and hiding in London? "What else did Jane say about Lady Tilbury the night she came to the Clifford School?"

Georgiana's brow furrowed. "Not much. Just that Lady Tilbury never leaves her country estate in Herefordshire, but that she'd come to London this spring with her grandson."

Her *grandson*? This was the first Benedict had ever heard of Lady Tilbury having a grandson. Lord Tilbury, who'd been a friend of his father's, had been killed in a hunting accident more than thirty years earlier, and Lady Tilbury had never remarried.

But perhaps Georgiana had it wrong, and the child Lady Tilbury had brought to London was her ward, or—

Benedict stilled, his eyes meeting Georgiana's. "How old is the child?"

Georgiana frowned. "I don't know. Jane didn't say, but young, I think. Jane said the boy was sickly, and Lady Tilbury had come to London to consult with Doctor Cadogan."

Benedict digested this, his heart racing. "Lady Tilbury's country estate is in Herefordshire, you said? Didn't Lord Draven's new housemaid also say she's from Herefordshire?"

"I think so, yes."

It wasn't that remarkable a coincidence, given how many people from Herefordshire came to London, but taken all together...

"Lady Tilbury never had any children, Georgiana. That boy isn't her grandson. When Jane told me Freddy isn't the duke's heir, I assumed she meant Lord Draven was Freddy's father, but—"

"But there was never anything between Jane and Lord Draven. She must have meant something else entirely." Georgiana's wide eyes met his. "Perhaps she meant—"

"That Freddy isn't the duke's *firstborn* son." If Clara and Kenilworth truly had married, and Clara had given birth to a son, then that child, and not Freddy, was the heir to the Kenilworth dukedom.

Georgiana grabbed Benedict's hand. "Lady Tilbury, who never leaves her estate in Herefordshire, suddenly appears in London with a boy who *isn't* her grandson, then Clara Beauchamp, who hasn't been seen in six years, is spotted in a carriage outside Lady Tilbury's townhouse? If Clara *is* alive, concern for her sickly child might have lured her to London."

"Lord Draven was attacked that same week, Georgiana. Mrs. Bury said she'd hired a housemaid from Herefordshire, and that she'd—"

"That she'd happened along at just the right time to accompany Lord Draven to Oxfordshire. If Clara really was in London, heard of Lord

Draven's attack, and feared for his life, she might have risked posing as a housemaid so she could come to High Wycombe to be with him. Jane said Clara had very fair hair—so fair it was almost white. Rachel has dark hair, but—"

"It might be a disguise."

"My God, Benedict." Georgiana covered her mouth with her hand. "I think...I think there's a chance Lord Draven's new housemaid might be Clara Beauchamp."

Chapter Twenty-three

Draven House looked even more silent and deserted than it had the day before. It couldn't have changed much in a single day, but somehow the sight of it made a shiver creep up Georgiana's spine in a way it hadn't yesterday.

"It looks a bit sinister, doesn't it?" She shifted uneasily in the saddle. "It's no wonder Lord Draven never comes here."

"It must have been handsome once." Benedict blinked up at the house, eyes narrowed against the glare of the early morning sun. "It could be again, with a family to breathe life into it."

Georgiana glanced up at the glassy windows peering down on them from above like a dozen sightless eyes. Lord Draven was behind one of them, lying still and lifeless in his bed. Would he or Clara Beauchamp ever get a chance to live a life here, after what Kenilworth had done to them?

She tapped her heels into the horse's flanks, breaking free of the tree line. They wouldn't get the answer standing here. "Shall we leave the horses with Peter?"

Benedict followed her toward the stables, but Peter was nowhere to be found. It was as clean and organized as ever, with every shred of hay in its proper place, but the few horses there were whinnying and tossing their heads.

"I don't like this. The horses are agitated. We need to get up to the house." Benedict leapt from the saddle and strode over to an empty stall, leading his horse behind him, but when he tried to swing open the stall door it refused to budge. "It's stuck."

"Is something blocking the door?" Georgiana dismounted and hurried over to Benedict.

He scaled the stall door and was about to drop down the other side when he froze, sucked in a breath, then let it out with a curse that made Georgiana stop in her tracks. "Jesus." His face paled as he stared down into the stall below. "Quickly, Georgiana. It's Peter."

Georgiana rushed forward as Benedict dropped down to the floor, dread pooling in her stomach. The stall door was too high for her to see over it, but she could hear Benedict dragging something across the floor. A moment later the door flew open, and what she saw on the other side made her gasp.

Peter was crumpled on the floor, blood running down his face. His white shirt was splattered with it, and it was pooling in the hay beneath him.

"Oh, no. No. Peter?" Georgiana darted forward and landed on her knees on the floor beside him. "Peter, can you hear me?"

Benedict caught Peter under his arms and heaved him to a sitting position, bracing his back against the wall. He tapped Peter's cheek until the boy's eyes fluttered open. "That's it. Wake up now, Peter."

Peter stared at them for a moment, his gaze unfocused, then he let out a low moan and raised his hand to the back of his head. "My...my head hurts."

"Don't touch it, lad. Let me have a look first." Benedict caught Peter's hand and lowered it to his lap, then brushed aside the blood-soaked hair at the back of his head and prodded gently at the injury. "It's not as bad as it looks." His face was grim as his eyes met Georgiana's. "Bad enough, though."

Peter winced. "Something hit me. Back of my head."

"Not something. *Someone.*" Benedict shoved the scattered hay aside with his boot, reached down and plucked up a shovel. "There's blood on the blade."

"It has to be Kenilworth." Georgiana scrambled to her feet. "Clara, and Mrs. Ellery and Martha. We need to go to the house at once, Benedict."

"I'm coming with ye, my lord." Peter braced his hand on the wall and tried to rise, but he only made it as far as his knees before dizziness overtook him, and he crashed back down to the floor.

"No, Peter. You're in no shape for it. Here." Benedict snatched off his cravat and handed it to Georgiana. "Stay here, and bind his wound as best you can."

"No!" Georgiana shot to her feet, her throat closing. "You're not going inside alone!"

Benedict grabbed her by the shoulders. "Yes, Georgiana, I am. There's nothing you can say to change my mind. You only waste time quarreling with me. Stay here and tend to Peter. I'll be back out to fetch you soon."

Georgiana stared up into those flashing dark eyes and could see at once arguing with him was pointless. So, she took the cravat without a word.

Benedict, who knew her well enough by now to be suspicious of such silent obedience, peered at her from the door of the stall, eyes narrowed. "I mean it, Georgiana. Stay here. Promise me."

Georgiana gave him a brief nod, but she said nothing. If Benedict had returned by the time she was finished binding Peter's wound, then she'd do precisely as he asked, and they wouldn't have a problem. If he wasn't back by then, well...

The less she said about what she'd do then, the better it was for them both.

Benedict hurried from the stables and Georgiana turned to Peter with what she hoped was a reassuring smile. She lowered herself to the floor beside him, folded the cravat into thirds, then pressed the thick pad of linen over the injury at the back of Peter's head. "Here. Hold that to your wound while I fetch some water."

She left Peter propped against the wall and searched the stables until she found a bucket half-filled with fresh water. She dragged it back to the stall with her and busied herself with cleaning and then wrapping Peter's wound. Benedict was right—the wound was nasty, but not life-threatening, and by the time she'd finished, Peter was breathing evenly and he'd regained some of his color.

But Benedict still hadn't returned.

"You'll have a nasty cut and a knot the size of your fist, Peter, but you'll be fine." Georgiana rose to her feet and dusted the stray bits of hay from her skirt. "Keep the linen pressed to it. I'll be back in a moment."

"Nay, miss." Peter shook his head. "His lordship said as you're to wait here."

"His lordship isn't here, Peter." Georgiana gave the boy a sweet smile. "Just stay here and rest. I won't go far."

No farther than the main house, at any rate.

She hurried from the stables and crossed to the drive that led toward the kitchen door at the back, her gaze once again on the windows, still staring blindly down at her just as they had before. Except this time Benedict was behind one of them, and he wasn't going to be pleased if he saw her coming toward the house—

She stopped, a frown on her lips as her gaze landed on a window on the second floor.

Was that...?

She thought she'd caught a glimpse of something moving behind it—a flutter of the drapes, or a shadow, perhaps? Before she could make out what it was, it disappeared. She waited, but she'd either imagined it, or whatever had been there was now gone.

Georgiana hurried toward the house, but she hadn't taken more than a few steps before pausing again, her gaze drawn once more to a flicker of movement at the window. She shaded her eyes with her hand and squinted up at it, just in time to see it shiver in its frame, as if it were—

"Dear God."

The horrified whisper had hardly left her lips before a deafening crash rent the air. Jagged glass exploded outward and plunged two stories down, shattering on the ground below.

Georgiana gaped in disbelief at the place where the window had been seconds before, her brain sluggish with shock. For a moment she could only stare dumbly between the heap of glittering shards on the ground and the gaping hole above, struggling to make sense of what she was seeing.

Two men were grappling in front of the broken window, their furious shouts echoing in the clear morning air. Georgiana stared up at them, her heart leaping into her throat. She'd seen men fight, but never before had she seen anything like this. One man had the other by the throat, trying to squeeze the life out of him, and the second man was struggling to shove the first one out the window.

Benedict and Kenilworth, each of them intent on killing the other.

A sound left Georgiana's mouth, either a scream or a whimper. She didn't know which, nor was she aware that she was running, flying across the drive, a spray of pebbles at her heels and words on her lips, a plea, a prayer...

The kitchen door was unlocked—*thank God, thank God*—and she burst through it, only dimly aware that it was empty, with Mrs. Ellery nowhere to be seen, and no fire in the huge stone fireplace. She darted around the corner and up a flight of narrow stairs to a dusty entryway dominated by a sweeping staircase surrounded by dark paneling, with a massive bannister of carved wood.

She must have run up the stairs, but she was aware only of the pounding of her heart, her desperate heaving breaths echoing in her ears, and the other sounds—another crash of glass, the dull thump of fists pounding flesh, a man's grunt of pain, all of it growing louder as she neared the second-floor landing. A few steps from the door she heard Benedict's voice, low and furious, and the duke's, louder and mocking, and a woman, her voice high-pitched and panicked, and the sounds of a scuffle, the heavy crunch of boots over broken glass.

Georgiana tried to prepare herself for what she'd find when she crossed the threshold, to brace herself for the nightmare she was certain was waiting for her on the other side of that door, but when she got there she stumbled to a halt, a scream trapped in her throat.

There was no way to brace yourself, no way to prepare for *this*.

There was shattered glass everywhere—fragments scattered across the floor or ground to a glittering powder, wicked-looking shards standing like a row of jagged teeth in the window frame, and—

Blood.

Benedict's hands were covered with blood, his shirt sleeve soaked with it from a slash on his upper arm, and streaming down his face from a jagged cut on his forehead.

Georgiana stared at him in horror, her heart trapped in her throat.

If Benedict noticed her in the doorway, he gave no sign of it. All his attention was focused on Kenilworth, who was clutching a bloody shard of glass in his hand. The two men circled each other warily, mere steps away from the open window, each waiting for their chance to strike.

"You're never going to see Jane or Freddy again, Kenilworth." Benedict circled closer, forcing Kenilworth to back up, closer to the gaping hole.

One stumble, a single misstep, a push at the right time and the right angle, and one of them was going to fall through it. Georgiana knew it, felt it in the deepest part of herself where her most unspeakable nightmares lived.

Please, please don't let it be Benedict—

"How do you intend to stop me, Haslemere?" Kenilworth laughed, but it was a mockery of one, twisted and ugly. "Jane is my *wife*, and Freddy my son. They *belong* to me, and there's not a damn thing you can do to change that."

"No?" Benedict bared his teeth in a savage grin. "The English courts don't take kindly to bigamists, Kenilworth, even if they do happen to be dukes. Your marriage to Jane is illegal, and will be dissolved as soon as your crime is discovered. I wonder what all your London admirers will think, to see the great Duke of Kenilworth brought so low?"

Kenilworth tutted, as if disappointed. "Do you truly think a worthless rake like you is going to be the one to bring my secrets to light? I've kept them for six long years, Haslemere. It'll take a cleverer man than you to expose me."

Kenilworth lunged forward suddenly, slashing with the shard of glass in his hand. Georgiana's heart dropped as the jagged edge came within inches of Benedict's wrist, but he jumped back just in time, out of Kenilworth's reach. He dragged a hand over his forehead, and his sleeve came away drenched with blood. "Half a dozen people know what you've done, Kenilworth. Do you intend to kill us all?"

"No, just you, Haslemere, and Draven, of course. He doesn't look like he's in much of a condition to defend himself, does he?"

Kenilworth jerked his head toward the bed. Georgiana followed the gesture, and for the first time noticed the dark-haired housemaid—Rachel, or Clara—was there, her body between Kenilworth and the bed in which Lord Draven lay, pale and haggard, but very much awake.

"Oh, I think Clara and Jane will fall into line quickly enough when I threaten to take their sons away if they don't." Kenilworth was creeping forward as he spoke, edging closer to Benedict, trying to maneuver him toward the window. "You see, Haslemere, bigamist or not, those two boys are still my sons, and therefore mine to do with as I wish."

"You're not leaving this room, Kenilworth, unless it's through the window." Benedict darted forward and slammed his fist into Kenilworth's stomach. Kenilworth grunted, staggering under the blow, but he managed to keep his feet.

"Not good enough, Haslemere. You look a little unsteady, my friend. Is the blood loss making you dizzy? Pity. It looks like you're the one who's going out the window." Kenilworth's lips split in a bloodthirsty grin as he leapt forward and landed a blow to Benedict's knee. There was a sickening crunching sound, and Benedict's knee collapsed beneath him, sending him heavily to the floor.

Clara screamed, but her terrified shriek was drowned out by Georgiana's panicked shout. "Benedict!"

"*No*! Get back, Georgiana." Benedict held out a hand to stop her. "Don't come any closer."

"Your whore is very loyal to you, Haslemere." Kenilworth advanced on Benedict with slow, lazy steps. Then with a casual air, as if he were brushing dust from his boots, he landed a vicious kick to Benedict's chest. "She's not a conventional beauty, is she? But I quite like her, all the same. Perhaps I'll make her my mistress after you're dead."

"You'd better make sure I'm good and dead first, Kenilworth," Benedict snarled, his face a mask of fury. "Because if you lay a single finger on her, I'll kill you."

"You're hardly in a position to make threats." Kenilworth prepared to deliver another punishing kick, but Benedict rolled to the side and managed to stagger to his feet before Kenilworth could get close enough to land the blow. "You only delay the inevitable, Haslemere. Anyone can see you're nearly dead already."

Georgiana looked from Benedict to Kenilworth, despair gripping her and nearly sending her to her knees. Kenilworth was right. Benedict, dizzy with blood loss, could hardly keep his feet. Kenilworth would bide his time until Benedict lost consciousness, and then he'd shove him out the window, and that would be the end.

No one could survive a fall like that.

She had to *do* something.

Think, think...

A weapon. If she could find a weapon, something to strike Kenilworth with, something heavy enough, the blow would fell him, and from there she might be able to push him out the window. He was much bigger and stronger than she was, but she was quick, and he wouldn't be expecting her to attack him.

Georgiana frantically searched the room until her gaze landed on the fireplace poker. It was leaning against the wall beside Lord Draven's bed. It was much closer to her than it was to Kenilworth, but as soon as she lunged for it, Kenilworth would guess what she was doing, and he'd attack Benedict again.

She bit her lip in an agony of indecision, but with Benedict's life hanging in the balance, she had no other choice but to risk it. She kept one eye on Kenilworth as she crept closer to the fireplace, but before she could take another step, she glimpsed movement out of the corner of her other eye.

It was Clara Beauchamp.

Her gaze caught Georgiana's, and she tipped her chin subtly toward the poker. Clara was standing right next to the fireplace, and Kenilworth seemed to have dismissed her as a threat, because he wasn't paying any attention to her.

Georgiana held Clara's gaze, and gave a tiny nod of her head. A moment of perfect understanding passed between them, and then...

Then it was happening.

Clara seized the poker, and with one mighty heave sent it flying across the floor toward Georgiana. It clattered to a stop at her feet and she snatched it up and whirled around, her heart racing, every bit of rage she possessed focused on Kenilworth.

She heard a shout, but she didn't pause. With as much strength as she could muster, she raised the poker over her head, and smashed it across Kenilworth's back.

Kenilworth made a strange sound—a grunt of pain and surprise—then he hit the floor with a deafening crash. If Georgiana could have managed a second blow even half as brutal as the first, she would have finished him, but her arms were shaking, so she fell to the floor beside him and without a moment's hesitation began kicking him toward the broken window.

One shove, her feet braced against his back, two...dear God, he was heavy, so heavy, but the blow had stunned him, and he didn't resist.

At first.

Another shove, another...closer, then closer still, slowly, painstakingly but inexorably closer to the edge...

Georgiana was so intent on shoving him *out* and putting an end to the nightmare that was the Duke of Kenilworth that she didn't notice he'd grabbed Benedict by the ankle until Benedict began sliding across the glass-strewn floor toward the gaping window, clutched in Kenilworth's grasp.

"Benedict!" The scream tore from Georgiana's throat. She grabbed him by the arm, but the combined weight of Kenilworth and Benedict was too much for her. Benedict tried to kick loose from Kenilworth's hold, but Kenilworth held him in the inhuman grip of a man who was destined for death, and determined to take his enemy with him.

There was a scramble of footsteps behind them, but Georgiana saw nothing, knew nothing other than Benedict. She held on with all her strength as she looked into the eyes of the man she loved.

She knew what he was going to do before he did it.

The only thing he could do to save *her.*

"*No!* Benedict!"

He tore his arm loose from her hold.

"No!" She scrambled for him, but it was already too late. Kenilworth's lower body had slipped over the edge. He was clawing at Benedict, holding on with every last vestige of his strength, mere seconds from falling to his death. In that last instant, Benedict's dark eyes met hers, and Georgiana saw a world of love shining in their depths.

There was a shout—Clara's voice—and a flurry of activity beside Georgiana, and then Kenilworth was gone, tumbling over the edge with a terrified cry. Georgiana's howl of anguish followed, torn from the very depths of her soul, and she squeezed her eyes closed, unable to watch, unable to bear seeing Benedict fall...

Except incredibly, Benedict's arms were wrapped around her. Somehow, he was there beside her, on his back, tangled in a panel of the heavy silk drapery from Lord Draven's canopy.

He gathered her against his chest, blood still gushing from his wounds, but alive—somehow, impossibly, he was alive and holding her close, his voice hoarse as he whispered in her ear.

It's all right. I've got you. We're safe. I love you...

He said those words over and over, his hands in her hair and his lips at her temple. At last the anguish, the unthinkable anguish of losing him faded, and Georgiana, overwhelmed with love and gratitude, buried her face in his chest, and sobbed.

* * * *

Clara Beauchamp was as accomplished a nurse as Mrs. Ellery had said she was.

The slash on Benedict's arm still throbbed, the cut on his forehead still burned, and his knee ached like the very devil even after Clara's ministrations, but he didn't give a damn.

He didn't give a damn about anything but Georgiana, who was safely pressed against him, her arm around his waist and his wrapped protectively around her shoulders. What he really wanted was to take her back to the gamekeeper's cottage where they might have some privacy, but there were, er...a few details to be managed first.

Like the dead duke on the front drive of Draven House.

The magistrate was on his way, and would no doubt demand a detailed explanation as to why the Duke of Kenilworth was lying under a shattered window with a broken neck.

As for Benedict, try as he might, he couldn't work up any regret on Kenilworth's behalf. The man was a monster, and Benedict felt only relief knowing Jane and Freddy were free of him forever.

"More tea, Lord Haslemere?" Mrs. Ellery had been fluttering around them for the past hour, pressing cup after cup of tea on them and doing her best to stuff them with scones and cakes. "The best cure for a shock, my lord, is food."

"More tea would be delightful, Mrs. Ellery. Thank you." Benedict would have preferred a few stiff fingers of brandy, but Mrs. Ellery had suffered a shock of her own, and he couldn't bear to refuse her.

She and Martha, the other housemaid, had been bound and gagged and shoved into a cupboard in the stillroom by Kenilworth after he'd attacked Peter in the stables. There'd been no one here to protect them, so he'd made quick enough work of the two women.

Benedict shuddered to think what might have happened to them—and to Clara and Draven—if he and Georgiana hadn't come along when they did.

As it was, Peter had been sent home to rest and recover from his injuries. Martha had declared the country a "wicked, horrible place" and begged to return to London at once—a request Lord Draven had quickly granted.

As for Draven, he'd been ordered to bed by his fair-haired nurse, her dark wig now discarded, and he'd succumbed to her commands with the air of a man who'd be pleased to have her order him about for the rest of his life. Clara had disappeared to his bedchamber with him, but now she'd reappeared again, just in time to save Benedict from another cup of Mrs. Ellery's tea.

"I beg your pardon, Mrs. Ellery. Lord Draven would like to speak to Lord Haslemere and Miss Harley, if you can spare them."

"Yes, yes. Go on, then." Mrs. Ellery waved the tea cloth at them in a motherly gesture. "I'll keep the tea hot for you, Lord Haslemere."

"Er, that's kind of you, Mrs. Ellery." Benedict nodded his thanks, then he and Georgiana followed Clara up the stairs to see Lord Draven. The earl had been moved to another bedchamber, and was seated before the fire, waiting for them. He looked pale and exhausted and much too thin, but his lips curved in a smile when he saw Clara.

"Well Haslemere, Miss Harley." He raised an eyebrow as Georgiana and Benedict sat on the settee across from him. Clara settled herself beside him and took his hand in hers. "I don't know how you two got tangled up in this business, but I'm damned glad you did."

Benedict looked at Georgiana, then back at Lord Draven. "It's a long story, Draven. I'd be pleased to tell it to you sometime, but perhaps for now I'll simply say we did it to help my sister, Jane, without having the least bloody idea what we were getting ourselves into."

Lord Draven chuckled. "It's a web with many threads, all of them hopelessly tangled. I've no idea how you managed to sort them all out, but we'll always be tremendously grateful to you both."

"We had our suspicions, my lord, but it was Kenilworth himself who untangled the final threads." Georgiana's gaze drifted to Clara. "You were married to the Duke of Kenilworth, Miss Beauchamp, and you have a son together?"

"Yes. His name is Augustus. He'll be seven years old in September." Clara gave Benedict an uneasy glance. "I realize you have a nephew who—"

"It's all right, Miss Beauchamp. I'm aware Freddy isn't the heir to the dukedom. I care only that my sister, Jane, and Freddy are safe. The title and fortune are your son's by right. You'll get no trouble from my family."

Clara sagged against Lord Draven, relieved. "Thank you, my lord. When you and Miss Harley came here yesterday, I thought...that is, I feared you were here at the behest of the duke, and I...I didn't know what to do. I was terrified, but I couldn't bring myself to leave."

"You heard of Lord Draven's, er...unfortunate accident while you were at Lady Tilbury's in London, Miss Beauchamp?" Georgiana asked.

"It was no accident, Miss Harley. I was set upon by half a dozen of Kenilworth's ruffians. I don't remember much, but I have no doubt they intended to kill me. Kenilworth came here today to finish the job, and drag Clara away again." Lord Draven's face was tight as he gripped Clara's hand. "I shudder to think what he would have done to her."

Georgiana let out a deep sigh. "The Duke of Kenilworth is not at all what he appeared to be, is he?"

"I'm afraid not," Clara said on a sigh. "But to answer your question, Miss Harley, I *was* in London with Lady Tilbury when Lord Draven was attacked, yes. I hadn't set foot outside of Herefordshire in six years, but Augustus was ill, and I couldn't bear to let him out of my sight, so her ladyship reluctantly agreed to let me come with her as long as I took care to stay in the townhouse."

Lord Draven raised Clara's hand to his lips. "It's a miracle Jane saw her at all. She came straight to me that night to tell me she believed Clara was still alive. Jane didn't know a thing about Clara and Kenilworth until then. She came because she knew how devastated I was over Clara's disappearance, and for no other reason. Your sister has been a good friend to me, Haslemere."

Benedict's mouth twisted. "If Jane had suspected what a scoundrel Kenilworth was, she never would have married him. There's no excuse for *my* not knowing, however. I should have protected her."

Clara's blue eyes softened. "You must understand, Lord Haslemere, what a deep secret it was. Only myself, my mother, and Kenilworth knew about the marriage. Neither my mother nor I breathed a word about it because Kenilworth claimed his uncle, the duke, would disinherit him if he found out the truth."

Lord Draven nodded. "It's true, Haslemere. Even I didn't find out about the marriage until much later, after Clara disappeared. I believed her to be dead by then, and so never suspected Kenilworth of bigamy."

Benedict stiffened at the reminder, and Georgiana reached for his hand. "Such an odd coincidence, that Jane happened to be driving by at the precise time Miss Beauchamp was in the carriage."

"Yes. It makes me believe in fate." Lord Draven smiled. "As you've probably determined, Clara never made it back to Herefordshire once she left Lady Tilbury's. She coaxed Mrs. Bury into hiring her as a housemaid, and came with me here, to Draven House. Perhaps I'm a selfish man, Miss Harley, but I'm very glad she did."

"So, you've been hiding in Herefordshire for the past six years?" Benedict could hardly believe it. "It must have been awful, living every day in fear Kenilworth would discover you."

"It was worrying, yes. I was more fearful on Augustus's account than my own, however. Lady Tilbury took good care of Augustus and me. She's a dear friend."

"Dear enough to lie right to my face for you." Georgiana smiled to take the sting out of her words. "Though I don't see that she had much choice."

"None at all," Lord Draven said, his voice grim. "I wish I'd ended Kenilworth six years ago, the night Clara disappeared. When I think of the heartache that followed not just for me, but for Clara and Jane…"

"The duel, you mean?" Benedict leaned forward. "I confess to some curiosity about that."

"My father put a stop to it the night of the Christmas party, but I followed Kenilworth to London, and challenged him again there. I assure you, I was in deadly earnest, Haslemere. If I'd had my way, Kenilworth would have died that night."

"I've no doubt. You thought at first Kenilworth had ruined Miss Beauchamp?"

"Yes. At the ball that night I saw Kenilworth force Clara from the ballroom. I suspected something was amiss, so I followed them to the library. From what I overheard, I assumed Kenilworth had seduced her. I didn't find out until much later he'd married her a year earlier, then run off to London to spend her fortune."

"I was entirely deceived in Kenilworth's character." A spasm of pain crossed Miss Beauchamp's face. "I fancied myself in love with him, but it was a short-lived delusion. By the time he returned to Draven House for the ball, he'd inherited the dukedom, and wanted nothing more to do with his common bride. He'd set his sights on your sister by then, Lord Haslemere, leaving me with nothing but an empty purse, and…" She hesitated, her cheeks flushing. "A child in my belly."

Georgiana gasped. "Oh, no. How dreadful."

"I'm afraid it was. Kenilworth was afraid the child would be a boy. A son with common bloodlines wasn't good enough to be the Duke of Kenilworth's heir, so he packed me up into his carriage, took me to Southampton, and loaded me onto a ship bound for North America. I suppose he thought I'd die on the journey."

"But you didn't, Miss Beauchamp," Georgiana said fiercely. "You survived, and here you are."

"Yes, thanks to Lady Tilbury." Miss Beauchamp dashed a tear from her cheek. "Once Kenilworth was gone, I sneaked off the ship and made my way to her in Herefordshire with the little bit of money Kenilworth had given me. With her help, I survived." Clara turned to gaze at Lord Draven, love glowing in her blue eyes. "Now I will reap my reward, undeserved though it might be."

"Not undeserved, love." Lord Draven cast her an adoring look. "Never that."

Georgiana turned to Benedict, a tremulous smile on her lips. "You saved Bene—that is, you saved Lord Haslemere's life, Miss Beauchamp. As far as I'm concerned, you deserve everything good that befalls you."

A lump rose in Benedict's throat at Georgiana's words, and he pressed a fervent kiss to her hand. "Fate, indeed. She's smiled on us both, Draven, and I, for one, intend to make the most of it."

Chapter Twenty-four

Mill Street, London
Ten days later

"You mean to tell me, Georgiana, that Miss Beauchamp saved Lord Haslemere's life with a *bedcurtain*?"

"Well, there was a bit more to it than that, but yes. Lord Haslemere was mere seconds from toppling out the window when Miss Beauchamp tossed him one of the bed hangings, and he crawled back in."

Emma plopped down on the window seat beside Georgiana. "That must have been an extraordinary bed hanging."

"It was. Heavy silk, attached to a monstrous oak canopy. Lord Draven *is* an earl, after all. Don't all earls have grand beds with silken bed hangings?"

"I don't have the faintest idea what earls have." Emma glanced at Georgiana out of the corner of her eye. "I think you're more qualified to answer that question than I am, dearest."

It was the fourth time Emma had offered Georgiana a not terribly subtle invitation to confide her adventures with Lord Haslemere, and the fourth time Georgiana had failed to do so.

There was a part of her that longed to rest her head on Emma's shoulder and release the unbearable tension that had been building inside her these past ten days—all her worries and misgivings, her hopes and dreams—but she hadn't any idea where to start.

With the murderous Duke of Kenilworth? With Clara Beauchamp and Lord Draven, and the love story that had risen from the ashes of a tragedy six years ago? With the newly widowed Duchess of Kenilworth, who'd gained her freedom on the same day her son had lost his title and inheritance?

Or did she start with Benedict, the charming rake who wasn't truly a rake at all, but a wonderful, honorable man who'd somehow managed to burrow so deeply into her heart she couldn't draw a breath without thinking of him?

It was all so complicated, and touching, and wretchedly emotional she was sure to end up dissolving into a sniveling puddle of tears right here. Emma would be shocked, and a scene was sure to follow.

Georgiana detested scenes, and so she said nothing at all about any of it, but gestured instead to the garden outside the window, hoping to distract Emma. "I mean to put the eldest girls on tidying up that garden at once. It'll be a lovely place for us to walk in the spring and summer, won't it?"

"Hmmm. Lovely, yes."

Georgiana waited, but Emma didn't elaborate. "These window seats are perfect, aren't they? So many handsome bow windows in one house, and each with its own window seat. It's lovely, isn't it?"

"Hmmm. Lovely, yes."

"So spacious, as well!" Georgiana went on, growing desperate. "Just think, Emma! Five large bedrooms on both the second and third floors, and all the common rooms on the ground floor besides. The attics will make a lovely schoolroom for the younger pupils, won't it?"

"Hmmm. Lovely, yes."

"For pity's sake, Emma!" Georgiana threw her hands up in exasperation. "Is that all you have to say?"

"Oh, did you want me to say something more, Georgiana? Very well, then. I'll say this. I'm extremely cross with you."

"*Me*? Why, what did I do?" Georgiana tried to summon some dignified outrage, but her voice lacked conviction. She knew what she'd done, and if she'd been in her right mind, she'd have known Emma would never let her get away with it.

"I've been gone from London for *ages*, Georgiana. Ages, with no one but—"

"Such dramatics, Emma. It's hardly been ages—"

"*Ages*, with no one but Lady Crosby for company. Lady Crosby, Georgiana, who for all her kindness is sixty years old if she's a day. I've tatted enough lace to last me a lifetime, and—"

"I don't see what's so terrible about tatted lace—"

Emma held up her hand for silence. "In that time, you've bested a wicked duke, saved his duchess, reunited an earl with his long-lost love, and fallen in love with Lord Haslemere, and you have the *nerve* to sit here and talk to me about gardens and window seats?"

"I don't see what's so terrible about gardens and—"

"Don't you *dare*, Georgiana Harley. I don't want to hear another word about window seats. I have only one day to spend with you, and you've already wasted most of it with your dithering. I demand to have the entire story this *instant*. Start with Lord Haslemere."

Georgiana stared at her friend with wide eyes. Emma didn't often fall into tempers, and one didn't like to argue with her when she did. She'd be gone soon, as well, back to Lady Crosby to finish whatever business she'd undertaken for Lady Clifford. If Georgiana didn't confide in her now, she'd lose her chance.

Emma took her hand and ducked her head so she could see into Georgiana's eyes. "Come now, dearest. I can't bear to see you looking so sad."

I'm not sad. I don't get sad, I don't weep, and I don't...I don't...

Georgiana tried to push the words off the end of her tongue, but her chin was wobbling, and tears were stinging her eyes, and...and... "Dash it, this is all Benedict's fault."

Once a lady wept for a man once, she was certain to do so again, especially a man like Benedict Harcourt.

Emma's eyebrow ticked up at Georgiana's use of his Christian name. "Dear me. What did he do?"

"Why, the most horrible thing imaginable!" Georgiana gave a pathetic sniffle. "I can hardly think it, much less say it."

"Oh, no. Is it as terrible as that?" Emma's eyebrow twitched, just as it always did when she was concerned. "Tell it to me quickly, like when you have the stomachache and Winnie makes you drink one of her dreadful potions."

"He tricked me!" Georgiana wailed, covering her face with her hands. "He's so much cleverer than I ever dreamed, Emma, and so funny and caring and lovely, and he has such handsome eyes and such a sweet smile, and before I even knew what was happening, he—"

Emma pulled Georgiana's hands gently away from her face. "He made you fall in love with him."

"I was *told* he was a rake! I was *led to believe* he was a rake, and he isn't! Or, he was once, I daresay, but he isn't now, and I—I was *duped* into falling in love with him, Emma!"

Emma rolled her eyes. "No one will ever accuse you of being a romantic, Georgiana. But I don't see what's so terrible about falling in love, unless... does he love you, too?"

Georgiana wiped her eyes with her sleeve. "He told me he did, but at the time we were...he said it under unusually intense circumstances."

"You mean he said it while the two of you were engaged in—"

"No! My goodness, Emma!" Georgiana blushed to the roots of her hair. "He said it right after he climbed back through Lord Draven's window, mere seconds after escaping certain death. I daresay he would have said he loved whoever happened to be on the other side of that window."

"Did you believe him to be sincere at the time?"

"I...did." But then, what did she know about declarations of passionate love? Not a thing. She did know about common sense, however, and she could easily believe Benedict's words had been the truth of a moment only.

"But you're no longer sure of him."

Georgiana sighed. "Let's just say it's far easier to believe he loves me when he..."

When he'd been holding her tightly in his arms, pressing kisses to her temple, and whispering in her ear. But that had been more than a week ago. She and Benedict had returned to London that evening. He'd left her at the Clifford School with a dozen longing kisses, but he hadn't repeated his protestations of love.

She hadn't seen him since.

He'd returned to Oxfordshire at once with Jane, Freddy, Lady Tilbury, and Augustus for a grand reunion with Clara and Lord Draven. Jane and Clara were both adamant the two boys would come to love each other as brothers, and Lord Draven had been anxious to express his gratitude to Lady Tilbury.

It was bound to be a joyous occasion, but it was one for family only, and Georgiana wasn't family. She wasn't...anything, and that wasn't even the worst part.

Not for the first time, Emma seemed to read her mind. "There's something else worrying you, isn't there?"

"I...I don't know how to fall in love, Emma."

"My dear girl, it sounds as if you already have."

"Very well, then. I don't know how to *be* in love."

Georgiana expected Emma to laugh, or shrug and say that was nonsense, that everyone knew how to fall in love, to be in love, but that wasn't what she did.

Instead, a shadow passed over her face. "It amazed me, how quickly Sophia and Cecilia fell in love. Like it was nothing, as easy as falling into a field of daisies, or leaping into a cool pond on a summer's day. I wonder what that must be like."

There was a note of awe in Emma's voice. She stared at Georgiana for a long moment without speaking, then she swallowed and turned away. "Love requires trust, and vulnerability. That's not something that comes easily to either of us, is it?"

"No." Georgiana bit her lip to smother the wretched tears that were threatening once again. She did trust Benedict, and she was grateful to him. Perhaps he would break her heart, but he'd brought her closer to love than she'd ever thought possible.

There was something—surely there was something meaningful in discovering one had a heart to break?

Emma tried to smile, but she looked melancholy as she rose to her feet with a sigh. "I told Lady Crosby I'd be back by now, but before I go, there's one thing I want you to think about."

Georgiana reached up to squeeze the hand Emma lay on her shoulder. "What is it?"

"You *do* know how to fall in love, Georgiana. You've already done that part. So don't give up now, dearest. You're halfway there."

Emma bent down to kiss her cheek, and then she was gone, leaving Georgiana alone in the window seat, staring out into an overgrown garden. She remained there for a long time, watching the shadows lengthen.

The building was perfect, everything Georgiana had hoped it would be. All she'd wanted when this adventure with Benedict began was this building, a school for her girls, but now…she couldn't pinpoint the moment when it ceased to be all she needed to make her happy.

But here she was.

It was getting late, and Lady Clifford would be expecting her home, but perhaps she'd take a little wander upstairs first. It might cheer her up, and in any case, she wanted another look at the bedchambers to see if they might fit a desk in with the beds.

She lit a candle, mounted the stairs, and wandered down a long hallway on the first floor toward one of the largest of the bedchambers tucked into a back corner of the house. It was a spacious room with an attached sitting area, and had likely served as a grand bedchamber for some Earl of Haslemere or other.

There were still a few stray bits of furniture lying about, so Georgiana set her candle on a dusty table and, starting from one corner of the room, began to measure off the number of steps it took to reach the other corner. One, two, three…

Ping.

Four, five…

Ping.

She looked up at the noise, frowning. Dash it, it was interrupting her count. How many steps had she counted off, four or five? She retraced her steps to the corner and began again. One, two, three—

Ping.

Georgiana froze mid-step, her head jerking toward the window. That sound, it was familiar, like...pebbles hitting the glass. She flew toward the window, her heart rushing into her throat as she pushed aside a dusty, tattered drape.

And there was Benedict, standing on the dim street below as if he'd appeared there by magic. He was gazing up at the window, and as soon as he saw her a breathtaking smile rose to his lips, and he clasped his hands to his chest like some lovestruck hero in a Gothic romance.

Then he crooked his finger at her.

Georgiana's knees were shaking as she ran into the hallway and down the stairs. She tried to tell herself to calm, to remind her heart he might have come here to tell her goodbye, but it continued to flop about in her chest like a fish out of water.

Or no, no *that*. That wasn't a romantic image at all.

A fish in love?

Oh, Emma was right. She was hopeless when it came to romance, but love...well, that was something else altogether, because as soon as she lay eyes on Benedict beneath the window, her heart sprang to instant life, soaring inside her with such power and grace she might have skipped the stairs entirely, and floated to the ground floor below.

Benedict was waiting for her at the bottom of the stairs, arms open wide.

Georgiana didn't hesitate. She didn't pause to think or doubt or reason, but flew down the stairs and threw herself straight into his waiting embrace. "You're back! Why didn't you send word you—"

That was as far as she got before Benedict's lips were on hers, his kiss deep and wet and desperate, as if he'd been waiting a lifetime to kiss her. "God, I missed you so much, princess," he choked out between kisses, burying his hands in her hair. "It's been weeks and weeks."

"It hasn't even been two weeks," Georgiana protested, grinning against his lips.

"This is no time for math, Georgiana." He let out a low chuckle, his hands falling to her waist to tug her against him. "Anyway, it feels as if it's been years. I've been dreaming about tasting you since I left Draven's this afternoon. The ride to London nearly drove me mad."

"You, ah...you missed me, then?"

"*Missed* you?" Benedict gave her an incredulous look. "There I was at Draven's, Jane happier than I've ever seen her, Draven and Clara annoyingly in love, and Freddy and Augustus like brothers already, and all I could do was pout and snap at everyone, because all I wanted was you."

Georgiana peeked up at him from under her lashes, suddenly shy. "Really?"

"Yes, *really*, you maddening woman. Jane finally lost patience with me. She said I wasn't fit for company, and sent me back here to you."

Georgiana toyed with the buttons on his coat, avoiding his eyes. "I thought perhaps you'd thought better of…that you'd changed your—"

"No." He tipped her chin up and gazed down at her with dark eyes so filled with love it brought tears to Georgiana's eyes. "Never. I'm afraid you're stuck with me, because I'm mad for you, Georgiana. I love you to distraction, and I intend to…are you crying? *Again*?"

Georgiana threw her arms around his neck. "I love you too, Benedict, more than I can ever tell you."

"Show me, then." He pressed another kiss to her lips, his eyes twinkling. "Marry me at once, and we'll get to work straightaway on giving Freddy and Augustus the cousins they're demanding. They've asked for six, all of them girls."

"What?" Georgiana gaped at him, her cheeks on fire. "No, they didn't! They're too young to ask for such a thing."

"Well, I might have helped them along a bit. Here, Jane sent you a letter." Benedict rummaged around in his coat pocket and handed it over. "And Freddy sent you this," he added, placing a thick, wooden object into her palm.

Georgiana turned the puzzle piece over in her hand and a laugh bubbled up in her throat. "Italy? He sent me Italy?"

"Well, you did say you fancied it. He was quite taken with you, you know, but then all of the Haslemere gentlemen end up smitten with exceptional ladies. He's anxious to see you, but he'll have to wait, because no one is more anxious than I am, and I need you all to myself."

"Indeed? How intriguing. What did you have in mind?" Georgiana asked, stroking her thumb over his bottom lip.

"Oh, I was thinking a wedding, followed by a marriage, a half-dozen children, and a school full of willful little girls." He caught her hand and pressed a kiss to the tip of her finger. "What do you think, princess? Do you think you'd like to be Lady Haslemere?"

Georgiana took his beautiful face in her hands and touched her forehead to his. "I'd like to be *yours*."

He groaned, and took her mouth again. When he broke away, they were both panting. "If we keep this up, Brixton will have my head."

"Daniel? What's he got to do with it? I hope you two aren't quarrelling again."

"We never *stopped* quarrelling. I went straight to the Clifford School when I arrived in town, searching for you. After delivering a great many threats and casting dozens of aspersions on my character, Brixton finally told me you were here, but if we don't return soon, he's bound to come after me. The man's a menace."

Georgiana tried to look stern, but her lips were twitching. "I think you both enjoy baiting each other. Daniel will be content enough once we're married, though. Who are you going to wrangle with then?"

"Why *you*, of course." He planted a sweet kiss on the tip of her nose. "Though I confess I have quite a different sort of wrangling in mind."

Georgiana rested a hand on his chest and felt the steady beat of his heart against her palm. His brave, true, honorable heart. "There's nothing I want more than a lifetime of wrangling with you, my lord. But are you certain you want a wife with such a sharp tongue?"

He gazed down at her with warm dark eyes. "I want everything you are, Georgiana. Your sharp tongue, your hazel eyes, and your insatiable appetite for preserves. I want everything with you."

"You have it," she whispered, her hands curling against his chest. "Everything I have, everything I am, is yours."

Georgiana opened her mouth to say more—to tell him he'd already given her everything, even those things she didn't know how to dream of—but her throat ached with happy tears, and her heart was too full for words.

So she rose to her tiptoes and pressed a soft kiss to his lips that said more than words ever could.

Epilogue

Mill Street, London
Two months later

"Faster, Lord Benedict—*faster*!" Sarah let out a delighted squeal, her arms tightening around Benedict's neck as he neared the newly planted quince tree at the bottom of the garden.

"For pity's sake, Sarah, will you hush?" Benedict came to an abrupt halt and peeked around the slender tree trunk, which wasn't yet large enough to hide their antics from Georgiana. "I told you, if Lady Haslemere hears us shouting and happens to look out the window, she'll scold us until our ears ring for running footraces in the garden."

Marriage hadn't tamed Georgiana's tart tongue. Benedict, who delighted in her scolds, wouldn't have it any other way. Lecturing turned her eyes the most fetching shade of mossy green.

"Eh, we're safe enough. She's all the way up in the attics with the little ones, teaching them their sums." Susannah dangled Benedict's pocket watch on the end of one finger, watching it swing back and forth with covetous eyes. She was meant to be timing the race, but she seemed far more interested in pilfering his gold watch than anything else.

"They're a dim lot, they are. She'll be up there with them for ages yet." Sarah bobbed up and down on Benedict's back. "I wish we had a bridle for him, Susannah. That would be capital, wouldn't it?"

"A *bridle!* You do realize I'm not actually a horse, don't you, Sarah?" Good Lord. Georgiana had warned him not to spoil these girls. Perhaps he should have listened to her.

"'Course I do," Sarah scoffed. "Yer Lord Benedict."

That wasn't quite right either, but Benedict spent so much time at the school the girls, who'd come to look on him as a sort of benevolent uncle, had given up on calling him Lord Haslemere. They'd settled instead on Lord Benedict, a moniker that never failed to make him smile.

They were the wickedest, naughtiest girls imaginable, of course, and took shameless advantage of him, but Benedict couldn't resist them. He wanted a half dozen more of his own just like them, all of them with Georgiana's hazel eyes.

"Never mind a bridle, Sarah. A handful of his hair will do just as well." Susannah gave an approving nod as Sarah grabbed hold. "Right, then. Once around the garden. If ye get back to the tree in less than three minutes, ye get to keep your guineas, Lord Benedict. Longer than that, and—"

"You lose, and we get to keep 'em. Giddyup, Lord Benedict!" Sarah dug her heels into Benedict's legs, shrieking with laughter when he took off like a shot. Susannah chased after them, hopping up and down and shouting as Benedict flew up the garden toward the fountain where all the walkways converged. He was just about to round the perimeter, panting with exertion and laughter, when a tall, slender figure emerged from the pathway leading from the back door of the school.

A tall, slender, *frowning* figure, her arms crossed over her chest.

Benedict came to a skidding halt just in time to avoid slamming into her, but not quickly enough to prevent Susannah, who was right on his heels, from crashing into him. She fell onto her backside with an ignominious thump and Sarah, whose balance had been upset by the sudden collision, dropped down on top of her.

Georgiana peered down at the two girls, her lips twitching. "Well, if that isn't a fitting end for a forbidden footrace, I don't know what is."

"Aw, we weren't doing any harm." Susannah jumped to her feet and dusted off the back of her skirts. "Were we, Sarah?"

"Not a thing, Miss...er, yer ladyship. Just having a bit of fun with Lord Benedict here."

Georgiana raised an eyebrow, and held out her hand.

Sarah and Susannah glanced guiltily at each other, then Sarah stuffed her hand into her skirt pocket, pulled out the two guineas she'd hidden there, and dropped them into Georgiana's palm.

Georgiana's fingers snapped closed around the coins. "Return Lord Haslemere's pocket watch to him this instant, Susannah," she ordered, waiting until Susannah reluctantly handed over the watch. "Thank you. Now, aren't you two meant to be in French class right now?"

The girls exchanged another guilty glance, then Sarah muttered, "Yes, ma'am."

"Then I suggest you get upstairs at once, before Madame takes a fit. You're already late as it is."

Sarah glanced at Benedict, who did his best to produce a forbidding frown. "Do as Lady Haslemere says, you mischievous imps."

The girls scurried off, leaving Benedict alone with his wife, who, despite her frown, couldn't quite disguise the amusement in her eyes. "Well, Lord Haslemere? What have you to say for yourself?"

"Not a blessed thing." Benedict held his hands up innocently. "Unless it's that the Clifford schoolgirls are the most ill-behaved in all of London. It's a scandal, the way they're constantly leading me astray as they do."

"*They* led *you* astray, my lord? How curious. I suppose they stole those guineas and your watch out of your pocket, too."

Benedict crept closer to her. "As to that, who can say?"

"I imagine *you* can." Georgiana's tone was stern, but there was no mistaking the twinkle in her eyes. "Really, my lord, I would think you'd have learned your lesson about spoiling those girls by now."

Benedict edged another step closer—close enough so her skirts brushed against his legs. "It's not me who needs to learn a lesson, Lady Haslemere. It's you."

"Me?" Georgiana pressed a hand to her chest. "Why, what lesson am I meant to learn, my lord?"

"Not to interrupt a footrace already in progress, of course." Without warning, Benedict lunged for her and swept her up into his arms. "Once it's begun, it must be finished. Fortunately, one jockey does as well as another."

"Benedict! Put me down!"

But Benedict didn't put her down. He raced down the garden with her laughing, shrieking, and squirming in his arms. Once they reached the quince tree, he set her carefully on her feet, her back against the trunk. "Ah. Now this is a proper reward for a race well run."

"There are a dozen little girls upstairs in the attics waiting for me to teach them their sums, Lord Haslemere." Even as the protest left her lips, Georgiana's arms were already stealing around his neck.

"I'm afraid they'll have to wait." Benedict braced his hands against the tree on either side of her head and pressed his body close to hers. "I'm not finished with you yet."

"You're never finished with…" Georgiana trailed off with a soft gasp as Benedict's lips found her neck.

"Damn right I'm not. I never will be." He brushed the collar of her gown aside until he revealed bare skin, then proceeded to nibble and lick and kiss her until she melted against him, a sigh of surrender falling from her lips.

"So sweet, princess." Benedict settled his hands on her waist and nudged a knee between her legs until her delectable curves were flush against the length of his body. "I could spend every minute of the rest of my life tasting you, and I'd die a happy man."

Georgiana's breath caught on a moan when he brushed his thumbs over her breasts, her head falling back against the tree. "But you can't...we can't..."

"Hmmm? Did you say something, Lady Haslemere?" Benedict sealed his lips over hers before she could answer, a desperate groan tearing from his chest as he delved into the sweet, hot depths of her mouth.

He took her mouth again and again, his blood surging. In an instant he was utterly lost in her, so much so things might have gotten scandalously out of hand if he hadn't dimly registered the sound of a window opening, followed by an explosion of high-pitched giggling.

He tore his mouth from Georgiana's and peered around the tree. Sarah, Susannah, and Abby were hanging out a window, giggling and nudging each other until they were in danger of toppling from the second floor into the garden below.

"Those troublesome girls have caught us out again." He pressed one final, lingering kiss on Georgiana's lips, then drew back. "Can't a lord kiss his lady in peace?"

Georgiana buried her face in his neck, her lips curving against his skin. "This is the Clifford School, my lord. Prying eyes are everywhere."

"This school needs a private garden," Benedict grumbled, dropping a final kiss on her forehead.

"A private garden, or a bigger quince tree. But you'll have all the privacy you require when we're at Haslemere House. Patience, my lord."

Benedict snorted. "If you think we'll have privacy with Freddy and Augustus running about, you don't know little boys as well as you do little girls. And that's to say nothing of Jane, Clara and Draven, Cecilia and Darlington, and Lady Tilbury. I'll never have you to myself for a moment with such a crowd interrupting us at every turn."

They'd planned to spend the school break together alone at Haslemere House, but then Jane had insisted she and Freddy join them so she might become better acquainted with her new sister, then somehow the invitation had been extended to Clara and Draven and Augustus, and now...well, all of bloody England was spending the month of June at Haslemere House.

"Oh, dear. I think I forgot to mention I invited Sophia and Lord Gray as well." Georgiana peeked up at him from under her lashes, biting her lip. "Are you cross with me?"

Benedict brushed a lock of hair back from her forehead. "No. I could never be cross with you, princess. As long as you're happy, I'm happy too."

Georgiana smiled up at him, the hazel eyes he loved so well glowing with love. "I *am* happy, Benedict. Happier than I ever believed I could be."

Benedict cupped her cheeks in his palms, pressed a tender kiss to her lips, and whispered, "And if I have anything to say about it, you'll stay that way, Georgiana. Forever."

Author's Notes

Evan Andrews. Eight Unusual Good Luck Charms: Symbols, Amulets and Other Talismans from Around the Globe. Feb. 2018, updated March 2020. https://www.history.com/news/eight-unusual-good-luck-charms.

Dr. William Cadogan was a prominent eighteenth-century London doctor who became governor of the London Foundling Hospital in 1749, and physician in 1752. http://www.bshpch.com/18th-century.html.

Romola Davenport, Leonard Schwarz, and Jeremy Boulton. The Decline of Adult Smallpox in Eighteenth-Century London. *Economic History Review,* Nov. 2011. https://www.ncbi.nlm.nih.gov/pmc/articles/PMC4373148/.

Caitlin Dempsey. Dissected Maps: The First Jigsaw Puzzles. Nov. 2015. https://www.geographyrealm.com/dissected-maps-the-first-jigsaw-puzzles/.

The Faro Ladies, a close-knit group of friends who ran gambling dens out of their own homes, were an institution in 1790s London. The three most infamous Faro Ladies were Lady Sarah Archer, Albinia Hobart (later Lady Buckinghamshire), and Lady Elizabeth Luttrell.

Cliveden House is located in Maidenhead, Kent, less than four miles to the west of the gamekeeper's cottage in Burham. Benedict and Georgiana likely wouldn't have passed Cliveden House on their route from London to Oxfordshire, but the author found the beauty and history of the house too tempting to resist. https://www.clivedenhouse.co.uk/the-house/.

Printed in the United States
by Baker & Taylor Publisher Services